THE COTERIE

GARY S GREGOR

Published 2021 by Next Chapter

Edited by Lorna Read

Cover art by Cover Mint

Back cover texture by David M. Schrader, used under license
from Shutterstock.com

Acknowledgments

A number of people play a role in getting an author's story from an initial idea to a published book. For some of them, that role is small, for others it is significant. All who contribute in some way, regardless the level of input, are important to me, and although it might be cliché, it is true that this book would never have seen the light of day without each of them.

If I must nominate just a few, I would start with my former colleagues in the Northern Territory Police Force. You wonderful folk are the inspiration for my characters and, while those characters are fictional, I occasionally draw on the personality traits of some of those I have met in the job. If you recognise yourself in any of them, please remember that you are there because you inspire me.

My beautiful wife, Lesley, who tolerates my long hours in front of the computer without complaint, I love you and I thank you, although I still insist my love of writing is not an obsession.

Last, but by no means least, I thank all at Next Chapter Publishing. The Next Chapter team took a punt on an unknown, and that's rare in this business. I hope I can justify your gamble. I know I'll never stop trying to honour that leap of faith; thank you.

This book is respectfully dedicated to the memory of police officers everywhere who have paid the ultimate sacrifice in the service of their communities.

Prologue

Eddie Dickson knew intuitively he was about to die. From the moment his assailant stepped from the dark, shadowy recesses of the portico, suspended above the entrance to the South Australian Police Headquarters building, it was certain. The realisation that he was going to die sooner rather than later was not a conclusion he reached at that instant, but from the moment his normally ordered, structured life began to unravel just a few days earlier.

Strangely, as he waited for the inevitable, it was the compelling desire to see the faces of those sent to kill him, and not his imminent death or how he might avoid it, that occupied his thoughts. For the moment at least, the rain had eased to a light drizzle but still the road was awash with the remains of intermittent heavy showers. The dark, nondescript sedan skidded to a stop a couple of metres from where Dickson stood at the curb, sending a filthy, black wash of gutter water over the footpath, soaking his shoes and the cuffs of his trousers.

Suddenly, he felt himself propelled, forcefully, towards the car. He glimpsed only a shadowy outline of the driver, and even less of whoever it was behind him doing the propelling.

This man was an anonymous force from behind. No image, no voice—just a sudden, violent shove in the middle of his back which sent him stumbling through the now open door and into the rear passenger compartment of the vehicle.

Pushed violently and uncomfortably to his elbows and knees on the floor of the back seat, the one thing Eddie Dickson did recognise was unmistakable: the cold, hard pressure of a gun barrel held firmly and steadily against the back of his head. One did not have to be a rocket scientist to know these people were not here to take him on a guided tour of the city. They were good, they were fast, and they were efficient.

Dickson knew he was dealing with professionals. He also knew what they had been sent here to do, and why.

Eddie Dickson might be many things, but defeatist was not one of them. Resistance, although desirable, would be futile in the circumstances in which he found himself. But, while he was still breathing, and as long as he maintained that most basic life-sustaining bodily function, there remained hope. Someone—he had long since forgotten who—once told him the secret to staying alive was to keep inhaling and exhaling. Simplistic in its logic, but well founded, he thought. At least until, and if, an opportunity to get free of his present predicament presented itself.

Eddie Dickson was not a young man anymore, but he was surprisingly fit and strong for a man of sixty-four. Unlike the majority of Australian men in his demographic, he preferred fitness to flabbiness, and he was not lacking in motivation when it came to regular exercise. As often as the prevailing weather conditions allowed, he rose early, often before dawn, and rode a pushbike. For two hours, he rode hard and fast around the many cycle paths that crisscrossed his home city. On days when the weather was not conducive to outdoor exercise, he followed a rigorous workout regime in a gym near to his home. Fitness was not so much an obsession as a desire to stay as healthy as possible, given his advancing years.

Dickson knew that in going one on one, he could handle himself with almost anyone, even someone many years younger than himself. These two characters, however, were very obviously not in the category of 'easy-beats'. Still, he would love to try. He liked to think, given the opportunity, he was physically capable of doing considerable damage to his faceless captors before they finished what they came here to do.

Eddie Dickson had killed men before, albeit a long time ago. Some he had shot; others he had dispatched at close quarters with a knife. A couple he sent into the next life with his bare hands. Accordingly, the prospect of killing another human being, although unpleasant and not something he hoped he would ever have to do again, was not alien to him. Given his current situation, he knew that the opportunity to revive these long abandoned but not forgotten skills, was not about to present itself. At least not while he remained jammed awkwardly, face-down on the floor between the front and rear seats of the vehicle. All he wanted now was to see the face of the man sent to kill him. He was not overcome with feelings of anger or hatred, or even helplessness. This moment had been coming for some time; he just never knew exactly when. Now he did.

The car pulled away from the curb and the anonymous assailant jammed a heavy, sodden boot hard into the back of Eddie's neck, forcing his face against the floor. A damp, musty odour flooded his nostrils. He hoped it wouldn't happen in the car. He didn't want to be found like that. If this is what it had come down to, he wanted his death to be, at the very least, dignified.

During the short journey, no one spoke. Any conversation would have been superfluous. These people knew where they were going and what was required of them. It seemed like they had been driving for only a few minutes when the vehicle slowed and came to a stop. He heard the rear door open, and a sudden gust of icy wind flooded the interior of the vehicle. As he was dragged unceremoniously backwards out of the car, he tried to turn and get a look at the man behind the wheel. He saw only a glimpse of a shadowy figure in a heavy coat with the collar pulled high and his face turned away, staring out at the darkness through the driver's side window.

Eddie Dickson had never before had a gun pressed against the back of his head. But then, he didn't need to see it to know what it was, or know it was the instrument by which he was about to meet his premature demise.

The prospect of dying had never been something Eddie feared to any great degree. It was more a case of the timing of his death that concerned him. He was not ready to die yet. In no doubt that it was about to happen, it was an immense sense of sadness rather than fear that accompanied him on the short walk to the centre of the park. There was more he wanted to do with his life. Places he wanted to go. People he wanted to see. Now, in his last moments of life, the realisation that he was never going to do any of those things filled him with almost overwhelming regret.

He peered into the cold darkness that engulfed the park ahead of him, hesitating for just a moment, briefly considering an attempt to turn on his attacker. If he was going to do it, it had to be now. Then, he felt a tug at his collar and he knew it was time. He began to turn and face the stranger tasked with the job of killing him. In the last few seconds that remained of his life, he wanted to face the man and tell him to go fuck himself and, if he got the opportunity, spit in his eye.

Then there was nothing. No sound, no pain, no awareness. Nothing. Just blackness. He never heard the footsteps as his killer walked briskly away towards the car that was waiting for him at the edge of the park. At that moment, as if by design, the heavens opened again and he never felt the cold rain as it fell on his back and soaked through his clothes. Eddie Dickson never did see the man who killed him.

Chapter One

The call came in the early hours of the morning, dragging Chapman Bouttell reluctantly into an unwelcome degree of alertness. Slowly, he surfaced from the shallow depths of what had been a fitful sleep. His mouth was dry and he needed the toilet. Fumbling blindly in the darkness for the telephone, something crashed noisily to the floor.

"Shit," he mumbled sleepily.

Finally, after expending a couple more expletives he would never use in mixed company, he found the telephone, thankful to be able to stop the incessant ringing.

"Hello," he groaned.

"Chap?" It was a female voice.

"Yeah."

"Chap, this is Jenny Patten, from Communications. I'm sorry to disturb you, but I'm afraid I have to call you on duty."

"Of course you do, Jenny. It's the middle of the bloody night after all. That's the only time anyone ever calls me," he said, with undisguised sarcasm. "What time *is* it by the way? My bedside clock is on the floor somewhere."

"It's a few minutes after four o'clock," she answered.

"That would be in the morning, right?"

The policewoman ignored the sarcastic jibe. "Why is your clock on the floor?"

"The display is too bright, it keeps me awake," Bouttell lied. "What have you got?"

"It looks like homicide, Sarge. One of our patrols found the body of an adult male with what appears to be a single gunshot wound to the head."

"Front of the head or back?"

"Back."

"Then that wouldn't just look like a homicide—it would *be* a homicide. It would not be a suicide, would it? Suicides don't shoot themselves in the back of the head. None that I've ever seen, anyway. Where is it?"

"Heywood Park, on the southern end of Hyde Park Road. Do you know it?"

"Yeah, I know it."

"We have officers there at the moment securing the scene. You have been assigned to take charge of the investigation."

"Shit!" Bouttell spat. "It's pissing down out there. Isn't anyone working in Major Crime tonight?"

"There's no Senior Investigator on duty. The Watch Commander nominated you."

"And who would that be?"

"Sergeant Turner."

"That would be right," Bouttell scoffed. "That prick hates me, I'm sure of it."

"Pardon?"

"Forget it, Jenny. Tell Turner I'm on my way."

"Your partner has already been notified. He's on his way to pick you up. He should be there shortly," she advised.

"Okay, thank you."

Bouttell reached for the bedside light, switched it on and dropped the receiver onto its cradle. He yawned, swung his bare legs over the side of the bed and slowly raised himself into a sitting position. He sat for a moment, silently cursing the arthritic twinge that burned deep in his hips and shoulders. He yawned again, ran his hands through his unruly hair and picked up the fallen clock.

"Shit!" he murmured. "Shit! Shit! Shit!"

Murder was bloody inconvenient. At least that was how Chapman Bouttell perceived it. The burden of being a Detective Sergeant, which in his case carried with it the responsibilities of Senior Investigator, did nothing to diminish this opinion. It wasn't the first time he wondered why most murders seemed to happen at night. Statistically, the hours between six p.m. and six a.m. were those in which a person would most likely expect to die at the hand of his fellow man. By contrast, death as a result of an accident was somewhat more considerate, not so selective as to the hour of the day in which it occurred. Accidents had the courtesy to distribute their circumstances with some degree of impartiality with regard to day and night. Not so with murder, Bouttell mused. Murder was bloody inconvenient!

Nonetheless, murder and the investigation of it was his job, and had been since his transfer to the Major Crime Investigation Section, MCIS, ten years earlier. The utter senselessness associated with the killing of another human being, and the curiously bizarre novelty that murder scenes presented when he first came to his current position, had long since left him. Even after all his years in the job, he still found the whats and the whys of every homicide investigation fascinating. And, despite the unpleasantness of being roused from his bed in the middle of the night, it was his job. It was just that, to be summoned to duty at such an hour, on such an abysmally cold and wet night, was, he assumed not unreasonably, damned inconvenient.

———

It was July. In Adelaide in July, it was most definitely winter, and Chapman Bouttell found little comfort against the pre-dawn icy chill as he waited on his front porch for his partner to arrive. Hoping he would not have to wait long, he tugged at the collar of his heavy overcoat, pulling it high around his neck, trying to burrow deeper into it.

The street light in front of his house emitted a hazy, indistinct glow and cast an eerie shadow over the front yard and the unkempt garden within its borders. His lawn needed mowing; he would have to do something about that, he thought. Or, maybe he should just pay someone to do it. He looked up into the dark, starless sky. It had started to rain again, and a bone-chilling wind whipped the steady downpour into all too frequent gusts of numbing spray from which his small porch offered precious little protection. He pushed back further into the shadows of the porch and hunkered even deeper into his coat. Any warmth, even imagined, had to be better than none at all.

Bouttell had not had a cigarette for over three years, but, waiting here for his partner in the bitter, pre-dawn cold and dark, the desire returned. He found that odd because he had never really craved cigarettes once he had made the decision to quit. He comforted himself with the realisation that if he still smoked, he would have to take his hands out of his pockets to enjoy one.

Incongruous thoughts of a long-abandoned bad habit were interrupted by the arrival of an unmarked police sedan. As it slowed and stopped at the entrance to his driveway, he braced himself against the elements and stepped from his porch. "Time to go to work," he muttered softly.

The car's heating system was noisy, but at least it was working, albeit inefficiently. Tepid air from the engine compartment seeped from the vents in the dashboard and circulated weakly through the interior of the vehicle. There was a damp, musty smell to the air and, even though smoking in police vehicles had long been banned in the interests of the health and safety, the interior smelled of it.

Bouttell settled down in the passenger seat and welcomed what little warmth there was on offer, but not the familiar odour. He glanced across at his partner. At thirty-eight, Detective Senior Constable Anthony Francis was twenty-four years younger than Chapman and considerably junior to him in length of service. They'd been partners for almost a year, and there were those within the job who considered Francis worthy of admiration for achieving that particular milestone. A long time ago, someone, Bouttell had long forgotten who, had described him as being a morose individual. At the time, he remembered being unsure of whether or not he should feel offended. Mainly because he had never heard the word 'morose' and had absolutely no idea what it meant, other than a gut feeling that it probably wasn't complimentary. By the time he had a chance to look it up and discover its meaning, it was too late to argue the point either for or against.

Chapman had seen many partners come and go, but none had remained with him for longer than a few months. Perhaps deservedly, perhaps not, he had earned a reputation of being often difficult to work with. It was not a reputation he enjoyed or encouraged. Rather, he lived with it in quiet tolerance. Needless to say, he was inwardly pleased to discover, a few months into their partnership, that Francis looked upon the relationship as a valuable learning experience.

Bouttell's preference was to work alone, much to the chagrin of his superiors, but he reluctantly and silently accepted that these past months working alongside Francis had been mildly enjoyable. Indeed, that was about excited as Sergeant Chapman Bouttell was ever going to get about working with anyone.

The two were, however, like chalk and cheese in their respective attitudes with regard to ambition. Whereas Bouttell maintained a somewhat casual detachment directly relevant to his years of service, twenty-seven in total, Francis epitomised the very definition of a career police officer. Unlike his more senior partner, Francis decided early that his destiny, like that of his father before him, lay amid the ranks of commissioned officers and it was to this end that he channelled all of his energies. Marriage had never been something he seriously considered. It wasn't that he didn't believe marriage and subsequent parenthood to be satisfying and rewarding. He was sure it was. Indeed, he was himself a product of just such a marriage.

For him, it was simply a matter of priorities. His job took preference in his life and he had long ago fully committed himself to it. It would be wrong, he reasoned, to have a wife and kids waiting at home wanting, perhaps even demanding, more of him than he was prepared to give. Whenever he was reminded of the high marriage mortality rate amongst members of the police force, and that was far too often for his liking, he always came back to the conclusion that bachelorhood was not something to be taken lightly. A perfect example of that logic sat next to him in the car.

Bouttell's marriage had gone the way of many others within the force. A once happy union had taken a slow, bitter and decaying spiral towards inevitable breakdown and ultimately, divorce. Francis decided early that there was no room in his life, at least in the foreseeable future, for external distractions such as marriage and the commitment it demanded.

They did not have far to drive, but it was not a journey warmed by jovial small talk. Francis was far too familiar with his partner's all too often sour disposition to expect him to engage in anything deeper and more meaningful than perfunctory conversation.

Operational procedure dictated a radio channel other than that used by General Duties units be used by members engaged in investigative roles. It was to this channel that both men directed their attention as they drove.

Chapman glanced at Francis and noticed his partner looking at him. “What?” he asked the younger man.

Francis smiled. “Good morning, boss.”

“You gonna sit there staring at me or watch the road?”

“Well, aren’t we just dripping with charm this morning?” Francis chided.

Chapman turned away, looked through the passenger window at the terrible night and, in spite of himself, smiled inwardly. “You’re gonna kill us both before we even get there if you don’t keep your bloody eyes on the road!”

Chapter Two

Heywood Park was a small, lightly treed public recreation area located approximately fifteen minutes south of the city centre and Police Headquarters. It was a park with which Chapman Bouttell was familiar. He'd been raised and educated in an orphanage just a few streets to the west of the park, in neighbouring Goodwood. As often as he saw an opportunity, he would go to the park with a couple of confidants to escape, at least for a short while, its regimented and often cruel confines. Confidants were few and far between and often hard to get within the orphanage atmosphere. This was a place where abuse, both physical and emotional, was to be expected by the young residents almost on a daily basis.

Chapman Bouttell had long forgotten the name of the Catholic order charged with running the orphanage, but it had the word 'Mercy' in it, he remembered; an oxymoron if ever there was one, he thought. Mercy of any degree following an indiscretion, regardless of severity, was rarely shown by those in charge.

New kids, wide-eyed and terrified, arrived regularly. Others, those who had reached the mandatory age where they were required to leave and make a life for themselves on the outside, were equally as terrified at what they might face beyond the orphanage walls. These young adults left through the huge front doors with their humble possessions clutched tightly in trembling fingers and an uncertain future ahead of them. Others were adopted, taken from the only home most of them ever knew to face an equally uncertain future as part of a family of strangers.

As a young lad, Chapman believed the adoptees were the lucky ones. They were the chosen ones; chosen to go to happy homes and to the arms of loving families to start their lives over with new-found parents who would care for them, nurture them, and love them. It was a nice thing to believe, even if it was nothing more than the wistful, albeit naïve musings of youth.

Conversely, the new arrivals were the sad, miserable souls who had suffered for most of their short lives and it was difficult for Chapman or any of the young, confused, scared residents to cement lasting friendships. However, on occasions, he was able to convince a co-conspirator that it was worth the risk to join him and slip away unnoticed for an hour or so. Inevitably, such illicit excursions into the glorious but scary freedom of the world outside the orphanage walls almost always resulted in discovery, punishable by a flogging with a well-worn razor strop: an implement of punishment with which most of the young residents of the orphanage were well acquainted, Chapman Bouttell more so than most.

Notwithstanding the oft-applied strop to his rear end, Chapman considered himself one of the luckier ones. He, for reasons he was never able to fathom, never suffered the sexual abuse that many of his fellow residents did. Punishment, regardless of its severity or how often it was applied, was never a deterrent for the young Chapman Bouttell. He learned the art of nonconformity from a very early age. It was an education that would stay with him for the rest of his life.

These days, progress in the form of ever expanding urban sprawl had swallowed much of what Chapman remembered of Heywood Park. Today, the park was slightly less than half its original size. It was not childhood memories, however, that brought him back to this place after all these years; it was murder.

A sole flickering amber street light, the earliness of the hour and the cold, stormy conditions cast a sinister ambience over the park. Bouttell looked up at the dark, leaden sky and rapidly building needles of rain stung his face. Away to the east, slender fingers of dawn's early light struggled to introduce another day upon the still sleeping state capital, as they probed tentatively above the crest of the hills fringing the eastern side of the city.

From somewhere even further away, he heard the long, low rumble of thunder. This was one of those times when he would have liked to summon those escapist skills which served him so well in his youth, slip quietly away and go back home to his bed.

Forcing himself to focus, his eyes began to adapt slowly to the dark, shadowy recesses of the park. Gone were the sounds of laughing, playing children who filled these grounds during daylight hours. Gone, too, were the proud mothers pushing contented, gurgling babies in strollers as they watched their older children, and their neighbours' children, run, jump, climb and scrape their knees. Life's innocence was still tucked snugly into warm beds.

The bullet had entered the victim's head at a point slightly below and behind the right ear, exiting in the hairline above the left eye. The absence of any trace of blood, long since washed away by intermittent showers of rain, left an ugly purple hole where the projectile had entered and plowed its deadly course through the brain, splintering bone and rendering tissue, before exploding out of the forehead.

Death would have been instantaneous. The victim had crashed face-down onto a cobbled walkway that wound its way through the park from Hyde Park Road on the northern side, to an easement access lane on the south side. Rivulets of rain dammed momentarily against the dead man's head, before finding the path of least resistance and continuing on their meandering way over the patchwork pattern of cobblestones.

If there was any positive aspect to the scene confronting the investigators, it was both the hour and the weather conditions acting in concert to ensure the curious remained soundly ensconced inside their homes. The negative, and there were always negatives, was that these same two conditions would guarantee that there would be no witnesses to events as they unfolded earlier.

This was murder, and walk-up-starts in murder cases were much too much to hope for. The easy ones came along from time to time throughout a homicide investigator's career, but not often enough for Chapman Bouttell's liking. Perhaps they would get lucky. Luck sometimes played a role in murder investigations; circumstances coupled with facts, unfolding neatly, leading to a conclusion with little more than routine effort by the investigators. As he looked down at the soggy, lifeless form at his feet, Chapman knew instinctively this was not one such occasion.

Sergeant Peter Turner, General Duties Watch Commander and thirty-three-year veteran in the job, was one of the first to arrive at the scene. A big, balding man, with a waistline rapidly approaching obesity, Turner was not one of Chapman Bouttell's favorite people.

In the context of his long career, Turner was a good cop,

right up there with the best. Twice commended for his actions in the line of duty, he had more than adequately proved himself on the streets and, for the most part, he enjoyed the respect of his colleagues. It was not, however, Turner's ability as a police officer which Chapman took exception to. Indeed, he was one of those who respected Turner's competency as an officer of the law. It was more the attitude Turner seemed to have adopted towards the job now, thirty-three-years later, as he approached the end of his career; that 'been there, done that, don't give a shit' attitude.

Unfortunately, it was not an attitude unique to Turner. Chapman had seen it before in other cops close to retirement. He guessed it was a subconscious thing and he doubted any of them were even aware of their somewhat blasé approach. Perhaps his fellow officers thought of him the same way. After all, he had twenty-seven-years in, and was getting close to the time in the job where he considered all cops should seriously consider retirement.

No one should stay around longer than thirty years, Chapman believed. Not unless you were a commissioned officer and spent your days polishing the seat of your trousers while firmly entrenched in the ivory tower, as the administration section was known. Then you could stay forty years if you wanted to. No one ever saw much of you, anyway, and many of the front-line officers who had been around a while soon forgot you were actually still in the job.

In Turner's case, Bouttell believed he had become way too complacent. He had got tired, fat, and lazy, and had overstayed his appointment by at least three years.

Chapman watched the big man approach, his massive shape looming out of the darkness. Turner positioned himself between the two detectives.

"What's your take on this?" Tony Francis asked the uniformed sergeant.

Turner removed his hat and ran a huge, pudgy hand

across his hairless pate. “Well,” he offered, “at first glance it looks like an execution-style hit.”

“Or a drug deal gone sour,” Francis suggested.

“Could be, mate, could be.” Turner shrugged. “Two of my blokes on routine patrol came past here about…” he squinted in the poor light at his watch… “forty minutes ago. They found the body when they shone their spotlight over the grounds.”

“Is the area secure?” Chapman asked.

“I’ve seen to that,” Turner confirmed. “My chaps have just finished placing a cordon around the park, and I have stationed a car at each end of this walkway. Don’t want any fitness freaks stumbling through here on their early morning jog.”

Chapman looked at Turner and then up into the black sky. It was raining more heavily now. “You’re kidding, right?” he said.

“Yeah, right,” Turner chuffed.

Chapman turned to his partner. “Tony, get a statement from the two officers who found the body. You know the procedure. Don’t forget to ask about any vehicles or people in the area at the time.” He watched Francis walk away towards the park entrance and then he turned back to Turner. “Have Forensics been notified?”

“They should be on their way as we speak. The Coroner’s Constable also, and the duty medical officer to verify death.”

The man, face down on the ground at their feet, was certainly dead; Chapman hardly needed verification of the obvious. However, procedure was procedure. That was the way things were done. There could be no gaping holes which a half-smart defence lawyer could drive a truck through if, and when, the case came before the courts.

“Have you looked around? Found anything that might interest us?”

“Yeah, I had a quick look around when I arrived.” Turner

nodded. "There is a wallet, over there in that garden bed." He pointed to a small patch of low, well maintained shrubbery a few metres from where they stood. "I haven't examined it, nobody has. Thought I'd leave that to you blokes. I assumed you'd want it photographed in situ. It may not even belong to this poor bastard." He nodded at the body. "I'm willing to bet it does, though. It may provide some identification. If it's empty, it could suggest robbery as a motive."

"I doubt it," Chapman said. "Unfortunately, it's never that easy." He gestured at the corpse. "What was this bloke doing here, anyway? Look at him—clean-cut, nice clothes. I don't think he was out for a leisurely stroll in the park on a night like this. And what self-respecting mugger would have the balls to ply his trade in this shitty weather? Most street thugs are pussies, they're tucked up all cute and snugly in their beds." He dropped to one knee on the wet cobblestones. "Shine your light here," he said. "Let's get a closer look at our friend."

Turner held the torch steady, focusing the light on the upper half of the body. The dead man was face-down on the walkway, his facial features partly obscured. As Chapman studied what he could see of the man's features, he suddenly felt something; something strangely familiar. He moved his face closer to the corpse.

"Hand me the torch," he said, reaching behind him.

"What's the problem?" Turner asked.

Chapman took the torch from Turner's outstretched hand and directed the beam into the lifeless face. "I'm not sure," he murmured, "but I think I've seen this guy somewhere before. How long before we get some floodlights here?"

"I requested a lighting plant, including a tent, as soon as I got here. It has to come from Star Force, and you know those girls, they're scared of the dark!" He chuckled at his own joke.

A feeling of uneasiness confused and unsettled Chapman Bouttell. He had always considered himself fortunate to possess an excellent memory when it came to faces, but there was something about the dead man that bothered him. He was certain he was not a recent acquaintance, but he had met him somewhere. Somewhere in his past. Where? His recollection was vague and strangely disturbing. What was it about the crumpled, saturated body at his feet that he found familiar?

Chapter Three

The media began descending on the park before dawn. Chapman never ceased to be amazed at how the press hounds found out about such events, almost, it seemed, before the police did. There were plenty of theories within the department as to how news, good or bad, managed to find its way to the various arms of the media as quickly as it did, and none of them had anything to do with efficiency. Not the least fancied of these was the offering of incentives by the media to a select few police officers in return for a discreet, timely telephone call.

It was a scenario that angered Chapman, and many other cops like him. However, wisdom born of experience had taught him that his opinions on the matter were never going to change the way things were. Personal profit was, and always would be, a powerful motivator. He considered the often-used term 'media circus' to be apt as he watched the rapidly building frenzy of activity just beyond the newly erected crime scene cordon.

Cameramen, reporters, sound crews and assorted media gophers jostled for the best vantage point, all vying for that exclusive interview or that classically gruesome front-page photograph. Over his years in the job, Chapman had known of more than one forensic photographer to be offered inducement to part with graphic photos taken in the process of evidence-gathering. Journalism, and the accompanying ratings which determined its worth, was stimulated by aggressive competition, and while there were always going to be a couple of bad eggs in the basket, he could only hope the vast majority of his fellow officers maintained a healthy strength of character and integrity when dealing with the media.

Detective Constables Grahame Smith and Bob Sanderson, the other half of Chapman's four-man investigation team, arrived with a portable lighting plant and a portable tent shelter which they had collected from the Star Force offices themselves. Apparently, unless there posed an immediate threat to life or property, Star Force was staying in bed.

Smith and Sanderson began the business of erecting the tent over the scene and firing up the lighting plant. Soon, the hum of the generator was just audible above the noise of the wind, which seemed to have intensified in the last few minutes. The immediate area around the body was instantly bathed in an artificial glow, adding a carnival-like hue to the macabre scene.

Next to arrive was a forensic specialist, a young man Chapman had seen around the corridors of Headquarters but had never actually met. He was new to the forensic unit and had, up until tonight, never worked on any of the same cases as Chapman. Both men nodded a greeting to each other and Chapman watched with interest as the younger man huddled under the tent and assembled his photographic equipment. Shortly after, he emerged from the tent and began photographing the area in the immediate vicinity, shielding his expensive camera equipment as best he could from the rain.

Eventually, he re-entered the tent and took more photos of the body from a number of different angles and aspects. Some would be enlarged and all of them would be studied in minute detail over and over again by Chapman and his team during the ensuing investigation. None of the photographs would find their way into the hands of the media without his express authority; not on his watch, of that Chapman was certain.

As Chapman waited for the photographer to finish his work, Tony Francis returned, together with Smith and Sanderson. They had managed to obtain two umbrellas and the four detectives huddled together under the barely adequate shelter. They made a pitiful-looking group, all of them soaked to the skin, and all of them hunkering down against the elements. This was one of the downsides to police work and, as they waited for the completion of the forensic formalities, Chapman massaged at an arthritic shoulder and wondered silently if, at sixty-two years of age, he might be too old to consider the merits of alternative employment.

Dr. Keith Rogers was one of five medicos employed by the state government and attached on a rotating roster system to the police department. Being called out to perform preliminary examinations and to certify death at scenes such as this, was just one of the duties that fell within his job description. His name had rotated to the top of the list and he did not look particularly pleased to be there.

With practiced experience, the doctor conducted a preliminary examination of the body, certified death, and, with extreme difficulty in the prevailing conditions, completed the obligatory paperwork. With a flourish, he signed the form and handed it to Chapman, who glanced at it briefly in the awkward light before placing it into a plastic evidence bag and tucking it away inside his very wet coat.

Rogers was not prepared to speculate as to time of death, due to the temperature of the body being so affected by the cold. Chapman would have to wait until an autopsy could be performed under controlled, clinical conditions.

As quickly as he'd arrived, Dr. Rogers left. Soon, the Coroner's Constable would arrive to take possession of the body and supervise its dispatch and transportation to the morgue. As the officer in charge of the investigation, only Chapman could grant such possession, and he was not about to do so until he was satisfied that a complete and thorough search of the area had been carried out and all possible evidence had been collected, bagged and tagged, and recorded on the crime scene running sheet.

Despite his moody disposition, and regardless of the difficult weather conditions, he would not cut corners or in any way compromise the thoroughness with which he conducted the investigation. He knew his general demeanor was not his most admired character trait and was considered by some to be arrogance. He was also aware that he was guilty at times of somewhat unorthodox methods, but what he was not, was casual in his approach to the way he went about his work. Although he had never really cared much about what others thought of him, the term 'arrogant' was not one that sat comfortably with him. 'Doggedly determined' would be a more apt description of his attitude to his work, he would have said if anyone ever asked. No one ever asked.

His task completed, the young forensic team member approached and waited at the edge of the light. "Great morning for it, fellas!" He smiled.

"Bloody beautiful," Francis answered. "Are you done here?"

"I am, unless there is anything specific you want photographed." He carefully began packing his camera and flash equipment into a specially constructed aluminum, foam-lined carry case.

Chapman indicated the nearby shrubbery. "Did you get some shots of the wallet over there?"

"Yes, several. I will get started on developing them first thing."

Chapman glanced at his partner. Francis glanced at Chapman, shrugged, and gave a knowing wink. Chapman transfixed the photographer with a withering glare. "What's your name, son?"

"Davis, Sarge. Paul Davis," the photographer answered, offering his hand.

Chapman ignored the gesture, stepped up to the young man and put one arm around his shoulder. "Well, Paul," he began. "You and I have never worked together before and this seems to be as good a time as any for you to start learning a little about the way I do things. I want those photographs on my desk by the time I return to the office. We owe it – *you* owe it – to that poor bugger lying on the wet grass in there." He thrust a thumb towards the tent. "Do we understand each other, Paul?"

Clearly intimidated, the young man lowered his eyes and fiddled nervously with the catches on the camera case. "Yes, of course," he said eventually. "I'll get started immediately." He turned and walked away into the slowly fading darkness.

"A bit hard on the lad, don't you think?" Francis asked.

"He's new. He has to learn," Chapman said dismissively. "Better he learns now, on his first job with me, than later." He moved to where the wallet lay open, upside-down in the garden bed. Carefully, he picked it up and turned it over. It was empty. There was no money, no credit cards, no driver's license, nothing. Not even the obligatory snapshot of a loving wife or girlfriend, or smiling children; nothing that would offer any clue as to the identity of the dead man. He handed the wallet to Francis. "I think we can eliminate robbery as a motive."

Francis examined the wallet. "Why? It *is* empty," he observed.

"Yes, but all traces of ID have been removed," Chapman

continued. "Some effort has been made to make a quick identification difficult. Why would a thief intent on grabbing some fast cash go to the trouble of removing all traces of ID? Shit, we don't even know if the wallet belongs to this guy." He hesitated. "Although, I'm with Turner. I'd bet my left nut it does."

"You've bet your left nut on things before," Francis smiled. "You should be careful, you might end up sounding like Tiny Tim."

"I'd still have the right one," Chapman said casually.

Francis turned the wallet over in his hands. "It could be a drug thing," he suggested. "Hiding the identity of a drug hit victim is often consistent with drug-related murders."

Chapman did not agree. The dead man was not the victim of a drug hit. Nor was this a mugging. His sixth sense, if such a thing existed, told him this was far more complicated than that. He ducked his head, stepped into the tent and looked down at the body. His partner stepped in behind him.

Relieved to be out of the rain, albeit temporarily, the two detectives stood together, their shoulders almost touching in the confines of the tent. The artificial lighting created by the small generator humming a short distance away filled the tent with warmth, more perceived than actual, and a thin fog of steam rose from the victim's wet clothes and quickly dissipated in the cramped space.

The victim was neatly dressed in a conservative suit under an equally modest yet fashionable overcoat. In life, this had been a man of neat, clean-cut looks. His shoes, although now sodden, appeared to be highly polished. It could easily have been the body of a businessman, a doctor or, dare he think, a cop. Maybe a husband, or father, or perhaps both. Whoever he was, Chapman Bouttell could not rid himself of the strange feeling of familiarity. He knelt again on the wet grass, close to the dead man.

"Who are you? Who the bloody hell are you?" he muttered softly to the body.

Chapter Four

There were a few police officers, perhaps more than were willing to admit, who found a morbid fascination with morgues and the procedures which took place within their walls. Chapman Bouttell was not one of them. Death in itself did not bother him unduly. He had seen more than his fair share of it and he had, he believed, become inured to it and thereby somewhat detached from the emotions it can, and often did, evoke in others.

The dissection of a corpse, however, was an entirely different matter. Post mortems were procedures that did bother him. It was not the body so much that unsettled him. The body was, after all, dead; an unthinking, unfeeling mass of flesh and bone and it was never going to do anyone any harm. The difficulty for Chapman was in maintaining that perspective, and he often found himself in awe of those who were charged with this unenviable task. To these folk, it was all so clinical, and so impersonal, to be almost matter-of-fact. To perform this kind of work every day took a certain type of character and he wondered if it was easy to switch off after spending all day slicing and dicing, up to their armpits in the blood and gore of what were once living, breathing, feeling human beings. He was certain he would never be able to mentally detach himself from the grisly task.

Mostly, it was the combination of the sickly, sweet smell of formaldehyde and body fluids which accompanied a dissection that got to him. It was a smell he had never become accustomed to and, after all his years on the job, he doubted he ever would. As a homicide investigator, his attendance at autopsies was a requirement of the job, and one which he undertook with no small amount of reluctance. Today was no exception. In truth, today was as bad as any of those he could remember. He was uncomfortable. His clothes were still damp, and he was tired.

He arrived at the city morgue directly from the crime scene, where he had left his team combing the grounds of Heywood Park in search of evidence. Morgues always seemed to be located in basements or lower ground floors of the buildings that housed them. Chapman often wondered about that —underground, but not quite underground, buried, but not quite buried. There were, he assumed, a number of perfectly logical reasons for them being situated where they were, accessibility and privacy being only two. Those morgues he ever had occasion to visit all had vehicle access ramps leading down to a discreet entrance, away from public scrutiny. It simply wouldn't do to wheel the hapless deceased through the corridors of the building, in full view of unsuspecting members of the public and staff alike.

And then, perhaps an oddity, perhaps not, morgues were all white; white ceilings, white walls tiled up to two thirds of their height, and white tiled floors. The only apparent concession to this starkness was the stainless-steel benches and gurneys comprising the sparse furnishings.

If it were possible for one to enter a morgue while oblivious to the procedures which occurred within, the combination of sterile surroundings and the odour permeating the air would, Chapman was sure, soon stimulate one's awareness.

He guessed there were things which could be done about the smell; improved ventilation for one. But, surely the appropriate authorities could improve the sombre and depressing ambience by introducing a more appealing decor? Appealing to whom, he wondered? White was cheap, and easy to clean, he supposed. And then, all things considered, those poor souls who unknowingly took up temporary residence in this place were in no position to complain about either the smell or the decor.

There were two separate sections to the city morgue, a department within the state's Forensic Science Centre. Both were located below street level and had separate entrances. There was a general section where victims of non-crime-associated death were brought, those who had died as a result of an accident, for example, and then there was a police section which accommodated the victims of crime.

The two sections were separated by administration offices and two comfort rooms where next of kin could wait and prepare themselves for the unenviable task of identifying the remains of a loved one. An internal access door led from the comfort room to the viewing room; a tiny airlock space with a glass window in one wall, beyond which lay the autopsy room. The viewing room and, to a lesser degree, the comfort room, were cold, clinical, impersonal places, and being there always made Chapman wish he was somewhere else. He hesitated in the airlock space between the two rooms and looked through the window into the autopsy room beyond.

Forensic Pathologist, Dr. Lee Richardson stood hunched over a bench on which lay the naked body of the man found in the park some ten hours earlier. On the far side of the room, beyond where the doctor worked, was yet another room; an ante-room which housed a wall of refrigerated drawers, twelve in all, resembling a huge filing cabinet. These drawers contained the remains of victims who had met a premature death as a result of a criminal offence.

Chapman could recall a time or two in his career when all twelve drawers were empty, but such occasions were rare and he found no solace in the fact that he had never seen all twelve occupied at the same time. Given the times in which he lived and worked, he rather thought he stood a better than even chance of seeing them all occupied before he ever saw them all empty again. The apprehensive familiarity with the victim which he had felt at the crime scene accompanied him as he pushed through the door leading to the autopsy room.

Dr. Richardson turned from his work and offered a smile and a nod of recognition as Chapman entered. A generally good-natured and pleasant individual, Richardson's smiling demeanor seemed incongruent here in this depressing place. He cast his eyes over Chap's damp and ruffled attire.

"Good morning, Chapman. You look like shit."

Very few people ever addressed Bouttell as "Chapman". His name was a combination of his mother's maiden name, Chapman, and his father's surname, Bouttell. As is the case with most names which, by their very structure, lend themselves to an abbreviated form, "Chap" or "Chappy" had long ago become the names by which he was more commonly known among his colleagues and friends.

Chap's overcoat was unbuttoned. He held it open and looked down at himself. The doctor was right. He looked like shit and felt much the same. "Thanks, Doc," he responded. "I've been on the job since four o'clock this morning. I'm wet, I'm cold, I'm tired, and I could use a stiff scotch about now, not to mention some good news from you."

"I'm afraid I haven't got much for you yet." Richardson shrugged. "As you can see, I'm still in the process of dissection."

Chap approached the table and looked down at the

remains of the murder victim. The smell, almost overpowering, invaded his senses, and he fought against the urge to throw up all over the shiny white floor.

The pathologist had opened the chest cavity from a point just above the sternum to just below the navel. The skin and flesh had been peeled back, exposing the rib cage which he had subsequently sawed through and lifted clear of the body, thus giving him unrestricted access to the internal organs. Most of these organs had been removed for closer clinical examination, and Chapman recognised a human liver resting on a set of scales sitting on an implement trolley next to the dissection table. He swallowed hard, unable to drag his eyes from the grotesque display.

An incision had been made just below the hairline at the back of the man's head and continued around the skull, ending just in front of each temple. Like the tough outer husk of a coconut, the scalp had been peeled forward over the skull and now lay across the top half of the man's face. It was an ugly, stomach-churning, surreal thing to see, but something Chapman also found hard to drag his eyes away from.

Like a lid to the cranium cavity, a circular piece in the uppermost section of the skull had been sawed through and removed. The brain now lay in a thin pool of clear, cranial fluid in a stainless-steel dish on the table alongside the man's head. If Chapman didn't know better, this could easily be a scene from some hideous 'B' rated horror film.

As his eyes wandered over the remains before him, he was even more convinced that, although necessary, autopsies were obscene, highly impersonal procedures.

"When Dr. Rogers returned from the scene," Richardson said, "he left some notes for me. When I discovered this was your case, I gave it priority. Had to pass a couple of cases on to others, who bitched and moaned they already have too much on their plate. But, I *am* the boss, and I guess that has its advantages."

"Is there anything at all you can tell me yet?" Chap asked.

"Not a lot, it's too early. He is about sixty years old, maybe a little older. Obviously very fit for his age. There is very little excess fat around the abdomen or the chest area and he has excellent muscle tone. This guy kept himself in pretty good nick. I've taken fingerprints, dental impressions, and samples to determine DNA. But, unless you've come up with any identification, we will have to wait for the system to run its course before we find out who this bloke is, or was."

"I've got diddly squat." Chap shrugged. "We found a wallet at the scene, near the body. We think it belonged to him, but it was empty, and there was no ID on the body. What about the bullet?"

"Also too early to tell," Richardson said. "I recovered a number of small fragments which I have already sent to ballistics for testing. Basically, the bulk of the round went straight through." He paused. "The caliber is for the folk in ballistics to determine but, if I were to hazard a guess, I would think a .38 or .357. I lean slightly towards the latter because it has the extra velocity required to send the projectile right through the back of the skull and out the front. The adult human skull is very hard, capable of withstanding considerable force. It has to—it's the only protection the brain has from external forces. It was almost certainly a very close-range shot. More than likely the muzzle was held up hard against the victim's head."

He leaned forward and turned the dead man's head to one side. With a gloved finger, he indicated the entry wound behind the right ear. "There are powder burns here that would support that."

"You know, Doc," Chap said, "it's strange. As I said, we found a wallet at the scene, presumably this fellow's, with all traces of identification removed. Up until an hour ago, there were no new missing person reports in the system which might have given us some idea who he is. And he was too well dressed and clean-cut-looking to be a homeless John Doe."

"Perhaps he just hasn't been missed by anyone yet," offered the pathologist.

"Maybe." Chap nodded. "Somehow, though, I feel as if I should know him."

"I've known you a long time, Chapman. You've got an excellent memory for names and faces. If you think you know this guy, you probably do." Richardson hesitated. "There is something I found which may be of interest to you. I don't know if it will help, but it struck me as unusual."

"I could use all the help I can get, unusual or otherwise," Chap said with interest.

Richardson turned back to the body, took a firm grip on the right arm at the wrist, lifted it clear of the table and turned it inwards.

"Here," he indicated. "Just above the elbow, at the back of the arm. What do you make of it?"

Chap took an involuntary step backwards, away from the table, and stared wide-eyed at the tattoo. In the shape of a diamond, it was small enough to be almost insignificant, but not to him. "Oh shit!" he heard himself murmur. "Oh shit!"

"Christ, Chapman, what's the matter?" Richardson appeared genuinely concerned. "You're as white as a ghost. What is it? Does that tattoo mean something to you?"

Chap steeled himself and took a pace forward, regaining his position closer to the table. He paused momentarily and then stooped to take a closer look at the strange little tattoo. "Show me his face, Doc."

Richardson dropped the man's arm and it slapped on the cold, steel table. He reached for the bloody scalp, gripped it tightly, and lifted it up and away from the upper face. He laid it back to its original position over the skull, exposing the dead man's features.

Immediately, Chap knew who it was and the recognition stunned him. "Eddie," he said, almost inaudibly.

"Jesus, you look terrible, Chap. Who is this guy?"

"Dickson, Eddie Dickson," Chap answered. "I've had a gut feeling, right from when I first saw him in the park, that I knew him from somewhere. The tattoo rang all the right bells. It's been a long time, but that's Eddie Dickson."

Chap turned away from the table, his mind racing, his stomach fluttering. He needed to get out of there. Suddenly, the fluttering turned to something more ominous and he fought against the urge to be sick. "I need your report as soon as possible, Doc."

Before Richardson could respond, Chap turned and walked quickly, head bowed, from the room.

Chapter Five

Finally, the heavy rain had eased. Now, only light intermittent showers fell across the city. Chap knew it would not stay that way. He had spent every winter of his life so far in Adelaide, and he knew that any respite from the freezing, drenching rain, typical for this time of the year, was only temporary. Dark, bulbous clouds suspended low in the sky promised an approaching night similar to the previous one.

Chap hated winter. He felt numb, confused and sad. He knew, however, it was not just the weather that stirred these emotions within him. It was the memories. Old memories which had lain just below the surface of his consciousness hit him every winter. Now, those memories flooded back and bathed him in a hollow sadness. A sadness accompanied by an emptiness that burned deep within his chest.

He knew he should have returned to the murder scene to check on his team's progress. From there, he should have returned to Police Headquarters to follow up on the latest developments, if indeed there were any. He did none of those things. Instead, shrouded in a fog of lethargy, he drove home. He needed a hot shower and a change of clothes. He needed a couple… no, more than a couple, of strong whiskies.

In his front room, Chap sat on an aging crushed velvet settee that had exhibited tell-tale signs of wear for longer than he could remember. He had showered and changed into a comfortable tracksuit. A phone call to his partner revealed that there were no new developments requiring his immediate personal attendance. He instructed Francis to dismantle the cordon around the crime scene, and he promised to explain his non-attendance when he returned to the office in the morning.

Chapman Bouttell was not a heavy drinker; not these days, anyway. There was a time when he could put the booze away with the best of them, but that was a long time ago. Nowadays, it was an occasional beer or two with colleagues, or a glass of warming whisky on a cold winter's night. This was one such night.

He took a long, slow slip from the glass, and the amber liquid burned his throat as he swallowed. He swirled the whisky in the tumbler, listening absently to the tune the ice cubes sang as they clinked against the glass. With his free hand, he rubbed his eyes in a futile attempt to wipe away the tiredness and the overwhelming feeling of depression threatening to overcome him.

The war in Vietnam was such a long time ago, over forty years. Chap had always imagined that those who were fortunate enough to survive the savage, senseless war, those just like himself, would live long, peaceful lives, dying only after attaining the respectability of very old age. That was the very least they deserved after surviving that hell-hole. It was what he wanted for himself and, up to this point, his life seemed to be heading in that direction. But, he knew a normal, happy, fruitful life post-Vietnam War was not something that came easy for many returned veterans. The suicide rate amongst Vietnam vets was disproportionately high, given the numbers who served. When compared to that of the general population, he remembered reading somewhere that the life expectancy of a Vietnam vet was approximately seventy-three years. How would they know that, he wondered? Only a handful of vets would have yet reached that age, even without the intervention of premature death.

Chap took another sip of his drink. Not so for Eddie Dickson. Like so many others, Eddie was never going to be one of those to make it to the estimated life expectancy.

He leaned back, his head resting on a worn, faded cushion, and he remembered.

The last time Chap saw Eddie Dickson was at Sydney's Mascot Airport in 1970. It was a long, slow flight on a military Hercules aircraft from Tan Son Nhat Airport in the city then known as Saigon. They spoke very little during the flight home. Mostly they slept, or pretended to, as each man dealt with his own mixed emotions. Mixed because they were going home alive, but six of their mates were not.

At Mascot, safely on Australian soil at last, they shook hands, exchanged awkward, uncomfortable embraces, and went their separate ways. The next time Chap saw his old friend was just a few hours ago, face-down in a suburban Adelaide park with a bullet hole in the back of his head.

Only four of them survived the war, four out of ten. A forty percent survival rate was hardly what Chap would have called acceptable. Had he known the odds beforehand, he might never have volunteered for the specialist unit. Now, and many times since, with the benefit of hindsight, he wished he never had. Given the nature of the duties they were required to perform, the attrition rate should have been obvious and predictable. But they were young, keen, and busting for a fight. The prospect of not coming home never entered their heads, or if it did, they never spoke about it.

He closed his eyes and allowed his thoughts to drift back across the years and linger for a moment on those who never made it home alive. He concentrated on their faces. Their images rose and ebbed in a hazy, disjointed slideshow. The images were not of men in their sixties, but young, ambitious, hungry soldiers, eager to play their part and take the fight to the enemy. Had they lived to reach his age, or that of Eddie Dickson, their faces would have changed with the passage of time, but their names would be forever etched in his mind.

Chap would never forget their names. 'Fergy' Ferguson, John 'Billy' Bunter, Ray Porter, 'Jock' McAndrew, David 'Girly' Galway and 'Big Fella' Colin Lewis. All dead. Six young, vibrant lives once filled with hope and promise, snuffed out in a few minutes of chaotic madness. These men came home in cold, grey caskets, strapped in the even colder cargo hold of a C-130 Hercules transport aircraft. They were robbed. Deprived of the chance to marry, raise families, and grow old with peace and dignity.

Chapter Six

Gunfire, incessant, deadly, and accurate, raked over them from an unseen enemy deeply entrenched in the jungle on the opposite side of the river. The metallic clatter of the Chinese-made Chicon 56 assault rifle, used by the North Vietnamese Army—NVA—was distinctive amid the cacophony of noise. Chapman Bouttell and the rest of his unit were in no doubt they were under attack by a far superior force of well-trained, disciplined enemy soldiers from the north.

The '*whump!*', '*whump!*' of mortar rounds exploding in their midst was deafening. They were taken completely by surprise. It was not supposed to be this way. The area was supposed to be clear of enemy troops. It was supposed to be a cold zone. They were not supposed to walk into a well-planned, well-executed ambush. They were all just days from heading home, their year-long tour of duty over. For each of them, the brutal, ugly war was over, or so they believed. Something went terribly wrong that day. Now, all these years later, Chap still didn't know what.

Although they were a tight, disciplined team, and had been even before they were deployed to Vietnam, this was the first and only time since they arrived in country that they had embarked on an operation as a complete unit and hence were all in the same place at the same time. Up until that day, they had worked together in small groups, or solo.

Conveniently ensconced in an area of comparative safety many kilometres from the site of the ambush, someone in a position of command decided this final mission was one which required the participation of every member of the unit. At the time, it was a decision which surprised each of them, given that this operation was, in truth, no different from any other they took part in, apart from it being their last before returning to Australia. But then, decisions made by senior military officers, most of whom had never experienced actual combat, were often considered questionable, particularly by those who were required to carry out orders derived from such decisions.

It was three-thirty in the afternoon. They were only three kilometres from their base camp. They walked in single file, each man separated from the man in front by several metres, along the bank of the Srepok River, a major tributary of Vietnam's Mekong River. Here, the jungle grew almost to the edge of the river. The trail they followed, although narrow, damp and spongy beneath their feet, was one they had used many times before. They were, for the most part, used to the occasional hazards associated with it. Occasionally, however, one of the team could be heard cursing softly as a misplaced foot sank to the ankle in sticky, clinging, odorous mud.

They had to cross the river to reach the opposite bank where they would then be close to the shores of Lac Lake, home for many generations to the native M'Nong people. This was the place which had been their unit's home for the last year. It was a narrow part of the Srepok, and they had crossed it many times before. Crossing the river always invoked a heightened state of apprehension as they would be exposed and vulnerable in waist-deep water.

Up until this point, it had been an incident-free operation, resulting in no contact with the enemy and hence no casualties on their side. Someone, somewhere, had passed on unreliable intelligence in regard to enemy movements and so the mood within the squad was light but not overly relaxed. There would be plenty of time for relaxation when they got back home to the real world.

They were all together, and rather than keep a specified distance from the man in front, as would be considered normal patrol formation, they had bunched up a little. Hence, conversation between them became more frequent and not as hushed as it should have been and indeed would have been on any of their earlier operations. They were, however, still alert. Aware that, although they had reached what they believed was a relatively safe area, they could not consider themselves to be out of danger, not yet.

Potentially, one of the most dangerous sections of the trail they followed was the river crossing. To keep their weapons dry, they carried them high above their heads and, as well as being awkward and uncomfortable, it made them fractionally slower to react in the event of an attack.

Although narrow here, this part of the river was not fast-flowing. The bed was rocky and uneven and staying upright required a degree of balance and concentration which meant some attention had to be diverted from the jungle, both behind and beyond.

Previous crossings here had always proved incident-free and, although they always stopped at the point they intended to enter the water and waited for a few minutes, examining the river and the jungle on the other side for any signs of trouble, they expected, and indeed saw, nothing untoward on this day.

Perhaps they were a little more relaxed than they thought they were. Perhaps, this close to their base camp, and another day closer to home, they were not as alert and attuned to their surroundings as they usually were. In hindsight, the silence should have been the thing which alerted them. Normally, there would be typical jungle noises all around; the rustle of small animals foraging for a meal on the forest floor; the twitter of birds calling from their perches high in the trees. But, on this day, there was a strange, unusual silence and no one noticed it. It would prove to be a fatal lapse in concentration.

James 'Jock' McAndrew was 'Tail End Charlie'. The affable, red-headed, freckle-faced Scot was the first to die. Jock was the last man in the line of ten and his job was to watch the trail behind them and alert the team should he spot a threat from their rear. 'Tail End Charlie' was not a coveted patrol position and McAndrew scored the role by the democratic process of elimination—he drew the short straw.

The Scotsman stood at the water's edge, waiting for the man in front to move further out into the river. Just before he stepped into the water, he turned slowly and closely examined the trail behind him one more time. Satisfied no ugly surprises followed them, he turned back to the river, moved cautiously forward, and joined his nine mates already in the water and strung out in a line ahead of him.

A mortar round, the first shot fired and the one that signaled the start of the ensuing slaughter, landed just a couple of metres from where Jock stood. The blast lifted him off the ground and hurled him backwards into the jungle undergrowth. He was dead before his body hit the ground.

Someone screamed. "Contact!"

Ryan 'Fergy' Ferguson, the man in front of McAndrew, spun around at the sound of the explosion. He knew instantly that the Scot was dead. One of McAndrew's legs had been torn from his body, thrown high in the air, and landed with a splash right next to where Ferguson stood. For a moment, he froze, unable to move, and stared at the gruesome sight floating in the water in front of him and slowly moving downstream with the current. It was a surreal moment. For a split second, everything seemed to go very quiet and still.

Then, suddenly, a cacophony of noise erupted, fracturing the silence.

Fergy was the next to die. Stitched across his back from left hip to right shoulder by a hail of 7.62 millimetre rounds, he fell face-down into the water and disappeared below the murky surface.

Suddenly, there began a mad, uncoordinated scramble as they turned mid-stream and made desperately for the bank where McAndrew had fallen. Fighting against the drag of the waist-deep water and the terrain of the rocky, uneven river bed, the going was clumsy and fatally slow. Mortar rounds erupted in their midst. Huge, heavy fountains of muddy, blood-stained water rained over them. In the centre of the river, the leader of the unit and its oldest member, thirty-five-year-old Sergeant Ray Porter, disappeared in a misty fog of red when a mortar round struck him in the middle of his back.

Chapman Bouttell was the third man in line to enter the water. He had almost reached the other side of the river when the first mortar exploded behind him. As he turned to look behind him, he saw Porter get hit and simply disappear in front of his eyes. One second he was there, then he was gone.

The two men in front of him, John Bunter, who had only seconds earlier stepped out of the water onto the opposite bank, and David 'Girly' Galway, both died in the first deadly salvo. Chap glanced back to his front in time to see them both go down under a deadly hail of bullets. They never stood a chance. Pieces of bone and bloody tissue flew haphazardly into the air as the high velocity rounds slammed into them, striking them in the chest and head.

Galway took a moment longer to fall than Bunter. He turned and faced Chap, a few paces behind him. There was now a gaping, jagged, bloody hole where, just seconds before, the left side of his face used to be. Even from where Chap stood, he saw Galway's one remaining eye begin to glaze over in death. Then, another hail of bullets riddled his back and he was thrown forward into the water. Chap stared in shock as Galway slipped beneath the surface. A washed-out pool of pink began to spread on the surface around Chap's knees and he instinctively stepped back in horror, almost losing his footing on the uneven river bed.

In the confusion of noise and panic, and driven by adrenaline coursing through his veins, Chap dived below the surface and struck out for the river bank behind him. He could not swim underwater while carrying his weapon, so he let it slip from his grip and it sank to the muddy bottom beneath him. His mind raced as he tried to comprehend what was happening. Just above him, through the shallow depth, he heard the muffled sounds of battle. Bullets entered the water all around him with a softened *"phhtt"*.

Chap surfaced only once on his desperate swim, just long enough to grab a much-needed lungful of air. In the brief moment his head was above water, he saw none of his comrades. The noise of the one-sided battle continued to rage around him. He ducked below the surface again and, although he swam with his eyes open, he was unable to see more than a few feet in front of him. When he involuntarily swallowed a mouthful of water, churned muddy and red with blood, it tasted foul and the urge to vomit was strong. He hoped he was heading for the river bank and not swimming either up or down stream or, God forbid, directly into the waiting arms of the enemy.

Presently, he felt the river bed rise against his knees and knew he had reached the bank. He waited below the surface; an eternity, it seemed, until he thought his lungs would burst. Then, when he could hold his breath no longer and was about to take another mouthful of putrid water, he kicked against the bottom, sprang from the water, and plunged headlong into the undergrowth beyond the trail they had all just traversed.

Now somewhat protected and hidden from view by the dense foliage surrounding him, he stumbled forward, deeper into the jungle. He did not know where he was going, only that he needed to put some distance between himself and certain death behind him. When he had advanced approximately three hundred metres, he stumbled across the remainder of his unit: Eddie Dickson, Charlie Cobb, Brian Elliott and Colin Lewis. They were hunkered down behind the butt of a huge tree which lay fallen on the jungle floor. They heard Chap approach before they saw him. He crashed noisily through the thick tangle of vegetation, and when he emerged into the tiny clearing where they sheltered, Eddie Dickson called out loudly, "Chappy… Chappy… over here!"

Chap collapsed to his knees, exhausted. He fell forward on his hands and now, on all fours, he sucked deeply at the humid air. Finally, he looked up at his friends. Each face looking back at him bore an expression of confusion and shock.

Brian Elliott seemed to be the only one still carrying a weapon. He stood protectively over Colin Lewis who sat slumped against the base of the tree behind which they rested. It was then that Chap realised Lewis was badly wounded.

'Big Fella' Colin Lewis, the biggest and toughest of them all, sat slumped on the jungle floor with his back against the trunk of the tree. His eyes dropped to his hands and he stared in shock and awe as his bloodied intestines slipped through his fingers. He moaned pitifully as he tried in vain to push them back into the gaping, jagged hole in his abdomen where gunfire had almost cut him in two. Only the Big Fella could have made it this far into the almost impenetrable jungle without succumbing sooner to his horrific wounds.

When Lewis eventually looked up and focused on Chap, it was his eyes Chap remembered most: wide with fear, and filled with the knowledge that death was only moments away. It was reaching for him, clawing at him, dragging him down into the depths of darkness from where he knew he would never return.

Suddenly, the pain kicked in. Lewis started screaming, a primeval, mournful scream which belonged in the depths of hell. It seemed to go on forever. Chap remembered how he wished he would stop screaming and then, moments later when he finally did, he wished he would scream some more.

The four remaining members of the unit stood and stared in numb, disbelieving silence at their dead comrade. Still confused and bewildered at what had happened back at the river, they could not look away from the face of their friend slumped on the ground at their feet. Finally, Charlie Cobb knelt down in front of Lewis, reached out, and closed the lifeless, staring eyes. When Cobb stood up, he was visibly struggling against a flood of tears threatening to overwhelm him.

The unit was a close-knit squad. They looked out for each other. Watched each other's back. They did it throughout their training back in Australia, and they had been doing it here in this Godforsaken country for the last twelve months. Cobb and Lewis, however, were particularly close. Whenever it was necessary for only two to go on an operation, Lewis and Cobb always seemed to pair off together. It was all about trusting your mate, and believing he would watch your back as diligently as you watched his. It was a creed which applied to all of them, but these two seemed to be more comfortable working together rather than with any other member of the team. It was not that they had never worked with anyone else, or didn't want to—it was just that the first time two men were required for an operation, it was Lewis and Cobb who put their hands up and from that time on, they almost always worked together.

"We need to take him home," Cobb said to the others. It wasn't a suggestion, it was a statement about how it was going to be.

Eddie Dickson, the next most senior man after Ray Porter, who never made it out of the river, looked at Cobb. "We can't do that, Charlie. Col has gone. So have the others. We need to get out of here. The enemy will know some of us got out of the river alive and they will be coming across after us. They're probably right behind us."

Each of them turned and stared back the way they had come.

"What about Colin?" Cobb demanded.

Dickson raised his hand to silence them all. He cocked his head in the direction of the river. "Just listen," he said. "The gunfire has stopped. They are coming now. We have to move out. When we get out of here, we will send someone back for Col, and the others. There's nothing we can do for any of them now. You know they would want us to get clear."

He looked around at the bedraggled remainder of the unit and noticed Brian Elliott was the only one carrying a weapon, an AK47 Russian made assault rifle. "Anyone else got a weapon?" he asked.

"I lost mine in the river," Chap answered.

"Me too," confirmed Charles Cobb. "The Big Fella too, I think." He looked down once more at his dead friend.

Eddie Dickson paused. "I lost mine escaping through the jungle. A lucky shot took it from my hands. I wanted to stop and pick it up but the fire was too heavy and I had to keep going. I think it was smashed but I was not fucking going back to find out."

"Have we all still got our knives?" Chap asked.

Each agreed he still carried his hunting knife strapped to his lower leg.

"Four knives, and one AK47," Brian Elliott said. "We'll never make it if we stand and fight. They've got us outnumbered and outgunned."

"Five knives," Chap corrected. "Col has still got his."

"Brian is right," Dickson said. "There's too many of them. Did any of you get a shot off?"

He was greeted with silence. "There you go." He shrugged. "Those we lost at the river died in the opening salvo. There were ten of us, and I don't think any of us had a chance to return fire. Jesus, it was a fuckin' massacre. Can we get a consensus here? Do we stay here and almost certainly die, or do we make a run for it?"

"Where do we go?" Elliott asked. "We obviously can't go back and cross the river."

"The tunnels," Chap suggested suddenly.

"What?" Cobb asked.

"The tunnels," Chap repeated. He looked around into the jungle in front of them. "You know, the old tunnel network we used to use. I think it is only a few hundred metres to our west."

"Are you sure?" Dickson asked.

"I'm certain." Chap nodded.

"Can you find it again? We haven't used it in months."

"I think so. It's our only chance to get clear. We can follow it and cross back over the river further upstream. When we get back to the village, we can call in an airstrike. I, for one, would like to see these arseholes blown to hell."

"Are you sure you can find it?" Brian Elliott pressed.

"We'll never know unless we try, and the alternative is not worth thinking about," Chap answered.

"Okay," Dickson said, "do we all agree?"

"Let's go," Elliott said.

Charles Cobb remained silent for a moment, and then he reached down and placed his hand on Lewis's shoulder. "We'll bring you home, mate. I promise." He straightened and turned to the others. "Okay, let's hustle."

"Chap, you take point," Dickson directed. "You can lead us to the tunnels. Brian, you and Charlie follow. I'll take the tail."

Charles Cobb protested, "No, Eddie! We've already lost one leader today. You stay in the middle with Brian. I've got the tail."

"Charlie, I…" Dickson began to protest.

Cobb reached out and snatched the AK47 from Elliott's hands. "Decision made." He looked at Elliott and slapped the banana-shaped magazine on the rifle. "Full?" he asked.

"Yes," Elliott confirmed. "Like everybody else, I never got a shot off."

"Right, fuck off, you lot! I'll drop back a bit, but for Christ's sake don't lose me. I'll never find the bloody tunnel on my own." He turned away and started to move off in the direction of the river before Eddie Dickson could object.

They watched Cobb hurry away, and then Dickson turned to Chap and Brian Elliott. "Okay, fellas, move out!" he reluctantly ordered.

Without warning, the jungle exploded around them. They all ducked instinctively as bullets whined and slapped into the canopy above, bringing twigs and jungle foliage raining down on them.

"Go…go!" Cobb screamed.

As one, they turned and raced off into the undergrowth, ducking and weaving through the thick vegetation. As they ran, each of them hoped Cobb was following.

They had waited too long around the fallen tree and Lewis's body, discussing their next move. Now, the enemy had found them. Once again, the familiar sound of the Chicom Type 56, spitting 7.62 millimetre rounds at a rate of sixty rounds per minute, chattered noisily from close behind.

As he ran, Chap found himself hoping he could find the tunnels. Suddenly, above the din of the gunfire, he heard someone yell.

"I'm hit! I'm hit!"

Chap stopped, turned around, and started to move towards the sound of the voice, only to run into Eddie Dickson who grabbed him roughly and held him back.

"Keep going, Chap!" Dickson yelled. "Charlie's down. Brian's got him. He's hit but he's alive."

Just then, Brian Elliott appeared from the bush, carrying Charles Cobb across his shoulder. Chap saw instantly Cobb was badly wounded in the upper legs. Chips of bark from tree trunks, small branches, and leaves rained down on them as the onslaught from automatic gunfire continued relentlessly.

"Don't stop!" Elliott yelled. "Don't stop! The bastards are almost on top of us!"

Again, they turned and raced away, weaving awkwardly through the dense jungle.

At one point, Chap stopped briefly, turned a full three hundred and sixty degrees and looked anxiously around, as if looking for a landmark which would indicate he was leading them in the right direction. Satisfied the tunnel was close, he moved a few metres to his left, turned around again, and stopped. He kicked at the deep leaf litter under his feet and found nothing. The tiniest hint of panic began to flicker deep inside his gut. What if he was wrong? What if the tunnel entrance was nowhere near here? He moved a couple of paces back, and to his right, and swept the ground once more with his boot. There! There it was! "Here!" he called. "It's here."

He dropped to his knees and lifted the rapidly deteriorating wooden cover concealing the entrance. Beneath the cover plate, a thick mass of cobwebs covered a small hole marginally wider than a man's shoulders and extending approximately three metres into the dark, damp earth.

Chap stared into the black pit momentarily, and then quickly brushed at the cobwebs with his hand. He knew if he hesitated, he might not be able to find the courage to enter the narrow shaft and time wasted thinking about it would surely bring the enemy right to them.

Chap was not one to suffer from claustrophobia but these cramped, hot, steamy labyrinths always invoked feelings of unease in him. This complex, abandoned long ago and falling into disrepair, had been declared clear of enemy presence some months previously. Initially shown the system in the early weeks of their deployment in country by the M'Nong people with whom they lived, Chap and his unit had used the complex only a few times. He was well aware that rats, snakes, spiders and scorpions, among other unsavoury members of the insect and animal community, lived down here in this dark, eerie, poorly ventilated underworld.

Vietnam was crisscrossed with a vast network of tunnels originally built by the Communist Vietminh following World War Two, when the country became a colony of the French. Covering many hundreds of kilometers, some tunnels were more elaborate than others, with areas beneath the jungle floor used for accommodation, kitchens, hospitals, workshops, military operations centres and ammunition storage.

Chap's job was to kill the people who built these subterranean mazes, but there existed a part of him that admired the commitment and the allegiance they bore to their country, their leaders, and to their faith in the Communist doctrine.

Following the defeat of the French and the subsequent onset of war between North Vietnam and South Vietnam, Ho Chi Minh, the leader of North Vietnam, ordered the expansion of the tunnel network. The work was carried out by the Viet Cong, who used them mostly during the day as sanctuaries, where they could rest before emerging under the cover of darkness to take the fight to their enemy.

Steeling himself, Chap lowered himself down into the hole, supporting his body weight on his elbows on the lip of the entrance. When all but his head and shoulders were in the hole, he tucked his elbows into his sides and dropped out of sight.

Halfway down one side of the shaft, there was a side tunnel which branched off to the left. Built to accommodate the much smaller Vietnamese, Chap's shoulders brushed against the sides of the pit. With some difficulty, he managed to manoeuvre his body into the shaft, where he paused to catch his breath and allow his eyes to accustom to the darkness which engulfed him. A strong smell of mildew and damp soil filled his nostrils.

He knew that, a few metres ahead, this side tunnel opened up into a man-made cavern, probably once used as a storage area. He remembered he could stand in the cavern, albeit stooped, and he remembered there were other spaces just like it at regular intervals along the length of the complex. It was the getting to each of these larger areas by crawling on hands and knees along narrow, uncomfortable connecting tunnels that he never got used to.

In the early weeks and months of their deployment, the tunnel was a relatively safe way to get to and from their base camp and avoid detection. However, the structure was old, and in many places some minor collapsing had occurred. Constructed a long time ago, it was sited too close to the river and, with the ravages of time and the yearly monsoon seasons, excessive dampness had seeped into the complex, leaving the walls and the low ceilings perilously close to total collapse.

As Chap lay in the side tunnel, waiting for his eyes to adjust to the darkness, he hoped he could remember which way to go to take them out safely. The enemy must surely be very close behind them. He turned slightly onto one side and called up into the thin shaft of daylight that filtered down to where he waited. "Okay, lower Charlie down!"

Awkwardly and agonisingly slowly, Dickson and Elliott lowered the badly wounded Cobb down the narrow shaft. With difficulty, Chap maneuvered Cobb into the side tunnel, dragged him deeper into the black interior and, as he waited for Elliott and Dickson to follow, he comforted Cobb, silently fearing his friend was not going to make it out of the tunnel alive.

The deeper they crawled into the tunnels, the darker it became. The only light they had was provided by a small torch carried by Brian Elliott. The batteries were low, but, with the aid of a small compass Elliott also carried in a pouch on his webbing belt, Chap was confident they were heading in the right direction. Getting lost down here was not an option, and something he did not want to contemplate.

They took turns carrying and sometimes dragging Cobb painfully, slowly, clumsily, through the stifling confines of the tunnel. As they moved ever so slowly forward, they encountered occasional pools of dirty, stagnant water which had to be crawled through. The stench in these places was almost overpowering, but they dare not stop or even think about turning back. They rested briefly when they reached each of the larger cavern areas, and Chap remembered, as they moved ahead again after each such rest, how Cobb's cries of agony increased in intensity, rising to screams of unbearable pain when, occasionally, someone slipped, stumbled on the damp, muddy floor and lost his grip on the badly wounded Cobb, dropping him to the floor of the tunnel.

Then there was the morphine. They had only a small amount, and he remembered how it induced a painless, delirious semi-consciousness. Until it ran out; then the screams began again and there was nothing they could do but listen to the mournful, harrowing cries echoing through the long, narrow tunnel and try in vain to comfort their friend.

And, there was the blood, so much blood. The field dressings they had packed into the wounds in Cobb's legs were soaked and now barely stemmed the flow. If they didn't get out of this place soon, their friend was going to bleed out, and this was not a good place to die.

Finally, they surfaced cautiously, a long way from the ambush site. They used the tunnels to escape that day, leaving behind them a heavy haze of blue gunsmoke slowly dissipating in the jungle canopy, the strong smell of cordite, and six good men.

Chapter Seven

Chap placed his glass on the coffee table, lifted himself wearily from the settee, and walked slowly across the room. He felt lightheaded and slightly unsteady on his feet. He hadn't eaten since dinner the previous evening and the whisky was beginning to have an effect. He stopped in front of the large, open fireplace. The flames had died down, and he stared into the crackling embers.

Above the mantelpiece hung a large, elaborate, gilt-edged mirror, one of the last remaining remnants of his long-ended marriage. He'd always hated the damn thing but he had never got round to discarding it. He took it down once, years ago, intending to get rid of it, but when he saw that the wall behind it was much paler than the wall surrounding it, he put it back again, opting for the lesser of the two eyesores.

He stared at the pale and drawn reflection staring back at him. The eyes were the eyes of a stranger, dark and empty. There were tears in there, somewhere in the haunted, hollow depths of his soul, but they would not come. Slowly, he reached across his body and pulled the sleeve of his tracksuit up over his elbow. Gently, he rubbed his fingers over the tiny, diamond-shaped tattoo.

Chap, Eddie Dickson and the others who made up the Diamond One team were trained specifically for the things they were required to do. Selected from the elite Special Air Services Regiment, they were taken to a top-secret location deep in the rain forests of far north Queensland. Here, they underwent three months of gruelling, intensive, morale-shattering training.

Notwithstanding, they were recruited from the ranks of the SAS, the best of the best. Such was the intensity of their training. There were some who never made the grade and were sent back to their regiments. The training program was tougher, both physically and mentally, than anything any of them had experienced before.

They came to their new unit already proficient in how to kill quickly, and silently; with their bare hands, a knife, a piece of wire, even a bootlace if that was all that was available. Now, those skills were honed to an even finer degree. They learned to sleep sitting high in the foliage of a tree. They learned to lie, unmoving, barely breathing, for hours, in leech and mosquito infested swamps. They learned to go for days at a time with little or nothing at all to eat, and just the barest amount of water to keep them from dehydrating in the steamy jungle. It was here, deep in the tropical rain forests of far north Queensland where they started their daily diet of fish and rice.

When the training was over, they were extremely fit, extremely angry, and extremely willing, ready and able to kill their fellow man. Not once during this three-month period were any of those who made it through told the full details of what would be expected of them, once they landed in the country to which they were assigned.

Before they left the training ground, a man whom their trainers intentionally gave no name to, and who offered none himself, came and tattooed each of them. Right there in the damp, humid jungle. They all wondered about it, but none shied from it. On the contrary, they were, to a man, strangely proud of it. It set them apart, made them different, special. That was the day each of them became members of the elite and highly secretive Diamond One.

Chapter Eight

When sleep finally overpowered Chap, it was shallow and haunted by dreams that came to him in a bizarre sideshow peppered with images of war and the faces of dying soldiers. When he woke, he had no recollection of exactly when during the long, restless night it happened, but he made a decision. Despite the bad dreams and the unwelcome, unheralded memories, it was a decision which came more easily and with more clarity than he might have expected. As he lay in his bed, staring through the dim light at the ceiling and listening to the rain drumming on the roof outside, his mind drifted again to those chaotic days so long ago.

No one knew the extent of his experiences in Vietnam. It was something he never discussed with anyone, not even his ex-wife with whom, in the early years of their marriage when their love was fresh and new and still exciting, he shared many confidences. She knew of his military service, of course, but she did not know—indeed no one knew—the exact nature of his duties during the twelve months he spent on active service in what many have labelled as history's most unpopular war. No one, that is, except the four survivors of his unit who came home and, of course, those who sent them over there in the first place.

It was not that he didn't want to talk about it; the so-called experts would insist there was plenty of evidence to suggest talking about these things to a trained counsellor was excellent therapy. But Chap had lasted this long without feeling the need to talk about it with anyone and he suspected he would continue to do so. In this case, however, things were different. There was a very strong reason why he elected not to discuss it and, at least in Chap's case, it had little to do with feeling the need or otherwise.

It was called a Secrecy Agreement. They all signed it. It demanded their ongoing silence in relation to their missions in Vietnam. A documented oath of silence warning that any breach would be met with official and emphatic denial, by both military and governmental authorities, that the top-secret unit ever existed. It promised swift justice and harsh penalties should such a breach occur. As young men, yet to be blooded in the art of war, these were intimidating threats which served as a strong incentive to remain resolutely silent.

Chap did his job. He kept his part of the bargain just as he and the others of his unit had agreed. Of course, he couldn't be sure this was the case with the other survivors, but he suspected it was. With the passing of the years, he learned to suppress the horrific, tormenting memories of the war. He learned to file them away in some distant, rarely visited corner of his mind. However, confining them in the far reaches of his consciousness and never speaking of them was one thing. Forgetting was something else entirely. He would never forget.

Chapman Bouttell was a man of his word. He was from the old school. A man who maintained a degree of honour he held dear. It was a characteristic trait he found sadly lacking in many of the people he came into contact with in the course of his present occupation. He gave his word all those years ago, and he would keep it. The sudden, unexpected emergence of his recently deceased friend, Eddie Dickson, had unfortunately served to bring the latent memories to the surface, but had done nothing to undermine his resolve to keep the secret.

For Chap, there was no real choice. He had to keep his word. He had worked hard for a lot of years, bringing killers to justice, so how could he now admit that, deep in his heart, deep within the core of his being, he believed himself to be no more of a man than those he hunted now in the pursuit of his present profession?

In his mind, the things he did back then amounted to murder. It mattered not what kind of spin his superiors might have put on it, or what the government of the day might put on it; it was murder, plain and simple. The things he did over there, the things *they* did, amounted to murder, and murder could never be justified, regardless of the circumstances that precipitated it. He had spent the last twenty-seven years upholding those principles and he believed he had a pretty good sense of what constituted murder and what didn't.

There was such a thing as justifiable homicide, he had seen that a couple of times in the job, but when he stripped away the veneer and broke it down to its essential components, the nuts and bolts of it, he could not justify the things they did by sugar-coating them with time-worn clichés such as 'acceptable conduct under the actions of war', or 'just a soldier following orders and doing his job'. What he and the others of his unit did amounted to cold-blooded, premeditated murder. They hunted men down and when they found them, they killed them. Men just like themselves; young, scared, perhaps with families pining for them, perhaps with sweethearts anxiously awaiting their return. They trained long and hard to do just that and they were very, very good at it.

Such is the nature of war that it has the ability to make men do things they would not normally do; things which, under different circumstances, any reasonable, thinking man would consider abhorrent. Things that might be, and often were, considered acceptable because they were acts committed in the name of war. What Chap's unit did, did not fall within those parameters. With the benefit of hindsight, there simply was no way he could excuse their actions, and it was not just the secrecy agreement he was a party to which guaranteed his continued silence, it was also about his own personal shame.

In 1969, Chapman Bouttell was twenty-two years of age. He was full of the gung-ho bravado that went hand in hand with being a young man serving his country in a war which he believed to be the right and proper course of action for a country perceived to be under threat of Communist rule. It was how they all felt. Their country needed them. There was not the slightest hesitation by any of them to put their hand up to go. They were doing their bit to bring the war to a speedier close; at least that was what they were told. They believed it because they were young and naïve. How could he admit now, all these years later, that they covertly followed enemy forces across the border into neighbouring Cambodia and killed them?

Cambodia's King Sihanouk, believing the United States would eventually be defeated and driven out of South Vietnam, and afraid such a defeat would lead to the subjugation of his country, had long and loudly declared Cambodia's neutrality in the conflict raging just beyond his borders.Forty years ago, Chap knew nothing of the politics behind Sihanouk's declaration. He had no desire to know. In truth, he had never heard of King Sihanouk. He did know it was forbidden to take the conflict beyond the borders of a neutral country, and the fact that elements of the Communist North Vietnamese Army sought respite and refuge from the fatigue of battle inside Cambodia, was of little concern to him. Even less so in the fact the Cambodians seemed to turn a blind eye.

In groups of twos, and threes, and sometimes alone, Chap and the others would slip undetected over the border into Cambodia. Silently, they made their way to where soldiers of the NVA rested from recent combat missions and refurbished their supplies from stores filtering down a tributary of the infamous Ho Chi Minh Trail, which meandered for hundreds of kilometres from Hanoi in North Vietnam to the south.

There were several such sanctuaries inside Cambodia. They were not static camps, but could be easily and quickly moved from place to place. They were also never so far from the border as to make it difficult to slip back across into Vietnam and take their enemy unawares. Such surprise attacks were becoming both more frequent and more costly in the numbers of casualties sustained by allied forces, and pursuit of the Communist-backed forces was often frustrated by their ultimate flight back across the border into 'neutral' Cambodia.

Ultimately, diplomatic ties between Cambodia and the United States were severed when several CIA plots dating from the early 1960s, designed to get rid of Sihanouk, were discovered. The king subsequently terminated all aid programs emanating from Washington, leaving little doubt in the corridors of power in the United States that the Cambodians were aware of the Communists' blatant disregard for their neutrality. The fact that the Sihanouk regime did nothing to curtail Communist troop movements within their borders and seemed to tacitly accept their relatively peaceful existence in the region, was considered by deskbound bureaucrats in Washington to be a deliberate snub to the United States administration. All diplomatic approaches to the Cambodians fell on deaf ears. Something had to be done. Chapman Boutell's unit was chosen to do it.

Classified top secret, the mission they were tasked with was given the code name Operation Diamond. Their job was to conduct clandestine operations inside Cambodia designed to confuse, disorganise, and hopefully terrorise the enemy.

Assigned the radio call sign Diamond One, the unit was given unlimited parameters within which to work. Their superiors didn't care *how* they did it, just so long as they *did* it. They were to track the enemy, find him, and kill him. In doing so, they were to cause him the most inconvenience possible. Most importantly, lest these forays into Cambodia become a matter of public knowledge, the rule was "don't get caught!"

They waited. In sniper's hides, and in meticulously planned and staged ambushes, they waited. While they waited, filthy, malaria-carrying mosquitoes buzzed and dive-bombed any piece of bare skin inadvertently left exposed. Muscles and joints silently screamed with the fire of cramp from endless hours without moving. Perspiration ran freely and the saltiness of it stung their eyes, attracting even more mosquitoes.

Sometimes there was only one of them, waiting for that one clear, clean shot. Sometimes there were two or three of them, working together in disciplined silence for much of the time. Minimal conversation between them was a definite requirement. They devised a series of hand signals which everyone in the unit understood. And they waited. Searching through telescopic rifle sights for the most senior enemy officer they could find.

It was imperative that the timing should be perfect. It always was. Eventually, the target was found, and a man died. One shot was all it took. Just one shot from a high-powered rifle fired by an Aussie Digger highly skilled in the art. One shot, and someone's husband, someone's father, someone's son died.

Then they fled. Like phantoms in the night, they vanished. Silent and fast, deep into the jungle. Melding, blending into the surrounding tangled undergrowth, back across the border into Vietnam. Then they did it again, and again.

Sometimes they set an ambush in the jungle on the Cambodian side of the border and waited for the unsuspecting enemy to enter the trap as they made their way wearily to their makeshift sanctuary. In the short ensuing firefight, they killed as many of the enemy as they could.

Sometimes they crept silently up to an enemy encampment and, just as silently, cut the throat of a sentry, leaving him where he lay to be found later by his comrades. Then again, they slipped away, back to the relative safety of the Vietnamese Central Highlands where they were harboured by the M'Nong people, one of the many Montagnard tribes indigenous to the mountainous region of South Vietnam.

The Montagnards were despised, persecuted, and brutalised by the Communist north for their allegiance to both Australian and US forces. Of a darker complexion, and with an entirely different culture and language to the Vietnamese, the Montagnard hill tribes were an asset of immeasurable value to the allied forces. It was not difficult for these immensely proud people to align themselves with US and Australian troops; after all, their allegiance was purchased. Paid for with school buildings and education for their children, new huts in their villages to replace those razed to the ground by the ruthless northern army, and money (lots of it), and rice (tons of it).

Chap and the men of Diamond One lived with the M'Nong for twelve months. They slept on mats on the ground in a communal hut for single men and boys of the tribe. They ate the same food as the villagers, mostly fish and rice with the occasional unidentifiable animal thrown in to add extra protein. They had to smell just like the Vietnamese. It was believed the enemy could always tell when American or Australian soldiers were nearby, because they could smell them. Apparently, Caucasians have an odour distinctly different from the Asian race. After a few weeks of eating the exact same diet, the men of Diamond One, if not looking Asian, certainly began to smell Asian.

The Montagnard people kept the tall, pale strangers who

had come into their midst from a land they had never heard of, hidden from the frequent and often violent searches conducted by North Vietnamese troops, and occasionally by a Viet Cong unit. Never, not once, did they ask for anything in return. The good fortune that came their way in the form of money, rice and other more tangible gifts was never asked for, but kept coming anyway. All they had to do was feed and hide the benevolent foreigners and provide occasional intelligence on movements of the NVA and Viet Cong, who they despised anyway.

Even in the face of summary execution and the brutal rape of their women, both common occurrences, they did not break. Not even the oldest and frailest among them and these were usually the ones who, with hands brutally bound behind their skinny, bony backs, were paraded in front of the entire village prior to being dispatched with a single bullet to the head.

Nonetheless, in Chap's mind, what Diamond One was required to do was not a lot different. They committed their 'crimes' in a neutral country; a country they had no authority or mandate to enter.

Protests by the Cambodian government, and there were many, were met with strong and firm denials that the allies would ever consider taking the war across a neutral border. It simply was not happening, was the adamant, indignant response from the corridors of power in both Washington and Canberra.

Their actions, however, had the desired effect. They did cause confusion, apprehension and fear amongst the enemy, and that was exactly what they were ordered to do. The hit-and-run tactics were not new initiatives; they were tried and true, having been used to great effect in past conflicts, albeit never in a neutral country. It was illegal under the terms of engagement relating to Australia's deployment in the war zone. It was illegal under the terms of the Geneva Convention. It was probably illegal under any international law Chap could think of, and some he couldn't. But this was Vietnam, and Vietnam was a dirty war.

Back home in Australia, and in the US, the tide of anti-war protest swelled and gathered momentum. Chap had no time for the long-haired, pot-smoking, rent-a-crowd protesters, and, as far as he could tell, that was what most of them seemed to be. Oh, he supposed there were a few well-meaning folks among them. Folk who might have lost a loved one to the war, for instance, or those who held strong anti-conscription beliefs. But, for the most part, he saw them as a bunch of brain-dead sheep following a handful of equally brain-dead politicians and assorted peace mongers, marching *en masse* through city streets and storming docksides, preventing vital supplies bound for the troops from being loaded aboard transport ships. Little did they know, but these misguided fools only made the job more difficult for those who served in the war zone.

In the face of all the media attention such protests attracted, if the actions of his unit ever became public, the world press would have a field day. The political ramifications would be felt in many countries and it was highly likely that even now, forty-plus years later, high-ranking military personnel and politicians, retired or otherwise, would be ducking for cover everywhere. The acronym CYA—Covering Your Arse—existed now, just as it did back then. Heads would roll, and it was conceivable some would even find themselves facing war crimes charges. The fact it all took place over forty years ago would not in any way lessen the severity of their acts, nor would it save them from eternal vilification, or prison.

It is conceivable that back then, when it was all happening, had the actions of Diamond One been exposed, entire governments may have fallen. Australian troops engaged in top secret, aggressive military action inside the borders of a neutral country, action sanctioned by both

Australian and American military commands and hence, by association, their respective governments, would be Christmas on a stick to the international media.

It may well be forty years later, and governments may have changed many times in the interim, but the gravity of what they did, and the consequences which would undoubtedly follow, could not be diminished. What the men of Diamond One did was wrong. It was illegal, and the naïvety of their youth was no defense. Murder was murder. So, Chap Bouttell would honour the secrecy agreement.

Chapter Nine

Chap drove to Police Headquarters early. It was a ritual he followed daily in an attempt to avoid bad-tempered commuters caught in the morning peak hour traffic snarl. It rarely worked. He had lost too much personal time already on the case and, in the interests of maintaining continuity, it was important that the investigation be kept moving.

The more time that elapsed without any significant breakthrough, the colder the trail became. Discovering the body was that of Eddie Dickson was a breakthrough, but the killer was still out there somewhere. Chap was determined to find who murdered his old friend, and why. Not just because it was his job, but because now, it was personal.

Important early investigations at the scene were hampered by the abysmal weather. Now, twenty-four hours later, the sun shone with early promise of a fine day. Chap was alone in the Homicide Squad Incident Room. Photographs taken at the murder scene were pinned to a large white display board fixed to one wall. His eyes wandered slowly over the pictures and lingered momentarily on the body of Eddie Dickson, face-down on the wet cobblestones in Heywood Park. They were good photographs, he thought. Two sets in all. One set he found in a folder on his desk when he arrived, and those he looked at now. The new guy in Forensics, Paul what's-his-name, had done a good job. Chap made a mental note to compliment him when next they met.

The crackle of a police radio drifted to him from the main squad room. Some units were being dispatched; others relayed the outcome of completed tasks to the Communications Centre. He glanced at his watch—6:50 a.m. In a few minutes, there would be a shift change. Cold, tired, midnight-shift members would gladly begin wending their way home through the early morning traffic build-up. Oncoming day-shift personnel would begin signing out weapons and checking occurrence sheets for any carry-over tasks uncompleted by the outgoing shift.

Slowly at first, the Homicide squad room would begin to stir with activity as detectives arrived and began thinking about their duties for the day. Coffee would be consumed in copious quantities, friendly back and forth banter would begin, and the solitude Chap had been enjoying would be consumed by the indecipherable hum of a dozen overlapping conversations.

Tony Francis was the first of his team to arrive. He was surprised to see Chap already in the Incident Room. He knew his partner was an early starter, but it was not often Chap arrived before him. Francis was followed soon after by Detectives Smith and Sanderson. They exchanged greetings and complaints about the weather as they jostled to be first to the coffee makings. Sanderson cursed his own clumsiness at spilling some of the hot brew on his tie.

"Shit! The bride just bought this tie for me yesterday," he groaned. "She told me not to spill coffee on it!"

The other detectives in the room laughed. Tony Francis sipped casually at his own coffee and moved to the front of the room. He stood next to Chap and studied the photos closely for a few moments. Then, without taking his eyes from the prints, he said, "I suppose it's too much to expect any good news might have come in overnight?"

Chap looked at the contents of his own coffee cup, sniffed at it suspiciously and placed the mug on a nearby desk. "I have a name, but nothing else," he said. "I'm waiting on the ballistics report and the results of the autopsy."

He turned to face Sanderson, who was still dabbing at the stain on his tie with a handkerchief. "Bob, I want you and Smithy to go back to the park. Conduct house-to-house enquiries on the same homes the uniformed boys covered. Make sure they didn't miss anything. There are more photos here on my desk. Take a good one from the folder and show it around. We have a name now, and who knows, we might get lucky. That name, by the way, is Dickson. Edward Dickson, probably more commonly known as Eddie."

The two detectives moved to Chap's desk and the photos that lay there.

"Oh, and before you go," Chap added, "thanks for sticking with it yesterday. Covering for me, I mean."

Smith shuffled through the photos in the folder, decided on one, and turned back to Chap. "No problem, boss. That's the kind of decent, upstanding blokes we are."

Chap smiled and watched as they left the room.

Francis moved away from the notice board and took a seat. He watched Chap quizzically. "You've got something, haven't you? We're all waiting for some clue to the victim's ID, and you already know his name. How does that work?"

Chap stepped across to the photo display. He reached up and unpinned one of the pictures; one of the photos taken at the morgue, an eight-by-ten of Dickson's right arm, showing the diamond-shaped tattoo at the elbow. He moved to where his partner was seated and handed him the glossy enlargement.

In silence, Francis studied the print. He did not notice as Chap removed his jacket and rolled up his right shirt sleeve.

When Francis looked up from the photo, his surprise was immediate. He stared at Chap's exposed elbow. His eyes moved back to the photograph, and then back to Chap's arm. The tattoos were identical. Finally, he lifted his eyes to meet Chap's. "I am, needless to say, lost for words," he said. "Would you care to explain?"

Chap took the photo from his partner's hand. He looked at it himself, then placed it on the desk in front of Francis. He took the time to straighten his shirt sleeve and button it at the wrist. He sensed his colleague's impatience.

"Well," Francis prompted. "Talk to me."

Chap would tell him only that which he thought necessary and sufficient to satisfy his colleague's curiosity. He would have to be convincing. Francis was way too smart to fall for any old snow job explanation. He would have to lie about some things, for the moment at least, but he could see no other way.

"I am a Vietnam veteran," he began, almost too quickly. He jerked a thumb at the notice board. "So was he. We served together, back in '69-70." He paused and looked at his partner.

"I never knew you were in Vietnam," Francis said, with genuine surprise.

"It's not something I talk about," Chap said, as if this response was self explanatory. "We were both part of a specialist unit," he continued. "There were ten of us. Primarily, our role was search and destroy—most of the time, well, all of the time actually, behind enemy lines. We hit them hard, and fast, and then got out. Our actions were designed to surprise, disrupt and confuse the North Vietnamese troops. We trained in Australia specifically for this work, and we were good at it. For the entire year of our tour of duty, that was all we did. The tattoo… this tattoo," he tapped the photo on the desk, "was an identification mark." He looked at Francis, searching for some reaction, any reaction.

"Don't stop now," Francis invited. "This is fascinating."

"None of us wore the standard issue uniform, dog tags, or anything else that might identify us to the enemy if we were killed or captured. We wore the traditional black pyjamas worn by the vast majority of the Vietnamese people and carried the barest minimum of supplies such as ammunition and medical gear. We carried the AK 47 Russian-made assault rifles so our weaponry would not betray our nationality in the event we were either captured or killed. The theory was, it would add to the enemy's confusion. They wouldn't know who attacked them. All they would know is that we were white, and we could be U.S. troops, Australian, or even Kiwis. It was all aimed at throwing their intelligence-gathering into disarray."

Chap walked across the room and busied himself with preparing a fresh cup of coffee. He needed these few seconds to collect himself. So far, he had been truthful, as he understood the truth to be way back then. He did, however, omit the part about stalking the enemy into neutral Cambodia. If he never mentioned it at all, he wasn't lying, he reasoned.

He returned to stand in front of Francis. "The tattoos were also for the benefit of our people, those who came to carry our bodies out. Should we not be able to get out alive, a recovery party would go in and retrieve our dead and, as we carried no form of identification, the tattoos would identify us, firstly as Australians, and secondly to which unit we belonged."

He paused and looked at Francis. Was he accepting this? Sure, why wouldn't he? It was plausible, and as close to the facts as he could get without disclosing the real purpose and locations of their mission.

"When I saw the body in the park, his face was familiar but I just couldn't place it. I wasn't thinking of someone I knew forty years ago. Then, at the morgue, I saw the tattoo and the penny dropped." He turned back to the notice board. "He's changed over the years. After all this time, it is to be expected, I suppose, but that is Eddie Dickson. There's no doubt. I haven't seen him since we parted company at Mascot Airport in Sydney the day we arrived home."

Chap paused and stared intently at the photographs. "And now," he murmured, "he turns up dead. Right here in Adelaide. Right here in my own shit pile."

Tony Francis had a look on his face displaying emotions somewhere between discomfort and compassion. "I'm sorry about your friend, Chap. Where was he from? Did he live here in Adelaide?"

Chap thought about the question momentarily. "I'm not sure," he responded. "It's been a long time. I think he was from New South Wales, or maybe Queensland. No, New South Wales. As I recall, I was the only South Australian in the unit."

"Maybe he still lived interstate," Francis suggested. "If he came by plane, there will be flight records. Why don't I do some checking with the airlines?"

Chap watched as Francis got to his feet. "Thanks, Tony, that's a good idea. In the meantime, I will rattle a few cages and see if I can hurry the autopsy and ballistic reports we're waiting on."

When Francis had left the room, Chap stepped again in front of the photo display and looked into face of his old friend. "I'll find out what happened, Eddie," he murmured softly, with genuine sadness. "I promise you, I'll find out what happened."

Chapter Ten

Chap was not expecting any real surprises from the autopsy or the ballistics reports and in that respect, he was not disappointed. As Richardson had suspected, the ballistics report confirmed the bullet that killed Eddie Dickson was a .357 caliber, fired at very close range. Chap was willing to bet the weapon from which it was fired was not going to be easy to locate.

Predictably, the autopsy report offered no case-breaking revelations. For his age, estimated by Richardson to be in the early sixties, Dickson had been a fit and healthy individual. There was evidence indicating that, at some point in his life, he had been a smoker but it was apparent he had kicked the habit many years ago. Also, there was no liver damage suggesting a lifetime of heavy drinking. By all accounts, it seemed Eddie Dickson had lived a healthy, disease-free lifestyle.

Frustrated, Chap tossed the report aside. Frustration was an emotion he was all too familiar with, even at the best of times. It came with the job. Questions needed to be answered. What was Dickson doing in Adelaide? Did he live here now?

If so, how long had he lived here, and why had he never contacted his old friend? Who killed him… and why?

In the fullness of time, all his questions would be answered, he was certain. It was early in the investigation. Information and evidence would come to light. Facts would emerge and the pieces would fit together, eventually. Unfortunately, 'eventually' was not soon enough for Chapman Bouttell.

This case was uniquely different from murder cases he had investigated in the past. This time, he had a personal involvement. There were those who would say he should distance himself from the investigation because of that involvement, but an old friend had been murdered and it mattered not one iota to Chap that forty years had elapsed since he last saw Eddie Dickson.

On more than one occasion they had saved each other's lives. With the other members of Diamond One, they supported each other, and stood side by side through the savage brutality of war. That alone qualified Eddie Dickson, and everyone else in the squad, as a friend. Chap could not, and would not, disregard that friendship just because Eddie was dead; he owed him more, much more than that.

War creates and cements friendships far stronger than anything else. Friendships which would stand the test of time and pay scant regard to the time that might elapse between meetings. The more brutal, the more savage, the more fearful the war, the stronger the bond between those who participated became. Every member of Diamond One shared the terrible secrets of their actions, and it was those things and more which made this case different.

Chap would have the answers, of that he was certain. What he was less certain of was whether he possessed the patience required to allow this case to unfold at its own pace. Sometimes, undue haste resulted in things being missed, important things. It was important to proceed at a pace where, hopefully, that might be prevented. And then, sometimes you had to make things happen. Perhaps this would turn out to be one of those times.

Chap sat at his desk in the Incident Room, shuffling through the growing pile of reports, photographs and investigation running sheets as they came in from his team on the streets.

Sitting opposite Chap, Tony Francis was speaking on the telephone, thanking someone on the other end of the line. He hung up and looked at Chap. "Some good news, mate," he said. "Dickson flew in from Canberra at ten p.m. last night. He booked and paid for a return ticket, including one night's accommodation at the Airport Motel." He looked down at the notes he had made. "Room seventeen. He was due to fly out again at 11:50 this morning."

Francis had a lady friend who worked in Reservations for the Virgin airline company. This was not the first time she had come through for him. Passenger lists are confidential, and never given out casually, and certainly never over the telephone. There were proper, procedural channels for getting access to such confidential data. But, they had been friends for a long time and Francis had gained her confidence. The lady knew, given his job, that if he asked for specific information in relation to a passenger list, it would be a genuine request and he would have a genuine reason for asking. And, because she suspected she might be in love with him, that may also have contributed to her willingness to disclose such information.

"All the way from Canberra," Chap mused. "That's interesting. It had to be something important to bring him all this way for just one night."

"Perhaps he was here on business," Francis offered. "Business people are always flying in and out."

"He arrived late at night, and was due to fly out next

morning," Chap reminded him. "I'm not a businessman, but I don't think business meetings are scheduled for the middle of the night, at least not the legitimate ones. Let's go and check out his motel room. Perhaps the cleaners are slack. You never know—we could get lucky."

Chapter Eleven

Canberra, the nation's capital, is for the most part, considered a government town. It is a city overburdened with politicians, public servants, foreign embassies and assorted consular officials.

As he and Francis left Police Headquarters, he wondered if they would find answers in Eddie's motel room. He hoped they would—an early breakthrough would be welcomed. The first twenty-four to forty-eight hours of an investigation were the most critical. The more time that elapsed without a significant breakthrough, the colder the trail became.

Outside, although the sun shone superficially, it was far from warming. A distinct chill blanketed the winter morning. Chap watched the pedestrians, their breath steaming in the icy morning air as they scurried, hunched inside bulky overcoats, their faces hidden behind woollen scarves, to their respective places of employment. Hot vehicle exhaust emissions billowing from congested city traffic condensed as they hit the cold air. Accompanied by a tuneless orchestra of sounding horns and the occasional squeal of brakes, traffic was building rapidly towards the morning peak hour.

Not blessed with a temperament conducive to driving in

heavy traffic, Chap rarely drove when he had a partner with him who could take the wheel. Unless he was working on his own, he much preferred to climb into the passenger seat and let someone else deal with the suicidal insanity of his fellow road users. Today, however, he chose to take the wheel and climbed into the vehicle before Francis could open the driver's side door.

As they drove, Francis made no comment. He simply closed his eyes, gripped the overhead hand-rest so tightly his knuckles turned white, and silently prayed they would reach their destination in one piece.

"Fucking rain!" Chap cursed, as the heavens opened again and they skidded through a corner just as the traffic lights changed from amber to red. Francis gripped the hand-rest a little tighter and prayed a little harder; just in case God might be temporarily preoccupied with business more pressing than keeping them both alive.

When they finally arrived at the Airport Motel, Chap glanced across at his partner. Francis looked pale but decidedly pleased they had reached their destination without major incident.

"Fucking rain!" Chap said again, in case Francis hadn't heard him the first time.

As suburban Adelaide accommodation options go, the Airport Motel was best described as average. Aptly named, it was situated on Sir Donald Bradman Drive, just a short distance from the entrance road to Adelaide International Airport. It offered relatively comfortable and reasonably affordable rooms for travellers who preferred to stay somewhere close to the airport and still be within a fifteen-minute taxi ride from the city to the east, and half that time from Adelaide's beaches to the west.

The Hilton Hotel it was not, despite the sign out front promising *Five Star Facilities*. At first glance, the somewhat bland, stark facade suggested the sign might be little more than over-ambitious advertising hype.

Chap turned off the street and stopped momentarily in front of the reception office. Full length drapes, which may have once been an appealing shade of blue, covered the large office window and were yet to be opened, presenting guests with a washed-out, tired first impression of their chosen motel. As he looked ahead, beyond the office, into the large courtyard-cum-guest-parking area, Chap wondered why places like this always looked so much better in the advertising brochures than they did once you arrived and it was too late to change your mind.

Tony Francis climbed out of the car and entered the building to collect the key. Chap drove on, into the guest parking area, found room seventeen on the ground floor of the two-storey premises, and parked in the vacant space reserved for the room's occupant.

In contrast to the external appearance of the building, room seventeen was spotless. The cleaner was obviously fastidious; a rare breed, Chap thought. There was nothing to indicate Dickson or anyone else had used the room recently. They searched it anyway, not expecting to find anything, and it lived up to that expectation. Perhaps Dickson's luggage would prove more fruitful, Chap wondered. He must have had some luggage, even for a one-night stay. They left the room as they found it and walked quickly to the office.

The motel manager, a short, obese, mustachioed man of indeterminable age, decided it was time to open the curtains. He stepped away from the window and greeted Chap and Francis in the centre of the customer area, with an obviously ingenuous smile. He was, he declared, with what Chap sensed was practiced politeness straight from the pages of the Motel

Manager's Handbook, only too pleased to be of assistance to the police.

When Eddie Dickson did not return to his room, and did not check out the next morning, his luggage, such as it was, was removed from the room and stored in a small storage area in the motel office for collection when the owner eventually returned. Dickson travelled light which, given his intended length of stay, was no real surprise. Just one small piece of hand luggage, which he could easily have taken onto the aircraft as carry-on baggage.

The manager scurried away with a comical, waddling gait to fetch the bag. When he returned, Chap accepted it from him, unzipped it, and emptied the contents onto a small, two-seater sofa positioned against the back wall of the reception area. Underwear, a clean shirt, toiletries, socks, all the things one would expect to find in an overnight bag, tumbled out. Dickson's return ticket was there, but nothing which would shed any light on where he lived.

What did they have? Canberra, that's all! A big bloody place, Canberra! Chap upended the bag again and shook it. Nothing else fell out. There was a side pocket, and two smaller pockets at each end of the bag. Systematically, Chap unzipped all three and rummaged inside each. All were empty. For a moment, he stood looking at the items that were lying scattered haphazardly on the sofa. Behind him, Francis questioned the manager. Chap slowly and methodically picked through the scant contents a second time. There had to be something. Something which would help them understand why Eddie Dickson came to Adelaide. He found nothing! "Damn," Chap muttered to himself.

Tony Francis moved up alongside Chap. The manager disappeared, presumably into his private quarters behind the office.

"Got anything?" Chap asked his partner.

"Not a lot," Francis answered, referring to his notebook.

"Dickson arrived and checked in at 10:20 p.m. Thursday, the night he died. The manager's wife attended to him. Apparently, he went straight to his room and left by taxi shortly after."

"What about phone calls?"

"The manager has gone out the back to get his wife. She handles the guest records." He indicated the spilled contents on the seat. "How about you? Did you find anything in that lot?"

"Just the usual stuff you would pack for an overnight trip," Chap confirmed. The disappointment was obvious in his voice.

Shortly, the manager returned, with his wife following close behind. She was, Chap noticed, not unlike her husband in stature and he was certain better lighting would reveal a faint wisp of moustache, also not unlike that of her husband. They made a most unattractive couple, Chap decided. If he didn't know better, he would have picked them for any profession other than the hospitality industry.

The wife had obviously been interrupted; probably watching morning television, drinking gallons of coffee and overdosing on ugly pills, Chap guessed. She had a look of annoyance on her face, seemingly directed squarely at Chap. She looked the type to delegate rather than participate in the duties her longsuffering, browbeaten husband was required to perform. Chap took an instant dislike to her and, it seemed, she to him.

"What's the problem?" she asked, with undisguised annoyance.

Chap reached inside his coat and produced his identification. He snapped open the wallet and held it open inches from her face, just in case she was blind as well as unattractive. "I'm Detective Sergeant Chapman Bouttell. This is Detective Senior Constable Francis. We are interested in anything you may be able to tell us about one of your guests, Mr. Edward

Dickson. He checked in late on Thursday night. Your husband tells us you were on duty at the time."

The woman moved her head and glared at her husband, who appeared to be cowering behind her; the look she gave him promised, "I'll speak to you later!" Then, she turned her attention to the sofa across the room and the spilled contents of Dickson's overnight bag.

Chap watched her eyes almost close in an angry squint. Her eyebrows, black, bushy and in serious need of a trim, almost met in the middle of her forehead. She looked away from the contents on the sofa and directed a withering glare at Chap.

"What's to tell?" She shrugged. "He was just another guest. His room was pre-booked and paid in full." She sniffed and flicked at a strand of untidy hair which fell across her eye. "Silly bugger never even slept in the bed."

"Did he make any phone calls?" Chap interrupted.

Her husband stepped out from behind his wife, and presented a telephone account printout. Unfortunately, Chap was not quite quick enough. The woman snatched it from her husband, who immediately resumed his subservient position behind his wife's more than ample back. "Well, let's see," she said, quickly scanning the document. The relevant information was circled in bold red ink. "Just two calls. Not paid for, either," she added, as an afterthought. "One is the number of a taxi company. I know that because we use it a lot as a service to our guests. I don't recognise the other number."

Chap reached across the counter. "May I?"

With a frown of reluctance she made no effort to disguise, and perhaps wondering if she should ask to see a warrant, she finally handed him the page.

Eddie Dickson had placed two calls from his room within minutes of checking in. The first phone number, the number the manageress had not recognised, caught Chap's attention. It was a phone number he was all too familiar with. He stared at the printout. The number should be familiar to him; it was the phone number for Police Headquarters.

Dickson flew all the way from Canberra, arrived late at night, checked into the motel, and immediately rang Police Headquarters. Then he called a cab and, soon after, left the motel. To go where, Chap wondered? Who did he meet?

Chap handed the page to his partner. "He rang the station, Tony." He turned back to the manageress, who was obviously becoming more agitated at the intrusion into her privacy. Perhaps they really had interrupted some inane morning show.

"What cab company is the other number for?" he asked.

"Suburban Taxis," the man blurted out from behind his wife.

She turned and gave her husband another withering look; this one would strip paint from a wall. He was going to pay for that later also, Chap surmised.

"Suburban Taxis," the woman echoed, turning the same searing look on Chap.

Chap was sure he could feel the skin starting to blister and peel from his face. "I would like to take the phone record with me," he said. It was not a question.

She stood tall and thrust her shoulders back, an air of authority about her which only served to accentuate her ample bosom. "That's motel property," she insisted.

"It's also evidence in a murder investigation," Tony Francis advised.

"Murder… murder?" she sputtered. "Well… no one said anything about murder!"

Chap took the paper from Francis and handed it to the woman. "Take a copy of this for your records. We would like the original. I'll see that you get a receipt for it."

The woman grasped the phone record from Chap's hand, turned and hurried from the room, brushing her husband roughly aside in the process.

Chap looked at Francis and they exchanged knowing smiles. He crossed back to the sofa and the contents of Dickson's bag. Slowly, he began replacing the items piece by piece, checking each again for anything he might have missed. There was nothing. He zippered the bag closed.

Then, there it was. He had almost missed it, a folded piece of paper, just one corner visible where it had fallen down the back of the cushion. He reached for it and unfolded it. It was handwritten and as he read the words, his heart pounded in his chest. He read the words again. Words, and a telephone number. He read the scrap of paper a third time, trying to comprehend the significance of what was written.

"I don't bloody believe this," he said finally.

"What?" Francis asked.

Chap handed the note to his partner who looked down at the words written there. When he had finished, Francis looked up at Chap, the surprise in his eyes obvious. Then he, too, re-read the note.

Detective Sergeant Chapman Bouttell
Major Crime – Police Headquarters – Adelaide

Beneath these words was the telephone number of Police Headquarters, followed by the extension number for the Major Crime squad room.

To say Chap was confused would be to grossly understate the obvious. None of it was making any sense. Did it mean Dickson traveled to Adelaide to see him? If so, why had he not let him know he was coming? He had the phone number, why didn't he call ahead? Why *did* Eddie Dickson come to Adelaide?

Chap was certain of one thing. Dickson's visit was not one of a social nature. This was not a pleasure trip. After all these years, he would not have come all this way to spend just a few short hours socialising and reminiscing about the old days. This was not about old times best left unremembered. If it were, he would have planned a longer stay, and he would have let Chap know he was coming. He knew how to find him, that was obvious; the number was right there on the tiny remnant of paper.

The more he thought about it, the more convinced he became that Dickson's visit, and his subsequent murder, were related. There was a link. Somewhere, there was a definite link. Chap had to find that link. Dickson's murder was premeditated, he was certain of it. But why? A thousand unanswered questions swam in his mind. Unfortunately, before this was over, he knew there would be a thousand more.

Lost momentarily in the turmoil of his thoughts, Chap did not hear the manager return with the original phone records. The short, fat man cleared his throat noisily.

"If it's not too much of an inconvenience," he said almost apologetically, "my wife would like a receipt for everything you take with you, as soon as possible. Company policy, you know."

Chapter Twelve

Chap's driving stint was over, part voluntarily and part on the insistence of his partner. Francis was going to drive now or he was going to walk, rain or no rain, he hastily informed his superior. Bouttell was never going to admit it, but the new driving arrangements suited him. He was happy to sit back and think about why Eddie Dickson came to Adelaide, and why he had apparently intended to make contact with his old friend. Of course, he could contemplate and drive at the same time, despite his ex-wife's insistence that managing more than one task at a time was far too much of a challenge for him, but he decided it was more judicious to concede to his partner's wishes.

At the offices of Suburban Taxis, it became instantly obvious that in times of inclement weather, cabs were the preferred mode of transport for the public. The place hummed with activity. Suburban Taxis was the largest of Adelaide's taxi companies and the typical winter weather had them operating at a frenetic pace.

The duty controller was an unhealthy-looking individual; grossly overweight with a bad case of smoker's breath and heavily nicotine-stained fingers. Chap's first impression of him was, if the stress of the job didn't kill him, the chain-smoking probably would. He looked decidedly unexcited by the prospect of searching through hundreds of dispatch records at the request of the police. His impatience was obvious.

Chap and Francis waited while a radio request to return to base was sent to the driver who had picked Dickson up from the motel the night he died. When he arrived, it came as no real surprise to them to discover the cab driver dropped Dickson at Police Headquarters. Given what they had already learned, it seemed to be the natural progression of things. The driver confirmed he dropped his fare off in front of Police Headquarters, but was unable to confirm whether Dickson actually entered the building.

Subsequent enquiries made later with the officers on duty at the front counter of headquarters, failed to establish whether Dickson was ever there on the night he died. Surveillance tapes of the reception area recorded at the time he was dropped off by the cab also confirmed there was no sign of Eddie Dickson inside the building.

Chap located the detective who took the call when Dickson phoned from his motel room. The junior detective insisted he informed Dickson that Chap was out on the road. Dickson told the detective he had just arrived in Adelaide, was on his way to Police Headquarters, and would wait until Chap returned to his office as it was urgent that he should speak to him. He insisted the message be passed on to Chap, and the detective recorded the call in the squad room message book.

Chap silently cursed his own omission. Once again, he had taken the squad room message book for granted. Nine out of ten times, he would check the book daily, and this was one of those times he had neglected to do so. As a consequence, he had missed the message from his old friend. Only by a few minutes, it seemed. It was not the first time he had been caught out by office procedure.

Chap and Francis were on duty that night and, for the majority of their shift, they were in the office preparing prosecution files for an upcoming court case. Towards the end of the shift, they had decided to brave the conditions outside and get a late evening snack and perhaps a half decent cup of coffee. The call from Dickson came in just after they left the building. When they returned some time later, cold and damp and with their hunger appeased, it did not occur to either of them to check the book. The detective who took the call had completed his shift and left for the warmth and comfort of his home. Chap and Francis finished their paperwork, logged off duty and went home themselves. When he left that night, Chap was not to know that, in just a few, short hours, he would become entangled in matters which would effectively change his life.

As was the case with all incoming calls to Police Headquarters, the first to receive such calls were the personnel on duty in the Communications Centre. As a matter of procedure, all calls were recorded. Ultimately, when the tape currently in use was filled, it was dated, and placed in storage in a large filing room adjacent to the Communications Centre.

A shiver travelled up Chap's spine as he listened to the voice from his past, a little surprised to find he still recognised it after all these years. He listened to the tape, over and over. As he listened, he thought he sensed some agitation, some urgency perhaps, in Eddie Dickson's voice. The call was brief and to the point but, save for the anxious tone, Chap was unable to distinguish anything overly untoward, and there was nothing in Dickson's words which would indicate the purpose of his trip to Adelaide. However, the recorded voice did confirm one thing. Eddie Dickson had travelled here specifically to see Chap. Now, Chap wanted to know why.

With the sound of Dickson's voice came the memories, some good, most bad. The good ones were of times of friendship and laughter; all too brief moments in an otherwise long and lonely twelve months of fighting and killing. The bad ones were of that very same fighting and killing, and of the terrible tactics they employed… memories of the hot rush of blood which accompanied the soft gurgling of an enemy soldier with his throat cut from ear to ear. Unable to resist, Chap found himself slipping back to a time he had long ago decided was best left buried in the deep, dark recesses of his mind.

Tony Francis spoke, dragging Chap back to the present. "What do you think?"

Chap lingered over the job of packing the tape away in its container and placing it in an evidence bag. "I'm stuffed if I know, Tony, I'm stuffed if I know. It's apparent now that Dickson came here to see me. But why? I don't know. It was important enough for him to travel all this way to see me in person. Why? What was so important that he would come all this way? We know he had the phone number, so why not just ring?"

"He almost made it," Francis nodded. "We know he got as far as the front doors, the taxi records confirm that much. Maybe someone followed him here, waited for the cab to leave, and then jumped him." He was speculating, but speculation was all they had.

"Or," Chap offered, "maybe someone was already here, waiting here for him outside the building."

"You mean someone was expecting him? Knew he was coming here, specifically?"

"Why not?" Chap continued. "When you think about it, it makes sense. If the killer was following him, he could have taken him in a couple of places, the airport for instance… or the motel. Why follow him all the way here and take the risk, a considerable risk I would have thought, of grabbing him in front of Police Headquarters? No, mate, I think the killer was waiting out the front for him."

Francis pondered this for a moment. "The risk is the same," he said finally. "Whether he followed him here, or was waiting here for him to arrive, it's still in front of Police Headquarters. But, I see your point… I think," he conceded. "You're saying, I take it, the killer had no choice but to grab him here, despite the risk involved?"

"Exactly," Chap acknowledged.

They left Communications Centre and headed along a long corridor to a stairwell which led back to the Major Crime squad room. Deep in thought as they walked, Chap's intuition began to dominate his thoughts. It was intuition born of years on the streets doing what he did. Doing what he loved. What he was best at. Investigating, sifting, probing. Looking for the logical but never overlooking the illogical. Examining the negatives, and putting himself in the place, in the mind, of the killer. The more he thought about it, the more he was satisfied with the scenario placing the killer lurking in front of the police building, waiting for his victim to show. It had to be the way it went down; it was the most logical. He talked to Francis as they continued.

"Remember Thursday night? It was a cold, wet, miserable night. It was pissing down outside, thunder, lightning, the whole shooting match."

"I remember," Francis acknowledged.

"Around the time Dickson's plane was landing, you and I went out for a meal. Remember the streets? They were deserted."

"What are you getting at?" Francis asked.

"Okay, let's assume, for the purpose of the exercise, that the killer knew Dickson was coming to Adelaide."

"Okay," Francis said. "I'm assuming."

"In that case, given the lack of traffic and people in

general about that night, and given the cover the storm would have provided, why wouldn't he grab his victim as he was leaving the airport?" Chap was theorising on the run. "Or, why didn't he follow him to the motel and grab him there? Why, for Christ's sake, did the killer pass on both of those opportunities in favour of taking the obvious risks involved in grabbing his victim in front of Police Headquarters? From under our very noses?"

"Why indeed?" Francis answered.

"Do I detect a hint of doubt in your tone?" Chap asked.

Francis paused for a moment. "What you're saying makes sense, to a degree. But are you sure we can eliminate a random act of violence? We both know there are more than enough weirdoes out there on the street. Why couldn't this be a random thing? Why couldn't he have been killed by some drug-crazed loon all strung out on dope?"

"I don't reject that theory completely, mate. But I think it's unlikely. Firstly, if committing murder just for the sake of it, or for money to score the next hit, was the objective, why pick your victim in front of Police Headquarters? Dope-heads are off the planet most of the time, but they're not so stupid as to attempt to score just metres from a hundred coppers. Secondly, mugging is out because mugging is a hit-and-run crime. It happens on the spot; the victim is left in the street, and the offender bolts from the scene."

Chap looked at Francis and could see his partner was slowly coming around to his way of thinking. "And," he continued, "muggers don't usually kill their victims. Not, that is, unless by accident during the committing of the offence. They certainly don't take them away, shoot them in the back of the head, execution style, and then take the time to remove all traces of identification."

"Okay," Francis conceded. "If we eliminate a random killing, and a mugging, and we assume the killer was waiting for Dickson out in front of the building, all that's left is… why?"

"You touched on it yourself earlier," Chap reminded him. "The killer had no other choice. He was expecting Dickson alright, but here, out in front of the building was the only place he *could* grab him."

They reached their office and sat behind their desks.

"Please continue," Francis invited. "I'm not sure I follow where you are going with this, but you have that familiar look on your face which tells me you've got the bit between your teeth."

"Well," Chap suggested. "What if the killer was expecting Dickson, knew he would be coming here, but… he didn't know him?"

"Now I really *am* confused," Francis admitted.

"What if they had never met?" Chap began to explain. "The killer didn't know what Dickson looked like! That's why he didn't grab him at the airport, or at the motel after he left the airport. Eddie Dickson wasn't the only passenger on the plane. If the killer wanted to follow him from the airport but didn't know what he looked like, who, of all the passengers, was he going to follow? It's the only scenario which makes any sense. The killer knew Dickson was on his way to Adelaide. He knew he was on his way here to see me. All he had to do was wait here. He knew Eddie would arrive eventually. It's reasonable to assume he knew Dickson would catch a cab. Remember the night? It was a bitch. It's not as though there would have been a crowd out front. It would not have been difficult to sit and wait for the taxi to pull up in front of the building."

Tony Francis picked up the theory. "And, if the killer *was* expecting Dickson, it's a safe bet he knew his name, if not his face. And, as you suggest, it's a safe bet he knew he was coming here to see you."

Chap leaned back in his chair and smiled across the desk

at his partner. "Good Lord! I do believe the lad's got it at last. We'll make an investigator out of you yet."

"Prick!" Francis laughed.

A uniformed patrol officer approached the desk and spoke to Chap. "Sergeant Bouttell?"

"That's me," Chap confirmed.

The officer held out some papers. "These just arrived for you."

"Cheers, mate, thanks." Chap took them and watched as the officer left the room.

"What have we got?" Francis asked.

Chap read quickly through the pages. "Fingerprint results," he answered. "It says here, Dickson was still in the army, a Major, no less. His home address is listed as Canberra. It looks like he worked there, too."

"Doing what, exactly?" Francis probed.

Chap scanned the papers more thoroughly. "According to this, he worked in Central Army Records Office, doing something with historical research. It looks like he was transferred there six months ago. It was to be his final posting prior to retiring from the army."

The irony of that did not escape Chap. Eddie Dickson had made a career out of the very establishment he himself couldn't wait to walk away from all those years ago. They shared the same memories, he and Eddie. It must have been difficult for his friend to keep those memories buried and still maintain an association with the institution responsible for causing them.

Chap knew there were some soldiers who, as a result of their experiences, became attached to the army. It was like an invisible umbilical cord. They often became dependent on, and unable to sever, the connection they felt. He'd found it easy to turn his back on it and the things the army required, indeed ordered, him to do 'for the good of his country'. Those things disgusted him now, and had for the last forty years. They filled him with anger and regret. He could see, however, there would be others who might not feel the same way. It might be easy for another person, a person like Eddie Dickson, for instance, to become emotionally attached to the army. Perhaps by maintaining that connection, by refusing to live in denial, and refusing to forget, was how he dealt with the memories.

In Dickson's case, his method of coping appeared to have worked for him. The last time Chap had seen him they were both 'baggy-arse' diggers, glad to be alive, and glad to be back on home soil. Now, after all these years, Eddie Dickson had attained the rank of Major, and Chap knew that officer rank was not handed out as readily and as willy-nilly as Corporal stripes seemed to be back in his day. Officer rank had to be studied for. At some stage of his career, post-Vietnam, Dickson must have attended Officer Training School. Chap looked down again at the report, and felt a strange mix of pride and sadness for his friend.

"Any family?" he heard Francis ask.

"No, it says he was single… no next of kin is listed."

"Pity," Francis said. "A wife might have been able to tell us why he wanted to see you."

Chap agreed. He sensed this case was not going to become any clearer until they knew why Dickson had made such an effort to see him; an effort which led him straight to his death. He was also not particularly surprised to learn Eddie was not married. The documents he read did not elaborate, other than to say he was single. They did not say 'divorced' or 'widowed', just 'single'. Chap dropped the report onto his desk and hoped the answers had not died along with his old friend.

The telephone rang with a familiar, solitary ring indicating an internal call from another extension somewhere inside the building.

Chap casually picked up the receiver. "Bouttell speaking."

Detective Superintendent George Baldwin, the Officer in

Charge of Homicide, and Chap's immediate superior, was on the line. Baldwin was not one of Chap's favorite people. The animosity between Chap and his boss was legendary, both within the squad and beyond. Chap made no secret of the fact he held little respect for the man he considered both pompous and arrogant.

Baldwin was an academic, somewhere in his early forties, Chap guessed, who wore his arrogance and an air of superiority as though they were a badge of honour. Chap thought he wore both like an ill-fitting jacket. Baldwin was one of those people the police forces seemed to be targeting in their recruiting campaigns these days. Those with university degrees who were considered potential leaders and would take the force in a new and exciting direction, a direction more in touch with the times and the community's expectations of modern policing.

Chap saw the new recruiting style as a crock of shit. He was one of those, and there were still a few in the job, who considered a good smack delivered to the side of the head and some worthwhile time spent in the slammer, went much further in educating some lowlife in the error of his ways than did a good behaviour bond and a few hours leaning on a shovel doing court-ordered community service.

Baldwin had a history of talking down to members of a lower rank than his own, and Chap knew the opinion he held of his superior was not unique to himself. It was an opinion shared by the vast majority of those who came into contact with George Baldwin. There were many in the job who had, at one time or another, found themselves on the receiving end of Baldwin's aggressive, belittling attitude, and believed he suffered from that age-old malady, 'Little Man's Syndrome'. A physically small man, Baldwin would never have made it into the job if minimum height requirements were still a condition of entry. He used aggression and disrespect for subordinates as a means of compensating for his considerable lack of physical stature.

It was not that Chap had any specific beef against academics in general. In truth, he held nothing but admiration for those who chose to better themselves by means of furthering their studies in an attempt to make a success of their lives. His partner, Tony Francis, was one such person. It was just that, every now and then, along came a character like George Baldwin. His rapid advancement through the ranks came about by sitting for every possible examination he could, while accumulating very little actual street-smarts. Chap reasoned this did not give him license for the arrogance and condescending attitude with which his superior carried himself.

On the other hand, Chap, and many others like him, learned his trade on the streets, where experience counted for something. He learned the lessons of policing the hard way. He believed, along with most of his colleagues, that the best cops, and by extension the best leaders of the future, were those who served their apprenticeship at street level; in the real world, the world of blood, guts, crime, and compassion, as opposed to between the covers of an operational manual or a text book on criminology.

He and Baldwin had crossed swords more than once, and Chap was extremely disappointed when Baldwin was appointed to the position of Officer in Charge of the Major Crime Investigation Section. For the most part, Chap was able to work around his boss, but, by the very nature of his work, he could not avoid contact altogether, and with considerable effort on his part, and precious little on Baldwin's, he managed to keep the relationship on a workable albeit uncomfortable level.

Chap's respect for Baldwin was minimal at best, but he simply went about his business and did his best not to aggravate an already sensitive situation. There were occasions, however, when he simply could not resist the overwhelming urge to torment the crap out of his superior.

"Come into my office, Sergeant," he heard Baldwin say on the other end of the line. That was all he said and then the line disconnected.

"Fuckin' arrogant prick!" Chap said, as he replaced the handset.

"That would be our esteemed leader, I assume?" Francis asked, smiling.

"How many other short, arrogant, up-themselves pricks do you know?" Chap responded.

———

George Baldwin's office was adjacent to the main squad room. The two rooms were close enough that he could have stuck his head into the squad room and called for Chap, but that was not his way.

Chap stood for a moment outside the closed door, and then knocked loudly, knowing it annoyed the hell out of Baldwin, who preferred visitors to tap lightly and then wait to be admitted. When he got no response from behind the closed door, it pissed Chap off. It was a game they played; who could piss who off the most? Chap knocked again, louder this time.

"Come in," Baldwin called.

The office was small, but functional, adequate for a room where Chap suspected very little work of any genuine consequence was ever done. Baldwin was seated behind his desk, hunched over, head down, writing something in a file.

Baldwin preferred his office door closed when he had someone with him. Chap left the door open.

"Shut the door," Baldwin ordered, without lifting his eyes from the file in front of him.

Chap reached behind him and slammed the door, way harder than was necessary.

"Sit," Baldwin commanded.

"Thanks," Chap said, to the top of his boss's head. "I prefer to stand." He was hoping not to be there very long.

Finally, Baldwin placed his pen on the desk and lifted his head slowly until his eyes met Chap's. "Where are you with this Dickson thing?"

Chap met Baldwin's stare with a noncommittal shrug. "You know as much as I do at this stage. You get a copy of the progress report. That's operational policy, remember?"

"Don't be a sarcastic prick. I was referring to your relationship with him."

Cooperating with Baldwin was not easy for Chap. He thrust his hands deep into his pockets and glared at his superior. "Relationship? What do you mean, relationship? I don't have a relationship with him, George… he's dead."

"Do you have to be such a rebellious arsehole? And don't call me George! It's 'sir', to you. Show a little respect!"

Chap ignored the reprimand. "We have established," he began, "with reasonable certainty, that Dickson came to Adelaide specifically to see me. Why? I don't know. I've had no contact with him for over forty years. We were both in the army. We served together in Vietnam—when you were still crapping in your Pampers," he added, for no particular reason other than it felt like the thing to say. "I have no idea what he wanted to see me about."

"Well," Baldwin interrupted, "it's all irrelevant now. I am closing down our involvement in the investigation."

The words hit Chap like a fist to the gut. For a moment, he was not sure he had heard correctly. No, he couldn't possibly have heard correctly. He took a step closer to Baldwin's desk. "What?" he asked, incredulously. "What did you say?"

Chap saw the slightest hint of a smile form on Baldwin's face. The smug bastard was enjoying this. This was his thing.

He loved it. The being in control. Being in charge. This was what he was born to do.

"As of now, and I mean right now... this minute... this case is out of our hands. I've just received, via the Commissioner, a directive from the Federal Police in Canberra, to forward all files pertaining to this matter to FEDPOL headquarters. They are taking over the investigation from this point on."

Chap was stunned. "Why?" was the only question he could think of to ask.

"*Why* is not important, Sergeant. I have been ordered to hand the investigation over. As such, I am ordering you to bring me everything you have on file that relates to this case... everything. I will see it is forwarded on to the relevant authority."

"This is bullshit!" Chap spat. "An old friend makes a special trip to see me. He is snatched from under our noses, and murdered. I don't fuckin' believe this. Did you remind the Commissioner that *we* are the relevant authority? This is our jurisdiction. Dickson was killed here, in Adelaide. What the hell's it got to do with the Feds?"

George Baldwin paused, placed both hands palm down on his desk top, leaned forward, and gave Chap a look that could in no way be misinterpreted as an invitation to join him for cocktails after work.

"Sergeant," he began, "I do hope you are not telling me how to do my job. This is the police force, not the bloody Boy Scouts! Perhaps you have forgotten that. We follow orders here, all of us. That includes you! Or do you consider yourself exempt from orders?"

"Do you at least know why the Feds want the case?" Chap asked.

"No, I don't, and it doesn't matter why they want it. It is no longer our concern."

"Well, it fuckin' concerns me!" Chap stated flatly. "Surely

you don't expect me to just walk away from this?"

"That's exactly what I expect you to do, Sergeant. And what's more, that is exactly what you *are* going to do. Do I make myself perfectly clear?" Baldwin pushed himself to his feet and stood as tall as his short, dumpy stature would permit. He thrust his shoulders back and glared up at his subordinate. A tiny fleck of spittle shone at the corner of his mouth. At that very moment, in that particular pose, he reminded Chap of the old cartoon character, Elmer Fudd.

"You're an arse-kissing prick, George. Those bastards upstairs tell you to jump and you say… 'Yes, sir, how high, sir?' …Jesus, you piss me off!"

The colour started at Baldwin's collar and moved upwards, over his ample chin, and continued to the top of his balding head. Chap could almost hear his boss's blood pressure rising. When Baldwin spoke, his voice rose at least two octaves.

"I don't have to take that shit from you, Bouttell! Get your ugly face out of my office, and bring me everything you have on the Dickson case. And I mean everything! You are to consider this matter closed." Almost as an afterthought he added, "Unless you want to find yourself facing disciplinary charges!"

Chap had nothing more to say, although he did feel somewhat aggrieved at the "ugly face" comment and momentarily considered exercising a right of reply. He stood for a moment, staring at the red-faced Detective Superintendent.

"What are you waiting for?" Baldwin said. "Get the fuck out of here, or so help me, I'll shoot you!"

Chap turned away, opened the door, and then turned back to face Baldwin. "I'd think twice about shooting me, George. I hear you only have eight toes now, following your training days on the pistol range." He walked briskly from the office, leaving the door open behind him, because he knew Baldwin hated that.

Chapter Thirteen

The directive stunned Chap. The more he thought about it, the more curious he became. Detectives, moving around the office, going about their business, spoke to him in passing, and most of the time he never even heard them.

Although not as emotionally connected to this case as Chap, Francis, too, was confused. However, it was easier for him to come to terms with the order to suspend the investigation. Francis was a 'by the book' cop. Orders which came from above were to be followed, regardless of how questionable they may appear. For Francis, that was just the way it was.

It was not the way Chap Bouttell looked upon this particular order. Something was wrong. Something was way out of kilter and did not sit right with him. Questionable directives from superiors were, by their very nature, there to be questioned. Not blindly followed without satisfactory explanation. Baldwin was not forthcoming with any explanation, satisfactory or otherwise, and Chap knew he could not simply walk away from this case regardless of his superior's insistence. Baldwin was a prick, and it was bad enough he was Chap's superior, let alone having to kowtow to the man.

For the Feds and the local police to cooperate on cases

occasionally was not unusual, but never at any time in his career had he known a case to be removed so abruptly, and so completely, from the hands of the authorities in whose jurisdiction it originated. The 'no explanation' thing was even more mystifying. Was Baldwin simply being his usual obnoxious self, or was there something more sinister at play here? Chap wanted to know, was more determined than ever to know, exactly what Eddie Dickson had been involved in that warranted the exclusive attention of the Federal Police.

Chap telephoned Communications and requested they call Detectives Smith and Sanderson in from the field. When they arrived some twenty minutes later, he was unable to answer any of their questions, or offer any reasonable explanation as to why the case had been taken out of their hands. He could give them only what he had been told by Baldwin. Sanderson was nonplussed about the directive, as was Smith to a slightly lesser degree. They were both good cops, and experienced investigators, but one less case on the books was one less on their workload. The value of an easing of the workload was never something to be underestimated, they reasoned.

Despite Baldwin's instructions, there was never any doubt in Chap's mind that he would stay on the case. He would find out who killed Dickson. Not because he was a cop and it was his job to solve murders, but because he and Eddie Dickson shared a history. Eddie had tried to reach out to him, perhaps to ask for help, and Chap felt he owed it to his friend to find his killer. This was not about being a cop, or not being a cop. This was an obligation he could not, and would not, ignore.

He hadn't seen Eddie in a very long time, but there was a time when he knew him like a brother. Even after all these years, there existed an unbreakable bond between all the survivors from his unit. It was a bond which promised, Chap knew, that if the situation were reversed and it was he who needed help, Eddie Dickson, and the others, would be there for him.

He thought briefly about going over Baldwin's head. There were other senior officers he knew who were more approachable and, thankfully, they were not all cut from the same cloth as George Baldwin. Lord knows there were more than a few old favours he could call in, but without really understanding why, he decided against it. The feeling that he was missing something was all-consuming, but skirting around Baldwin's authority could, and almost certainly would, create waves which might conceivably make more trouble for him than he could effectively handle.

Ultimately, the course of action he opted for came more easily than he might have imagined. He decided to carry out discreet inquiries on his own. It seemed to him that he might have a better than even chance of finding out what was happening if he made those inquiries without the knowledge of the Department and, in particular, without the knowledge of George Baldwin.

It would not be easy without the benefit of the extensive facilities of the job which would be at his disposal as a matter of course during an official investigation, but he would not allow that to deter him. He would not leave this case alone, regardless of the consequences should Baldwin learn of his actions, and regardless of what he might discover as a result of his intended, unauthorised investigation.

As ordered, Chap passed the Dickson file to Baldwin, but not before he had copied the contents. One complete copy of everything in the file he kept for himself. Exactly what he was going to do with it he was not sure, he had not thought that far ahead as yet, but he kept it anyway.

There were other cases backed up behind the Eddie Dickson murder which he could, and probably should, involve himself in, and the smart thing to do would be to forget about the Dickson case and move on to other matters. But that was the smart, conformist thing to do, and he suspected that digging around in this case when he had been expressly ordered not to, would more than likely unearth some things he may well wish had stayed buried. Right now, however, Chap was not feeling particularly smart or conformist.

Francis and the others on his team would soon forget Eddie Dickson; he was, after all, just another case number to them. Chap would not forget. He had to do something. He could not turn his back and pretend it never happened. There was a connection between Dickson's visit and his subsequent murder. There had to be, and George Baldwin was sadly mistaken if he thought Chap would simply accept the sudden, unexpected turn of events and go about his job as though nothing had happened, as if he had never heard the name Eddie Dickson.

Chap had contacts, many of them. You don't spend nearly thirty years in the job and not establish a good network of contacts on both sides of the law, unless of course, you were a cop like Baldwin. Baldwin couldn't establish contact with his dick on a dark night.

One of those contacts worked in the South Australian offices of the Australian Federal Police and it was necessary now, Chap believed, to make use of him. However, he had to do it covertly. He had no desire to place himself in a position of confrontation with Baldwin, who would, without a moment's hesitation and with a vast degree of delight, welcome the opportunity to bring formal disciplinary charges against him.

Deception with discretion was the key. It would not be easy. How could he covertly investigate Dickson's murder and still be seen to be supposedly actively involved in other unrelated cases? He would not be able to fool his partner for one, and he did not want to. Tony Francis deserved better that his deceit. Also, as discreet as he may be, it would only be a matter of time before Baldwin got wind of what he was doing and then the excreta would really hit the portable wind turbine.

The answer came suddenly. He would take leave; he had plenty of leave time accrued. Taking holidays had never been high on his priority list over the last few years, certainly not since his divorce. Under normal circumstances, he wouldn't know what to do with himself if he were away from the job for more than a few days. Now he did. The time he had accrued was more than enough to carry out his inquiries, and he knew he could still move about the office and use the facilities, not to mention stay out of Baldwin's way, without raising too many concerns. There were those who said he virtually lived at the office, anyway, and staying out of Baldwin's way was something he was well experienced at.

Baldwin would approve his application in a heartbeat—he would endorse anything to get Chap out of what little hair he had for a while. Chap was certain Baldwin held him directly responsible for the stomach ulcer with which he suffered constantly and miserably. Baldwin would use his absence as an opportunity to relate to anyone who would listen, even those who had no desire to listen, that Sergeant Bouttell spat the dummy at being ordered off the case. Such was the conniving character of the man.

Chap's team was, to say the least, surprised. It took some explaining, but he eventually convinced them that his getting away for a while was the best course of action. The death of his friend had upset him, and then there was the sudden, unexpected pulling of the case from under him. He needed some time off, he explained. Time to think things through. Time to think about where to next? Maybe, he confided to his partner when the other members of his team were out of earshot, he would make a few discreet inquiries of his own.

Tony Francis was worried. He spent time trying to dissuade Chap from his intended course of action, making a point of reminding his partner of the consequences, should he be discovered by George Baldwin. His concerns fell on deaf ears and, ultimately accepting he could not dissuade Chap, he wished him well.

"How long will you be gone?" Francis wanted to know.

"I don't know." Chap shrugged. "As long as it takes. A week, maybe two, I really don't know. As long as it takes to find out who killed Eddie Dickson, and why."

He requested leave effective immediately, and personally took the application to Baldwin's office. He waited patiently, quietly exasperated, while Baldwin took his own sweet time to read through the application. Enjoying himself at his sergeant's expense had to be the highlight of his day thus far, Chap thought. Being the knob-head he was, Baldwin was obviously going to drag this out and milk it for all it was worth.

Sensing his lingering over the application was annoying Chap, and annoying Chapman Bouttell was like cocaine to an addict, Baldwin couldn't get enough of it. Finally, he placed the application on the desk in front of him, removed his glasses, and looked up at his senior investigator. "What the fuck is this?" he asked, poking at the paper with his glasses.

"You took long enough to read *Gone with the* fuckin' *Wind*," Chap said, with exaggerated sarcasm. "It's an application for leave. I'm sure you've seen one before. As I recall, there's a requirement that one fills one of those out when one requests leave."

"Don't get smart with me, Sergeant. Give me one good reason why I should approve this."

"Only one?" Chap scoffed. "I'll give you more than one. Firstly, I have more than thirteen weeks' leave accrued and now seems like a good time to take some of it. Secondly, you have been on my back for the last six months to take leave, obviously in an attempt to get me out of what little hair you have left. Thirdly, I would have thought you would be as thrilled to get rid of me for a while as I am to see the back of you. Last, but by no means least, the weather has been so bloody nice lately I thought I would take the opportunity to improve my golf game."

"You don't play golf!" Baldwin responded.

"Oh, yeah, that's right, I don't," Chap said. "And, the weather is not really nice at all. It's freezing cold and raining like a bitch. Jesus, George, just sign the damn thing and let me get out of here!"

"It remains my deepest regret that I haven't yet found a way to get rid of you from the job permanently," Baldwin continued. "But let me make one thing perfectly clear. If I find out you are using this as an excuse to snoop around in the Dickson case, as I suspect you are, I am going to get my wish. If I find out you are sticking your nose into this matter in contradiction to my direct order, I promise you I will have your badge. I'll escort you from the building myself. Do I make myself perfectly clear?"

"Yeah, yeah, I got it. Sign the bloody form."

George Baldwin was not going to be hurried, certainly not by the likes of Chapman Bouttell. Bouttell was anxious to leave, and Baldwin could see it. He would sign the application, of course, but he would do it only when he was ready. He would savour this game a little longer. Inwardly, he was thrilled at the prospect of having Bouttell out of the way but, for the moment, he was enjoying the position of power he held over his subordinate. Chapman Bouttell was the person he most despised over all others. He leaned back in his chair, breathed deeply, and thrust out his chest which, much to Chap's silent amusement, made him look like he had a really nice set of knockers underneath his shirt.

"I'm warning you, Sergeant, if you continue to investigate this case while officially on leave, your arse will be hanging out in the breeze. I will not protect you. Indeed, I will be the first to applaud when you come unstuck. Do you understand me?"

Chap almost laughed. "Most people have to work at being

a prick, George. With you, it comes easy. For Christ's sake, sign the damn form. The longer I stay in this office, the worse my rash gets." He looked around the room. "Are there fleas in here?"

There was that colour again, rising slowly up from Baldwin's neck. Chap loved this part. The red face, the soaring blood pressure, the burning ulcer—life really didn't get any sweeter than this.

With a sudden flourish, Baldwin signed the leave application, pushed it roughly across his desk and glared up at Chap. "Get out of my office!" he barked.

Chap reached out, picked up the form and looked at it. Satisfied, he turned sharply and walked quickly from the room, leaving the door open behind him.

Chapter Fourteen

Chap needed to see Sally. How long had it been? A week? Longer? He felt a comfortable warmth deep inside whenever he thought of her. Sally was good for him. She made him laugh, something he didn't do a lot of when he was not around her. Sally Prescott evoked feelings in him he thought he was no longer capable of feeling, and too many cold, wet nights had passed without the warmth of her body next to his.

A menacing growl of thunder rumbled from somewhere in the distance as he hurried from the headquarters building. His thoughts lingered on Sally, and he smiled. Then, just as quickly, he was angry with himself for having left it so long without seeing her. He hardly noticed the rain as it drummed cold and heavy against the pavement, sending tiny explosions of water over his shoes as he walked. Dusk had closed around the city early, as it did this time of year.

Sally Prescott was not the kind of woman to complain about how long it had been since they were last together, although he suspected she silently wished things were different, a little more permanent, perhaps. She was a good woman, and there were times when Chap thought himself undeserving of her affection. It was not that he treated her badly; on the contrary, whenever they were together he always made a special effort to be considerate and loving toward her.

Chap Bouttell was not now, nor had he ever been, one to follow the 'sensitive New Age guy' mantra, but he was also not totally without feelings. He had not yet admitted it to himself, perhaps because he was afraid of the consequences, but it was just possible he was in love with Sally Prescott. Following his divorce, love was an emotion he thought he would never experience again and the fact that he hadn't, until recently, was not something which had ever really bothered him.

Sad circumstances three years earlier had brought them together. Sally had owned a restaurant, jointly with her husband of twenty-five years, James Prescott. An armed hold-up, late one Friday night, went horribly wrong with tragic results. In a split second of madness, James Prescott was shot through the heart while resisting a drug-crazed gunman intent on getting enough cash for his next score. James Prescott died right there on the floor of his restaurant. Chap was assigned to the case in the capacity of lead investigator. It turned out to be a long and difficult investigation.

His relationship with Sally began slowly and innocently. Almost a year passed before they advanced to the all-important first date stage. Chap knew he was attracted to her long before that, but Sally was the grieving widow and he was determined to keep the relationship in perspective. He watched her closely over the course of the investigation and, as he got to know her better, he occasionally found himself wondering if he would, one day, love someone as much as she obviously loved her late husband. It was a question which both frightened and excited him.

Chap never really allowed himself to get close to anyone in a romantic way and that was, as his ex-wife took great pains to point out to him many times, the reason she could no longer stay in a marriage devoid of true affection. Chap knew it was his inability to display real affection which finally drove her away, and he was afraid, if he ever got too close to anyone else, he might find himself repeating the mistakes of the past.

Those first, tentative, nervous steps outside the bounds of their cop/victim relationship seemed to work for both of them and, although progress was slow, the mutual attraction grew stronger. Chap needed to be sure he was more than just a shoulder to lean on. More than just a comforting friend on whom she could unburden her grief. He also needed to be sure Sally was not rebounding from the tragedy of her husband's death, and so he was deliberately cautious.

From a tiny seed planted in the fertile soil of their growing friendship and watered with the tears of her grief, a romance blossomed. Together, they nurtured it, cared for it, and allowed it to develop at its own pace. It felt comfortable, for both of them.

There had been no romance of any real consequence in Chap's life since his divorce. There were others, not many, and most were unattached policewomen with whom he came into contact within the course of his job. They came and went from his bed, and his life, from time to time but none had lasted more than a few weeks. Why? Chap didn't know the answer to that question, and he was reasonably sure he didn't want to know. He suspected that if he analysed it too deeply, he would find that he was one of those men who found it difficult to fully commit to a relationship. One of those men who wanted the side benefits a casual relationship might offer, but not the long-term commitment that is often expected from the lady involved.

There was nothing wrong with any of the women he'd dated since his divorce; on the contrary, they were all nice, stable, attractive, single women. But for Chap, and for Chap there always seemed to be a 'but', they were all looking for more from a relationship than he was prepared to give. Until now, perhaps. His relationship with Sally felt different from all the others. He couldn't put his finger on what the difference was, exactly; it was a feeling deep within him which he felt not only when he was with her, but when he was alone and she occupied his thoughts, as she did now.

As he hurried to his car, he cursed himself for not having the foresight to buy flowers. Sally loved flowers. She insisted on a solitary, fresh flower on every table, every day, in her restaurant. Not the artificial, plastic, dust-collecting type, but real, fresh flowers. It was just one of the many little things she did which brought a personal touch to each table setting and helped to make her business the success it had become.

Since the death of her husband, Sally Prescott had worked tirelessly, devoting most of her time and energy into continuing and maintaining the popular, middle-class eating establishment she started with her husband.

The restaurant, aptly named Sally's, was a place for romantics. The age of the romantics was of no consequence; couples of all ages came. The atmosphere was warm and inviting, the lighting soft, and the menu diverse, ever changing, yet affordable. Chap loved to go there, primarily to see Sally, but it also beat the hell out of cooking for himself.

When Chap did not see her car parked in its usual place, he was not overly concerned. He was early; it was just five-thirty, and the restaurant did not open until six.

There were lights on inside the building. Chap knew the chef, François, would be in the kitchen preparing for the coming night's meal orders. François was actually French born, as opposed to many of the egocentric, wannabe chefs who would have the public believe they were truly French, spoke with appalling French accents, and struggled to make a decent omelette. Hiring François was, Chap thought, another example of Sally's determination to run an honest, genuine, transparent business.

As the front doors were still locked, Chap entered through the back. The jovial chef welcomed him warmly. "*Bonjour*, Chapman." He always referred to Chap using his given Christian name, pronouncing it 'Shackman'. "Welcome, *mon ami.* It 'as been too long, no?" He crossed hurriedly to Chap, embraced him warmly, and immediately proceeded to kiss him on both cheeks.

François did this every time they met, and it always made Chap feel mildly uncomfortable. What was the cheek-kissing thing the French do? Was he supposed to reciprocate? Chap had never kissed François in return, and he was not about to start now, regardless of what might or might not be protocol in France.

He offered François one cheek, and then the other. "Yes, François, it has been too long," he said, disengaging himself from the Frenchman's embrace. "How are you?"

François smiled. "I am well, thank you. It is not so good to complain, I think." He took Chap's elbow and ushered him through the kitchen, awash with inviting aromas, to a small, intimate cocktail bar adjoining the main dining area.

The restaurant had become a place where Chap always felt welcome. It was a sanctuary, a place where he could escape the stresses associated with the job, and from people like George Baldwin. He had been there many times over the preceding three years and he and François had become warm acquaintances, despite the awkward cheek-kissing thing. Perhaps someone should tell the bloke that, when Australian men meet, they just shake hands.

As the jovial, smiling chef left to return to his preparations for the evening meals, Chap made his way behind the bar and helped himself to a whisky, pausing to place a fifty dollar note on top of the cash register. It was a practice he knew irritated Sally. She insisted he was not to pay for drinks, or meals, when he visited her here, but free food and drink was not an arrangement which sat well with Chap. He preferred to pay his own way, and being in a relationship with Sally did not change that mindset.

Drink in hand, he returned to the customer side of the bar and chose his usual stool, tucked neatly into a secluded corner at one end of the small bar. Neil Diamond sang *Play Me* softly through the in-house sound system. He sipped his whisky, strong and warm, and listened for a moment, drifting with the melody. The liquor softened him. He felt the tensions of the previous hours begin to thaw, and he relaxed, indulging himself in the warm, comfortable ambience of the moment.

For the first time since the Eddie Dickson saga began, he felt able to detach himself from everything the previous days had offered. It was a nice feeling. But, he knew it would not last. It would not be wise to become too complacent. This case was far from over, despite the ranting, threats and orders from George Baldwin. He sat, lost in his thoughts, watching the ice cubes swim and clink together in his glass.

He did not hear Sally enter the bar. She approached softly from behind, gently encircled him with her arms, and kissed him lightly on the neck. His senses swam with the scent of her perfume. He leaned back into her, feeling the pressure of her firm breasts against his back. Words at this point seemed unnecessary. He turned on his stool to face her, and placed his hands around her waist, pulling her closer. She gazed warmly into his eyes and smiled. Slowly, he pushed her away from him and held her at arm's-length, drinking in the pleasure of her from the top of her head to the tips of her toes.

At fifty-six, Sally Prescott had long ago left behind the cuteness and naivety of adolescence, and was still several years short of the timeless beauty which seemed to accompany the elegance of women of more mature years. What Sally Prescott was, Chap thought as he gazed at her, was an extremely attractive, refined woman who looked after herself.

She was one of the few fortunate women who required the barest minimum of attention in the form of makeup to look their best.

Gently, Chap pulled her to him. In his position on the bar stool, she was only slightly taller than him, and he stared up into her green eyes. Warmly, gently, he kissed her. As their mouths came together, there was no doubt in his mind that his feelings for Sally went far deeper than mere affection.

Finally, Sally cupped his face in her hands and smiled. "Hi," she whispered throatily.

"Do I know you?" Chap responded.

"No, I do this to every strong, virile-looking man who comes in here."

"You think I'm strong and virile?"

"With your clothes on, yes." Sally smiled. "But, don't forget, I've seen you naked and there are a couple of adjectives other than 'strong' and 'virile' I could use to best describe that image."

She picked his glass up from the bar and, without taking her eyes from his, she sipped the drink. "I was beginning to think I was never going to see you again," she said, pouting.

Instantly, Chap felt like a first-grade jerk. "I'm sorry," he said. "I'm really sorry. I've been so busy, time just seemed to get away from me." It was a lame excuse, and just looking at her now made him all the more annoyed with himself.

Perhaps sensing his discomfort, Sally leaned close and kissed him quickly. She left him, and moved behind the bar where she proceeded to pour herself a glass of her favourite Chablis. "Apology accepted," she said. "At least it will be if you tell me you can stay and have dinner with me."

Chap smiled, handed her his glass, and talked as he watched her freshen his drink. "Okay, I'll stay and have dinner with you. Then, if you are a very good girl, I might just avail myself of some of that wonderful after dinner comfort I know you are so good at dispensing. This tired old body of mine could use a bit of comforting… for the rest of the night, perhaps?"

"Do you mean 'for the rest of the night' as in 'all of the night – right through until breakfast'?"

"That depends," Chap shrugged. "What's for breakfast?"

Sally smiled, tilted her head in just the way he had come to love, and, in a feigned display of coyness, she batted her beautiful eyes. "The same as that 'after dinner comfort' I know you like so much."

"I'm hungry already," Chap smiled.

Chapter Fifteen

The evening was filled with the hushed sounds of quiet, intimate conversations and soft mood music as the many diners enjoyed the relaxed, inviting atmosphere. The subdued lighting cast a warm, unobtrusive ambience over the dining room and the adjacent cocktail bar. It was made even more pleasant with delicious food, compliments of François' excellent menu, and good wine, compliments of Sally's small but selective wine list.

Later, when only a handful of diners remained, lingering over coffee or perhaps an after-dinner drink, Chap sat at the bar and sipped brandy, waiting for Sally to complete her closing duties. Now, Engelbert Humperdinck singing *After the Loving* wafted softly through the restaurant sound system.

With the pre-dinner whisky, a bottle of wine over dinner, and now a snifter of brandy, Chap was beginning to feel a little light-headed. He stared into the brandy balloon, swirled the warm, golden liquid around in the glass, and gently tapped his foot in time to the music. He wondered if it was the alcohol or the effect Sally was having on him that made him feel this way.

He was not drunk. Overindulgence in alcohol was a

pastime best left to the young, he thought. Drunkenness was something he hadn't been guilty of for a long time. Tonight, he was intoxicated with the mood of the evening. Soon, he knew, he was going to have to make some life-changing decisions with regard to Sally Prescott.

He was nearing the end of his police career and, when that day came, he would have to find something, or someone, to help him fill his days. Police work was all he really knew and thoughts of what he might do when retirement came was not something he had spent a lot of time considering. He could kill a man, he knew how to do that; or at least he used to know how to do that. But killing people was not a particularly good option for a career change, he mused.

Back at his home, Chap lit a fire, and they sat close together on the sofa, drinking coffee and talking softly as they stared into the hypnotic flames crackling warmly in the fireplace. In a moment of comfortable silence, he found himself hoping this night would never end. Such was the effect Sally Prescott had on him.

The atmosphere did not exactly lend itself to convoluted, perhaps complicated conversation, but Chap felt the need to talk to her about Eddie Dickson. He had to talk to someone, and Sally was the obvious person to unload on. He couldn't, and wouldn't, lie to her. To avoid doing so, he neglected to explain his actual duties in Vietnam. He wanted to tell her the truth, all of it, and although omitting certain parts of his life was technically not lying, Sally was an astute woman and he wondered if she suspected he was not completely forthcoming. He desperately wanted to tell her everything, to hold her close and purge himself of the secrets which lay buried deep within his very being. Perhaps, by doing so, he might be able to lay the ghosts of the past to rest, once and for all.

He told her only as much as he had told his partner. Sally listened attentively, holding his hand and occasionally gently touching his cheek. Soon, he would be totally honest with her, but not yet, not tonight. First, he had to face the truth of his actions himself. He had spent the preceding forty years pushing the outrage deep into the dark recesses of his memory where he did not have to deal with it; fooling himself he was succeeding.

It took the death of Eddie Dickson to remind him of the fact that, although he had been running from the past all these years, he never managed to put any distance between then and now. The memories were still there, perhaps not buried as deep as he might have thought.

Now, it was time to stop running. Time to stop hiding. Time to turn and face the demons which, in reality, were not all that far behind him. Just because one did not regularly focus on events of the past didn't mean those events no longer existed. It was time to come to terms with it. Take ownership of it. Deal with it and finally rid himself of the cancerous guilt slowly eating away at him. If he were to contemplate the possibility of a future with Sally, he had to do it from a position of honesty. It was the right and proper thing to do for her, and even more so for himself.

It would happen, he thought. When he found the killer. When he had put all the pieces of the puzzle together. Then, and only then, would he find the absolution and self-acceptance he needed to tell Sally the whole truth. He hoped she would forgive him. Without her forgiveness, he would never be able to forgive himself.

Their lovemaking was always good for both of them, and tonight was no exception. Much later, as they lay in his bed, their legs entwined and their bodies still damp with perspiration, Sally made him promise they would see each other more often. It was a promise he made gladly.

At some point through the night, as she slept beside him, he asked himself why he had never made more of a commitment to this woman. The answer came immediately. He was afraid. Afraid of losing something special. Special to both of them. He'd lost someone like Sally once before; the woman he married. He remembered how deeply it hurt. While he knew he had long ago recovered from that particular hurt, the memory of it was enough to make him afraid of suffering it again.

Following his disastrous marriage, making the decision to commit one's life to harmonious union with another was one Chap hoped he would never have to face again. Now, as he listened to Sally breathing softly beside him, her arm flung casually across his bare chest, he knew believing he would never have to make such a decision again was based on his inner fears. The time was fast approaching, if it hadn't already arrived, when such a decision would be thrust foremost into his mind and there would be no avoiding it. Sally moved in her sleep, murmured, and nestled even closer against his body. As he listened to her soft murmurings, he also knew he no longer wanted to avoid it.

Chap woke to the aroma of eggs, bacon, toast and coffee drifting down the hall to the bedroom. It was late, and the soft, green glow from the clock-radio beside his bed indicated it was almost nine-thirty. He sat up with a start and realised he did not have to go to work today. He was on leave. He could stay in bed all day if he chose to. He stretched, yawned, and relished the thought of doing just that.

He had told Sally at dinner the previous night that he had taken leave so he could use the time to investigate, unofficially, the Eddie Dickson murder. Sally knew how he felt about George Baldwin, and she also knew that if he investigated the Dickson case in direct contravention of Baldwin's orders, he was going to find himself in more trouble than he could effectively handle. But, she knew Chap well enough to know nothing she could say would dissuade him. He had earned a reputation built on the foundations of his own determination and he was not one to be deterred from a course he set for himself, regardless of how ill-advised that course of action may be.

Sally left him at midday, but not before another short but passionate dalliance which began in his kitchen soon after they had eaten breakfast, and concluded in the bedroom. She had bookwork at the restaurant to attend to, and Chap had an investigation to plan. It would have been unproductive but nonetheless easy for her to forget the bookwork, and he the investigation plans, and spend the rest of the day together. As they collected their respective clothing, haphazardly discarded along the hallway, and dressed, they considered it momentarily, and finally compromised, agreeing to meet again that evening. Sally would leave the restaurant in the capable hands of François. They would buy a take-away, overdose on tasteless, artery-hardening junk food, and watch a movie in front of the fire. They would compensate for the bad junk food by drinking a good bottle of red wine. Chap found himself anticipating the pleasure of it. Perhaps there was something to be said for the retirement thing.

As if on cue, the rain stopped. Outside, Mother Nature struggled to present a fine but cold afternoon. Chap waited on his porch and watched Sally reverse out of his driveway, oblivious to the fact he was not the only one watching her leave. Sally tooted once, waved, and drove away.

Someone else, further up the street, out of sight and hunched low in the front seat of a nondescript dark sedan, also watched as Sally Prescott drove from his house.

Chapter Sixteen

It was inevitable that Chap would go to Canberra—he had to start somewhere. Canberra was where Eddie Dickson lived and worked. If he were to find clues, and there were always clues to be found regardless of how insignificant they may seem, he was sure he would find them in the nation's capital.

He booked a flight for the next morning, leaving the return date open, not knowing what he might find, or how long he would be there. He would need to visit Dickson's workplace—CARO—Central Army Records Office. He hoped the relevant authorities had not already been censored by the Federal Police. When it came to soliciting information from the military, particularly in regard to one of their own, he was going to have to bluff his way. It would be difficult, maybe impossible, if the Feds had already cautioned the military into silence.

He sat at his kitchen table, drank coffee, and read and reread his pirated copy of the Dickson murder file. Searching for something. Anything. Any clue he could use as a starting point. He found nothing.

Sergeant Reg Brennan was a twenty-year veteran of the Australian Federal Police, attached to the South Australian office. Chap and Brennan had worked together occasionally on matters of South Australian-based drug importation cases which had their origins in another country and thereby fell foul of both federal and state laws. It was not a close working relationship and he and Brennan were more co-operative acquaintances than they were social friends. They did, however, each share a mutual respect for the other's ability.

Chap found his federal counterpart at work when he placed a call to the Federal Police Adelaide office. The two men agreed to meet at Brennan's office. During the short drive, Chap considered his options, finally electing to let the cards fall where they may and play them as they were dealt. He would not disclose to Brennan too much of what he already knew about the case because he wanted to see if Brennan, and by association the Federal Police, was already aware of Eddie Dickson and his fate. If so, it stood to reason Brennan would also be aware that the investigation had been taken out of the hands of the local police.

Meeting with Brennan was a gamble, but one Chap was prepared to take. He needed information and an informal chat with Brennan offered some chance of getting it. Brennan would either cooperate or he wouldn't. Chap was banking on the former. If Brennan clammed up, or claimed ignorance, it would be because he knew Chap had no right to be asking. The two were not that close as friends for Chap to ask Brennan to keep quiet about his enquiries. If it went that way, it would only be a matter of time before George Baldwin found out he was conducting his own unauthorised investigation.

The two men shook hands, exchanged greetings and, as opposed to skirting around the issue, Chap decided to jump straight in at the deep end. He proceeded by giving Brennan details of the information he required, watching his counterpart closely for any reaction. Then, he waited while Brennan, seemingly none the wiser, made a series of phone calls and computer searches. His apparent cooperation led Chap to assume he was not aware of the Dickson case; at least not yet.

From his conversation with George Baldwin, Chap understood the case files would be sent directly to Federal Police Headquarters in Canberra. It came as a complete surprise when Brennan informed him that, apparently, no one in the Canberra office was aware of the case. If they were, they were not letting on, even to their South Australian office. Brennan could find no record of Eddie Dickson either in the Adelaide files, or the Canberra headquarters.

Now Chap really was more confused than ever. No one in the Federal Police organisation was aware of the name Eddie Dickson. It was Sunday, however, and perhaps those with any knowledge of the case were not on duty. On Chap's insistence, Brennan did some more checking with other sections of his department. The results were the same. He could find no one, in either the Adelaide or Canberra office, with any knowledge of the Dickson murder.

What was going on, Chap wondered? The strange was getting stranger by the minute. It was possible a 'no comment' order had been placed on the Dickson file, in which case Brennan's loyalty would lie with his employers and he would not disclose anything to Chap, even if he found information relevant to the case. However, if that was the situation, why not simply tell Chap such an order was in effect and he was bound to comply with it? Why bullshit around with all the phone calls and computer checks? They were both cops. Why not just tell him the case was subject to a confidentiality order and no comment was to be made? Chap was aware of confidentiality orders, and the seriousness with which they were treated. He had encountered such orders a few times in his career, but why one would be applied to the Dickson case was a mystery.

There was another explanation which crossed Chap's mind briefly. One he did not want to think about. What if it was true? What if the Feds really did have no knowledge of Eddie Dickson? That would indicate George Baldwin had lied to him. Chap did not like Baldwin, but he could see no reason, in this instance, anyway, why he would lie. Unless he was telling him what he himself believed to be the truth. Could that indicate that someone even higher up the chain of command had lied to Baldwin? In any event, Chap was even more convinced that this case was far more involved than a straightforward murder enquiry. Something was definitely not right.

Could it be that no one had any actual control over the case? Could it be that someone in a position of authority far above that of George Baldwin used the Federal Police story as a diversion, with the express intention of stalling the investigation? If so, why? Was it possible that someone, somewhere, had effectively halted the investigation? Who would do that? It would take, Chap reasoned, a person of some considerable influence. It was a theory far too outrageous, he decided, to be worthy of serious consideration.

Mystified, Chap could not understand why he should suddenly think of Charles Cobb and Brian Elliott. As an afterthought, he asked Brennan to carry out Motor Vehicle Registry checks on both. Now, he wanted to know where the remaining two survivors of his old unit were. He didn't know why he wanted to know, but something deep inside him niggled at him.

Chap had always been one to trust his instincts, and this was an instinctive thing. He wanted to know where Cobb and Elliott lived. Perhaps he should make contact with them. It had been a long time, but he figured they would like to know about Eddie. Maybe it was time they all reconnected. Eddie was gone, and none of them were getting any younger. Who knows? Perhaps if they had been in regular contact with each other, and talked about their past amongst themselves, it might help him to understand, even accept, what they all did over there all those years ago.

It would be good to see Cobb again; to see how time had healed his horrific injuries, both physical and emotional. Chap never saw him again after the medevac chopper picked him up from their base camp in the remote mountain village and flew him out of the area. He heard later that after receiving emergency surgery at the field hospital in Nui Dat, Cobb had been shipped home to Australia almost immediately, his condition critical, but the early prognosis was cautiously optimistic.

Guilt again washed over Chap; guilt for not following up on Cobb, Elliott and Eddie Dickson. They shared something special, unpleasant, ugly even, but nonetheless special. It was not right that he had lost all contact with his old friends.

Eddie Dickson's murder brought him to the realisation that it was time to put things right. He had fought alongside these men, in a war seemingly all of their own; such was the secrecy and isolation within which they operated. Their war seemed to each of them to be disconnected from the war waged between North and South Vietnam. They had left six men behind and now, Chap would put things right. Only four had returned. Four out of ten. Now, one of the last four was dead.

Time was going to kill them all, sooner rather than later. Now, there was a sense of urgency about his decision to re-establish contact with Charles Cobb and Brian Elliott. How would he find them today, forty years later? Married with families, perhaps? Maybe they had grandchildren? Would they be happy and content with their lives post-Vietnam, or would they to be haunted by ghosts from the past? When he concentrated, Chap could see their young faces in his mind. Young, strong, and brave. Although they showed no outward signs of fear, he knew they were frightened, scared to death; they were just like him.

Four decades had gone by and, of course, they would be older now. Perhaps, as was the case with Eddie Dickson, he might not recognise either of them at first. But, whether or not he would recognise them now was of little consequence. The inevitable change in appearance which accompanies the aging process could not alter what they shared. The deep sadness he felt over the death of Eddie Dickson was eased slightly by the anticipation of seeing Cobb and Elliott again.

Lost in his thoughts, he did not notice Brennan had spoken until the federal officer nudged him.

"Hey, Chap," Brennan said. "Come on back. Stay with me if you can."

"Sorry," Chap apologised. "Did you find anything?"

"It took longer than I thought but I think we may have something."

"Really? What?"

"Well," Brennan continued. "I came up with a number of Cobbs, and a number of Elliotts. However, only one Charles Cobb, and four Brian Elliotts." He handed Chap a computer printout list of names and waited while he glanced through the names before he spoke again. "I did a computer cross-reference between the two names, looking for similarities, on the off-chance we might get a match."

"And…?" Chap asked hopefully.

Brennan looked down at some other papers he held. "We have one Charles Cobb, and one Brian Elliott, who both share some commonality."

"Commonality?" Chap's interest rose.

"Well, it seems both are around the same age, and they both served in the army back in the sixties." He paused. "And, this is strange…"

"What? What is strange?" Chap interrupted.

"It says here," Brennan tapped the paper he was holding, "under 'distinguishing marks and scars' that Cobb had extensive scarring about his legs and abdomen, consistent with some sort of major trauma to the lower body. It also says both he and Elliott had the same small diamond-shaped tattoo on their right elbow. What could that be about? Some sort of club membership badge or something?"

Chap lowered his head and rubbed his eyes. "Yeah," he murmured. "Something like that."

He allowed Brennan's words to sink in for a few moments. Eventually, he realised the federal cop was staring at him. He lifted his eyes and looked directly at Brennan. There was something else, something Brennan had not yet disclosed. Suddenly, Chap was overcome with an unexplainable sense of impending grief. He didn't want to know the rest, but he asked anyway. "You said they 'had' the same tattoo—what do you mean 'had'?"

"They're both dead," Brennan answered with a shrug. "Recently. Both of them. Shot at close range in the back of the head."

"Jesus Christ," Chap whispered, barely audible. "Jesus bloody Christ!"

Brennan took a step closer to Chap. "Shit, Chap, you are as white as a ghost. Are you okay? Is there a connection between these two and the Dickson killing?"

Chap's mind raced. He breathed deeply, trying to slow his rapidly accelerating heartbeat, trying to assemble his scrambled, disjointed thoughts into some sort of order before he spoke. It was still best, he thought, to keep quiet about exactly what he knew, but he needed to allay Brennan's concerns. "I don't know," he began. "There may be a connection. I'm not sure, not yet." He turned to leave, and stumbled slightly.

Brennan reached for his arm and steadied him. "Are you all right, Chap?"

"Yeah… I'm fine. Sorry… just a bad night's sleep. I'll be

okay. Tell me," he paused. "Why would Cobb and Elliott be in your computer records, anyway? I mean, other than in the Motor Vehicle Registry?"

"It's a new system we have now," Brennan began to explain. "All our computers are programmed to cross-reference certain personal characteristics which appear. In this case, the criminal offence records instigated a flag in the MVR records linking Cobb and Elliott, as entries of significance. When I punched them in, it indicated similar characteristics; namely, their deaths by identical methods… a single gunshot to the back of the head. But, that's just the start. Having got that far, we can isolate them even further from all those who died in a similar manner, by another cross-reference relating to identifying marks and scars, etcetera. Cobb and Elliott both had the same strange, diamond-shaped tattoo, just behind their right elbow. There is a sketch of it here, take a look." He handed the paper to Chap.

Chap knew exactly what the tattoo looked like, but feigned interest, anyway. He stared at the small diagram on the page. Finally, he looked up at Brennan. "How come we don't have the same sophisticated computer technology you guys have?"

Brennan smiled. "Because we are the Feds, Chap. We are the Feds, and you blokes are merely the local state boys. You know how it works. The bigger the boys, the bigger the toys."

"Yes, I do," Chap said. "It's a shame, though. We are all on the same side, after all."

"There are some I've met in this game who would argue that point with you, Chap," Brennan said.

"I know," Chap agreed. "I think we might have met some of the same people. What about someone else who might have the same tattoo?" he asked.

"If he, or she, were dead, and if the cause of death was the same, or very similar, the computer would link them with Cobb and Elliott." He indicated the page Chap held. "These two seem to be the only ones with the same tattoo. If there are others, they are still among the living."

That explained, Chap thought with some relief, why his name did not pop up on the federal system. He had the same tattoo, but there was one distinct difference; he was not dead. Although Eddie Dickson was, it was too soon for his name to appear in the system. In a day or two it would, when the records were updated.

"I don't suppose there is anything in there in relation to a suspect?"

"Nothing," Brennan answered. "Offender outstanding—investigation ongoing in both cases."

"Why am I not surprised?" Chap scoffed. He offered his hand to Brennan. "Thanks, Reg, you've been a big help. I appreciate it."

Brennan shook hands. "Any time, Chap. Let me know how things pan out."

"I will, mate," he lied. "Thanks again."

Chap sat in his car in front of the Federal Police building and read through the papers Brennan had copied for him. Cobb and Elliott were dead. He struggled to comprehend it, even though he knew it to be true. The proof was right there in his hands. The pages fluttered slightly with the trembling of his fingers. Shot. Both of them. Just like Eddie, shot in the back of the head. What the hell was happening? This was now far more sinister than he would ever have imagined when he started probing into Dickson's murder. Now, there was a connection between his three old friends which went much further than their shared war experiences. Chap had to find that connection if he was ever going to find the answers.

He would love to see the ballistics report on both deaths. However, even without it, he was willing to bet the murder weapon would prove to be, if not the same as the one used to kill Dickson, then of the same caliber. He felt numb. He put the papers on the seat next to him, rubbed his eyes, and then massaged the incessant arthritic twinge in his shoulder. Damn the cold, wet winter!

The case was gathering momentum, albeit slowly, building piece by piece into something he didn't want to speculate on. Chap never had any reason to assume his three former army buddies had maintained contact with each other since the war, but it was beginning to look very much like they might have.

Were they mixed up in something illegal, something that finally caught up with them—drugs, perhaps? No, surely not. They were all killed in the same way; a bullet to the back of the head. And, it seemed, all within a short while of each other. They had to have been in contact, it was the only thing that made any sense. If they had been living separate lives, without any contact, then there had to be something in common, some connection that resulted in them being killed. Something in common—what? The painful twinge moved to the opposite shoulder and he rubbed it vigorously.

Suddenly, a cold shiver, like icy fingers running down his spine, roused realization. *He* had something in common with each of them, a diamond-shaped tattoo, among other things. Could it be? Could this madness possibly have some connection to his old unit, Diamond One? If there was a link, whatever it may be, wherever it might lead him, he was determined to follow.

Then, there it was again, that icy shiver; worse this time. "Shit!" he murmured. That was it! There was the link! Three of the four surviving members of Diamond One had been slain. All of them shot dead! The last to die, Eddie Dickson, was trying to reach him when he was killed. Why? What was Dickson trying to do? Warn him, perhaps? Did Eddie know that Cobb and Elliott had already been murdered?

The questions that raced through his mind came in no

particular sequence. They rushed at him, absent of any form or logical order. If the same person was responsible for all three murders, and he suspected that would prove to be the case, was the killer now coming after him? Is that what Eddie was trying to tell him?

Instinct—or perhaps it was paranoia—caused him to look around. He glanced first into the rear vision mirror and then out of the windows to his left, and right. Only occasional Sunday traffic ambled by. The city was quiet, peaceful, harmless.

He peered again into the rear vision mirror and then, he saw it. In the distance behind him, a car parked at the kerb. Why should that bother him? Why were his eyes drawn to it? Was there someone sitting behind the wheel? It was too far away to see clearly, but the car looked familiar… somehow. Had he seen it before? No, maybe not. He was imagining things. His mind was playing tricks. What was so strange about another car parked at the side of the road? Chap shook his head as if to clear it of irrational thoughts.

Despite the cold, a bead of perspiration formed at his temple and slowly ran down the side of his face, over his chin and disappeared beneath his collar. Why was he sweating? With the back of his hand, he wiped at the path it had taken. This was crazy. He felt mildly embarrassed at his apprehension. He wound down the window and let the cold breeze fan his face. Trying to relax, his heart racing again, he focused on regulating his breathing. He had to think. This whole business was getting uglier by the minute.

He looked once again into the rear vision mirror. The other vehicle was gone. If it passed him, he never saw it. It must have turned around and driven in the opposite direction. Angry with himself for his foolish paranoia, he started the engine and pulled away from the kerb.

Chapter Seventeen

Later, at Chap's home, he and Sally were sitting together, Sally's head nestled comfortably on his shoulder, watching some inane comedy she found only mildly humorous and Chap even less so. She sensed something was bothering him. Thinking perhaps he may have fallen asleep, she lifted her head from his shoulder and nudged him with her elbow.

"What?" Chap asked, startled. "Is it time for bed already?"

"No, it's not time for bed." She turned to face him and kissed him lightly. "What's wrong, Chap? You've hardly said a word all night. Is something bothering you?"

Chap did not want to concern her with things he did not yet fully understand himself. However, she deserved better than his silence. He picked up the television remote, clicked the off button. He got up from the sofa, and walked across to the fireplace, added another log and watched the sparks crackle and disappear up the chimney. When the embers finally turned to flames, he turned to face Sally. She was watching him, concern etched on her face.

"I had a talk with a federal police officer this morning," he began. "I've worked with him a couple of times in the past.

He did some checking for me on Eddie Dickson, the man who was murdered a couple of days ago."

"This would be the case you're working on but not supposed to be working on, and will probably get you fired when your boss finds out?" she interrupted.

Chap smiled weakly. "I found out," he continued, "that two men, both from interstate, and both former friends of Dickson's, were killed in a similar manner just recently."

"And this is bothering you why?" she asked

"I think… no, I'm sure the three murders are connected somehow. I also think the same person is responsible."

What Chap deliberately omitted to tell her was that he knew all three victims when they were all in the army and served in Vietnam together. Earlier in the day, he had a momentary thought he might possibly be the killer's next target and he did not want Sally to arrive at the same conclusion. It was out of a desire not to alarm her that he was selective in how much he told her. Besides, he didn't know if he *was* a target. He was more than likely overreacting, so why cause her worry unnecessarily?

This case was occupying his every thought, particularly since he learned of the deaths of Cobb and Elliott. He was distracted, and it showed. He never told her about the vehicle outside the Federal Police building, and the driver he suspected was watching him. He never told her because he wasn't even sure he *was* being watched. It was just a feeling he'd had at the time and now he felt silly about it. He only saw the car briefly, and it was too far away to see the driver clearly. The more he thought about the car, the more he came to believe he was mistaken. Why then could he not stop thinking about it? No small part of his success as an investigator was based on his ability to trust his instincts. Despite the fleeting vision of an innocuous looking vehicle parked in the street, his instincts told him he should be concerned. Should he once again trust his instincts, or was he overreacting? This damn case was making him jumpy.

He told Sally he was going to Canberra to follow up on the case. She did not take it well. She had been looking forward to spending a good deal more time with him while he was on leave. She had arranged for François to take care of things at the restaurant, and this was an opportune time to spend some quality time together, just the two of them.

To make matters worse, Chap could not tell her when he would be back. Sally had seen him this way before. Determined and committed. She saw it for the first time when he investigated the death of her husband, and she knew she could never dissuade him. If he had to go to Canberra, she would have to accept it, albeit reluctantly. He had to see this thing through to the end or it would consume him.

Chap could tell by the look in her eyes how hurt she was and it was almost enough for him to abandon his plans. But something pushed him on. He didn't know exactly what it was; not yet, anyway, but he would. He couldn't, wouldn't, let Eddie down; Cobb or Elliott, either. He was certain Eddie Dickson had been coming to him for help and he could not, would not, turn his back on his old friend. He liked to think Sally admired and respected his determination, but she was hurt, and her disappointment was obvious. He crossed back to the sofa, sat, and took her in his arms.

"You are not going to Canberra right now, are you?" she murmured softly against his neck.

"Not right this minute. Why, what did you have in mind?"

"Oh, I don't know, how about a lovemaking marathon?"

"A marathon!" Chap smiled. "What's the matter, three-and-a-half minutes of quality sex not good enough for you anymore?"

"Come on, old man… you can do it."

They made love, right there on the floor. The dim light from the flickering fire cast dancing shadows around the room and over their bodies. Sally made love with an intensity he had not seen in her before; desperate, clinging, almost like it might be the last time they made love. Chap sensed a hint of desperation, urgency, and maybe even fear in her passion.

When it was over, she left. She didn't want to stay the night. She explained that she knew it would be much harder to leave him in the morning. In a way, Chap thought it was probably a good decision. He needed to be clear-headed the next day. He kissed her warmly as she prepared to leave, and then stood on his porch in the cold and watched her drive away.

Back inside, he poured a strong whisky, settled again on his sofa, and sat in the hollow darkness of the room. He left the room lights off, the only light emanating from the slowly dying fire across the room. A warm afterglow from their lovemaking lingered with him, and he found something mildly hypnotic about the quiet, dimly-lit room and the softly crackling fire. The ambience carried him on a wave of nostalgia to another place—a long ago, hostile, sad place. He drifted to Vietnam.

Chap's flight departed at seven a.m. He made it with twenty minutes to spare, enough time for an expensive cup of tasteless airport coffee before he boarded. He felt both anxious and enthusiastic. Although, with the bit between his teeth and ready to run with whatever he might find, he also felt the very first symptoms of fear from somewhere deep inside. He recognised the feeling even though he had not felt fear for many years. It was a strange feeling, a mildly uncomfortable mixture of anxiety and apprehension. It was not a feeling he savoured, but he welcomed it nonetheless, because he knew from days long gone that feeling this way would keep his mind alert and focused.

The flight was not direct, and included a short stopover in

Melbourne. Passengers travelling to the Victorian capital disembarked here. Those travelling on to Canberra remained on board. Chap spent the entire flight, including the stopover, engrossed in his unauthorised copy of the Dickson murder file.

The man in the seat next to him slept, snored annoyingly and, despite the early hour, smelled strongly of beer; no doubt the residual effect of a night he would probably regret later in the day. Chap was tempted to nudge him and stop the snoring, but if the bumpy landing didn't wake him, he doubted a poke in the ribs would. Strangely, Chap felt a touch jealous. He did not know the man and did not know the circumstances leading to his current condition, but he looked as though he didn't have a care in the world, and Chap thought that might be a nice place to be.

When he left Adelaide, it was raining, and it was cold. Canberra was worse. Here, it was close to freezing. Just two degrees above, the pilot announced as they made their approach. However, it was only ten o'clock in the morning. It had all day to get better, or worse.

No appointments preceded his arrival into Canberra. He decided it would be prudent not to telegraph his visit. He planned to make his way to Central Army Records, where Eddie Dickson worked, and when he got there, let things take their own course. He didn't know what he was looking for and had no real place to start, but Canberra was where Dickson lived and worked, so he figured it was as good a place as any.

First, he checked into the Holiday Inn, chosen at the recommendation of his cab driver. It was, the cabbie explained, central to where he wanted to be and it was comfortable without being excessively expensive. He had to watch the pennies; there would be no job to go back to if George Baldwin found out what he was up to. He was not looking for luxury; this was not a holiday. All he needed was somewhere to sleep and have a meal.

Inside the offices of Central Army Records, Chap noticed a number of civilian employees engaged in reception and front office duties. These would be Public Service personnel employed by the Department of Defense to fill jobs which would have once been performed by members of the military. It was a modern management practice employed by all government departments and police forces throughout the country, designed to free up their members for performance of the tasks for which they signed on in the first place.

Chap paused just inside the front doors, and looked around the foyer. He spotted a pretty young civilian receptionist behind a long counter. She looked up from her work and smiled at him.

"Good morning, sir," she greeted him with a practised smile. "Can I help you?"

Chap produced his identification and introduced himself. "My name is Detective Sergeant Chapman Bouttell, I'm with the South Australian Police. I am making enquiries into the death of Major Edward Dickson who I understand worked here."

The smile with which the receptionist greeted him faded quickly. "Excuse me, sir," she said. She reached for a telephone and punched in a short, internal extension number. After a few seconds of speaking in hushed tones to someone in another part of the building, she hung up the phone, got up from her seat, and walked to the front of the counter. "Would you please follow me, sir?" She turned away immediately, and began walking smartly across the foyer. She was a tiny little thing, Chap observed, and fast on her feet. He hurried after her as she led him to a lift and pressed the up button.

They made the short ride in silence. Chap stood behind, and slightly to one side of her, and discreetly looked at her. She was petite, and pretty, and he found himself wondering why they never had people like her around when he was in the army. Life as a young, single soldier, overflowing with an abundance of testosterone, might have been much more enjoyable.

The lift stopped at the third floor. This was obviously where the brass was housed. Here, starched, crackling uniforms with shiny buttons and highly polished shoes scurried about with a definite air of purpose. There were no Public Servants here, but there was another reception area where several computers screens blinked and keyboards tapped softly under the fingers of uniform-clad soldiers—all female, Chap noticed. Hooray for equality of the sexes in the services, he thought.

With only military personnel working in this section, he guessed this would be the hub of the office. Without stopping at the reception desk, his escort led him into a long, carpeted corridor and stopped outside an office door which carried a small brass plaque announcing that, beyond, there was to be found a Lieutenant Colonel Frederick W. Baxter.

A strong feeling of anticipation washed over Chap. The girl did not knock, but opened the door and walked into what Chap saw was a small but obviously functional outer office. Another pretty, uniformed lass, wearing the rank of Corporal on her sleeve, sat behind a desk. She looked up as they entered the office but did not smile. The greetings were becoming decidedly cooler, Chap observed. His pretty escort gave his name to the Corporal, turned away, and walked quickly from the room without so much as a friendly goodbye.

An atmosphere of unease hung heavy in the air and settled like a fog around him. He'd sensed it when he first arrived at the building, and it had followed him to the third floor. It was quiet… no, not just quiet… it was depressingly quiet.

The Corporal did not speak directly to Chap. Instead, she pressed a button on an intercom and announced his presence to her superior.

Lieutenant Colonel Frederick W. Baxter was a big man. Seated behind a huge desk, his body filled the high-backed, leather-bound chair. When he rose, and offered his hand to Chap, he stood well over six feet tall. Aged somewhere in his mid-fifties, Chap guessed, the Colonel presented an imposing figure. His hair was thick, but cut short at the sides in what Chap could only describe as military style. It was a look Chap remembered from his army days, and not one he would be eager to revisit.

Above the left-hand breast pocket of Baxter's immaculately pressed uniform shirt, he wore campaign ribbons from places Chap did not recognise; probably from countries like East Timor, or Iraq, or maybe Afghanistan. Here was a man, it occurred to Chap, stoically proud of his career and his service to his country. Chap accepted the proffered hand and was not surprised to find the Colonel's grip strong and firm.

"Sergeant Bouttell, I presume?" The distinguished soldier smiled. "I'm very pleased to meet you."

"Thank you, Colonel. I hope my calling on you without an appointment hasn't caused you too much inconvenience."

"Not at all." He gestured to a chair in front of his desk. "Please, have a seat."

Baxter waited until Chap settled himself, and then resumed his own seat. "I assume," he began "you are here with regard to Major Dickson." It was a statement rather than a question.

It never occurred to Chap that the colonel would be aware of Eddie Dickson's death. He assumed he would be the one to break the news. He should have known better. Today was Monday. The murder had occurred the previous Thursday. Of course he would know by now. It would also explain the atmosphere which greeted him when he arrived. Eddie Dickson must have been well liked within these walls.

Colonel Baxter noticed the questioning look in Chap's eyes. "We were notified this morning," he confirmed. "At least, the rest of the staff were. I was contacted at my home yesterday. Everyone is in a state of shock. Major Dickson was a very popular member of our team."

For the moment, Chap decided against revealing he knew Dickson. He would play this as the homicide cop investigating any other murder. "I will not keep you long, sir. However, there are some questions I need to ask."

"I hope I can answer them for you."

Chap hesitated for just a second. "Can you tell me why Major Dickson was in Adelaide?"

"We are off to a poor start, I'm afraid," Baxter said. "I have no idea what he was doing in Adelaide. The truth is, I wasn't even aware he went to Adelaide until I was informed of his murder." He shifted in his seat. "Before he left on Thursday, he submitted an application for a rest-day on Friday. We work on the flexi-time system here. He was owed the day so, naturally, I approved it. It was straightforward, really. I spoke to him briefly, but he never mentioned anything about travelling to Adelaide. Our office is closed over the weekend, so he was officially due back at work this morning." Baxter leaned back in his chair as if inviting the next question.

There was something about the Colonel that stirred something deep within Chap. Baxter appeared too calm, too cool, a little too detached, perhaps. It was that gut feeling again. "Who notified you of his death?"

"Our Military Police," Baxter answered. "They came to my home yesterday. I'm told they were notified by the Federal Police here in Canberra. It's standard procedure, not to mention protocol, for the Military Police to be notified in matters concerning military personnel."

"Did they give you any details regarding his murder?"

"Only that he was shot, sometime last Thursday night, not long after he arrived in Adelaide. Robbery, as I understand it."

Chap could easily have told Baxter he did not believe robbery to be the motive behind the Dickson's murder, but he didn't. There was something about the Colonel that made him cautious. Those instincts again. He decided to dig a little deeper.

"Tell me, can you ever recall, at any time, Major Dickson mentioning my name?" He watched Baxter's eyes looking for any sign of reaction, a blink, a pause, anything. He saw nothing.

"I'm afraid not," Baxter answered. "Not that I can recall. But then, Major Dickson was the type of chap who kept pretty much to himself. As far as I am aware, he had a very limited social life, and very few close friends. In fact, apart from the occasional, obligatory Officer's Mess functions, I never saw him outside the work environment. By all accounts his private life was exactly that—private."

Why did Chap get the feeling Baxter was not being completely honest? Perhaps he wasn't. Perhaps it was just his imagination playing tricks on him. The feeling was strong, however. Colonel Baxter knew Eddie Dickson better than he was letting on, of that Chap was convinced.

"What did Major Dickson do, exactly?" he queried.

Baxter shrugged. "Historical army research, nothing particularly exciting, I'm afraid. He was updating all the army's historical records, transferring them from bulky, deteriorating paper files to computer discs."

"Sounds like a pretty big job," Chap mused.

"Somewhat daunting, I suppose," Baxter conceded. "Our army history dates back a long time. But he loved the work, and had a particular penchant for computer technology. I was very pleased with the progress he was making." Baxter leaned forward, interlocked his fingers and leaned his elbows on his desk. "Marvellous things, computers. I don't know how we managed so long without them. Never could quite master them myself, never really wanted to. Nothing quite beats a pretty secretary, I say." Baxter smiled.

Chap wanted to bring the conversation back to the subject at hand. "My investigations indicate his trip to Adelaide was decided on rather suddenly. Are you sure he never mentioned his intention to fly to Adelaide?"

"Quite sure," Baxter replied. "I didn't ask his intentions and he didn't offer. I'm not in the habit of asking my staff what they do on their own time."

Chap looked across the desk at Baxter. There was an air about the Lieutenant Colonel which had not escaped Chap's notice. Was it arrogance or confidence? He wished he could put a finger on just what it was about this particular career soldier that concerned him.

"Do the names Charles Cobb and Brian Elliott mean anything to you?"

There! There it was; an ever so slight flicker of the eyelids. Baxter recognised the names, Chap was sure of it.

"No," Baxter answered quickly. He shifted in his seat and cleared his throat. His body language betrayed him. "I can't say I have ever heard the names. Are they people I should know?"

"No, not necessarily," Chap responded. "Unfortunately, they both met the same fate as Major Dickson. I am working on the theory that, in some way, the three deaths are connected. I guess I was hoping the Major might have mentioned them to you at some stage."

"I don't seem to be of much help to you, I'm afraid," Baxter apologized, as he got to his feet rather hurriedly.

The conversation was obviously over, whether Chap wanted it to be or not. "On the contrary," he lied, getting up himself. "You've been very helpful. I wonder, though, before I leave, if I may have a look around Major Dickson's office?"

"Well… I suppose that would be okay. No one else has

been in there yet, and I guess, as you're involved in the investigation, it shouldn't be a problem. My secretary will show you to his office. If there is anything else I can do for you, please don't hesitate to ask." He pressed a button on his intercom and asked his secretary to show Chap to Major Dickson's office. Again, he offered his hand. Chap shook it firmly, and as he turned to leave the room he wondered, just for a moment, if he could be wrong about his feelings in relation to Baxter. He thought not.

The Colonel stepped around his desk and accompanied Chap as far as the door. "Perhaps we'll meet again." He smiled.

"Perhaps we will, thank you." Chap smiled back.

"You're welcome, Sergeant. May I say again, what a tragedy it is about Major Dickson, and his two old friends." Baxter turned away smartly, reached out and closed the door.

Chap stared at the closed door. He knew it! He knew he was right! He should have known his intuition would not let him down, it rarely did. Baxter had lied; not about everything, perhaps, but lied nonetheless. He said it was a tragedy about Eddie Dickson and "his two old friends". Old friends. What two old friends?

Chap tried to recall everything that was said during their short conversation. He was sure he never mentioned that Dickson, Cobb and Elliott knew each other, let alone were friends. No, he never mentioned it, or even hinted at it, other than to say that Cobb and Elliott had met the same fate as Dickson. That was where any association between the three ended. Maybe Baxter assumed they were all friends. Had Chap said anything which might lead Baxter to draw such a conclusion? No, no way. The Colonel was good, Chap would give him that, but he had slipped, badly. Where Baxter's *faux pas* left him now, he didn't know. He only knew it removed any doubts he might have had that Baxter knew more than he was disclosing.

Baxter's secretary moved from behind her desk to stand at

Chap's side. Her voice, accompanied by a gentle hand on his arm, brought him back from where his thoughts had taken him.

"Sergeant Bouttell, is there anything wrong?"

"Oh… I'm sorry," Chap apologised. "No… no, nothing's wrong. Sorry, I was lost in my thoughts."

"If you'll follow me, sir, I'll take you to Major Dickson's office."

This girl was also exceptionally pretty, a feature Chap hadn't noticed when he was first ushered into the office. Twenty years younger, and he would have followed her through the gates of Hell. She wore a name tag pinned neatly above a firm, well-rounded breast. For an instant, their eyes met, and he smiled at her. She glanced away immediately and he thought he saw a hint of pink flush rise in her cheeks.

"Thank you, Corporal… ah…" he looked down at her breast, "ah… Kelly."

"You seem a little distracted, sir. Are you sure you are alright?"

"Yes," Chap confirmed, "I'm fine. Please, after you."

Chap followed Corporal Kelly from the room. It was only a short walk to Eddie Dickson's office but, from where he followed, a few paces behind her gently swaying bottom, it was not an unpleasant walk. At his age, he reckoned he should have felt ashamed of himself, but he didn't. It was nice that a pretty girl could still turn his head. Corporal Kelly stopped outside another closed door where another brass plaque, just like the one on Colonel Baxter's office, proclaimed they had reached the office of Major Edward Dickson.

Chap paused outside the door and looked at the plaque. He had never thought of Dickson as "Edward". It had always been "Eddie". As he stood there looking at the nameplate, he felt a strong sense of remorse. Eddie Dickson would never again return to this office. He would never again return anywhere. It seemed… no, not seemed… it *was* such a waste.

"How well did you know Major Dickson?" Chap asked the Corporal.

"He worked directly for Lieutenant Colonel Baxter," she answered. "I liked Major Dickson, all the staff did. He was nice, you know… fun." Her voice began to waver, ever so slightly. "When we heard the news this morning, we were all devastated. I still can't believe it. It seems so… I don't know… so surreal. I expect him to walk into the building at any moment."

Corporal Kelly's eyes began to glisten. Chap hoped she was not going to start crying. She noticed him watching her and once more, she averted her eyes. He had embarrassed her again; he was starting to get good at that.

"Did he have a secretary?" he asked finally.

"No," she confirmed, gathering herself. "Major Dickson was an extremely capable officer. He was an excellent typist in his own right. Besides, his job profile did not allow for a personal secretary. You would have seen the typing pool when you came in. Most of the officers working here sent their typing to the pool."

"Including Major Dickson?" Chap asked.

Kelly nodded. "Occasionally, if he got behind in anything, but that was not very often. As I said, he was a competent typist and usually did all his own paperwork."

"Do you know where he lived?"

"I don't know the address, but it is out in Belconnen. That's a suburb about fifteen minutes from here," she explained "I can check with Personnel and get it for you if you would like."

"I would appreciate that," Chap smiled.

"I'll leave it at the reception desk downstairs. You can collect it when you leave. In the meantime, you are welcome to look around in the Major's office. I'll leave you alone to do that. If you need anything, just pick up the phone on Major Dickson's desk and dial 'one', that's my extension." She smiled, and Chap decided she was even prettier when she smiled.

"You've already been a big help, thank you."

Corporal Kelly turned to leave, stopped, and paused with her head bowed. Then, she turned to face Chap. He noticed the slight glisten in her eyes was back.

"He only had a few months to go, you know," she said. "He was due to retire from the army in about six months, I think." She turned and walked away.

Chap watched her leave. A thousand questions raced through his mind. For a man who kept to himself, as Colonel Baxter would have him believe, Eddie Dickson seemed to have more than endeared himself to those within his work environment.

Pieces to the puzzle. Now, he had a few more pieces. Not many, but a few more than he had before he got here. The problem was getting the pieces to fit together. Which piece went where? How many more pieces were there? Where did Lieutenant Colonel Frederick W. Baxter figure in the overall picture? He fitted somewhere, Chap figured. He was certain of it. He opened the door and stepped into Eddie Dickson's office.

Chapter Eighteen

The office was larger than Colonel Baxter's, and that surprised Chap. He stood just inside the open doorway and looked around the room and he could see why Eddie had needed the extra space. The walls on either side of the room were completely taken up with bookcases, which were filled from floor to ceiling with books and files. Directly across the room, opposite the door, a large, polished, timber desk sat in front of a panoramic window spanning the full length of the rear wall. The top of the desk was neat and orderly.

Chap smiled to himself. Typical of Eddie, he thought; a place for everything, and everything in its place. On one end of the desk there was a computer terminal and keyboard, with a printer sitting neatly next to the monitor. Somewhere nearby there would be a hard drive, probably underneath the desk, Chap decided. This was where his old friend Eddie Dickson had filled his working day.

He walked slowly across the room and stopped in front of one of the bookcases. His eyes wandered over some of the titles. There were books on military weaponry through the ages, historical books on great military battles and on warfare in general. There were books on wars he had never heard of. Some had small pieces of paper protruding from their pages, bookmarks indicating a particular page or passage of significance.

He noticed a complete volume of books on the statistics of past wars. He picked one from the volume, opened it and flicked through the pages. It contained statistics on casualties —dead and wounded—civilian and military, how much ammunition was expended, how much each war cost the particular countries involved. Page after page of numbers, meaningless to most people, but not to someone like Eddie Dickson. It was his job to know and understand the significance of the statistics. He replaced the book and ran his fingers over the spines of the remaining books in the set.

As his eyes wandered over the assortment of titles, Chap couldn't help but feel a new respect for Dickson over and above that which he had held for him as a young combat soldier. He felt a sense of achievement and accomplishment, on behalf of his old war buddy. Eddie Dickson had come a long way in the last forty years, and Chap was proud of him, and for him. He wished he could have had the opportunity to tell him that.

Unless Baxter was wrong, and someone had been into the office and tidied it, he could only assume Dickson had maintained the neat, tidy, meticulous ways Chap remembered from his past. Orderly, and regimental, were words that sprang to Chap's mind.

He moved across to the desk. On the end opposite the computer, there were two correspondence trays, one marked *In* and the other marked *Out.* Both trays contained paperwork, and Chap took a few moments to read quickly through them. He did not know exactly what he was looking for, he was just hoping something might jump out at him; something out of the ordinary. He had been a cop long enough to know clues could be found anywhere, sometimes in the unlikeliest of places. If there were clues to be found in Eddie Dickson's office, he was determined to find them.

He walked around the desk and looked at the obviously well-used chair in which Eddie had once sat. He lowered himself into it, and discovered, despite its creased, well-used appearance, it was comfortable. It had a swivel-base on a set of casters, and he pushed himself away from the desk and turned to face the window. Outside, the ashen sky threatened more rain. The view was, by any standards, uninspiring. But this was a military building, on a military base; it was not designed for taking in the aesthetics the view beyond the window might offer.

Directly below where he sat was the building's car park, beyond which stood an identical building to this one. Typical government sameness, Chap thought. In the far distance, he saw what he was sure would, on a clearer day, be picturesque hills and in the near distance he could make out the now famous and extraordinarily expensive flagpole which stood atop the equally famous and extraordinarily expensive Parliament House.

He pushed the chair back to the desk and cast his eyes slowly around the room again. On either side of the door, a number of pictures on the wall caught his attention. He got up and crossed the room to where he could better study the pictures. They were not paintings, or prints, but actual photographs, enlarged and framed, depicting scenes from the Vietnam War. Vivid images frozen in time.

There was the iconic Iroquois helicopter in full flight, obviously taken from the door of another chopper flying in close formation. What a magnificent machine the Iroquois was. Affectionately known by all Vietnam Veterans as Huey, it flew men into battle, re-supplied them while they were there, and then flew them out again. At times, way too often, it was both a flying ambulance and flying hearse. Many veterans still referred to the Vietnam conflict as the Helicopter War and

Huey was the star of the show. The *whup…whup…whup* of the Huey's rotor blades was a sound unique to the Iroquois. When it was heard in the distance, long before you ever saw the familiar silhouette in the sky, every digger knew Huey was coming to get you.

Beneath this photo was a picture of the U.S. military's Cobra Gunship, a flying arsenal with a frightening array of weaponry. Crewed by only two, this chopper was feared by everyone who had the misfortune to be on the receiving end of its massive firepower.

On the other side of the door there were more framed photos. One depicted Vietnamese villagers standing amidst the smoking ruins of what were, shortly before the photo was taken, their homes, basic that they were. The desperation, hopelessness and pure, unadulterated fear in their faces was clearly evident and frozen in the photograph for all time.

Chap wondered if Eddie Dickson took the photographs. He remembered someone in Diamond One had a camera with them, but he couldn't remember who. Theirs was not a tourist jaunt, after all, and there were not a lot of photo opportunities which would make for nice memories at some time in the future. He figured the photos were examples of many others which would surely adorn other walls in this building, as well as walls in buildings just like this one. He cast his eyes again over the scenes depicted, and his mind swam with hazy, disjointed memories. Would he ever forget the horrors of that place? He thought not; it was the price he was condemned to pay for the things he did. He looked down at his hands and noticed they were trembling just a little.

War, any war, had the sad and unfortunate habit of profoundly affecting people's lives long after the last shots were fired. It mattered not that Chap had lived his life following the war with the ability to suppress his memories; suppressing was not the same as forgetting. These last few days had enlightened him to the reality of those memories. The war, and his involvement in it, would never be forgotten. The truth was, he now knew he had not managed to put the experience behind him as well as he believed he had. It was there, always there, closer to the surface than he would ever have admitted to, and that both saddened and frightened him.

He turned slowly and looked back at Eddie Dickson's empty chair, imagining his friend sitting there. He closed his eyes, breathed deeply and realised, at that precise moment, it would be very easy to cry. Chap had never considered himself to be a particularly emotional person. His childhood in the bleak environment of the orphanage, the war, and now his job, had stood him in good stead when it came to controlling his emotions. Emotional cops do not make good cops. Was he beginning to learn more about his own inner self? If so, some might say it was a good thing. But, if that was the case, why did it make him feel so bad? He opened his eyes, crossed the room again, and resumed his seat in Eddie's chair.

There were two sets of drawers in the desk, and no locks on either of them. He began with the drawers on his left, going through them from top to bottom. He was not surprised to find them equally as neat and tidy as the desktop. A legacy of years of military order and discipline, he thought. He found stationery, pens, pencils, erasers, paper clips, staples—everything one would expect to find in an office desk drawer. There were, however, no clues. No evidence. The matching set of drawers on his right proved just as frustrating.

There had to be something. Somewhere, there had to be a clue. He needed a starting point, and it seemed it was not to be found in Eddie Dickson's office. There was a reason why Dickson made a hurried trip to Adelaide, and there was a reason for his murder. There was a reason why Cobb and Elliott were also murdered. There had to be a point from which to begin, there always was. One clue, one piece of evidence, was all it took, and then, hopefully, it would all start to make sense.

Eddie Dickson's office was exactly what it appeared to be —a place where a senior army officer conducted historical military research. It was nothing more than that, and no matter how thoroughly Chap searched it, it was never going to offer him anything more. In frustration, he slumped back in his old friend's chair.

He picked up the telephone and dialed 1. Immediately, Corporal Kelly answered.

"Corporal Kelly. How may I help you?"

"Corporal Kelly, Sergeant Bouttell. I was wondering if I could get access to Major Dickson's computer?"

"I'm sure that would be okay," Kelly said. "I'll be there in a few minutes and get you set up."

"Thank you." Chap replaced the receiver and stared at the blank screen of the computer terminal.

When Corporal Kelly arrived back in the office, she accessed the files Dickson had been working on. All Chap found was historical military records, hundreds of them. There was nothing there that would help him. He looked in other places on the system, including the email inbox, deleted items file and sent items file. It seemed that this was not a computer used for personal purposes, or if it was, Dickson had wiped it clean of all search history

It was here at this computer, Corporal Kelly explained, where Eddie Dickson scanned hard copy files of historical records, transferred them onto the unit's hard drive and then backed them up onto disc as well as an external hard drive. Thousands of pages of army records, once stored in aging, dust covered boxes, were now saved electronically where they would withstand the ravages of time and free up storage space in the basement of the building. As soon as one box was completed, another was brought from the basement and the process continued.

For Chap, his frustration was giving way to helplessness. His instincts told him there may be a connection between the work Dickson was doing and his subsequent death. But instinct was all it was. He had nothing else.

While Corporal Kelly busied herself logging off and shutting down the computer, Chap leaned back in Dickson's chair and revisited a theory which had occurred to him a couple of times, but he had dismissed because it made no real sense to him. What if all three men were killed because of their actions in Vietnam? The theory made no real sense because they had survived forty years since the war. If someone wanted to kill them for what they did back then, why weren't they killed years ago? And why wasn't *he* killed? After all, he was there, too. If someone wanted to silence them, afraid that what they were ordered to do might become a matter of public knowledge, surely they would all have been disposed of years ago. Besides, they all signed secrecy agreements. Chap had kept his silence, and he had no reason to believe the others hadn't kept theirs.

It had to be something else. Who would want to kill them just to guarantee their silence? It was crazy. It had to be something else.

"Is there anything else you want to see?" he heard Corporal Kelly ask.

Chap got up from the chair. "No, I don't think so, thank you."

They moved together towards the door.

"What sort of person was Major Dickson?" Chap asked. "Did you know him very well?"

"Not really," Corporal Kelly said. "He was very popular with everyone, jovial and friendly. But, he mostly kept to himself. He seemed to be a very fit man, for his age." She hesitated and looked at Chap. "Oh… sorry. I mean… he…"

"Don't be sorry." Chap smiled. "Sixty is the new forty, you know."

Corporal Kelly lowered her eyes, a light flush rising on her cheeks. "He rode a pushbike to work almost every day. Weather permitting," she added, as an afterthought.

"I can't remember when I last rode a pushbike," Chap said. "Sounds like hard work to me. How was his demeanor lately? Did he seem different in any way, preoccupied perhaps?"

She paused for a moment, thinking. "Well, now that you mention it, he had been acting a little strange the last couple of weeks."

"Strange?"

"Not *strange,* strange." She shrugged, as though searching for the right words. "Just… not his usual, cheerful self. He was a bit moody… and quiet."

"Do you have any idea why?" Chap pressed.

"No, not really, but I think it had something to do with a fight he had with Lieutenant Colonel Baxter."

Chap's interest suddenly intensified. "Major Dickson had a fight with Colonel Baxter?"

Obviously embarrassed, Corporal Kelly became hesitant, fearing she had spoken out of turn. She felt a certain loyalty to her boss, Colonel Baxter, and she was torn between that loyalty and her respect and liking for Eddie Dickson.

Chap reached out and placed a hand on her arm. "Your loyalty is admirable, but this is very important. What did they fight about?"

"Well," she began to explain, "it wasn't a physical fight as such, more an argument, a heated exchange."

"What was the argument about?"

"I don't know. They were in the Colonel's office and the door was closed. I was away from my desk for a few minutes and had just returned. Major Dickson must have arrived while I was away. I heard raised voices from the office and recognised Major Dickson's voice. A few seconds later, the Major stormed out of the office. He nearly knocked me over in his rush."

"Did you form an opinion as to what they were arguing about?"

"No, I did not!" Corporal Kelly answered a tad harshly. "And I don't wish to speculate. It was none of my business, and I prefer it that way. You may have noticed I am only a Corporal. I like my job and I want to keep it."

"I apologise," Chap said. He silently wished she had heard more of the argument. This was an interesting turn of events and it would have been nice to know what the two antagonists were going at each other about. He could see Corporal Kelly was already having some regrets about telling him as much as she had and was plainly concerned she might be placing her job in jeopardy. It would simply not do for the Colonel's personal secretary to disclose the content of what would surely be considered a private and confidential conversation to an outside party.

If Corporal Kelly knew any more about the argument, and from her demeanor Chap doubted she did, she was not about to tell him. He had learned enough, however, to reaffirm his suspicions that Colonel Frederick W. Baxter knew more about all this than he was letting on.

"Do they call you 'Ned'?" he asked the pretty Corporal.

"I'm sorry?"

"You know, like Ned Kelly, the bushranger?"

"My father calls me 'Ned' sometimes. Why?"

"No reason," Chap smiled. He reached into his pocket and removed a contact card. He wrote the name of his hotel on it and handed it to her. "Thank you for all your help. If you think of anything else that might help, you can contact me at this hotel."

She took the card, glanced at it, and tucked it away in her uniform pocket. "I have asked Personnel to put together some information from Major Dickson's file. Obviously, we can't release anything relating to his military records, but there will be some things relating to his personal life—address, date and place of birth, that sort of thing. It should be at Reception when you leave."

"Thank you," Chap said again and he turned to leave. "I can find my own way out."

On the ground floor, he stopped for a moment and spoke briefly to the women who made up the typing pool, a small team of skilled young ladies who, to the last, spoke affectionately of Eddie Dickson. As they spoke, a couple dabbed at moist eyes. They had all learned of Dickson's death just that morning and the news had obviously had a profound effect on them. It warmed Chap to think that the man he once knew to be capable of acts of savage brutality had a side to him which endeared him to those with whom he worked. It was a side Chap had never seen in the time he knew Dickson. Every member of Diamond One had been hand-picked to do one thing; kill the enemy, as quickly, efficiently, and as silently as possible, and Eddie Dickson was as good at it as any of them. Perhaps this endearing quality he displayed later in life was his way of compensating for the brutality of his past.

True to her word, Corporal Kelly had gathered the information he sought and he collected it from the main reception desk as he prepared to leave the building. He asked the girl behind the desk to order him a taxi. As he waited, he flipped through the few pages of personal information in the file.

"Thank you, Ned," he murmured to himself as he read.

Chapter Nineteen

Eddie Dickson lived alone in a subsidised government army house. Chap was surprised, because army houses were usually reserved for married members. Single members, as a general rule, were housed in barracks-style accommodation within the base precinct. But then, Eddie Dickson was an officer, not a rank-and-file soldier and this was not the 1960s. Times had changed, and today's modern army bore little resemblance to the army Chap remembered.

The documents supported what Corporal Kelly had already told him; Dickson was due to retire in the next few months. A waste, Chap thought, a lousy, pitiful waste. A productive, dedicated forty-five years of service to the army and his country gone in an instant. Again, the questions surfaced. Who? Why?

When his cab arrived, he returned to his hotel and lingered in a long, hot shower. He leaned forward, his back to the spray, playing the water over his aching shoulders.

Already, the night temperatures promised to drop below freezing and he dressed accordingly. He wished he didn't have to go out into the cold, but he wanted to, needed to, look inside Eddie Dickson's home.

A house key was attached with adhesive tape to the inside cover of Dickson's file. Chap pulled the key free and smiled at the efficiency of Corporal Kelly. In a leather-bound guest folder provided by the hotel, he found a phone number for the taxi company and ordered a cab.

Thirty minutes later, the taxi pulled up in front of a small, plain, unpretentious house on a street amidst similar looking houses, west of the city. They were all army homes, Chap guessed; neat, tidy, comfortable, and practical. This would be one of perhaps several small enclaves dotted around the capital.

Chap glanced at his watch and saw it was almost six-thirty. It was already quite dark and very, very cold. He paid the driver and, as he got out of the cab, his breath clouded in the night air. He watched the cab pull away and thought of places he would rather be—at home on his lounge floor with Sally, for instance. It had not yet been twenty-four hours and already he missed her.

He walked into the driveway of Eddie Dickson's residence and looked around the front yard and its well-kept garden. A homeowner's garden will tell you a lot about those who tended it, some believe. Eddie's was well manicured and maintained. It was as he would have expected, given what he had come to learn about Dickson in the last few hours. He paused, and thought briefly about his own scruffy, weed-dominated garden back in Adelaide and was even more convinced that a garden will speak volumes about its keeper.

As he approached the small front porch, he saw the checkered police tape crisscrossed across the closed door. He stepped onto the front porch, fumbled with the key in the rapidly fading light, and opened the door. Ducking low under the tape, he reached inside, found the light switch, and flicked it on.

The front door opened directly into a small lounge area. He stepped inside and closed the door behind him. Just inside the door, a bicycle leaned incongruously against the wall. Chap was no expert on pushbikes, but it seemed to be one of those multi-geared road bikes which more and more people seemed to be taking to these days instead of running or walking. It looked to be in well-maintained order, and would be, he guessed, the bicycle Corporal Kelly referred to earlier.

In most respects, the room was not unlike Eddie Dickson's office—clean and orderly. The furnishings, such that they were, were modest but practical. If anything at all was lacking in the presentation of the room, it was the decorative touch only a woman can provide.

Chap walked slowly around the room, looking for anything that might help. This was a government-built home, it was simple and uncomplicated. There were no open fireplaces here but there was a gas heater against one wall. Above the heater there was a mantelpiece on which sat a number of framed photographs. They reminded him of those he had seen earlier in Dickson's office. However, these were not enlargements but normal size snapshots in inexpensive, self-supporting frames. He crossed the room and stood in front of the mantelpiece.

The first picture which caught his eye was an old one. It was a group photograph of all ten members of Diamond One. He picked it up and studied it closely. The image took him back to their mountain hideaway and the Montagnard tribe who provided them with a sanctuary.

Now he remembered. Brian Elliott had a camera. He smiled, remembering how long they all had to stand there while Elliott gave the chieftain an impromptu lesson in photography, and how long it took to convince the old man the camera was not the invention of the devil and would not explode in his hands when he pressed the shutter.

Chap's eyes lingered over the young, smiling faces in the photograph and he was suddenly filled with immense sadness. These men, no… these boys, so young, so brave, and so naïve, were all too good to die the way they did. As he studied each face in turn, it reminded him he was now the only one of the ten still alive. A sobering thought, one which sent a shiver down his spine.

There was another photo, this one of more recent times. A photo of Eddie Dickson, Charles Cobb and Brian Elliott. He looked closely at the photograph and saw, in the bottom corner, the date the picture was taken. Obviously, the three had been in touch as recently as a few weeks ago. Had they maintained contact all these years? In the photo, they were all smiling at the camera, their arms around each other's shoulders. They looked happy. Chap wondered where the photo was taken and was instantly sorry he had not known any of them in latter years. Had he kept in touch with them, would his face also be smiling back at the camera? Would his arms be around the shoulders of his buddies?

He glanced briefly at the other photos on the mantelshelf. There were a couple of scenery snaps of places he did not recognise. Holiday snaps, he guessed. He moved away from the mantel, turning his attention to a small bookcase on the other side of the room. It contained a number of books, most of them on matters military, not unlike those in Dickson's office. There were magazines, lots of magazines, on computer science and related subjects. There was nothing which might shed any light on Eddie Dickson's murder.

There were three bedrooms in the house. The first one he entered was small and empty. There was no bed, no wardrobe, no furnishings of any kind. He left, walked a few paces down the hall and found the second room. It offered little more than the first—one single bed with a mattress that looked as though it had never been slept on. This was a room that was almost never, if ever, used. Eddie Dickson was, apparently, a man who held little stock in personal possessions. In a single, built-in wardrobe recessed into a wall in one corner he found sheets, and several blankets. Like the mattress, the bedding appeared to be new. Dickson was also not a man who entertained house guests, it seemed.

Chap was beginning to form a mental a picture of his old friend by now. Eddie Dickson was, for all intents and purposes, a loner. He was not married, he lived alone, and seemed to have few close friends, with the possible exception of the late Charles Cobb and Brian Elliott. He did not seem to be one who enjoyed a full social life, but one who was perfectly comfortable with his own company.

The third and largest of the three bedrooms, obviously Dickson's own, contained more furniture than the other two but was by no means lavish. A double bed, another built-in wardrobe, and two small bedside tables. On one of the tables sat a hardcover book—*Tobruk*, by Australian author Peter Fitzsimons. Chap picked it up and opened it where a bookmark had been inserted to mark the place Dickson had got to in his reading. Eddie was never going to finish this book, Chap thought. He replaced the book and crossed to a bay window which looked out onto the neat front yard and the street beyond. He stood for a few moments, staring out into the dark, cold night, lost in his thoughts.

Then he moved back to the bed and searched through the contents of both bedside tables. He found only socks, underwear, half a dozen neatly folded handkerchiefs, and a few dollars in small change casually discarded in a glass ashtray. He slid open the door of the wardrobe, this one larger than the one in the second bedroom, and found clothes: civilian shirts and trousers, and a range of army clothing; two heavy parkas, a couple of woollen jumpers. Several pairs of shoes, civilian and military, were lined up neatly beneath them. He rummaged through the pockets of each piece of clothing and found nothing.

Resuming his walk-through, he found a small, compact kitchen off the rear of the lounge. He searched the cupboards here and again found nothing out of the ordinary. He found the bathroom and did likewise, and then he searched a linen cupboard in the hallway. Out of sheer frustration, he even lifted the lid off the toilet cistern and peered inside.

He returned to the kitchen and opened the refrigerator. It contained the usual staples one would expect to find in a refrigerator belonging to a man of simple needs. On the bottom shelf was a six pack of beer. Chap would have preferred a whisky about now but, given he had not discovered any other alcohol during his search of the house, it seemed Eddie Dickson was a man who preferred beer, and then not much of it. He reached into the fridge, removed a can from the plastic carry holder, yanked at the ring pull, and took a long mouthful. Although the weather was not conducive to drinking ice cold beer, he savoured the taste. Prowling through Eddie Dickson's house had left him warm and flushed.

Sipping occasionally at the beer as he went, Chap walked slowly through the house one more time. Slowly, room by room, looking, touching, lifting, examining.

He went out the back door and instantly felt the chill of the night. A light on the outside of the door illuminated a compact, neat backyard and a small garden shed against the back fence. It was typical of the sheds which could be found in millions of Australian backyards. Usually, they contained the family lawn mower and assorted gardening implements. Perhaps an old suitcase or two filled with family mementos, or several dusty cardboard boxes filled with all manner of bits and pieces, most of which could be classified as superfluous junk and of significance only to the owner. Hunched over against the cold, he crossed the yard to the shed. It was unlocked and inside he found a single, low wattage light bulb hanging from the ceiling.

The shed was almost empty. He found the obligatory lawnmower, a leaf rake, a handful of basic tools and some garden pesticides. Chap looked at his watch and was surprised to see it was 8:30. He took a last, quick look around the tiny shed, turned off the light, closed the door, and returned to the house.

Inside, out of the icy night air, he stole another beer from Eddie Dickson's fridge and went into the lounge. He hadn't eaten since he left Adelaide and the beer aroused his hunger. He used Eddie's telephone to phone a taxi, sat on Eddie's sofa and drank Eddie's beer, while he waited for the cab. Smiling faces in framed photographs looked down at him from the mantelpiece.

The beer was nice, but it was cold, too cold. Chap needed a whisky, a strong whisky, and a hot meal. He stared at the smiling photographs and realised, once again, he also needed some answers.

Chapter Twenty

Chap was tired. The early morning flight, the visit to Central Army Records Office and his search of Eddie Dickson's home had left him exhausted and frustrated. All these things only compounded his already moody disposition.

He showered again, standing for a long time under the spray, hoping the hot water would reinvigorate him. It didn't. Now, he sat on the edge of his bed flicking through the pages of the Dickson file and searching his mind to find a common thread connecting all that he now knew. His mind was crowded with thoughts of his three former comrades. His efforts to make some sense of it all had, to date, been to no avail. On the surface, there appeared to be nothing to be found. But there was something. There was always something. He had been investigating murders long enough to know there was always something. He just had to find it. A strange sense of suspicion in regard to Colonel Baxter troubled him. Where did Baxter fit in the picture?

With the exception of murder committed in the heat of the moment on impulse, without premeditation, people were not murdered without motive. That was one of the very first things he learned ten years ago when he first joined the Major

Crime Investigation Section. Killers almost always had a reason for murder, and Chap knew these murders would be no exception. All he had to do was find a motive and then there was a better than even chance the motive would lead to a perpetrator. When he thought about it quickly, it sounded easy.

The similarities between all three deaths were not coincidental. For Chap, that was a given. Someone, the same person, he was willing to wager, had murdered all three. The who and the why were not a given.

It was obvious from what he had already learned that Eddie Dickson had demonstrated that he was an extremely capable and efficient army officer, well liked and respected by his colleagues and apparently by all who knew him. Had Dickson been mixed up in something, along with Cobb, and Elliott, which eventually got them all killed? So far, Chap had found nothing to indicate Dickson was anything other than what he appeared. He was unable to form a similar opinion of Cobb and Elliott as yet, simply because he had no information on their lives over the last forty years. He wanted to think these two would prove to be as squeaky clean as Eddie Dickson appeared to be. Nonetheless, they were all dead. Someone had killed them. Not randomly, but in cold-blooded, premeditated murder.

Adding to Chap's concerns was one Lieutenant Colonel Frederick W. Baxter. There was definitely something about Dickson's commanding officer that niggled at Chap and aroused his suspicions. The fight, for instance, or, as Corporal Kelly more accurately described it, the heated exchange between Baxter and Dickson. What the hell was that about? From what Chap understood, arguments seemed to be uncharacteristic to both men. However, something happened between the two of them which precipitated the unpleasant exchange. It was possible that whatever it was might be totally unrelated to Dickson's death, but Chap did not think so. What was the connection between Baxter, and Dickson, other than their working relationship? Did Baxter kill Eddie Dickson? Did he also kill Charles Cobb and Brian Elliott? If so, why? The fruit salad of campaign ribbons on Baxter's chest indicted he had most likely killed before in the actions of war, but was he capable of killing now? These questions, and a hundred others, filled his mind as he headed downstairs to the motel dining room.

He was eating late, and was relieved to find the restaurant still open for business. Only four guests were still inside, lingering over the last of their evening meals before retiring for the night.

Chap sat on a stool at the small bar and ordered a steak and a whisky. He sipped slowly at his drink while he waited, and still the thoughts peppered his mind. Two whiskies later, his dinner arrived and, as he was ushered to a table at the window, he looked out into the freezing cold, black, shadowy night beyond the large windows. He looked beyond his own reflection, into the darkness, and his mood slipped into one of reminiscence. He lingered on a scenario which had crossed his mind earlier; was it possible he could be the killer's next victim?

He pushed thoughts of his possible premature demise from his mind, and turned to thoughts of Sally Prescott. Would she cope if he were killed? He remembered all too vividly how the murder of her husband affected her, and how sometimes, in quiet, reflective moments of her own, she still grieved for him. Her love for her late husband gave rise to a selfish jealousy in Chap. Would she feel the same way if he were killed? It was a sobering thought.

Having been raised in an orphanage, there was no one to grieve for him. No parents, no siblings, no close friends, other than Sally. He had some mates in the job, of course, but none of them were so close that he socialised with them outside the confines of the workplace. Could life's circumstances be such that Sally Prescott would lose the only two men she ever loved at the hands of a murderer? If fate deemed that he was to look death in the eye once again, Chap was prepared, if not willing.

Unless circumstances are such that a person arrives at the decision to end their life by their own hand, people do not generally wish to die. Chap was no exception. He was not afraid of death; he had seen too much of it and had been the cause of too much of it, so the prospect of dying did not concern him greatly. It comes to everybody sooner or later. He just wasn't ready yet.

If the probability of his imminent death confronted him, he would resist it with every ounce of his being, and use every resource at his disposal to avoid it; but, if it was unavoidable, he knew he could, and would, face it with a dignified preparedness. It was not heroic—it was realistic. There seemed to be little dignity in protesting, or begging for mercy, if indeed death was inevitable. What he was not prepared to do was submit to it without knowing the reason behind it. If he was going to die, he was going to know the reason why.

Mysteriously, his thoughts turned briefly to Adelaide, and the car he spotted parked on the street behind him when he visited the Federal Police building. Was he being paranoid? Was he letting all this get to him?

It was unusual for him to have such feelings. He had always adopted a clinical approach to any investigation he was involved in and was able to stay emotionally unattached without compromising his focus on the task at hand. But not this time. He admonished himself for what he considered to be a weakness—he *was* emotionally attached to this case. It *had* become personal. He knew mistakes were easily made when one allowed emotions to dominate an investigation.

He stared into the blackness beyond the window, and found himself wondering if there might be someone on the other side of the glass, freezing his butt off, watching him. Was he being followed? He looked away from the window, shook his head as if to clear his mind of negative thoughts, and swallowed the last of his meal. This whole business was making him crazy.

He pushed his plate to one side, and sipped at a glass of very ordinary red wine which came complimentary with the meal. He had finished half of the wine and couldn't remember doing so. He shuddered at the acidic taste of it and wondered how he couldn't remember drinking it—it was bloody awful! House wine, poured from a cardboard cask no doubt, he surmised.

The waitress appeared at his table bearing an expression announcing she would rather be anywhere else other than here. She collected his empty plate without speaking and the disinterested look became more intense when Chap ordered another whisky.

Until now, it had not occurred to him that he was drinking more lately. He needed to watch that, and not revisit bad habits he had abandoned a long time ago, he thought. It was important he stay clear-headed and focused. The whisky arrived. He took a sip, and returned his attention to the window and the illusions the dark night beyond offered.

An image approached the window. Initially, he thought the reflection beyond his own was that of the bored waitress returning. Lost in deep thought, he did not hear her approach. One second he was alone, and then she was there, standing beside him.

It was not until she spoke that he realised it was not the waitress. He turned away from the window and looked up into the eyes of the very pretty Corporal Kelly.

In another time, another place, perhaps in another lifetime, if he possessed any male charm or base animal magnetism at all, Chap might have been encouraged and flattered at her unexpected, unannounced appearance, at night, at his motel.

"Sergeant Bouttell," Kelly greeted him.

"Well, Corporal Kelly!" Chap half rose from his seat. "This is a surprise. A pleasant one, I might add. I certainly never expected to see you here."

She looked very different out of uniform; younger somehow, if that were possible. Chap hadn't found her to be unpleasant on the eye before, and she looked even better in civilian attire, or mufti, as it was sometimes referred to by those in the military. He wondered if she had a boyfriend, and then he wondered why he would ask himself such a question. Of course she would have a boyfriend. With her looks, she would almost certainly have a retinue of testosterone-charged young roosters following her around. He glanced at her hands. She had long, slender fingers devoid, he noticed, of any rings which might indicate a husband or fiancé tucked away somewhere. If indeed there was someone special in her life, Chap considered him to be a very lucky man.

"I hope I haven't interrupted your meal," Corporal Kelly apologised.

"No, not at all, in fact I've just finished." Chap looked past her, searching for someone who might have accompanied her. He didn't know who, if anyone, he expected to see. He was so surprised to see her, it was more of a reflex action rather than an expectation of her being with someone. He saw only the waitress busying herself behind the bar and casting occasional furtive glances his way. It was only now, as he looked around the room, that he realised the last of the diners had left and he suspected the waitress was hoping he would, too, so she could lock up and go home.

"I'm alone," Corporal Kelly confirmed, as if reading his mind.

"Why is it that I get the distinct impression that our meeting like this is more than just a pleasant coincidence?" Chap posed.

"It's not a coincidence." She smiled, seeming a little

embarrassed. "I've been ringing, on and off, for most of the evening. They kept telling me you were not in your room." She gestured to the empty chair opposite. "May I?"

"I'm sorry," Chap blustered, as he half-rose again from his chair. "Please, sit down. Can I get you something to drink?" He leaned forward across the table as she sat and said quietly, "I'm afraid the wine is not very good, bloody awful, in fact."

"No, thank you. I can't stay long, but I had to speak to you before you went back to Adelaide. The reception people didn't know when you would be back. I assumed you might have gone to Major Dickson's home and I decided to take the chance and come here and wait until you returned."

The waitress approached the table. The look of disdain on her face did not escape Chap. He knew what she must be thinking; he was old enough to be the girl's father. Maybe even her grandfather. What was he doing meeting a pretty young girl at his motel at night? He decided to let her stew in the juices of her own moralizing.

"Would you like anything else to drink?" the waitress asked.

"No, thank you." Chap smiled and winked. "We're fine."

With a disapproving flick of the head, the waitress turned and hurried back to her bar duties.

Chap smiled at the pretty young Corporal. "That will give her something to think about for a while," he said quietly.

Corporal Kelly lowered her eyes, and the pink glow from earlier in the day flushed her cheeks once again.

"Your timing is perfect," Chap continued. "I arrived back about forty minutes ago. Another forty, and you would have had to wake me." He shifted slightly in his chair. "Now," he said directly. "It must be just a couple of degrees above freezing out there. Not the sort of weather to be out for a casual drive, and I'm sure it's not my good looks and charming personality that brings you here, so please, feed my curiosity. Why are you here?"

"I wanted to apologise for this afternoon," she began. "When you asked me about the argument between Major Dickson, and Colonel Baxter. I was a bit short with you. I was abrupt, and I'm sorry." She lifted her eyes and looked directly at Chap.

"You came all the way over here just to apologise?" Chap raised his eyebrows. "Forgive me, but I find that a bit hard to believe."

"Well," she explained. "It's not that far really, I live nearby."

"There's no need," Chap insisted. "I've done a little time in the army, half a lifetime ago, and I've been in the police force for more years than I care to think about. I understand your loyalty. In fact, I find it commendable."

"Thank you," Corporal Kelly responded. "But it's not a matter of loyalty. The truth is, I honestly don't know what they were arguing about. I was shocked to hear them like that with each other. From what I have noticed, they have always had a good relationship, and some might consider that unusual given the difference in their rank."

"Funny," Chap interrupted. "I got the impression from Colonel Baxter that their relationship may have been a little strained."

"What do you mean?"

"Well, I'm not sure, exactly. After speaking to Colonel Baxter, I formed the opinion that there was definitely some tension between the two."

"If there was, I never saw it—quite the opposite, in fact. I would have said they might even have been quite good friends."

"Really?" Chap was surprised. "I also got the impression that Major Dickson was a bit of a loner."

"I can't comment on what he was like outside the office," Kelly said. "But at work he was always very friendly, even with Colonel Baxter."

What Chap was hearing only served to confirm what he already suspected. Baxter had lied. The Colonel knew much more than he had disclosed and Chap wanted to know just how much more. He sensed that wasn't all Corporal Kelly wanted to say.

"There is something else," she confirmed.

"Go on," Chap prompted.

"With the news of Major Dickson's death this morning, and then your visit, I completely forgot about it until you left."

Chap's sixth sense was with him again, and a cautious anxiousness swept over him. "Please," he invited, trying not to display his eagerness. "Continue."

"It was last Thursday," she began. "I was taking Major Dickson's application for a flexi-day back to his office. Colonel Baxter had approved it. It was a few minutes before I went to lunch and Major Dickson was not in his office. His door was open, but he was out. I knew he could not be far away because whenever he left the office, even for a few minutes, he always locked the door."

"Why would he do that?" Chap interrupted.

"I don't know." She shrugged. "He always locked his office door when he left the room."

"Perhaps he just forgot to lock it this time," he suggested.

"No," she insisted. "Major Dickson was a creature of habit. It was an idiosyncrasy those of us in the rank-and-file joked about sometimes. He never forgot. But the unlocked door is not the issue. I was due to go to lunch and I was meeting someone. I decided not to wait for the Major to return. I went into his office to leave the application on his desk." She paused.

"And?" Chap pushed.

"I went into his office and put the application on his desk. I was about to leave when I noticed a large envelope lying on his desk."

"I'm sorry," Chap said. "I'm afraid I don't see the relevance."

"Well, in itself, that is not unusual. It was just that I assumed it was outgoing mail because it was addressed and stamped. We have a policy here that all outgoing mail has to be at reception by midday each day to catch the mail collection at 12:30. I didn't know where the major was, or how long he would be gone, so I thought I would take the letter with me and leave it at reception so it would not miss the mail pick-up." Corporal Kelly hesitated. "When I picked it up, I noticed it was not sealed and assumed it was not ready to mail yet, so I put it back on the desk."

"Then what?" Chap asked.

"Then nothing. I left, went back to my own office and went to lunch."

Chap was confused. Perhaps he had missed something. "I'm afraid I still don't understand how any of this helps."

Corporal Kelly continued. "Today, when you came to see Colonel Baxter, your name never registered with me, not at first. We had all just heard about Major Dickson and I guess I wasn't thinking clearly."

"I can understand that," Chap acknowledged. "It must have been quite a shock."

"It was not until you left and gave me your card, that it dawned on me."

"What dawned on you, exactly?"

"The envelope, on Major Dickson's desk—it was addressed to you."

Stunned, Chap slumped back in his chair. It must have been for just a few seconds but it seemed like many minutes. He must have looked to Corporal Kelly like a stranded fish with his eyes wide and his mouth agape. This was incredible! Had he heard her correctly? He knew he had, but the significance of her words was not immediately apparent. The revelation, however, was.

Eddie Dickson had intended sending him something in the mail. Or had he? Perhaps he had it on him when he flew to Adelaide, in which case it was long gone by now and he might never know what the envelope contained. Would it have provided some answers? Chap was now sure of one thing. Long gone or not, he had to find that envelope.

"Are you sure it was addressed to me?" he asked, finally.

"I'm positive. As soon as I read your name on the card you left, I knew it was the same as the name on the envelope. Chapman Bouttell, it's an unusual name."

"I never found any envelope when I looked through his office this morning," Chap said. "Do you know what happened to it?"

"I anticipated you would ask, so I did some checking."

Chap wanted to jump up and hug her. This could be the breakthrough he was hoping for. He was overwhelmed with optimistic enthusiasm. "That's great. What did you find out?" he pressed.

Corporal Kelly leaned forward slightly and placed both hands on the table in front of her as if studying her nails. "There's a book," she began. "We keep it at reception. It's called a Mail Movement Record. The member on duty at the front desk has the responsibility for maintaining it." She paused, but only long enough to see Chap's expression was urging her to continue. "In it, the member records the movement of all mail, in and out of the building."

"You mean the contents of the mail?" Chap asked.

"No, obviously not the contents; no one is authorised to open any mail except the person to whom it is addressed. The member on duty records the date, and time, the correspondence came into, or went out of, the building. Security was tightened up considerably following the 9/11 bombings. In relation to outgoing mail, the details from which office it originated, and to where it is destined, are recorded."

Never before had Chap ever been so enthusiastic about departmental office procedure. "And…?" he urged.

"The envelope was not recorded in the book." Kelly shrugged.

Suddenly Chap's new-found enthusiasm began to wane. "What does that indicate exactly?"

"It means the envelope never went out with the normal outgoing daily mail. Not on Thursday, or Friday, and not today. I checked. If Major Dickson mailed it to you through our internal office system, it would have been recorded."

"Could it have been overlooked somehow? Mistakes do happen, you know."

"It is the same member every day who keeps the record. That's office policy, and it's designed that way so mistakes don't happen. The girl with that responsibility is very efficient. If the envelope was overlooked, it would be the first time she has ever done so. As well as her other duties, she has been keeping the record for a long time. She knows how to do it, and she does it well. Besides," she added as an afterthought, "Colonel Baxter is a stickler for efficiency. Mistakes under his command are very rare, almost nonexistent."

For a few moments, they sat in silence as Chap absorbed this new information. Finally, he looked at Corporal Kelly and watched as she shifted in her seat, perhaps finding his silence a little uncomfortable.

"If," Chap began finally, "a piece of mail originates from an office in the building, in this case Major Dickson's office, and it travels to reception where, for some inexplicable reason, it is overlooked by the lass who is charged with keeping a record of it, how would Colonel Baxter ever know, regardless of his efficiency requirements? How would he ever know the said piece of mail ever existed in the first place?"

Corporal Kelly nodded. "He wouldn't know," she confirmed. "But if you are suggesting it might be easy for the girl to make a mistake and not be too concerned, because her mistake might never be discovered and thereby she would have no real incentive or motivation to keep an accurate record, you are wrong. You have to accept my assurance that efficiency around our office is the way I tell you it is, and you have to accept that the girl in question does not make mistakes."

"I'm sorry. It sounds like I'm being super-critical of your office staff and I don't mean to be. I guess I'm just trying to eliminate all the negatives."

"I understand." Corporal Kelly smiled.

"Okay," Chap continued. "Let's start from scratch. I accept that the envelope was not in the outgoing mail, and I know it was not in Major Dickson's office this morning. That brings me back to my original question. What do you think could have happened to it?"

"I don't know. I can only assume he took it with him when he left that day."

Chap suddenly felt stupid; profoundly dumb, in fact. Of course! That was it! Eddie Dickson took the envelope with him from the building! He cursed his own lack of initiative. "Shit!" he cursed.

"Pardon?" Corporal Kelly said.

"Oh… sorry," Chap apologised.

This damn case was really getting to him. He was missing vital signs that lay right in front of his eyes. He was a better investigator than that. He lowered his head and rubbed his eyes.

"He mailed it himself," he said quietly, more to himself than to Corporal Kelly.

"Excuse me?" he heard her say.

"Sorry, I was thinking aloud," he apologised once more.

"Do you think the envelope is important?"

"I don't know," Chap lied. "It could be." He pushed away from the table and got to his feet. "Listen, I want to thank you for coming over here, especially on a night like this." He moved around the table to where she sat and held her chair as she rose.

"Well," Corporal Kelly said, "I liked Major Dickson, everyone did. What happened to him was terrible. I just hope, in some way, I have been able to help."

"You've been a great help," Chap said. "I really appreciate it."

It was not his intention to appear rude by hustling the Corporal on her way, but he wanted to get back to his room, to the telephone. Once more under the withering, disapproving gaze of the waitress, he escorted Kelly to the door of the restaurant and, for a few moments, he stood and watched her walk through the freezing air to her car. When she had driven away, he stepped out into the night himself. The cold hit him with a vengeance as he hurried to his room.

The envelope was not found on Dickson's body, it was not with his belongings from the Airport Motel, and it was not in his office or in his house. Eddie Dickson must have mailed it himself when he left his office. Either that, or the killer had it. Chap preferred to believe Dickson mailed it sometime after he left his office and before he was killed. That was the positive option to believe. If he mailed it around midday on the day he died, and if Australia Post was at its most efficient, it could be in Adelaide right now, waiting for him.

He found his partner, Tony Francis, at his desk. The telephone reception was bad due to the weather, and Chap drummed his fingers on the bedside table, once again cursing the winter.

"Hello… hello… Tony, is that you?" he called down the line.

"Hey, Chap," Francis acknowledged. "I can hardly hear you. Where are you calling from, China?"

"It's the bloody weather," Chap said. "I'm in Canberra, but keep that under your hat. I don't want Baldwin to know I'm here. I'll explain when I get back home."

“Okay,” Francis agreed. “It’s under my hat. Now, why did you call?”

“I want you to check my desk, Tony. I’m looking for an envelope, official-looking, addressed to me, and possibly postmarked from Canberra.”

“I don’t have to check,” Francis said. “It arrived today, by registered mail. I signed for it myself. It’s sitting on your desk as we speak.”

Chap felt a feeling of relief mixed with anticipation and excitement. He heard Francis speaking. “What… what did you say?”

“I said, do you want me to open it?” Francis asked.

“No,” Chap said, a little too quickly. “No, I want you to hold onto it. Keep it safe. Don’t leave it lying around on my desk. And, for Christ’s sake, keep it well away from Baldwin’s prying eyes.”

Francis glanced around the room and lowered his voice. “I assume this has to do with the Dickson murder. You know, Chap, if Baldwin finds out, he is going to blow a gasket.”

“I’m relying on you to ensure he doesn’t find out.”

“He won’t hear it from me, mate,” Francis promised.

“Thanks, I’ll see you soon.” Chap dropped the receiver.

Chapter Twenty-One

Chap never really expected to learn from Francis that the envelope had arrived at Police Headquarters. Hoping it had, was a long shot at best. At that very moment, it was on his desk in the Major Crime office in Adelaide. Could it be possible his luck was changing for the better? Could this be the break he so desperately needed? His emotions oscillated wildly between anticipation and curiosity. Anticipation, because finally, he might have the first real lead in the case. Curiosity, because he had no way of knowing what the envelope contained.

It had to be more than mere coincidence that a man he hadn't seen for forty years dies while trying to reach him, and, possibly aware his life was in danger, mails a mysterious envelope to his old friend at Police Headquarters! Why? Did the envelope contain the same information Dickson wanted to convey in person? Did he mail it because he knew there was a chance he might not get the opportunity to deliver it himself? The questions tumbled over each other like waves on a beach.

The urge to catch the first available flight back to Adelaide was strong, but his enquiries in Canberra were not yet completed. When they were, he then needed to travel on to Sydney before heading home.

He was tired and, fortified with more whisky than he intended, he thought sleep would come easy. He was wrong. Restless with anticipation, he tossed and turned for hours in his bed, his imagination creating scenario upon scenario, each more bizarre than the one preceding it. His arthritic shoulders burned and ached as the cold seeped through to the bone, adding to his sleeplessness. He ran the case through his mind a hundred times and when he was finished, he ran it through another hundred times. Finally, in the early hours of the morning, overcome with fatigue, he slipped into a fitful sleep.

He awoke thick-headed and confused. It felt like he had only slept for a few minutes. Every bone and muscle in his body screamed at him to pull the covers over his head and go back to sleep. However, as appealing as it was, he knew he couldn't; that there were things he had to do.

He lingered under the scalding spray of the shower, finishing under the freezing spray from just the cold-water tap. The needles of icy water blasted away the fog of sleeplessness and left him refreshed and ready. He hated those tiny coffee sachets they put in motel rooms, but this morning he drank two cups.

It was possible, he reasoned, that Sergeant Reg Brennan of the Adelaide office of the Federal Police was wrong; or had lied to him. Perhaps someone from his Canberra office did have knowledge of the Dickson murder and had instructed Brennan to tell Chap nothing. It was also possible that whoever Brennan spoke to had never heard of Eddie Dickson —a communication breakdown, that sort of thing, not without precedence in a large police organization.

As he was already in Canberra, he decided it would be remiss of him not to check personally with the Federal Police. It would be taking a risk. Too much nosing around by an out-of-state detective in a matter which may well have been flagged as confidential, might arouse suspicion and get back to all the wrong people—George Baldwin, for instance. He weighed the risk against the information he might uncover and decided it was worth taking the chance.

He got as far as the head honcho in Criminal Investigations and then hit a brick wall. It was as though Eddie Dickson had never existed. There was no record of Eddie Dickson, and no record of any murder file having been forwarded from Adelaide. If such a file was to be forwarded to the feds, as George Baldwin would have him believe, this was the department to which it would be sent.

Was everyone lying to him, or was there really no record of Eddie Dickson in any Federal Police investigation? What was going on? This was the place. This was where Baldwin said the file was to be sent. Surely it would have reached here by now. Inter-jurisdictional matters could prove difficult at times, Chap understood, but this was ridiculous. There was a stench threatening to derail his determination to find answers and the deeper he dug, the worse it smelled.

If the weather bureau was to be believed, Sydney was warmer than Canberra, but not by any great degree. When he arrived, and walked from the terminal looking for a taxi, he was greeted with a freezing onslaught of wind driving a blast of icy sleet into his face. His clothes, still damp from the prevailing conditions in Canberra, clung to his body, adding to his discomfort and ensuring his mood was not about to improve anytime soon.

When he entered the New South Wales Police Major Crime offices in central Sydney, he figured the annual budget allocated to run this squad might easily outstrip the budget required to run the entire South Australian Police Department. The size of the place and the sheer number of personnel staggered him.

He located the lead detective responsible for the initial investigation into the deaths of Charles Cobb and Brian Elliott, and the same brick wall he hit in Canberra had moved to Sydney. Both Cobb and Elliott were killed within hours of each other, and just a few days before Eddie Dickson met his fate in Adelaide. It soon became apparent that the investigations into these two murders lasted about as long as his own did in the Dickson murder. The investigating detective was ordered by his superiors to forward the Cobb and Elliott files to the federal police in Canberra. Why was he not surprised?

He thought about what he had learned thus far. Police from two different jurisdictions believed investigations into all three murders were being capably carried out by their federal counterparts and those same federal counterparts were denying *any* knowledge of *any* investigations into *any* of the murders. This was not just a brick wall. It was a mountain of stone. Right then, and there, Chap decided if he couldn't go through the wall, he would go around it. It might take a little longer, but he would get to the bottom of this thing if it was the last thing he ever did.

Could it be that no one, anywhere, was conducting any investigations into the murders? Were these deaths being deliberately ignored and swept under the carpet? Surely not! If that were the case, what happened to the files? They had to be somewhere. Someone had to know of their existence. Someone had requested them. They were forwarded to someone. But who…? Where? Could it be that both the Sydney, and Adelaide, homicide chiefs had been duped? Chap thought about that for a moment. In the case of George Baldwin, it was a distinct possibility. Baldwin was a fool, and Chap knew he was one who could very easily be conned into giving up the Dickson file. He did not know the Sydney homicide boss and, as such, couldn't make the same judgment about him. In any case, it would have been unfair to assume the Sydney chap was as easily fooled. Nonetheless, he could not discount the possibility that he, too, had been taken in by a fabricated but plausible story.

Then, there was Lieutenant Colonel Frederick W. Baxter. Chap had already decided the colonel was not as squeaky clean as his shiny brass buttons and chest full of hero medals might suggest. He was now certain Baxter's relationship with Eddie Dickson was not as amicable and pleasant as it appeared to their staff, particularly in recent days. Corporal Kelly attested to that when she heard them arguing. Baxter made a mistake. He inadvertently let on that he knew Dickson, Cobb and Elliott were all friends. Chap didn't yet know how the good Colonel Fred was involved, but involved he was. Baxter was up to his knees in it. Way up over his gleaming, spit-polished dress shoes.

Anxious to get his hands on the envelope, the return flight to Adelaide seemed never-ending. Sound, restful sleep had eluded him since all this madness began and he took advantage of the flight to catch up on lost down time. For the first time in recent days, he did not dream of war. Instead, he dreamed of Sally Prescott. Pleasant dreams of happy, laughing times and dreams of loving.

From somewhere, a soft voice came to him through the haze of sleep. "Excuse me, sir," he heard the voice say. Someone gently shook his arm.

Chap opened his eyes and saw the friendly smile of the flight attendant.

"Please fasten your seat in the upright position. We will be landing in a few minutes," she ordered sweetly.

He glanced at his watch. Ten minutes to ten p.m. Through his window, the sky was black. He could see no stars above, and no lights below. A solitary white strobe light flashing every few seconds on the end of the wing drew his focus. He wondered if Eddie Dickson might have looked out of the window at the same dark nothingness as his flight made its final approach into Adelaide, unknowingly nearing the fate that was to meet him a short time later. It would have been a flight just like this one which brought Dickson to Adelaide.

Chap moved his seat, locked it in the upright position, checked his seat belt was fastened, and craned his head to look around the seats in front of where he sat. Some were occupied, some were not. He turned in his seat and looked along the aisle behind him. He found himself wondering just where Eddie Dickson might have sat on his flight and immediately felt it strange that he should think of that. Was he, perhaps, sitting in the very same seat number Eddie had occupied on his flight from Canberra? Such thoughts, confusing and disjointed, had occupied Chap's mind constantly these last few days.

The aircraft banked out over Gulf St. Vincent and commenced its descent into Adelaide.

As soon as he had disembarked, he telephoned Tony Francis, only to find his partner was not in the office. He was on duty, out on the road somewhere, Chap was informed. He left a message for Francis to meet him at Sally's.

Chapter Twenty-Two

When Chap arrived at the restaurant, it was closed. There were times when the prevailing weather conditions were such that potential customers much preferred to stay in the comfort of their own homes as opposed to venturing out into the cold and wet night. This was one of those nights. The last of Sally's clientele, the few who were brave enough to endure the conditions, had finished their meal and left, allowing Sally to close earlier than usual.

François, the chef, had also left for the evening and Sally sat alone at the cocktail bar. studying the night's receipts. A glass of chardonnay sat at her elbow. She reached for it, took a sip and spotted Chap standing in the kitchen doorway watching her.

"Mmm... the face is familiar," she said. "I can't remember the name, though."

"I'm Bruce," Chap said, "Chap's twin brother."

"Twin brother? I didn't know Chap had a twin brother." Sally placed the receipts on the bar and took another sip of chardonnay.

"Oh yes, that's me... Bruce." Chap leaned against the door frame.

"Where is Chap?" Sally played along.

"He couldn't make it. He's busy. He asked me to come over and take care of your needs."

"My needs?"

"Well … yes… your needs. Chap said you have… ah… particular needs."

"Particular needs?"

"This is a little embarrassing, but he told me you were a bit of a sex kitten and you needed some good, old-fashioned loving on a pretty regular basis."

"A sex kitten, eh?"

Chap nodded. "That's what he said."

Sally smiled. "Did he also tell you that what *he* lacks in endurance, *I* make up for in ingenuity and athleticism?"

"No, he didn't tell me that, but if endurance is what you're after, I'm your man." Chap moved across to where Sally sat and watched as she seductively crossed her beautiful legs.

"Really… endurance, huh? Now you have my undivided attention."

"Yes." Chap smiled. "In fact, I don't want to be one to toot my own horn… so to speak, but, I've heard it said that some of the ladies in the circle I mix with refer to me as 'The Six Minute Man'!"

Sally opened her arms and invited him in. "That would be a small circle, I suspect. Welcome home, Chap."

Chap stepped into her embrace and kissed her. He had only been gone a couple of days and he realised now just how much he had missed the smell of her hair, the soft scent of her perfume, and the warmth of her arms.

"I missed you," she whispered into his mouth.

"I hope so. I missed you, too."

They disentangled themselves and Chap said, "How come you're here all alone with the back door open? Do you realise how dangerous that is?"

"François just left, and I was half expecting you," Sally explained. "Would you like a drink?"

"You were expecting me?" Chap reached for his wallet. "A whisky would be nice."

"Well, more hoping, really." Sally reached out and took his hand. "Your money is no good here, Chap. How many times have I told you that?" She moved behind the bar.

"I'm not a gigolo." Chap shrugged. "You can't buy me with cheap whisky."

"Oh, there's nothing cheap about my whisky, and you will pay alright, just as soon as I get you home."

Chap laughed. "You better make that a double, it sounds like I'm gonna need the energy." It had been a long time since he ever felt as good as he did when he was with Sally.

Sally poured a generous measure of whisky into a tumbler, dropped a couple of ice cubes into the glass, and handed it across the bar. "How was the trip?"

Her question immediately renewed his anticipation regarding the mysterious envelope. Sally came back around the bar and resumed her seat next to him.

"It was productive, I think," Chap answered. "I expect to know more a little later. If you are not in a hurry, I need to wait here for Tony Francis. Eddie Dickson mailed something to headquarters from Canberra on the day he was killed. It arrived today, and I asked Tony to bring it here to me. I'm hoping whatever it contains will shed some much-needed light on exactly what is going on."

"Okay," Sally said. "Let's wait." She raised her glass and smiled.

They waited, exchanging small talk interspersed with occasional endearments not unlike those one would expect from lovers several decades younger. Forty-five minutes later, Tony

Francis arrived and entered through the still open rear door. Chap watched as he entered the bar.

"Hi!" Chap greeted his partner. "Wanna drink? Sally's in a generous mood and she's been plying me with booze. I think she has an ulterior motive."

Francis smiled. "No thanks, Chap. I won't stay. It's been a busy day, I want to get home to a nice warm bed, it's bloody cold and wet out there." He turned to face Sally. "Hello, Sally. You are looking stunning, as usual."

"Why, thank you, Tony." She looked at Chap. "I can't recall the last time *you* said I look stunning."

Chap reached across and took her hand. "That's because there are simply no words to adequately describe your beauty."

"You're so full of it, Chapman Bouttell." Sally laughed. She stood up and kissed Francis lightly on the cheek. "It's lovely to see you, Tony. You know, I'm still waiting for you to join us for dinner one night."

"I know, I know," Francis answered. "But, if I spruced myself up for dinner with you, I'm not sure the old fella here could handle the competition." He jerked a thumb towards Chap.

"I'm a woman of very simple needs," Sally said. "And besides, I have never been big on fancy packaging." She reached out and touched Chap gently on the face. "And, I suspect the old fella can handle just about anything he sets his mind to."

Francis reached into his pocket and withdrew his mobile phone. "I'm just gonna call a cab. My car's out of action for a few days. I bummed a lift from the office with one of the uniformed patrols."

Chap raised a hand to stop him dialling. "Don't call a cab, mate. Take my car. I'll get a lift with Sally. We're going home together, anyway, and this way we don't have to take two cars." He fished in his pocket and handed his keys to Francis. "I'll pick my car up from you tomorrow."

"Are you sure?"

"I insist," Chap said. "The deal's done. Take my car."

"Okay, thanks." Francis looked at Sally. "Tell me you're not going home with this broken-down excuse for a police officer? You know, you really should set your sights higher!"

Chap smiled. "Enough of this nonsense." He looked impatiently at Francis and said, "Did you bring the envelope?"

"Of course." Francis dug into the pocket of his overcoat.

Sally got up from her stool. "I'll leave you two to your police business," she said. "I've got a couple of things I need to do in the kitchen before I lock up."

Both men watched as she turned and walked quickly from the bar. When she was gone, Chap took the envelope from Francis's outstretched hand. The name and address on the front of the plain brown envelope were handwritten. Chap stared at his name. It was just as Corporal Kelly had said. It was his name, and it was addressed to Police Headquarters. He turned it over in his hands and looked at the back. It was as if some strange, telepathic power would reveal the contents to him without him having to open it. He felt a shiver of anticipation, yet he delayed opening it. He turned it over again and re-read the front of the envelope, his eyes lingering over his name, handwritten by Eddie Dickson not long before someone put a gun to the back of his head and pulled the trigger.

Tony Francis watched in silence as Chap studied the envelope. Finally, sensing his partner might like some privacy, he shuffled and cleared his throat in an attempt to get Chap's attention. "I gotta go, mate," he said. "I appreciate that you might like a moment to yourself, Dickson being a friend and all, so I'll get going. I know officially we're off this case, but if that envelope offers any clues and you need anything, let me know." He rattled the car keys. "And thanks for the loan of the car. I'll try not to ding it."

Chap laughed. "Thanks, Tony. I think I would like to be alone, if you don't mind. Oh… and… hey, listen. I really appreciate you hanging on to this for me." He waved the envelope at Francis. "In effect, you're guilty of aiding and abetting me in acting against a direct order. You stuck your neck out for me and I appreciate it. Thanks again."

"What have I done?" Francis shrugged, feigning innocence. "Some mail arrived at the station for you while you were on leave. All I did was deliver it to you. I have no idea what that envelope contains, and if anyone should ask, I have no idea what it's in connection with." He turned to leave. "Don't forget, stay in touch."

"I will," Chap promised. "Give my heartfelt regards to George Baldwin," he added, with undisguised sarcasm.

Chap watched as Francis walked out of the bar. He heard his voice as he went through the kitchen and said goodbye to Sally. When he heard the back door close, he turned his attention back to the envelope.

Chap didn't know what it was, exactly, that made him look up. It was just a feeling, a strange, foreboding feeling. He found himself staring at the large, double glass front entrance doors of the restaurant and he didn't know why. He watched Tony Francis hurry across the small car park, his coat collar pulled high against the rain. He saw the tail lights flash as he pressed the remote to unlock the vehicle. The interior light glowed, and Francis climbed into the sedan, closing the door behind him.

Suddenly, time stopped. There was a brilliant flash of blinding white light. The front doors of the restaurant imploded and seemed to rush straight at Chap. A deafening cacophony of noise accompanied by an explosive spray of broken glass and a blast of searing hot air hit Chap, hurling him backwards off his stool. Instinctively, he threw his hands up to protect his face from the deadly, hurtling slivers of glass indiscriminately peppering the room around him.

It happened in an instant; a blinding, deafening millisecond, but seemed to be happening in agonizingly slow motion. Then, he was on the floor. The blinding light was gone. In its place, a dense, heavy, black cloud of dust and minute particles of debris floated seemingly weightlessly in the air. The noise, too, was gone. Now, there was just a numbing silence.

Perhaps he was deaf. Perhaps he was dead. How did he get on the floor? Chap lifted his head, slowly pushed himself to a sitting position, and slumped with his back against the bar. No, he was not dead. Not deaf, either, it seemed, as the numbing silence was replaced by a soft ringing in his ears which climbed quickly to a piercing whine.

He turned his head slowly and looked towards the entrance doors. There was nothing there! Just a black hole where the doors should be. Except for the screaming whine in his ears, everything around him seemed to be bathed in an eerie silence. He shook his head slowly, in a vain attempt to silence the ringing.

Cautiously, he pushed his hands against the floor and tried to raise himself to his feet. He got no further than his knees when he collapsed back against the bar, cracking his head in the process. All around him, he could feel the floor was awash with pieces of broken glass varying in size from large shards, to needlelike slivers. Small pieces pierced his palms and he grimaced at the stinging. Confused and disorientated, he tried to focus. What happened? Something exploded. Was it in the kitchen, a gas cylinder perhaps?

From somewhere beyond the depth of the incessant ringing in his ears, he thought he heard a voice. He immediately thought of Sally. He tried to remember which way she went when she left the bar. Then, with a sickening feeling of dread, he recalled her saying she had to check on something in the kitchen. Was she still there? He heard the voice again. Someone was calling his name. Someone was touching him, trying to lift him from the floor. Sally… it had to be Sally.

Groaning with effort, and leaning against the bar, he managed to drag himself to his knees once again and then climbed slowly, awkwardly to his feet. He stumbled and almost fell as a wave of dizziness washed over him.

Anonymous hands snatched roughly at him, supporting him. He grabbed for the bar top, collapsed against it, and waited for the dizziness to subside. It was lighter now, and an orange glow flickered through the room. It seemed to be coming from far away—outside, perhaps. Someone was standing in front of him, holding him. The whining in his ears continued, but through it, a little clearer now, he could hear the distant voice.

He wanted to sit, and looked around for a stool. For the first time, he began to notice the carnage around him. His stool, and the one Sally had been sitting on earlier, were lying against the wall on the other side of the small room. Sally's face came slowly into focus in front of him. She was alive!

Chap blinked a couple of times, trying to focus on Sally's face. Her lips were moving. Was that Sally's voice? He leaned closer, his face just inches from Sally's. She stood in front of him and was clasping his arm in a vice-like grip. Relief overwhelmed him. Sally was alright. His legs almost collapsed under him and he leaned against her. Why wouldn't the damn ringing stop?

Then, he noticed a strange taste in his mouth. It took him a few seconds to realise it was blood, his blood. He put his hand to his face and when he took it away it was covered with blood. It had to be his blood, yet he felt no pain. He felt his face again, probing with his fingers, and found, high on his left cheek, a cut just below his eye. Blood flowed freely down his face, over his lip, and into his mouth. It tasted salty, and metallic. He spat clumsily and a crimson spray of spittle flew from his lips.

He turned and slowly cast his eyes around the room again. The lights were still on. He didn't know why that should strike him as odd, but it did. Something was telling him it should be dark.

"Chap… oh, Chap!" he heard Sally cry. "Oh Chap… your face. Chap… oh, dear God… Chap, can you hear me?"

When Chap spoke, he did not recognise his own voice. "I'm alright," he spat, and blood trickled onto his chin. Not at all confident that he was indeed alright, he tried to focus on Sally's face. "I'm alright," he repeated. "Are you hurt? What happened?"

"I don't know. There was an explosion," Sally answered. "Here, let me look at your face." She dabbed gently at his face with a napkin she grabbed from the bar.

Chap took the cloth from her and pressed it firmly against his cheek. He reached for her, placed his free hand around her waist and crushed her tightly to him. "Jesus, Sally. Thank God you're alright. What happened? I thought you were in the kitchen. Did the gas explode?"

He turned and looked anxiously toward the rear of the bar, toward the kitchen. "Oh shit, what about François? We have to help him!" He moved to step away from Sally and rush to the kitchen. Sally held him tighter, restraining him.

"François is not here, Chap, he went home before you arrived."

Chap shook his head again, trying to remember. He stared at the doorway to the kitchen. There was no smoke back there. No fire, and no apparent damage, none that he could see, anyway. Sally's voice came to him again.

"No, Chap," he heard her say. "It wasn't the kitchen, it was outside."

He turned and looked at Sally, uncomprehending. "What?"

"It was outside," she indicated, pointing to the front of the building. "An explosion, in front of the building. It was your car, Chap. Your car blew up!"

Images came to Chap, playing and flickering in slow motion. He saw Tony Francis walking towards the car, saw him unlock the car. He saw the flash of the tail lights as he pressed the key remote. He saw his partner climb into the driver's seat.

It was outside? The explosion came from outside? Sally was right. That was why the front door imploded into the building; the blast came from outside! He stared out through the jagged hole in the front wall into the dark, smoke-filled night beyond. Then, a cold shiver of fear travelled along his spine and the hair at the nape of his neck tingled. Suddenly, he was alert, and very afraid. "Tony," he muttered, almost in a whisper.

Beyond the wreckage of shattered glass and the twisted door surround, Chap's eyes were drawn instantly to the fire raging outside. His car was burning. It was completely engulfed in flames. Against the darkness of the night, a thick plume of smoke, blacker than the surrounding sky, curled, spiralled and clawed its way skyward as it rose above the distinctive shape of his vehicle. Every window in the car had been blown out in the explosion.

Chap stared in horror as flames, bright orange and yellow against the dark sky, danced a crackling, spitting, macabre jig from within the vehicle. He could not see Francis. An animal sound he did not recognise as having come from himself, surfaced from somewhere deep in his being. It was a pitiful, gut-wrenching sob of shock, recognition, and disbelief. It flowed wretchedly from his throat, accompanied by a tiny rivulet of saliva mixed with blood, which ran from the corner of his mouth and hung momentarily suspended from his chin before falling to the front of his shirt.

Instinctively, he wiped at his chin with the bloody napkin, unable to tear his eyes from the burning car outside. He had to get himself together, had to move, had to do something. He heard someone speak, and suddenly realised it was his own voice.

"Sally, call the police, give them the address and tell them an officer is down. Tell them to send an ambulance, and tell them to hurry. Then check on your customers, see if any of them are hurt."

Sally took his arm and shook him gently. "There are no customers, Chap. We are closed."

Chap looked at her and began to surface slowly from the fog into which he had been hurled. "That's right, that's right," he murmured. "Okay, call the police and ambulance. Don't forget, tell them 'officer down'. That will get them moving."

Sally's eyes betrayed her fear. "Are you okay?" she asked.

"I'm okay," Chap said. "Hurry, make the call."

Chap watched her cross to the telephone. She picked up the receiver and immediately found no dial tone. The phone was not working! She looked desperately at Chap. He reached into his pocket and tossed her his mobile phone. As she dialled, she glanced at him and smiled wanly. Chap nodded and smiled back. It was a forced smile designed only to give Sally some reassurance.

Supporting himself with one hand against the wall, Chap moved cautiously towards the front door, and stepped outside. It had started to rain again, and as he approached the burning car, the heat drove him back. Every time he got close to the vehicle, the flames and the smoke forced him to retreat. The smell of burning flesh flooded his nostrils. He covered his nose and mouth with his hand. In desperation, he looked back at the restaurant, searching for a tap and hose, anything he could use to fight the flames. There was nothing.

The rain was having no effect on the fiercely burning fire. Finally, Chap gave up trying to get any closer to the car. There was nothing he could do. Tony Francis was dead. Nothing could have survived the explosion and ensuing inferno.

Chap stood in the driving rain staring at the burning vehicle. In the distance, he heard the sound of sirens approaching. At some point, he had lost the napkin he had been using to stem the flow of blood from his face, and he was bleeding freely once more. He tasted the diluted, watery mixture and spat into the windswept rain. He reached into his pocket and pulled out a handkerchief. It was as wet as the rest of his clothing, but he pressed it against his face anyway.

Suddenly, he realised he was shivering and knew it was only partially from the cold. Shock was setting in. He needed to get out of the rain and try to stay warm. As he was about to turn away from the scene in front of him, he felt a tug on his arm and heard Sally's voice behind him. "Come inside, Chap, you're soaked. You need to have your face seen to, and you need to stay warm. Please, come with me." She held an umbrella over them both and pulled his arm firmly.

An ambulance and fire truck pulled up within seconds of each other, their flashing red and blue strobe lights adding a macabre carnival like glow to the car park and surrounds.

"There's nothing you can do here, Chap," Sally insisted. "Come on, let's go inside."

Understanding hit him hard. "That's my car… oh shit, that's my car. That should have been us! Oh, sweet Jesus… you and I could have been in that car… oh, Jesus!"

When he turned and looked at Sally, she wanted to sob at the sheer desperation and helplessness she saw in his eyes.

"Come on, Chap, come inside, you need to stay warm."

Chap looked at her through dark, hollow eyes. Sally had never seen him look so deeply shocked and traumatised. "Please, Chap, you can't stand out here in the rain. There is nothing you can do, Tony is gone."

Chap nodded slowly, and allowed her to lead him back toward the restaurant. "Where's the bloody police?" Sally heard him mumble. "They're not here yet. Did you call them?"

"I called Triple 0, they'll be here any minute," Sally assured him.

Chap turned his head and looked at the roadway beyond the burning car. "Always the last to arrive," Chap said, with no small amount of cynicism. "Never a bloody copper about when you need one." He stumbled and almost fell. Sally had an arm around his waist and clutched him tightly.

Chapter Twenty-Three

Police crime scene tape strung around the scene glowed luminous in the portable lighting, and a tent had been erected over the charred and blistered remains of the vehicle and its macabre contents. Sally had retrieved one of the stools from where it had been hurled by the blast and now, Chap sat against the bar and looked out at the temporary shelter. Police forensic technicians, working under floodlights, entered the shelter where they examined the car. The shell of the vehicle would be taken away to a secure location for even closer forensic examination.

Chap's face had begun to swell around his injury, and his cheek bore an uncomfortable wad of dressing put there by an ambulance officer. Paramedics wanted to take Chap to hospital for closer observation and further treatment, but he refused, and there was nothing they, or Sally, could say or do to change his mind.

The media began to gather almost simultaneously with the first of the police patrols. Funny about that, Chap thought. He watched as still-cameras flashed and television crews filmed. Three uniformed police officers were assigned to keep the press throng at an acceptable distance from the scene, and they did not look at all thrilled with the job they were given.

Slowly, confusion faded into some semblance of structure and order. The scene began to take on a quiet, sombre tone. A police officer was dead, and that made this different from any other death. There were those who would say it shouldn't be that way, that all deaths should be treated the same, but try telling that to cops who have just lost one of their own.

The police at the scene—and there were a lot of them—were subdued as they went about their assigned tasks. Chap took a moment to look around at the uniformed and plain-clothes police in attendance. Some, those not actually engaged in a specific task, were huddled in small groups, talking quietly, their heads almost touching. Some chanced furtive glances his way. News travelled fast within the ranks when one of their own went down.

Some police cars, obviously out of their designated patrol areas, drove slowly past the scene before moving on. Some might see that as morbid curiosity on their part and perhaps, to a small degree, it was. Chap saw it as nothing more than a show of respect for a fellow officer killed in the line of duty.

Sally was right there, offering support and comfort, plying him with hot coffee and insisting it was far better for him than the whisky he asked for. Two blankets left by the paramedics were draped around his shoulders and a degree of warmth was returning to his numb and trembling body.

Slowly, he was regaining his full senses. The ringing in his ears had eased considerably and the tremors brought on by a combination of shock and the cold had subsided. Gingerly, he prodded at the thick dressing on his face. The attending paramedic had assured him it was just a flesh wound and would not require suturing. It was one of those wounds in the soft, fleshy part of the body that bleed like hell at the time but resulted in little if any lasting damage. It might leave a small scar, the medico stated, but a slight blemish on an already time-worn, weather-beaten countenance was the least of Chap's concerns at the moment.

He could have, and probably should have, gone to the hospital and given his statement to his colleagues later, when he was feeling better. He could even go home now if he chose. Lord knows he wanted to, but he stayed. He needed to see this through and he needed to do it now. He felt he owed his partner at least that much. After all, if he hadn't offered Francis his car, he and Sally would be dead now and not Tony Francis. They had escaped certain death in the explosion and inferno that followed and the realisation of that fact started a renewed bout of trembling.

He couldn't remember exactly when she did it, but Sally had organised a couple of tradesmen to make temporary repairs to the damage so the restaurant would be secure until she could arrange more substantial and permanent repairs. Chap watched them for a moment as they worked on the shattered doorway. As he watched, George Baldwin pushed rudely past the workmen and entered the restaurant. As he approached, his feet crunched over the broken glass still covering the floor. He stopped in front of Chap, their faces inches apart.

A wave of nausea washed over Chap. He tried to get to his feet. He needed to get to the toilet. He couldn't get up, his legs felt weak. He was not going to make it. He leaned forward, gagged noisily, and threw up on George Baldwin's spit-polished shoes.

Baldwin stood in front of Chap with his head bowed, staring at his soiled shoes. Chap leaned forward on his stool, both hands on his knees, and looked at the mess on the floor and on Baldwin's shoes. Both men raised their heads simultaneously and looked at each other. The expression on Baldwin's face was not one of sympathy for Chap's condition. "Fuckin' hell!" he cursed, as he shook first one foot and then the other.

Chap offered Baldwin a half-smile. “Hello, George. Glad you could make it.”

George Baldwin looked back down at his shoes and then again at Chap. “What are you doing here? Aren’t you supposed to be on leave?”

“I’m fine, George, thank you for your concern. I *am* on leave as you well know. I’m here visiting a friend.” Chap turned to Sally standing alongside him, her hand resting on his shoulder. “Sally, meet George Baldwin. George, Sally Prescott.”

Sally inclined her head towards Baldwin. “Hello.”

“Good evening, ma’am.” George nodded and looked again at his shoes.

“Sorry about the shoes, George. It’s just a mild touch of nausea. It came over me just as you walked in the door. Imagine that. It’s gone now. I feel better already.” He glanced down at Baldwin’s feet. “Nice shoes, though. Never mind, I’m sure you can get them looking good as new in no time.” Chap’s attempt at a smile was not reciprocated.

“What happened to your face?” Baldwin asked, as if noticing the bandage for the first time.

Chap lightly touched the wadding on his cheek. “The door blew in on me, George. Surely you noticed there was no door when you came in, and you’re standing ankle deep in broken glass. Crunching around all over the crime scene. By the way, I know I’m on leave, but does this constitute being injured in the line of duty?”

“You know, Bouttell, I don’t have to stand here and listen to your sarcasm. I’ve got work to do. In case you hadn’t noticed, a police officer died here tonight. I want you out of my way, and out of my sight. You are officially off duty, and not required here. Go home. I will send someone to your house in the morning to take a detailed statement from you.” George Baldwin looked at Sally. “We will need a statement from you, too, Ms. Prescott. Please leave your home address with one of the detectives before you leave."

"Of course," Sally said to Baldwin's back as he turned and walked away.

Chap and Sally exchanged glances as Baldwin hitched the legs of his trousers up above his shoes and shuffled away, mumbling incoherent obscenities which Chap assumed were directed at him.

"Who *is* that bloke?" Sally asked quietly.

"That's George," Chap smiled at her. "He's nobody."

"He looks like Elmer Fudd," Sally said.

"He gets that a lot." Chap smiled.

"He acts like he's somebody important."

Chap shrugged. "Really? I can't say I've ever noticed that about him." He got up cautiously from the stool. "Well, my dear." He took Sally's arm. "Why don't we get out of here? I could use a hot shower."

"Why don't I drive you to the hospital?" Sally said. "You really should get checked over."

"Why don't you drive me home, and *you* can check me over?"

"You are as stubborn as you are handsome, Chapman Bouttell. Okay, I'll drive you home, but first I have to speak to the men working on the door, and I have to call François to come over and look after things until the place is secure."

"You think I'm handsome?"

Sally smiled. "No," she called over her shoulder, as she walked away to talk to the tradesmen. "I just said that to make you feel better."

Sally was right, Chap thought. He probably should have gone to the hospital for a check-up, but she was also right in regards to his stubbornness; there had been many times when his obstinacy had overruled his better judgment.

Outside, the scene was crawling with detectives and forensic specialists. He knew that many of them were not working when the explosion took place, but would have been called on duty as soon as it became clear that a fellow officer was involved.

It was possible that the explosion that killed Tony Francis was an accident, but Chap thought that more likely than winning the lottery without buying a ticket. Although a rare occurrence, this was not the first time a cop had been killed, and he knew it wouldn't be the last. It was, however, an occasion of such gravity that every available detective, on duty or otherwise, was called to assist. There existed a special bond of allegiance between police officers, not unlike the camaraderie Chap remembered from his time in the army. Losing one of their own was more than enough incentive for the closing of ranks in a show of support and solidarity.

While he waited for Sally, he took the time to look around him at the damage to the restaurant. Surprisingly, apart from the front door, which took the full force of the blast, there was very little, if any, real structural damage inside. It would take the workers some time to complete the task of erecting thick wooden security panels in the gap where the double glass doors had disintegrated. Sally would have to arrange to have new doors installed before she reopened for business. Chap gazed around at the glass-littered floor and wondered how he had managed to escape more serious injury. It was only then that he remembered the envelope. He patted his pockets under the blanket that was still draped around his shoulders; it was not there. Gripped with a brief moment of panic, his eyes searched the bar and the floor. He could not see it anywhere.

He patted his pockets again in case he'd missed it the first time. Then he swivelled on the stool and looked behind him. There it was, on the floor near the kitchen doorway. It appeared undamaged, albeit covered in glass fragments. He had forgotten all about it in the chaos and relief flooded over him as he gingerly stood up and stepped across to retrieve it.

He was surprised to notice the disorientation and discomfort he had been feeling was now only minimal. The dizziness had all but gone, and he stooped to pick up the envelope. He examined it for a moment, turning it over, satisfying himself it was not damaged and, as he turned, he found himself face-to-face once again with George Baldwin.

"Jesus!" Chap jumped involuntarily. "Are you trying to give me a heart attack?"

"I should be so lucky," Baldwin said. "What's that?" He indicated the envelope in Chap's hand.

"This?" Chap waved the envelope. "It's an envelope, George."

"I can see that, Bouttell. What's in it?"

Chap held the envelope in front of Baldwin's face. "Look, George, it's addressed to me. See, that's my name on the front. It's private mail. What's inside it is none of your business. Are you the Postmaster General now?" Chap tucked the envelope away in his jacket pocket beneath the blankets and out of sight.

Baldwin, looking miffed, said, "I thought you were going home?"

"I am, very shortly. Have you found Tony's killer yet?"

Baldwin ignored the jibe. "Before you go, tell me what Francis was doing here tonight."

"As a matter of fact, he was off duty, so that is really none of your business, either." Chap patted the blankets covering his chest. "This envelope arrived at headquarters for me and, as I was on leave, he thought he would bring it to me. He was just delivering some personal mail for me, George."

Baldwin stared silently at Chap. It was a look which plainly said he didn't believe a word his sergeant was saying. Chap returned his gaze and, when he thought enough silence had passed between them, he smiled at his superior. "Will there be anything else?"

"There will be, Sergeant, there will be." Baldwin turned sharply, and quickly crossed the room. He once again pushed rudely past the two door repairmen and walked back outside into the wind and rain, pausing under the shelter of the portico to pick up the umbrella he'd left just outside the door.

Chap watched him walk the few paces needed to cross to the temporarily erected shelter, lower his umbrella and disappear inside. Experienced crime scene investigators, all going about the business of investigating and gathering evidence, methodically and efficiently, created an illusion to the unsuspecting that the whole affair was under the disciplined control of Detective Superintendent George Baldwin.

"Hmph!" Chap scoffed to himself. "You are such a wanker, George."

Chapter Twenty-Four

Sally drove Chap home and escorted him directly to the bedroom. On the way, Chap looked longingly at the whisky bottle on the lounge room sideboard.

"You don't need that," Sally admonished. "You need sleep. Besides, you shouldn't mix alcohol with painkillers."

He leaned against her and clumsily attempted to nibble at her ear. "Would you like to know what I *really* need?"

Sally smiled. "You only *think* you need that. You are still suffering from shock." She pushed him gently onto the edge of the bed and removed his damp shoes and socks, followed by the rest of his clothes.

Soon, he was naked between the sheets and he heard himself mumble something about how her naked body next to his would surely hasten his recovery. He thought he heard her laugh and then he was asleep.

Sally tucked the blankets tightly around his body and sat for a moment, listening to him snore softly. As she watched him sleep, her thoughts turned to her late husband. She was falling in love with Chapman Bouttell, she was certain of that now. It was a realisation that filled her with a strange, nostalgic sadness.

While Chap slept, Sally reluctantly returned to the restaurant. François was there, and although she knew he would never complain, she felt bad about leaving him to handle the security arrangements. She would check in on Chap later in the day.

Chap woke at 2:30 in the afternoon. For a long time, he lay in bed, the events of the previous night slowly replaying in his mind. He touched his face and felt the bandage. It had not been a terrible dream. Tony Francis was dead.

In the confusion and shock of the night before, the enormity of the situation had not truly manifested itself until now. Now, in the light of a new day, and with his mind somewhat rested with sleep, it came to him in all its terrible realism. He wanted to cry but tears would not come. Tears for anything never came easy for him and, not for the first time, he wondered why.

Tony Francis had been his partner longer than anyone else. Francis was a cop, a man he liked and respected. Hell, he more than liked him. He was a good cop. The sort of cop a partner could trust and rely on when things got rough. A little too orthodox, a tad too 'by the book', perhaps, and Chap was never one for things orthodox, not these days, anyway. Besides, he felt he had Francis coming around slowly to his way of doing things. Chap knew one thing for certain; he was going to miss him.

He stood under the shower long enough for the hot spray to refresh and revive him. The bandage became soaked and he peeled it off. The bleeding had stopped, and most of the swelling had disappeared. When he stepped from the shower and looked in the mirror, he was pleased to see he had suffered no lasting physical damage over and above that with which he had been born.

No one had come to take a statement from him as yet, unless they had and couldn't rouse him. He guessed Baldwin would have assigned someone to take his statement by now, but Chap's health and wellbeing would be the last of Baldwin's concerns. Whoever scored the job must have elected to let Chap sleep and, while that was a decision he welcomed, he didn't want to be in that someone's shoes when Baldwin discovered his statement was still not forthcoming. That poor bastard was going to pay a hefty price.

A gnawing hunger reminded him that the last time he had eaten was when he grabbed a snack on the flight from Sydney. So much for a nice dinner at Sally's.

Sally must have left during the night, he guessed. He would have to cook his own breakfast. Chap's culinary expertise fell a long way short of Sally's, or François's and, despite his hunger, he was not inspired to cook. He compromised, and settled for three slices of hot, buttered toast and lots of coffee. He chewed on a piece of toast, sipped at his coffee and stared at the envelope that lay on the table where Sally had casually discarded it after removing it from his wet clothes. He swallowed the toast, took another sip of his coffee and lowered the coffee mug to the table. Finally, he reached out, picked up the envelope and read again his name on the front. Only another bomb could delay him any longer. He wiped his butter knife on a serviette, slipped it under the sealed flap and tore open the envelope.

There were two pieces of paper inside, both neatly folded. One piece, smaller than the other and folded inside the larger piece, fell out onto the table as he began to unfold the pages. He picked it up, and as he looked at it he felt a feather-soft bristle in the hair at the nape of his neck.

It was handwritten, in the same hand as the name and address on the front of the envelope. It was not a letter, as such; more like a short, handwritten note to him, from Eddie

Dickson. Chap picked up his coffee, sipped, and began to read.

> *Chappy – Charlie Cobb and Brian Elliott are dead. They're after me next. I'm on my way to you to explain. I am mailing this to you in case I don't make it. The ambush in Vietnam was a trap, a set-up. Our own people sent the bastards to kill us! We were all supposed to die that day. I stumbled across the original Operations Order made between ASIO and the CIA. It should have been destroyed but somehow it wasn't. This is big, Chap! High-ranking security officials, and politicians, were involved. The bastards were trying to kill us! I'm being followed. I know you will know what to do with this if I don't reach you. Start with my boss, Col. Baxter. I think he's involved somehow. Be careful, buddy, they will come after you. I'm sorry, Chap. - Eddie*

Chap looked at the name at the bottom of the page: *Eddie.* Slowly, he read the note again, and there could be no misinterpretation of its content; it read the same the second time.

Thunder may have crashed outside his kitchen window, lightning may have struck his roof, and Satan may have sat down at the table directly opposite him and spread himself some toast, but Chap would not have noticed. He was oblivious to everything around him. He felt numb. This was a mistake. It had to be a mistake, a terrible mistake, or else a sick joke. Chap read the note for a third time and then, somehow, he just knew it was no mistake. It was no joke. This was real. He lowered the note to the table and turned his attention to the larger piece of paper.

It was old, the edges discoloured with age. He picked it up and unfolded it, not wanting it to be what he knew it would be. And, there it was. He couldn't believe he was actually holding it. A strong feeling of dread washed over him, and his hands began to tremble slightly.

Positioned at the top centre of the page was the CIA logo—an eagle's head behind a shield. The document was headed *OPERATIONS ORDER*. Underneath the heading, in bold red letters, the words *CONFIDENTIAL* and *TOP SECRET* were blazoned.

He turned it over, looked at the back, and then the front again. It appeared to be original, not a copy. In the top left-hand corner, he read the date: June 7th, 1969. Chap stared at the date with a foreboding anticipation, and began to read the text of the agreement.

Eddie Dickson was right—it was a bilateral operations order between the CIA and ASIO. The message it intended to convey was clear. The opening paragraph was taken up with a preamble dealing with the political sensitivity of the document and to the importance placed on its destruction at the completion of the operation detailed therein.

A covert, special operations military squad commanded by the CIA and comprising members of the United States Special Forces, referred to only as T Force, was to plan, and initiate an ambush against a target code named 'Tattoo'. A set of map coordinates designated the spot at which the ambush was to take place.

Outside, a sudden, brief lull in the wind and rain arrived and the room fell eerily quiet. Chap looked up from the page. It seemed his breathing was the only sound he could hear. He looked nervously around the room. When he finally returned his attention to the document, the code name 'Tattoo' burned into his consciousness, and he knew instinctively that the map reference given was the exact location where his unit was ambushed forty years ago.

The ambush was to take place as the 'target' returned from their final operation inside neutral Cambodia. Special emphasis was made of the map coordinates and to the importance given to the fact that it was imperative the ambush take place on the Vietnamese side of the border.

Chap swallowed hard as he read on. All members of the target were to be 'neutralised'. Chap knew exactly what 'neutralised' meant. The order confirmed the target would be clothed in Vietnamese dress and not outfitted in military attire and that, following the success of the operation, confirmation of the identity of the target should be made by confirming the existence of a small, diamond-shaped tattoo just above, and behind, the right elbow of each body.

He stared at the last two lines in the document.

In the interests of both United States and Australian national security, it is imperative that all members of 'Diamond One' be completely neutralised.

At the bottom of the page there were two signatures. Signed in ink, the signatures had faded with the passage of time but were still legible. Underneath each signature was typed the signatory's name, and the position he held in his respective organisation.

Chap did not recognise either name, but each held a position of high authority. The first signature was that of the CIA's Associate Director for Operations for Military Affairs, attached to some place called National Clandestine Services. The second signature was of someone in the Australian Office of the Director-General—ASIO.

He let the paper fall to the table, and he sat stunned, staring at the two pages in front of him. It was true! Eddie Dickson's note was true! No one was to be left alive! He picked up the operations order and looked again at the top of the page. The document originated from the Executive Office—CIA Headquarters, Langley, Virginia.

He dropped the order back on the table and shook his head in utter disbelief. "Jesus Christ," he murmured. "Jesus bloody Christ." It couldn't be true, could it? But there it was, right in front of him. Documentary proof that, in 1969, a conspiracy existed between Australia and the United States to kill every member of Diamond One!

For forty years, Chapman Bouttell had lived with the memories of that day. In the early years following his return, the memories manifested themselves as dreams and sometimes the dreams manifested themselves as nightmares. Either way, they were vivid, haunting, and they came far too often. As the years passed, they became less regular and he was able, for the majority of the time, to enjoy reasonably undisturbed, dream-free sleep.

The memories never completely faded, and many a psychiatrist would attest that memories never disappear. They simply fade into some deep corner of the subconscious where they lie undisturbed until something triggers their return to the conscious mind. For the most part, and for many years, Chap's memories had stayed in his subconscious and had caused him few problems. Until now. Now, they were back with a vengeance.

Now he knew why Eddie Dickson was murdered. Dickson had found the operations order in the course of his work and he was going to tell all. He must have told Cobb and Elliott, and so they were silenced also. It was all starting to make sense. Not one single member of his unit was supposed to survive that day. With them all dead, there could never be any risk of the job they were ordered to do across the border in

Cambodia ever becoming public knowledge. The official line would simply be ten more Aussie Diggers killed in action.

The Australian public would be understandably saddened, and the radical anti-war protesters would take to the streets in even larger, rowdier and more riotous numbers. But, in time, the death in battle of ten of the country's finest would fade into the public's collective memory, only surfacing on occasions such as Vietnam Veterans' Day, Anzac Day and Remembrance Day. For the general population, life would go on and the media would turn its focus to more current news stories.

Slowly, through the numbing fog of disbelief and outrage, the true significance of the document began to surface. It was dynamite; a political bombshell, the likes of which he doubted had ever been seen, at least in this country. While the document made no mention of either the United States Government, or the Australian Government, in particular, it would be naïve to believe either was unaware of its content. No government was without its political scandals from time to time, but while the reputations of the individuals involved may be sullied, and their careers may well wind up in the toilet, governments, for the most part, survived.

This was no exception, in that it was obviously not the same two governments in power today as it was forty years ago, but this *was* different. Stupid decisions were made and would continue to be made by governments and security organisations all the time, but this decision, this agreement, this horrendous, unbelievable pact made between ASIO and the CIA, had resulted in the cold-blooded murder of six Australian soldiers in 1969, and was continuing today with the recent murders of Charles Cobb, Brian Elliott and Eddie Dickson.

A clap of thunder crashed outside. Startled, Chap jerked in his chair. Rain followed almost immediately, and he listened as it drummed noisily on the roof. A feeling of loss, hopelessness and despair overwhelmed and threatened to consume him. What was he to do? How was he to deal with this newfound knowledge? How long had Eddie Dickson known about the operations order? Dickson intimated in his note that Colonel Baxter could be involved. Was he? Then, there was Cobb and Elliott; what about them? Who killed them? It was more than Chap could comprehend. He slumped forward over the table, his forehead resting on Eddie Dickson's handwritten note.

He had to start thinking like a cop, logically and systematically. He had in his possession documentary evidence proving the United States military was involved in the deliberate, calculated massacre of Australian soldiers with, he assumed, the full knowledge and approval of the Australian government. The consequences of the content of the document becoming a matter of public knowledge were, to say the very least, explosive.

Chap pushed himself upright and rested his elbows on the table in an effort to stop shaking. It was not fear which caused him to tremble; it was outrage, disgust, and an overwhelming sense of loss at the needless execution of his mates.

What did frighten him, however, was the enormity of what he now knew. He could easily see the leverage a person with such knowledge might possess and how dangerous this information was.

Six men had died in 1969 as a direct result of the document which lay on his kitchen table, just inches away. Now, another three had died since it surfaced from where it had lain in obscurity for the last forty years. He paused. Only three? Cobb, Elliott, and Dickson—that was all, surely? His thoughts turned unexpectedly to Tony Francis. No. Not his partner. It was not possible. His death could not be related, could it?

Chap suspected, without having the facts at his disposal, that Tony Francis was murdered. The car explosion was no accident. Until now, however, he had not spent any time analysing his partner's death. Caught up in the shock of it all, he had not given any thought to a motive behind the car bombing. He supposed that, on a subconscious level, he assumed Francis was a victim picked at random by some crazed lunatic with a grudge against the police, or perhaps the world in general. Then, it came to him; surfacing through the fog. The answer was right there in the forefront of his mind! It was *his* car! The bomb was in *his* car! Chap loaned Francis *his* car! The blast was not meant to kill Tony Francis, it was meant to kill *him*!

Suddenly, it was starting to come together. Now he was starting to think like a cop. He picked up the note from Dickson and quickly scanned it, his eyes skimming over the words until he reached the last line: *Be careful, buddy, they will come after you.*

Yes, *he* was the target, not Francis! Eddie was right, they had come after him. But they got the wrong man. By now, he guessed his partner's name had been released to the public, and the killers would know they had failed. They would try again. Chap had never been surer about anything in his life. They would rightly assume that, because he was still alive, he still had the document and it had not been destroyed in the inferno. His task now was to stay one step ahead of his would-be assassins until he could figure out firstly who they were and, secondly, what to do with the information now in his possession.

Chap could now add Francis's name to the list of those killed because of the operations order signed by two of the world's closest allies back in 1969. This thing, this obscene piece of aging paper, was the catalyst for six murders in the jungle of Vietnam all those years ago. Now, having lain dormant and forgotten for forty years, it had surfaced like some evil, all powerful entity and claimed another four lives, so far!

It seemed impossible that Francis's death was linked to the others, but Chap knew it was. The coincidence was too strong to ignore and the thought of that fatal connection only served to reinforce the belief he now held; that he who had possession of the document, held two things—immeasurable power and a better than even chance of dying, sooner rather than later.

Chap was not prepared to die simply because he was now in possession of this piece of damning evidence. The document, and the revelations it contained, had come to him unsolicited and the prospect of him dying because of it was not an option. To protect himself, he had to protect the document. As long as he had it, he would stay alive. He took little solace in the fact that, in all likelihood, they would not kill him until they had retrieved the document and overseen its destruction. After that, he would have to be silenced. The evidence would be gone, but they could not afford to let Chap live with the knowledge he now had. These people would stop at nothing to keep the secret buried. The body count was rising, but Chap had no intention of letting his own demise add to the toll.

He was the only person left alive who could, and would, expose the truth about the conspiracy, and he had the proof to back it up. Whoever the killers were, they would want to get their hands on the order for no other reason than to ensure its destruction once and for all.

He needed copies of both Dickson's note and the Operations Order. He decided on three sets, the original, and three copies. The originals he would place in a safety deposit box with his bank; if not safe there, they would not be safe anywhere, he reasoned. He would keep two copies for himself, and the third he would lodge with a lawyer.

Solicitors had never been Chap's favourite people, particularly defence lawyers and, after twenty-seven years in the police force, it was indicative of that dislike that he could think of only a couple of members of the legal fraternity he believed he could trust.

The one he chose would not know what he had, because, like the originals he would lodge with the bank, the solicitor's copy would be sealed in its own separate envelope and would be accompanied by instructions authorising the envelope to be opened only in the event of his death. Someone would come after the documents, or him, or more likely both. He needed some bargaining power— to bargain, if necessary, for his life.

Now Chap was scared, and he was not afraid to admit it. He had no way of knowing who he was dealing with or when they would come. He knew only that they *would* come.

It occurred to him to go directly to the authorities with his newly acquired knowledge. He was, after all, a cop who had in his possession evidence of multiple murders. But who would he go to? His superiors? Definitely not George Baldwin; Baldwin would have him up on charges in a heartbeat. The Federal Police, perhaps? Or his local member of parliament? Who could he trust?

Withholding evidence of a crime was an offence in itself, one that had always stirred his anger, and while he believed he may well live to regret it, he felt it was an offence he had no choice but to be guilty of.

Chap sat in front of his computer and began to type a full account of his unauthorised investigation into the death of Eddie Dickson. He left nothing out. He included his trip to Canberra and Sydney, and his discoveries at the Federal Police office in Adelaide where he first learned of the deaths of Cobb and Elliott. He also included his involvement with Diamond One and all three of the deceased during the war in Vietnam.

He wrote about Francis, and how he suspected the promising young cop was killed by mistake because of the existence of the operations order. He put down everything.

Finally, he added instructions to both the bank and the solicitor he had selected to the effect that, in the event of his death, his investigation account and the documentation was to be forwarded to all sections of the media. When he was finished, he made three copies of the originals and sealed each copy in a separate envelope. He quickly wrote a covering letter outlining his instructions to the solicitor he had chosen and placed it, along with one of the sealed copies, in a larger envelope and addressed it.

As an afterthought, before shutting down the computer, he scanned Dickson's note and the operations order into the computer system and saved a copy to the hard drive.

Satisfied, he leaned back in the chair and listened to the rain outside as if noticing it for the first time. He tried to reassure himself that he was safe as long as he had control of the documents.

He picked up the telephone to call a taxi and was in the process of dialling when he suddenly dropped the receiver back onto its cradle. What if his phone was bugged? They could follow the taxi and intercept it before he got to the bank with the originals. What if they were already waiting outside his house? No, why would they wait outside? If they knew he was home, why not come straight in and finish the job? If they did come now, they would get the right man this time, and they would get all the documentation; originals and copies. No, he was being paranoid. He didn't think they were outside waiting for his next move. These were people who had shown they were prepared to make the first move. They made it fast, and without warning, and so far, their modus operandi had proven to be effective every time.

He picked up the envelopes and carried them to his bedroom, where he shrugged into a heavy jacket and tucked them out of sight in an inside pocket. He opened the drawer in his bedside table, took out his off-duty revolver, and clipped the holster onto his belt beneath the jacket. As he turned to leave the room, he glanced into the full-length mirror on the door of his closet. The face he saw was that of a stranger. The skin around the edges of the cut on his cheek had started to yellow and his eyes conveyed a dark, hollow, haunted and weary look.

Different people react to fear in different ways. Where some will sweat and tremble in relative silence, others will scream and weep in a frenzy of panic. Chap had never been one to openly display any signs of fear. He was not prone to panicking, nor was he to weeping fits of frenzied screaming. He had learned at a very early age how to mask the physical manifestations of fear, but the face he saw looking back at him from the mirror was the face of a frightened man.

He walked from the bedroom and, as he started down the hallway, he decided to use his mobile phone to ring for a taxi. As he reached into his pocket for the phone, a loud knock at the front door startled him. He immediately forgot the phone and reached for the security of the .38 snub-nosed revolver resting snugly against his hip.

With one hand on the grip of the gun, prepared to use it if threatened, he stepped quickly and silently to the door. There was no security peephole in the door but, through the frosted glass side panels, he could see the blurred, indistinct shapes of two people.

"Who is it?" Chap called.

"Bennett and Thompson, Sarge," he heard one of the shapes answer. "Baldwin wants a statement from you."

Chap reached out and opened the door. There on his porch stood Detectives Joseph Bennett and Les Thompson, two of his colleagues from the Major Crime office. "Hi, fellas." He half-smiled. "I was expecting you guys earlier."

"Well," Thompson began, "Baldwin wanted us here at first light this morning, you know what he's like, but we were both at the scene last night and you were not looking well, so we fed him a line about you having to go to the hospital for a check-up. We said you would not be available until now. We thought you could use the rest. I thought the prick was gonna have a stroke."

Chap smiled and stepped aside. "We couldn't be that lucky, could we? Come on in." He looked at his watch. "Here's the deal. I'll give you a detailed statement now if you boys give me a lift when we're done. I need to get to the bank before it closes and, as you know, I no longer have a car."

"Yeah," said Joe Bennett. "Damn shame about Tony. We've got every available man working on it and the off-duty guys have all been called back in. Don't be surprised if Baldwin recalls you from leave."

Chap led the detectives into the kitchen. "Actually, I would be surprised. He won't call me back. George and I share a mutual dislike for each other. He will never admit it, but I think he considers me some kind of threat to his authority. Sit down, fellas, let's get this over and done with."

Chapter Twenty-Five

Detectives Bennett and Thompson dropped Chap at his bank, just a street away from Police Headquarters. After completing what he considered to be an inordinate amount of paperwork, he was assigned a safety deposit box. A stern, ramrod-straight, senior bank employee led him to a large walk-in vault deep in the bowels of the bank building. The banker stood silently at a discreet distance as Chap locked the original of the operations order and Eddie Dickson's note securely away and slid the long, narrow container into its niche in a wall of similar security boxes.

The relief he felt was immediate. They could come after him now, and he would welcome it. There was a part of him that was looking forward to meeting up with those responsible for the killings. Now that the incriminating documents were safely locked away, he felt relatively safe. Should it come down to negotiating for his life, and he suspected it might, the documents were the ace up his sleeve.

When he left the bank, he hurried the short distance to Police Headquarters, hugging office and store overhangs in an attempt to avoid the rain that was still falling heavily. Late afternoon was upon the city, and the sky was darkening rapidly. Soon, the mad scramble of afternoon rush hour would begin and thousands of city workers would jostle and scurry as they made their way to their cars, or to catch buses, trains, or trams, to the safe, warm comfort of home and hearth. Little did they know, Chap thought as he pulled his collar up around his neck, hurried across a busy intersection, and ducked under the portico of the headquarters building. Little did the unsuspecting public know.

He found the Major Crime office unusually quiet. There were a lot more members around than he would usually expect to find at any one time and he recognised many who he knew would normally be off duty.

There was none of the usual banter, laughter and recycled bad jokes. Detectives stood or sat around, talking quietly amongst themselves and as he stepped into the room, most of those present fell silent as they looked up and acknowledged him with a nod or a wave of the hand. Many seemed confused and lost for something to say. Tony Francis had been a popular member of the squad and, somehow, at a moment like this, words seemed inadequate.

Chap made his way across the squad room, directly to George Baldwin's office. As usual, the door was closed. He paused in front of the closed door for a moment, turned and looked back into the squad room. He smiled, winked at the faces staring pensively back at him, and knocked loudly on the door. When he received no response, he shrugged and knocked again, louder this time. Almost half a minute passed with still no invitation to enter. He had lifted his hand to knock a third time when he heard Baldwin's voice from inside.

"Come in."

Chap opened the door and walked into his superior's office. He found Baldwin in the same, familiar position as the last time he was in this office, bent forward over his desk, writing in a file.

One day, Chap was going to sneak a look at that file. He was sure it was the same file Baldwin appeared to labour over every time someone entered his domain. Chap was convinced it was nothing more than a folder filled with meaningless papers designed to make him look busy and efficient. The suspected ruse had never worked with Chap at any time in the past, and it was not working now.

True to form, Baldwin made him wait. Eventually, he put down his pen and looked up. He wore bifocals perched on the end of his somewhat ample, bulbous nose and he peered across the top of the frames at Chap and frowned. "I'm busy, Sergeant." He pointed at the file on the desk in front of him. "What do you want?"

"You know, George, if that's a prosecution file you are working on, the statute of limitations is going to be up before you finish it." He smiled and nodded towards the file.

Baldwin pretended to ignore the sarcasm in Chap's words but he could not disguise the slight flush of annoyance that rose in his cheeks. "What do you want?" he persisted.

"If it's not too much trouble, I would like to be brought up to date on Tony's murder."

"Murder?" Baldwin queried. "Who said anything about murder?"

Chap shook his head in frustration. "Oh, for Christ's sake, spare me the platitudes. We both know the car bomb was no accident. My car was old, and sometimes a bit hard to get going on a cold morning, not unlike your good self, George, but it was never going to blow up without outside assistance."

"You are on leave, Bouttell. Why don't you go away and enjoy the rest of what's left of it? Everything is under control."

It was just the sort of condescending attitude and response Chap did not want. He clenched his fists at his sides, turned, took two steps towards the still open door, reached out and flung it shut with such force that a plaque hanging on the wall nearby crashed noisily to the floor. With his jaw set and determined, he turned back to face Baldwin, who had removed his glasses and was fiddling with them nervously.

Chap crossed back to the desk and leaned across the top of it, bringing his face only inches from his superior's. He stared at Baldwin for a long time, refusing to blink. As he stared Baldwin down, he was certain he could feel a subtle breeze from the superintendent's rapidly fluttering eyelids. Finally, he spoke directly but quietly to him.

"Outside, in the squad room, I walked past a number of detectives who I know would normally be off duty today, and there's a couple more I know who were away from the job on leave, myself included. You have called them in to assist with the investigation. Why not me?" He leaned even closer to Baldwin.

Baldwin dropped his spectacles onto his desk and squirmed uncomfortably in his seat as he struggled to maintain his composure. "You are emotionally involved," he began to explain. "And you are suffering an injury." He glanced at the small Band-Aid on Chap's cheek. "I decided it was in the best interests of the investigation to leave you out of it."

Chap was angry. He felt cheated. He was a senior investigator with many years of experience and Tony Francis was more than his partner, he was also his friend. He felt he deserved to be included in the investigation of his death. "I was his partner, you moron," he hissed. "I have as much right as anyone, more than most, to be involved. Just who do you think you are?"

George Baldwin sat back in his chair as if to put as much distance between himself and his sergeant as he could. Chap

Bouttell intimidated him, always had, and although he fought hard not to let it show, he failed miserably. Feeling decidedly uncomfortable, he wiped at a bead of perspiration which rolled down his face. He needed to gain some measure of control over the situation he found himself confronted with.

"What do you mean, 'Who do I think I am'? I know full well who I am, Sergeant. It would seem, however, that you may have forgotten. So, let me remind you." Baldwin sat more upright in his chair, his confidence beginning to return. "I am, first and foremost, your immediate superior. Secondly, I have assumed full responsibility for investigations into last night's unfortunate incident, and that includes assigning who will work the case. What that means, Sergeant Bouttell, is that you are *off* the case. In fact, you were never *on* it."

Baldwin paused momentarily. "Now," he continued, "if there is nothing else you would like me to bring you up to date on, I have work to do." He picked up his discarded spectacles, placed them back on the end of his nose, and reached for the file on his desk. "Close the door on your way out... gently," he added, as he leaned over the file.

"You can't do this, George," Chap said, to the top of his head.

It was the last straw for George Baldwin. He slammed his pen down on the desk, and, like an out of control missile, it bounced high and hurtled towards Chap, missing his wounded face by inches. The sudden outburst momentarily startled even Baldwin himself. He thrust himself back from his desk and attempted to stand. He was not going to be spoken to like this by anyone, least of all Chapman Bouttell. He moved so quickly that his chair toppled over and somehow became entangled around his legs. His composure, if he ever had any in the first place, dissolved into a tirade of abuse, some of it directed at the upturned chair, most of it directed at Sergeant Chapman Bouttell. He kicked out at the chair, sending it slamming into the wall behind him.

With all the slamming, banging, crashing and cursing going on in the room, Chap half expected a dozen detectives, with weapons drawn, to kick down the door and charge into the office. As he stared at the ruddy face of the Detective Superintendent, he thought that if the drama unfolding before him weren't so serious, it would be almost comical.

"I can do any damn thing I like, Bouttell!" Baldwin screamed, spittle flying from his lips. "Now, you listen, and you listen good. I ordered you to stay away from the Dickson murder, but I know you well enough to know you can't help yourself. I don't know what you're up to yet, but I will find out, and I'll tell you this, for the record. When one of my investigators is blown from here to eternity in the middle of the night, and I find you less than thirty metres away sipping scotch, it strikes me as more than mere coincidence."

"Whatever are you suggesting, George?" Chap interrupted, his sarcasm obvious.

"I'm suggesting Detective Francis went to that restaurant to meet you for some reason and, for his trouble, got himself killed. That makes you a prime witness. You know more than you are letting on, of that I *am* certain. I'm going to nail you to the wall, Sergeant, you can count on it. Just as soon as I can prove you know more about the circumstances surrounding last night's events than you disclosed in that piece of crap statement I just read. And, if you are withholding information pertinent to this investigation, I promise you, you will wish you had chosen another career!"

Chap absently touched his pocket where he had earlier placed his two copies of the documents. "You're full of shit, George," he responded gruffly. "Tony had finished work and met me at the restaurant to deliver some private mail that arrived at the office for me. I told you that last night. And, you seem to be forgetting one important thing. It was *my* car. The bomb was in *my* car. Even a fresh-faced rookie could figure out it was *me* who was supposed to die in the explosion, not Tony Francis."

"A pity it wasn't," Baldwin mumbled.

"What?" Chap asked, suspiciously.

Baldwin ignored the question. "You are in this up to your neck, I know you are, and it's going to be your undoing. Think about this over the next few days. As of this moment, you are suspended from duty pending a full investigation into your involvement in these matters." He stood, thrust his shoulders back, puffed his chest out, and glared up at Chap.

At that moment, Baldwin more than ever reminded Chap of an angry Elmer Fudd from the old Bugs Bunny cartoons. He wanted to laugh but managed to control the urge. "You can't suspend me, George. I'm not on duty, remember? I'm on leave." With that, he turned and walked smartly from the office, leaving the door open as he left. As he walked away, he could hear the familiar mumblings of discontent coming from his superior's office, and he smiled.

He crossed the squad room to his desk and sat. Around him, detectives went about their duties, for the most part trying to ignore him out of a feeling of discomfort. Occasionally, someone would approach and offer their condolences over the loss of Tony Francis. It was not Chap's loss alone. Everyone in the squad, and indeed throughout the department, felt the loss of a fellow officer. Francis was not married, but he did have a family in his parents who had now lost their only son.

It was depressing. He felt frustrated. He wanted to help with the investigation, but to do so, he would have to reveal what he had learned from the documents sent to him by Eddie Dickson. Somehow, he knew Eddie Dickson's murder was connected to Tony's and he wondered if perhaps he had bitten off more than he could chew. If he came forward with what he knew, Baldwin would have his justification for carrying through with his threat to suspend him. Chap was withholding vital evidence, and Baldwin would not stop until he had made good on his threat and had him drummed out of the job in disgrace, experience and a twenty-seven-year good service record notwithstanding.

Perverting the course of justice was a serious criminal offence and right now, Chap was guilty of it. As much as he wanted to be a part of the official investigation, he had to continue on with his own unofficial, private investigation, and hope for the best. It was too late to turn back now. He picked up the telephone on his desk, dialled for an outside line, and telephoned for a taxi. Sooner rather than later, he was going to have to get another car.

Chap was followed when he left headquarters, he was sure of it. He noticed the other car as he climbed into the taxi in front of the building. It was parked some distance away, at the kerb. It seemed to be the same car he thought he saw a few days earlier when he left the Federal Police building. Was his imagination playing tricks? He could be wrong, but his instincts told him otherwise.

The cab driver, a stocky man of Middle Eastern appearance, reset the meter and as he pulled away from the kerb, he asked, "Where to?"

Chap glanced quickly out the rear window and saw the other car was also pulling away from where it was parked. Although the driver maintained a distance behind them sufficient to remain unidentifiable, there was no doubt in Chap's mind. He was being followed.

He flashed his police identification card at the cabbie and asked him to make a few evasive driving manoeuvres, like slipping quickly down a side street and then doubling back. He glanced again out the rear window. The suspect vehicle was still there.

"Okay," Chap said quietly. "Let the games begin."

"What?" the driver asked nervously.

"Nothing." He asked the cabbie to contact his dispatch operator and order a second taxi to meet them in a narrow service lane which ran behind Police Headquarters. Then he instructed him to circle the city centre a couple of times, and see if he could lose the following car in the process.

The cabbie seemed to accept this as both an invitation to demonstrate his ability as a wet weather rally driver, and a licence to break every traffic rule in the book while a police officer rode in the seat next to him. This would be something to tell his fellow cabbies next time they all queued at a rank waiting for a fare. He tramped on the accelerator; the tyres spun uselessly on the wet road surface for a few seconds before finally gripping.

The vehicle snaked along the road, seemingly out of control, for about fifty metres and then took off at a speed that had Chap wondering if his life was about to end trapped inside a pile of broken and twisted metal. Perhaps this wasn't such a good idea after all. He grasped the dashboard in front of him, his knuckles white with his vice-like grip. Suddenly, all thoughts of shadowy villains in pursuing vehicles were forgotten and his concentration was centred on surviving the next few frantic minutes.

When the driver finally screeched to a halt behind the headquarters building as instructed, another taxi was waiting. Chap dug into his pocket for money and tossed a couple of notes at the driver without speaking. He was afraid that if he opened his mouth to speak, only unintelligible mumbling would emerge from his throat. He got out of the cab, paused unsteadily, and looked up and down the laneway. Satisfied his driver had lost the tail, he climbed into the second taxi and was somewhat relieved to see his new driver was a lady. He smiled cautiously at her and instructed her to depart as rapidly as she dared, moving into the quickly building afternoon traffic.

Glen Osmond Road, a major arterial road into Adelaide from the eastern states, was a short ride southeast of the city. Being a main access road, it was peppered with motels, all displaying large, garish neon signs welcoming visitors to the delights of Adelaide. Chap had no preference as to which motel he stayed in. Some were better than others, and while their individual facades varied in style and presentation, they all offered the same thing: a room on a busy, noisy thoroughfare, at a price which far exceeded the true value of the quality and comfort promised.

They drove outbound along the road for a few minutes, their progress slow and intermittent due to traffic build-up, traffic lights, and lousy weather. Up ahead, Chap saw a sign which read Park View Motel, and he directed the driver to pull into the entrance. As he paid the lady cabbie and got out under the shelter of the office awning, he wondered at the name, Park View Motel. Somewhat inappropriate, he thought, given there were no park views to be had. No matter—he was not here for the scenery.

At the office, he checked in for one night, purchased a copy of the *Advertiser*, the city's daily newspaper, and retired to the relative solace and modest comfort of his allocated room. He could have gone directly home when he left police headquarters. He could also have stayed at Sally's place; he knew she would be more than pleased to have him staying with her. Under normal circumstances he would have enjoyed that, too, but his life was in danger, there was no getting away from that, and he was not about to put anyone else's life, particularly Sally's, in jeopardy. Now, the game had begun in earnest. Now, it was the hunter and the hunted, and in this game, Chap was both of the above. Someone was going to considerable effort to follow him and he was not going to make it easy for them.

If whoever they were spent the night wondering where he was, or what he was doing, he reasoned he had them at a disadvantage, albeit only a slight disadvantage. It was time for him to transfer the confusion—from his mind to theirs.

Chapter Twenty-Six

After phoning the restaurant and getting no answer, Chap finally found Sally at her home. She had decided to use the inconvenience of the previous night as an excuse to carry out extensive renovations she considered long overdue but had never seemed to get around to commencing. The restaurant would remain closed for at least three weeks, she informed Chap.

She surprised him when she mentioned François had made her an offer to buy the restaurant. He first asked after her husband was killed, thinking that to continue may hold too many sad memories for her. Sally was not ready to sell back then; this was a business she and her husband had started together and built from the ground up. She felt she owed it to his memory to continue running it on her own.

François had been with her all this time and knew the business inside out. He had made offers from time to time, only to be disappointed when she refused to sell. Now, she felt differently. Time had passed, she had worked hard to build the restaurant into a very successful business and perhaps the time was right to move on.

Then, there were her feelings for Chap. Those feelings ran

deep, and she knew it was possible she was in love with him. Falling in love with anyone after the death of her husband was not something she wanted to happen, and falling in love with Chap Bouttell in particular was never on her agenda. While he had never actually declared the depth of his feelings for her, she believed he felt the same way she did. It was an awkward situation and one she knew she should have discouraged early in their relationship. But, when such feelings surfaced, as they were always going to, they were difficult to disregard.

She knew Chap planned on retiring in three years, and the thought of them spending the rest of their lives together had begun to have a certain appeal. She had wanted to tell him all this some time ago, but had always managed to restrain herself. In her heart, she suspected it might never happen.

Chap was genuinely happy that she had decided to sell the restaurant. He did not want her going back to work so soon after the events of last night, and he thought the idea of selling to François was a wonderful idea.

Sally wanted to know where he was, and wanted to join him. Chap had a difficult task dissuading her. He was working, he explained, and he was close to something. He asked her to trust him, and bear with him for a while longer. Finally, reluctantly, she agreed. As he was lowering the receiver at the end of their conversation, he thought he heard her say softly, "I love you, Chap."

The motel had its own small cocktail bar and restaurant attached to the office. Somewhat tired-looking and aesthetically unpleasing, it fell well short of the standard he had become accustomed to at Sally's. For the moment, however, Chap sought solitude, not aesthetics.

He chose not to enter, fearing he may find himself at the bar seated next to a fast-talking, over-enthusiastic, travelling sales representative, feigning interest in the latest electronic gizmos and gadgetry set to revolutionise the way the world watches television, or does the household laundry, or accesses the internet.

Instead, he decided to walk the short distance to the Akaba Hotel, a large hotel/motel complex which had, over many years, become a well-known landmark close to the city. The rain had eased temporarily and he welcomed the respite. From the bottle shop, he purchased a small bottle of whisky, and on his way back to his motel, stopped at a suspiciously unclean-looking take-away shop where he ordered a hamburger with all the trimmings. He was set. He had the necessities of life as many people perceived them— alcohol and junk food.

Back in his motel room, he unwrapped the greasy hamburger with its attendant overripe tomato and limp lettuce. Just looking at it was sufficient for his appetite to leave him. He discarded it in the bin after a couple of tentative bites. He did, however, manage to drink most of the whisky.

It was the sunlight that woke him. It streamed through a small section of the heavy curtains; in the middle, where the two drapes did not quite meet. At first, confused and disorientated, he momentarily forgot where he was, and the sunlight appeared, somehow, alien. It seemed like ages since he had seen the sun that bright in the morning. He lay still in bed and listened to the rapidly increasing hum of passing traffic. Making a conscious effort to ignore the sounds of passing motorists from outside, he listened instead for the sound of rain on the roof, and was mildly relieved that, for the moment anyway, the rain had ceased.

Slowly, he dragged himself into a degree of awareness, and looked at his watch. Seven-fifteen a.m. He threw the blankets off, swung his bare legs over the side of the bed and waited for a wave of light-headedness to subside. Got to back off a tad on the whisky, he decided.

His holstered weapon sat on the bedside table, on top of his personal copies of the damning documents. He pushed the weapon aside and picked up the envelope. As he held it, the events of the recent past flooded back.

So much time seemed to have elapsed since he was awoken from his bed that cold, wet night almost a week ago. He put the envelope back on the bedside table, picked up the newspaper he had discarded the night before, and glanced again at the headlines.

The death of Tony Francis had captured the interest of everyone. Television stations carried the story as their lead-in news item, and it occupied the entire front page of the paper. Chap looked at the photograph of what was once his car, taken by some diligent news person before the vehicle was covered and eventually removed from the scene by the forensic personnel. There was a small tarpaulin draped over the driver's side of the burned-out wreck, inviting the reader to speculate as to what ghastly sight might lie beneath.

Soon, the press hounds would be after him, if they weren't already. They would know by now that the car belonged to Chapman Bouttell, the dead cop's partner. They would come looking for him en masse, for his comments. That was all he needed; an unruly hoard of media vultures hounding him day and night, digging deeper than he would find comfortable.

Chap rose naked from the bed, shivered in the chill morning air and padded across to a small mini-bar in one corner of the room, where there was an electric jug complete with all the makings for tea and coffee. He flicked the switch on the jug, hurried back to the bed and climbed back under the covers, waiting for the water to boil.

Last night, secreted away in his nondescript room, in an even more nondescript motel, had done him the world of good, except for the whisky. His actions, his thoughts, his feelings were all calculated now. Gone was the trepidation and anxiousness of the past few days. As the time-worn cliché would have it, he was cool, calm and collected. He was ready. That nerve-tingling, hair-bristling excitement which always accompanied the chase was with him again. He had not felt that way since he left Vietnam. It was with him now, as though it had never left. Perhaps it never had. Perhaps it had just lain dormant, deep within him, awaiting the events of the past week.

As he focused on his emotions, he understood why he loved his work so much. They had trained him well back then; the thrill of the hunt, the painstaking patience of the stalk, and the sudden rush of adrenaline-soaked fear that always came with the ultimate contact.

He showered and dried himself vigorously. The whisky-induced lethargy was gone. His mind was sharp and focused. His senses alive and attuned. This was what it had come down to. This is what it was all about. Now, he recognised the face staring back at him from the mirror. He smiled knowingly at his reflection.

Chapter Twenty-Seven

Outside, the rain had stopped, at least momentarily, but the air was still icy cold. Despite the chill, the sun shone brightly through breaks in the heavy clouds, offering false promise. As Chap stood under the faded canopy of the motel office waiting for his taxi, he looked to the sky, ruing the fact that the consistent sunshine which accompanied spring was still several weeks away.

The cab took him to a car rental firm where he rented a car, opting for an open return date hoping, albeit a little *too* hopefully, that his insurance company would play ball and cover the cost. As he prepared to leave the vehicle rental yard, out of habit he checked the rear vision mirror and it occurred to him he was no longer concerned about whether or not he was still being followed. He thought it unlikely, as he was sure he had given any shadow he might have had the previous afternoon the slip. But, strangely, it didn't seem to matter anymore. That he and the anonymous motorist tailing him would meet eventually was, he thought, inevitable. It would be a meeting Chap looked forward to.

He had decided that, whoever these people were, he did not have to chase them, they would come to him. He had something they wanted; wanted badly enough to kill for. All he had to do was wait, and he was good at waiting. He had slept well for the first time since the night Dickson died, and the tingle of anticipation down the spine that he always got just before the hunt, was back. He was alert. He was ready. There would be no more hiding.

"Bring it on!" he said aloud as he drove from the yard.

As he drove away, he again reviewed his options. First, he could simply go the authorities with all he now knew, and lay it all out on the table; Vietnam, the ambush, the murders of Cobb, Elliott and Eddie Dickson, and the murder of Tony Francis. He could produce his copies of the documents as evidence to back up his story. However, should he choose that route, George Baldwin would have his badge, and Chap refused to give him the satisfaction of being the one to take it from him. When the time came for him to leave the job, he would gladly hand over his badge, but it would be on his terms, not George Baldwin's.

There was also his ongoing health and wellbeing to consider. If he chose to go to the authorities, revenge would be swift. Chap had never really considered himself to be afraid of death, but if it came, or more accurately *when* it came, he wanted his demise to be at the right time, not prematurely. Whoever these people were, they would not tolerate exposure without extracting vengeance on the person responsible. They would come for him, and he was prepared for that, but he was not going to make it easy for them.

The second option was to get on a plane, return to Canberra, and pay Colonel Baxter another visit. And, if necessary, shake the truth out of him.

This option, however, was one he considered only briefly. If Baxter was involved somehow in all of this, as Dickson had intimated in his note, wouldn't confronting him about it be playing into their hands? It would be unwise, Chap reasoned, to go charging headlong into uncharted waters without first checking what lay beneath the surface.

There remained a third and, it seemed, the only alternative option available to him.

He held all the cards, or in this case, all the documents. He had the upper hand and they, the enemy, would want to negotiate, and they would want to do it soon. They did not know him, or at least he thought they didn't know him and, as such, they did not know which way he would move. They would know of his police background and they would know he was dogged and determined. But, they had no way of knowing what he might do with the information Dickson had sent him. Would he sit on it and do nothing, hoping that to do so would keep him alive? Would he gamble with his life and go to the authorities, or perhaps the media?

Chap was certain of one thing; they would not sit around waiting for him to make the first move. He was not going to make himself hard to find, but conversely, he was not going to place an open house sign on his front door. He would go home, and he would wait. They would come. They obviously knew where he lived, and they would come. Soon.

As he parked the rental car into his driveway, there were no obvious signs of anything out of the ordinary. However, as he had now moved into a heightened state of alertness, he sat for a moment and studied the front of his home before he got out of the car. When he was satisfied everything was as it should be, at least externally, he got out of the car.

With a hand resting on his holstered weapon, he walked cautiously to the porch and checked the front door. It was locked, just as he had left it. He checked the windows in the front, and then completed a slow, thorough search around the perimeter of his house. Although cautiously relieved when he found no immediate signs of forced entry, he was not prepared for what he found when he retraced his steps and entered through the front door. He was not prepared, but neither was he surprised.

The lounge was the first room he saw. It was trashed. They had been there, and they had left a calling card. The drawers in the sideboard had been pulled out and tossed aside. The contents lay strewn about the floor. The cushions on the sofa and chairs had been sliced open and the foam and felt padding protruded from the ugly gashes.

Chap stood in the doorway and cast his eyes over the mess around him. Quietly, and deliberately, he un-holstered his weapon. Silently, he stood and listened for any sound inside the house. Was there still someone inside, lying in wait in another room perhaps? He thought not, but was not about to take any chances. Cautiously, he stepped further into the room, placing his feet with care so as not to trip on any of his belongings haphazardly discarded around the floor.

A slow, careful, room by room search verified what he already suspected—he was alone in the house. All the other rooms were intact. Nothing seemed to be disturbed or out of place. His computer, on which he had stored a copy of the documents, was just as he had left it. The storm of senseless vandalism had been confined to the one room.

Chap holstered his gun and returned to the scene of devastation in the lounge room. What at first glance seemed to be the results of a frantic, violent search was, he believed, nothing more than a welcome home, a calling card from his enemy. That was how he had to think of these people now; they were the enemy.

The fact that the other rooms in the house remained untouched was proof to him that whoever came to his house never intended to search for anything. If this was their idea of a thorough house search, they were demonstrating an unbelievable degree of incompetence, and Chap suspected these people were anything but incompetent. This was their way of letting him know they were around, and they knew where he lived. They wanted him to know they knew where to reach him, and could, any time it suited them. They were intimidating him; at least that was their intention.

If it was an attempt to frighten him, it failed. Any fear he might have felt earlier had left him. He felt angry, yes; and he felt violated. But he was not afraid, not anymore.

However, he would not let his anger consume him. He had to maintain his composure. He knew now that the inevitable confrontation was not far away. When it arrived, it would be a moment requiring strong, cool nerves. Chap was prepared.

He spent the next thirty minutes trying to restore some semblance of order to the room. As he replaced the ripped cushions, he thought of his ex-wife. She had spent almost every day for two weeks, all those years ago, searching every furniture outlet she could find for just the right lounge suite. Chap wondered what her reaction might be if she were to see it now. She would be mortified, he concluded; she would also make sure he knew she was mortified.

With time, rather than serious effort, he finally had the room looking the way it was before, albeit slightly the worse for the unsightly cushions. Other than the damage to the sofa, the intruders, and he guessed they would be in the plural, had caused him little inconvenience. He stood back and surveyed the room.

Across the room, on the sideboard, now intact with drawers re-inserted, stood a bottle of whisky. He was contemplating a small nip when he noticed the note for the first time. It was behind the whisky bottle, resting against a heavy glass tumbler. Amidst the mess he walked into, he had not noticed it until now. He strode across to the sideboard and reached for the note, picking it up by one corner so as not to disturb any fingerprints.

There were just two lines, handwritten.

Sorry we missed you.
Be in your home at 6.00pm. You will be contacted.

Chap turned the page over, looking for a signature. The reverse side was blank. Why was he not surprised? He glanced at his watch. Ten minutes past noon. He had almost six hours to wait. He stepped to the window, pushed the drapes aside and looked out into his front yard and the street beyond. The morning sun had disappeared behind heavy, swollen clouds. As he watched, it began to rain once again.

Chap left the drapes closed. This, in conjunction with the dull, ominous skies outside, made the room dark. He flicked the light on a tall standard-lamp next to one of the lounge chairs and a soft glow, which barely reached into the far corners, cast an ominous, almost eerie ambience across the room. The embers in the fireplace were cold and he busied himself cleaning away the ashes, resetting, and lighting the fire. Then, with the heat from the fire beginning to warm the room, he sat, made himself comfortable facing the doorway, and stared into the dark, flickering shadows dancing around the room.

For the second time that day, he un-holstered his weapon. He placed it on the coffee table in front of him and glanced again at the whisky bottle on the other side of the room; he could use a drink about now. He quickly dismissed the thought. This was not the time to cloud his mind with alcohol. He closed his eyes and leaned back against the headrest. He would also not allow his mind to become cluttered with questions he could not answer. He would simply sit, and wait.

He must have dozed. He did not hear the car pull up in front of his house. It was the sound of footsteps crunching on the gravel driveway that roused him. Now he looked at his watch, angry at himself for having slept. It was six o'clock exactly.

"I like punctuality," he murmured, as he straightened in his chair, reached forward and picked up the gun from the coffee table, fully prepared to use it should it become necessary.

He rose slowly from the chair, stepped around the table, and crossed silently to the window. Carefully, he drew the drapes aside a fraction and looked out into the street. Beyond the glow of the street lights, it was dark and it took a few seconds for his eyes to adjust.

Then he saw it. The same car again, parked outside on the street, directly in front of his house and illuminated by a dim overhead street light. Chap was in no doubt it was the same car. He stared at it, the familiarity of it still with him from the two previous times he had seen it.

Suddenly, a sensor light mounted above his front door flicked on and flooded the porch. He dragged his eyes from the car, and craned his neck to get a view of the man standing on his porch. He recognised him immediately, and knew instantly from where he remembered the car.

"You!" he gasped incredulously.

His mind raced and filled with questions, all demanding answers. Chap let the drape fall and he stood motionless, in shocked disbelief. "No, it can't be," he said quietly to the empty room. "I don't believe this."

A sharp rapping on the door snapped him into alertness. It was loud, and seemed to echo throughout the entire house. Chap lifted a corner of the drapes again and looked at the man. He had to be making a mistake, surely. The car parked in front of his house could not be the same car that had been following him. Through the fog of confusion, he knew it was. He dropped the curtain, crossed back to his chair and sat facing the door.

His visitor knocked again. Chap raised the weapon and

aimed at a point just above the middle of the door, about chest height. He moistened his lips with his tongue and softly cleared his throat. “It’s open,” he called loudly.

He watched the knob begin to turn and then the door swung slowly open.

Stony-faced and determined, Chap watched Dr. Lee Richardson enter the room.

The pathologist was smiling. It was not a “happy to see you, Chapman” smile, but more a cautious, wary smile. Nonetheless, he was smiling, and that in itself was disconcerting to Chap. In truth, it was enough to really piss him off.

Richardson saw Chap sitting facing him; almost simultaneously, he noticed the gun pointed at his chest. Suddenly, the smile disappeared. He did not look at Chap; he looked directly at the gun, his eyes fixed and wide. He gave the door a gentle push and allowed it to close with a soft click behind him. Richardson stood for a few seconds, staring at the gun in Chap’s hand. Then, he took a couple of tentative steps from the entrance foyer into the dimly lit lounge room. Finally, he spoke, softly, and with a slight but noticeable falter in his voice. “Good evening, Chapman.”

He took another couple of slow, cautious steps into the room. The gun in Chap’s hand never wavered from a point somewhere around mid-chest. He paused, as if satisfying himself Chap was not going to pull the trigger—not just yet, anyway—and then he moved further into the room until he stood directly in front of the detective, only the coffee table separating them.

“We need to talk, Chapman,” Richardson said, his eyes still focused on the gun.

Chap stared at the pathologist. He wanted to jump up, fly at him and tear the answers from him. Instead, he sat, silent and watchful, staring at Richardson, searching for any sign of weakness. What he saw in the pathologist’s eyes was more than cautious wariness. It was fear.

Finally, reluctantly, Richardson took his eyes from the gun and looked directly at Chap. Not wanting to spook him, he made a slow, slight gesture at the gun and spoke, quietly and deliberately. "You don't need that, Chapman. I only came to talk."

Chap did not move and, more importantly, the gun did not move from its point of aim. His hand was steady, his index finger rested on the trigger guard, and his knuckles were white where he gripped the weapon firmly. Just a slight deviation of the finger, a few grams of pressure, and Richardson would be dead. Chap felt a surge of nostalgia wash over him; it was amazing how the art of killing flooded back to him.

Perspiration was beginning to glisten on Richardson's upper lip. "Please, Chapman. Put the gun away. You're making me nervous." Slowly, he took the lapels of his jacket in each hand and opened his coat, exposing his shirt to the waist. "Look, I'm not armed," he continued. "I don't even own a gun, for goodness' sake. I really just came to talk."

"So, go ahead," Chap invited. "Talk."

"Jesus, Chapman. I'm terrified of guns, always have been, ever since I was a child. I can't even bear to hold one. Every day, I deal with the damage guns cause and that has only made my distaste for them worse. Please, put the gun down."

"I'm not interested in your insecurities, Doc. Say what you came here to say and then get out of my house," Chap insisted, sternly.

"May I at least sit?" Richardson asked nervously.

Chap stared at Richardson. Richardson's eyes swung back to the weapon. Finally, satisfied the pathologist would be less of a threat sitting than standing, he motioned with his free hand. "Sit on the sofa behind you."

Richardson took his eyes away from the gun, turned his head, and looked at the sofa behind where he stood. Slowly, he lowered himself into the seat, his eyes wavering between

Chap's, and the barrel of the gun as it followed his every movement.

Satisfied that Richardson was unarmed and of little threat to him, Chap lowered the weapon to his lap. He released his grip on the butt, and rested his hand lightly on top of it. If need be, he could raise it, aim and fire in an instant. He was a good shot. At this range, a blind man couldn't miss.

Visibly relaxing ever so slightly, Richardson shifted back in his seat. He glanced at a cushion next to him and fingered the ugly rip where some of the stuffing still protruded. "I'm sorry about this," he said. "They were not supposed to cause any damage, just mess the place up a bit."

"Who are 'they'?" Chap asked.

"Well… yes," Richardson began. "A legitimate question; sadly, however, one which I am unable to answer. A couple of characters, their identities unknown to me, whose job is to follow orders. That's all I can tell you about them." He ran his hand over the damaged cushion again.

"Whose orders?"

"Actually, mine," Richardson confirmed.

"Are you telling me you gave the order for a couple of common thugs to come into my home, trash my belongings, and you expect me to believe you don't know who they are?"

"Not exactly common thugs, Chapman." Richardson sounded mildly offended. "A little shady, perhaps, but not common thugs. I know it sounds confusing, but yes, that is what I'm telling you. I don't know their names."

"You have been following me. Why?"

"I, too, was following orders. You see, I'm not a lot different from the fellows who visited your home last night. Somewhat higher up the pecking order, I hasten to add, but nonetheless accountable to an even higher command. My job was to watch you and attempt to establish whether or not you had the document in your possession."

Now we're getting to the nitty-gritty, Chap thought. "What document?" He feigned ignorance.

"Come on, Chapman." Richardson smiled. "Naivety is not a suit that fits with your reputation. I know you received a document in the mail, as recently as Tuesday. It was sent to you through the post by your late friend Eddie Dickson and delivered to you at Ms. Prescott's restaurant by Tony Francis. I also know you made at least two copies of the document, one you deposited with your bank, and the other with a solicitor. I know you well enough to make an educated guess that there are more than likely other copies secreted away somewhere." Richardson watched Chap, looking for some response, some verification in his eyes that he was right. He saw nothing but cold, hard, unblinking eyes staring back at him.

"If you know all that, why bother to have my home ransacked?" Chap posed.

"Please, Chapman, hardly ransacked." Again, Richardson sounded affronted. He made a sweeping gesture around the room. "This was just a message. Confirmation, if you like, that there are people watching you, and that they have the ability to get to you at any time and in any place." He paused momentarily. "As you now know, the visit was confined to this room only. They were the specific instructions. I know you are not so stupid as to conceal the document in your own home, especially given the sensitive nature of its contents."

Chap decided it was time to change tack. "Who killed Eddie Dickson?"

"I'm afraid I can't help you there, either." The pathologist shrugged.

"Who killed Tony Francis?" Chap continued. Then, he saw it. There it was; an almost imperceptible movement in Richardson's eyes.

"Ah… yes." Richardson faltered slightly. "A dreadful shame about Tony. I liked him. He was a good police officer."

Chap moved the gun in his lap just enough to catch Richardson's attention. "Who killed him?" he asked again.

"I don't know who killed him, Chapman, and that's the truth. If you want me to speculate, then I suspect it was the same people responsible for Dickson's murder."

"Why Francis? He was not involved in any of this bullshit." Chap felt his anger rising.

Richardson shifted slightly in his seat and glanced again at the gun in Chap's lap. "Your movements have been closely monitored," he began to explain. "Including your recent trip interstate. In particular, your visit with Colonel Baxter in Canberra. We discovered, too late as it turns out, that Dickson had already mailed the document to you. It was apparent it would arrive here before you returned and, when it failed to materialise in your private mail here at the house— we checked, by the way—we were left with only one alternative; Dickson addressed it to you at Police Headquarters."

"So, you watched my partner," Chap concluded.

"In a word, yes. He was kept under surveillance, and his phone calls were monitored. We know you called him from Canberra, we know the document arrived in Adelaide, and we knew he was bringing it to you at the restaurant."

"You monitored his phone calls? How could you do that at Police Headquarters?"

"That's not my area of expertise, so I can't tell you how it was done, only that it was done."

Chap could not believe what he was hearing. He only knew, at that moment, that he hated the man seated across from him. He wanted to raise the gun and send a bullet crashing through the pathologist's face.

Richardson sensed his anger and glanced nervously at the gun. "Chapman," he said hurriedly, "you are selling these people short. They are not in the business of killing people unless it is considered necessary in the interests of national security. All I'm prepared to tell you, at this stage, is that your telephone conversation with Francis in regard to the document's arrival did not go unnoticed."

"So, you killed him." It was a statement rather than a question

"Well… no," Richardson stammered. "That is, not me personally, I…"

"You knew about it, you arsehole!" Chap interrupted. "That makes you just as guilty. Tony Francis didn't have to die. He didn't even know what was in the envelope. When he passed it on to me, it was still sealed."

Richardson dropped his eyes once again to the gun, and noticed Chap was now holding it off his lap. "You're right," he admitted. "Tony was not supposed to die in the explosion." He paused. "You were."

He looked into Chap's eyes and saw them harden visibly. "He was not supposed to drive *your* car. He was only supposed to drop the document off to you. It was then supposed to be destroyed in the explosion and ensuing fire after you left the restaurant."

"Along with me," Chap added.

"Along with you," Richardson conceded.

"Who planted the bomb?"

"I don't know, Chapman. I honestly don't know."

"I drove my car to the restaurant. When was it planted?"

"I assume it was planted while you were in the restaurant with your lady friend."

Chap thought about that for a moment. The restaurant was closed, the outside lights were turned off, and he recalled the car park was very poorly lit at night. It was dark, and raining heavily. It would not have been difficult to attach an explosive device underneath the car and not be seen. It had to be triggered by remote control as there would not have been time to wire a bomb to the ignition system.

"It would seem," Richardson interrupted his thoughts, "that your partner was killed by mistake."

Chap allowed these words to penetrate. He felt sick. He felt the bile rise in his throat. During his time in Vietnam he never wanted to kill anyone. He did it because it was his job and because he believed, albeit naively, what those who trained him told him; that what he did made a difference.

Despite his aversion to the act of killing, back then it came easily to him because he was well trained at it and had killed many times during his twelve-month tour of duty. Since then, in his twenty-seven years on the job, he had never discharged his weapon in anger, and had taken it from his holster on perhaps only two or three occasions. Now, however, at this very moment, he wanted to kill Dr. Lee Richardson and felt he could do it with very little regard for any consequences that might follow. The temptation was strong.

The two men sat in silence for what seemed to Chap like a long time. He found himself waging a battle against the feelings and urges rising within. This whole business was beginning to take on the momentum of a runaway train, careering downhill at a breakneck pace, gathering even more speed as it went unchecked. His mind was a tangled confusion of known facts, unanswered questions, and no small amount of speculation. He had little idea how any of this began, and even less as to where or when it was all going to end—if, in fact, it ever *was* going to end. Chap was sure of one thing, however. Whatever was happening, whatever he had unwittingly stumbled into, it was bigger than he could ever have imagined.

Richardson's eyes darted constantly from Chap's face to the gun, now resting back in the detective's lap. He was terrified of the weapon, and was trying very hard to remain composed and in control. He hoped his eyes did not telegraph how he really felt.

Finally, Chap spoke, deciding to push a little harder. "Who are you working for?"

"What?"

"You heard me. Your employers, who are you working for?"

"I work for the state, Chapman. You know that. I'm a government pathologist."

"Don't fuck with me, Doc, you know what I mean."

Richardson shrugged. "Who I represent is not important at this stage," he said. "Suffice it to say that the command structure has been in place for a long time and it conducts business on a need-to-know basis. I couldn't give you names even if I wanted to. The security of the system is foolproof. One can never divulge that which one does not know. When they want me to do something, I am contacted anonymously and told to collect instructions at a certain drop point."

"Where's the drop point?" Chap interrupted.

"I've only been contacted perhaps half a dozen times in the last forty years, and each time it was a different location. I told you, security is tight."

"Only half a dozen times in forty years?" Chap repeated incredulously. "Perhaps you are not as high in the pecking order as you think you are."

"I can't explain the logic behind their modus operandi, Chapman," Richardson responded.

Chap didn't know why, but for the most part, he believed the pathologist. At the same time, he suspected Richardson hadn't told him everything he knew. "Do the names Charles Cobb and Brian Elliott mean anything to you?" he asked.

"I'm afraid I've never heard of either of them," Richardson answered, a little too quickly for Chap's liking.

He was lying now, Chap was convinced. Richardson continued before Chap could challenge him. "If it's all the same to you, Chapman, can we get back to the business at hand?"

"Which is?"

Richardson's impatience was obvious. "The document," he answered.

Chap stared intently at the eminent forensic pathologist. It was far too late to pretend he knew nothing of the document, but he feigned ignorance anyway. "What document?"

"I want it," Richardson insisted. "The original, and all copies you might have made."

"Of course you do," Chap said.

"I'm serious, Chapman."

Chap almost laughed in the doctor's face. "Yeah, right," he chortled. "And the minute I hand them over, I'm as dead as all the others. No way, Doc! No… fuckin'… way! It ain't gonna happen. At least while I have what you want, there's a chance I'll live to enjoy my old age." He sat back deeper in his chair. "You are right, though," he continued. "There are copies. The original is lodged in a safety deposit box with my bank, and there is one copy with a lawyer I know, complete with instructions to be opened only in the event of my death. Right now, the document is my life insurance."

This was the first time Chap had actually admitted to having the document. It made little sense to pretend anymore. They, whoever 'they' were, knew he had them, and besides, he was anxious to see the back of the pathetic creature sitting opposite.

"Come on, Chapman," Richardson persisted. "Be reasonable. What would there be to gain by killing you? We know you would have taken precautions with regard to the document, in the event of your death."

"You got that right," Chap acknowledged. "It's like I said, the document is my life insurance policy. As long as I have it, I figure I stand a better than even chance of staying alive."

Richardson sighed deeply. "I must admit, it would be ludicrous to expect you would simply hand it over without resistance. Besides, we have no way of knowing how many copies you might have made."

"I guess what we have here, Doc, is a stalemate." Chap smiled confidently. "And you're right. Simply handing it over, like it was nothing important, really would be ludicrous."

"Speaking for myself, I never thought you would. There are, however, those who don't know you as well as I do, and I am required to at least go through the motions of negotiating some sort of agreement with you that is acceptable to both parties."

It gave Chap little consolation to learn that his death was perhaps not imminently planned. There would be negotiations first. He was smart enough to realise that his departure from this earthly life was high on their priority list, regardless of the outcome of any negotiations which may or may not take place. But he would have to face that prospect when it came; in the meantime, his continued health and wellbeing seemed to be assured, at least in the short term.

"Well, you came all the way over here in this shitty weather," he said, with undisguised contempt. "I suppose I should at least hear your sales pitch."

Richardson leaned forward in his chair. "Chapman," he began, "you are a good cop, intelligent, and astute. I'll come straight to the point."

"I wish you would," Chap interjected.

"I am authorised to make you a substantial offer for the unconditional surrender of the document. *Unconditional*," he emphasised. "That means the original, and *all* copies. You can walk away from this a wealthy man, Chapman. I'm sure you would agree a policeman's salary will never make you rich. One hundred thousand dollars, Chap—it's a lot of money." He paused and waited for a response.

"We live in expensive times, Doc. A hundred grand does not make any man wealthy."

"The amount is negotiable," Richardson added.

Now Chap was certain these people would not kill him; not yet, anyway, much as they might like to. They didn't dare kill him for fear of the document and its contents being exposed. The instant Richardson tried to buy the document from him, he knew he was safe, albeit temporarily.

As the situation stood, Chap was more of a threat to them dead than alive. Right now, these bastards would be afraid he might accidentally cut himself shaving and bleed to death. Of course, inwardly, he was pleased they had chosen the path of conciliation and arbitration... Oh well, let's not put too much of a spin on it, it was reverse blackmail, pure and simple. He never asked for money but they were prepared to pay for his silence, anyway.

Another part of him felt insulted. One hundred thousand dollars did not seem like a lot of money for his life. He was worth more than that, surely? He shook his head and glared at Richardson. "Now, listen to me, you sanctimonious prick!" he spat between clenched teeth. "You go back to your people, and tell them I can't be bought! You tell them I am holding all the cards. You might think you are in control of this situation, but in reality, you know you are not. I am! Do you understand that? I've got the document, and as long as I have it, I'm in control!"

There was venom in his voice which did not escape Richardson, and the doctor's fear became more evident. "I'm just the messenger, Chapman," he offered, as though it might go some way to appeasing the cop with the gun.

"Jesus Christ," Chap continued. His tone was a degree calmer now. "We are talking about murder. Not just Tony Francis, Eddie Dickson, Charles Cobb and Brian Elliott, but all the others in my unit. Jesus Christ, who do you people think you are?"

"I told you I know nothing about those people you named," Richardson said, again a tad too hurriedly. "I'm just a small cog in a big wheel, bigger than you or even I can imagine."

"I don't believe this shit," Chap said, more to himself than to Richardson.

"They don't want the document made public, Chapman. I don't know why, I just know they want it, and they want it so badly they are prepared to kill, if necessary, to get it. You have already seen that firsthand. To them, you are just another obstacle to be overcome."

Just for a moment, Chap returned to the jungle. The screams of his mates echoed in his ears as they lay dying on the banks of the Srepok River and on the damp jungle floor. He felt the bile rise again in his throat. In his eyes, Richardson was nothing less than a traitor. It would be so easy, oh so easy, and maybe even pleasurable, to lift the gun from his lap and send the eminent pathologist straight to hell.

"How the fuck did you get involved in all this?" he wondered aloud.

Richardson paused, considering the question, and Chap thought he noticed a glisten of moisture in the doctor's eyes.

"It's a long story, and not one I'm particularly proud of."

"I've got time," Chap responded. He sensed Richardson wanted to talk but was weighing his options, wondering whether it mattered or not if Chap knew how he got involved. He also sensed Richardson may well have wanted to unburden himself for a long time.

Richardson cleared his throat. "They bought my soul a very long time ago," he began, speaking in almost a whisper. "Now they have come to collect it." He paused and looked at Chap.

"Go on," Chap prompted.

"In one form or another, I have been working for the government for more years than I care to remember. I'm seventy years old, Chapman, and I am not in the best of health. These are things that have weighed heavily on my mind since I first got involved back in the Sixties.

"When I first graduated from university as a doctor, I was young, ambitious and, in hindsight, extremely foolish in some of the career decisions I made. The war in Vietnam was in full flight. In some military and government circles, chemical warfare was touted to be the new atom bomb, and there was a covert push by the Australian government to recruit keen, enthusiastic young doctors and get them into the area of chemical and biological research. The money was very good, compared to that of a first-year intern. So, when I was approached, I jumped at the opportunity. I naively saw it as a way of using my knowledge as a doctor to serve my country. Perhaps I should have just joined the army and volunteered to become a front-line combat soldier. I might have slept much better all these years."

"Don't bet on it," Chap said.

"Well… perhaps not. I guess you chaps had it pretty bad," Richardson continued. "Anyway, once I was accepted…"

"By whom?" Chap interrupted.

"ASIO, the Australian Security Intelligence Organisation. As an organisation, they were in their infancy, less than twenty years old. They were into everything and espionage was not their only area of expertise. They worked closely with the CIA in America and some of us went there to further our careers. Opportunities abounded. I was sent to CIA headquarters in Langley, Virginia. The U.S. Congress had authorised millions to be spent on research as well as new and improved espionage and counterespionage techniques and, as such, the CIA budget was almost limitless."

Chap had no idea where these reminiscences were heading. "Get to the point," he insisted.

"There's not a lot more, really," Richardson said. "I went through a familiarisation program, and was then assigned to the medical research lab at Langley."

Chap raised the gun and aimed at a point between Richardson's eyes. The pathologist was holding back and Chap was determined to know the truth. And, he would know it right here and now.

Richardson raised his hands in a gesture of surrender, real fear evident in his eyes.

"There is more, Doc, I know there is," Chap said. "You're holding something back. Now, here's the deal. I have been a cop for a long time. I have seen every dirty trick in the book when it comes to murder. Believe me when I tell you I know how to get rid of a body where it will never be found, and I know how to ensure your sudden disappearance will never be connected to me. Believe me also when I tell you I *will* shoot you right here, right now, if you don't start levelling with me. I want the truth. This is your last chance. What's it gonna be?"

Richardson stared at the barrel of the gun pointed at his head and he began to tremble. "Okay… okay… there is more. Just put the gun down, Chapman. You're scaring me."

"I will more than scare you if you don't start telling me the truth," Chap promised. "Now, start talking."

Richardson sighed wearily. "Okay, I expect you will find out sooner rather than later. But put the gun down, please."

Chap slowly lowered the gun back to his lap, and Richardson relaxed slightly. "Have you ever heard of the Phoenix Program?" he asked.

"No, what's the Phoenix Program?"

"It was put into effect in 1967 and ran until 1972. It consisted of a Special Operations Group that was part of the CIA's Special Activities Division during the war in Vietnam. Their job was to identify and neutralise civilians who gave support for the National Liberation Front in South Vietnam. The National Liberation Front was, of course…"

"The Viet Cong. I know, I was there, remember? What exactly do you mean, 'neutralise'?"

"Among other things, it meant the infiltration of groups identified as supporting the NLF and, sometimes, the assassination of certain individuals."

"Are you saying that this Special Operations Group had something to do with what happened to my unit?"

Richardson hesitated.

"Well?" Chap pushed.

"Yes, they were involved."

"You are fucking kidding me! Where do you fit into all this?"

"I worked with them for a while," Richardson admitted. "I was transferred to National Clandestine Services out of the Executive Office. I acted as a sort of liaison between the CIA and ASIO."

"Jesus," Chap cursed. "National Clandestine Services, Executive Office, CIA, ASIO—what the fuck did you get yourself into?"

Richardson ignored the interruption. "From time to time, I was required to carry out certain duties related to my profession. I did whatever was asked of me without question. Remember, I was young and ambitious," he added, as if his youth and ambition might offer some justification for his actions.

"What exactly did those certain duties consist of?"

"They varied," Richardson continued, "and I'm not inclined to relate all of them to you now. Needless to say, I considered the things I did to be my patriotic duty. I was then, and am now, a believer in mutual Australian-American security collaboration."

Chap was stunned. The man sitting across from him must be stark raving mad. "How can you sit there and tell me you considered it your patriotic duty to murder your own people? We are talking about brave young men who risked their lives every day because their country asked them to. How the fuckin' hell can premeditated, cold-blooded murder be justified under the guise of a 'joint security venture'? Jesus Christ, it's madness! This is insane!" He shook his head in disbelief. "They brainwashed you, you gullible prick, and they called it a familiarisation program! Jesus, Doc! I gave you credit for more brains than that."

If Richardson took Chap's tirade as an insult to his intelligence, he did not show it. "It's not my job, and never was my job, to criticise, or to question. It was just to follow orders. You were a soldier and now you're a cop; you know all about orders."

"Tell me about the ambush." Chap changed tack again.

Richardson shifted uncomfortably in his seat and clasped his hands on his knees. His face conveyed a look of resignation. The ambush was something he was never going to avoid having to explain at some point and, with a gun pointed at him, now seemed like as good a time as any.

"It was a CIA-planned and executed operation as part of the Phoenix Program," he began nervously. "In fact, the operations carried out by your unit were at the instigation of the CIA in conjunction with ASIO. The U.S. government and the Pentagon were copping a lot of flak from the world press, and the public, about the escalation of the war. The seemingly indiscriminate carpet bombing of North Vietnam, and Hanoi in particular, which claimed hundreds, if not thousands, of innocent civilian lives, alleged atrocities carried out by U.S. troops against civilians, and the list goes on. U.S. troops were taking a pounding by the North Vietnamese Army who, afterwards, simply scampered over the border into neutral Cambodia believing they would not be pursued." He paused.

"Go on," Chap prompted.

"Pursuing the enemy into Cambodia and taking the fight to them in a neutral country would bring about world condemnation. The U.S. administration could not afford any more negative publicity and embarrassment."

"So, they conned the Australian government into doing their dirty work for them," Chap concluded.

"The U.S. government passed the buck to the Pentagon, and the Pentagon passed it to the CIA, with instructions to come up with a solution," Richardson elaborated. "The CIA got together with ASIO and soon after, your unit, Diamond One, was raised."

"What about the ambush?" Chap pressed.

"Your unit had been in Vietnam for a year. Your tour of duty was over. You were all due to fly home within days of returning from your last mission."

Chap nodded as he remembered how excited they all were about going home.

"While it was accepted that the job you did was satisfactory, it was also accepted that, in reality, it had no real effect on the original problem. The enemy was still using Cambodia as a sanctuary, and there were rumours doing the rounds of the media contingent in Vietnam that we were into something we shouldn't have been into. There was nothing specific, just rumours, but it was feared that to continue your operations would ultimately result in the exposure of Diamond One and the reason behind their formation. Someone, somewhere, made a decision that yours was to be a one-off unit. The clandestine operations into Cambodia were to cease, and you would not be replaced." Richardson paused.

"And, to ensure our silence, we were all to be 'neutralised'," Chap added.

"Unfortunately," Richardson continued, "it was decided it was too much of a risk to have you all return home and expect you to live normal, respectable lives while you carried around the knowledge of the things you did in the name of war. It was feared that, one day, one or more of you would talk and it would all become a matter of public knowledge. They couldn't take that risk."

"We all signed secrecy agreements before we even went over there," Chap reminded him. "It meant something to us. But obviously not to them."

"They were designed for no other reason than to give you all a false sense of security," Richardson explained. "It was important for you to believe you would all survive to go home."

"Are you saying it was decided before we even left Australia that none of us would return?" Chap asked incredulously. The very thought sickened him.

Richardson shrugged. "I can't be sure. The actual agreement was not signed until near the end of your deployment, but I suspect that was the scenario."

"I would think that the escape of four of us would have caused considerably panic," Chap suggested.

"That was the case, yes," the pathologist agreed. "Fortunately, for the four of you, that was when the secrecy agreement came into play. You were a well-trained, disciplined unit, and the risk involved in killing you all later, on Australian soil, was too great. It was decided to let you all go home and rely on your sense of patriotism and respect for the secrecy agreement you all signed."

"They were taking a hell of a chance, wouldn't you say?" Chap asked.

"Yes, they were," Richardson agreed. "But one they had no option but to take. By the time you escaped the ambush, disappeared into the surrounding jungle, made your way back to your mountain base, and ultimately back to the nearest Australian Fire Support base to await evacuation, it was impossible to get at you without the operation being exposed. Before the powers-that-be could regroup and counter with another plan, you were all shipped home and subsequently scattered in different directions. The job of neutralising you then became far too risky. Of course, you were all closely monitored over the ensuing years. It was a gamble to rely on your continued silence but, under the circumstances, they had little alternative."

Richardson waited for some response from Chap, who sat riveted, listening intently to every word.

"Who, or what, was T Force?" Chap asked.

"They were a CIA-led force of crack U.S. military commandos attached to National Clandestine Services. For all intents and purposes, they don't exist and never did."

"Jesus fucking Christ!" Chap spat. "This is unbelievable! You know all this stuff and yet you say you know nothing about the deaths of Dickson, Cobb and Elliott—how is that?"

"I never lied to you, Chap. It's true, I never knew about Cobb and Elliott. And I only learned of Dickson when I was given this assignment. But you don't have to be a rocket scientist to figure out they were the three others who escaped the ambush with you."

Then, suddenly, realisation smacked Chap between the eyes. Finally, it was clear. For a small cog in a big wheel, as Richardson described himself, he seemed to know an awful lot about that day in the jungle. Instinctively, his hand circled the butt of his weapon. The movement did not escape Richardson, and Chap saw the pathologist's eyes widen with fear.

"You were there," Chap said, just above a whisper. "You bastard, you were there!"

Again, Richardson raised his hands in a defensive, surrendering gesture. A tiny drop of spittle formed at the corner of his mouth as he began to speak haltingly. "Yes… yes, I was there. B… but not as a combatant, my role was as a medic… I was a doctor. My… my job… was to treat any members of T Force who might be wounded, and to confirm the success of the ambush in respect of the death of all members of your unit by identifying the bodies."

"How were you supposed to do that if you didn't know any of us?" Chap posed.

"By the tattoo you all wore," Richardson said.

Instinctively, Chap tucked his right arm closer to his side. "You know about the tattoos?" he asked cautiously.

Richardson averted his eyes and stared vacantly at a point somewhere across the room. "Yes," he confirmed softly, almost apologetically. "I should. I put them there."

"What?" Chap exclaimed.

"I… I'm not surprised you don't remember. It was a long time ago. We were all forty years younger. I didn't remember any of you from back then, either. I was never privy to any of your personal details. I was there just long enough to apply the tattoo to each of you and then my job was done, at least for the time being."

"Until later," Chap added, "when they took you back to identify your handiwork."

Richardson averted his eyes again. "Yes," he confirmed.

Chap was incensed. For all the years of his police service, he had admired and respected the man who sat opposite him; a man who had, by all appearances, dedicated his life's work to the medical profession. Richardson was applauded, even honoured, by his colleagues and the public alike. But in reality, he was just a shell of a man, a puppet who danced to the music of others. He had sold his soul to the devil, and now he was a disgrace to his profession.

Chap felt disgusted. Dirty. Somewhere along the journey of Richardson's narrative, the hatred he felt earlier had given way to pity. He still wanted to shoot him, right there and then, no longer out of hatred, but because now he saw him as a pitiful, wounded animal. Whatever happened from this point on, Richardson's career was finished. Chap would see to that.

"I know what you're thinking," Chap heard Richardson say, "but this thing is bigger than both of us, and neither of us is indispensable. They want the document. Do yourself a favour, take the money. Retire. Go fishing. Put the past behind you. You've managed to do that for the last forty years, you can do it again."

"And how do you suggest I live with my conscience?" Chap asked.

"With a hundred thousand dollars, and your police pension, I would suggest that most people would not have too much difficulty living with their conscience."

Chap glared across the space between them. "That's because for most of your life you have dealt with dead people. Dead people no longer have a conscience. I'm not most people," he hissed. "I'm a cop, a damn good one. I've spent half my life putting the scum of society, scum like you and those you work for, behind bars."

Richardson got to his feet, somewhat unsteadily, and Chap's fingers again wrapped around the butt of the gun, ready to react in an instant.

"You have twenty-four hours to make a decision, Chapman," Richardson said. "I trust, for both our sakes, you will make the right one." He adjusted his coat.

"And if I don't?"

"That," Richardson confirmed, "would be most unwise."

Chap stared at Richardson's back as the doctor turned and walked across the room. When he reached the door, he turned slowly and looked back to where Chap still sat with the gun in his hand. "You know where to find me," he said. He opened the door and stepped out into the cold night.

Chap sat and stared at the door as it swung closed behind Richardson. "Oh, yes," he murmured to the empty room, "I know where to find you."

Retire—go fishing—put the past behind you. Richardson's advice echoed in his mind. "I hate fishing!" he announced aloud to the empty room.

Chapter Twenty-Eight

Chap lost track of how long he sat in the deepening darkness. He looked across at the fire and stared into the hypnotic flames. Then, he looked down at the glass sitting in a wet ring of condensation on the coffee table. He could not recall getting himself a drink. He reached forward, picked it up, and sipped the whisky. The ice had melted and it tasted weak, watery. He lowered the glass, rose wearily from his chair, and stepped across to the fireplace.

With a brass fire-iron, he stood and prodded the embers, sending a shower of sparks up the chimney. He was engulfed by mixed emotions: anger, lots of anger, confusion, frustration and, even though he hated to admit it, there was fear.

There had been a tingle of fear ever since the Eddie Dickson thing started. It was not a hand-shaking, leg-trembling, can't-think-straight kind of fear, nor was it as omnipresent as the fear he had known in the past, but it was there, nonetheless. As he stood in front of the fire, staring into the flames, he felt surrounded, smothered by an aura of depression.

A single bead of perspiration appeared on his forehead, rolled down between his eyes, down the length of his nose where it hung suspended for a second, and then dropped onto his chest. These were not new feelings for him. Over the years, he had experienced them all at one time or another. They were accepted as a consequence of his job as a police officer. Although he had known many moments of apprehension throughout his career as a cop, he could not remember ever being truly afraid. Not like the fear he knew in the jungle. That dry-mouth, damp-palms fear, its vice-like grip tightening around his chest, squeezing, pressing, tighter and tighter, making it difficult to breathe.

By his very nature, he was, most of the time, a level-headed, calm, clear-thinking individual, except perhaps when he was in the presence of his boss. George Baldwin had the seemingly effortless ability to bring out the worst in people, Chap included. Baldwin notwithstanding, Chap refused to allow himself to be consumed by the feelings washing over him. For a year, in Vietnam, he lived every day in the face of imminent death. He lived with and controlled the emotions then, and he would do so now.

He left the fireplace, crossed slowly to the window, and parted the drapes. A heavy film of condensation clouded the glass and he wiped his hand over the dampness. Outside, the street was deserted. No lights burned in the house across the road. There was just the dull glow of the street light, its image now indistinct through the foggy window. At that moment, Chap felt truly alone. He shuddered involuntarily, kidding himself it was from the cold, but, in reality, he knew he could no longer believe fear had not returned to his life—with a vengeance, it seemed.

Twenty-four hours. That was all the time he had. He glanced at his watch. Twenty-four hours from when? From when Richardson arrived, or from when he left? What was he thinking? With all that was going on in his mind, why was he concerned about thirty minutes either way? He shook his head, as if it might clear his mind of trivialities.

Twenty-four hours was more than enough time to gather the documents and hand them over. Plenty of time, if that was what he intended to do. It wasn't. There was no way he was going to give them what they wanted. To do so would surely be the precursor to his premature death. They would kill him, of that he had no doubt. They had already proved they were prepared to go to any lengths to keep the documents from falling into the wrong hands.

The ensuing hours would be a game of bluff, and Chap believed he held the advantage. They would wait the full allotment of time before moving against him and he figured that gave him a distinct edge. He would not, however, sit and wait for the next twenty-four hours to pass without doing something to bring this thing to some kind of conclusion. The days of sitting in a sniper's hide waiting for the enemy to show his head were long gone. He had to take the initiative. He had to become the aggressor.

He dropped the drapes, crossed back to the fireplace and dropped another log onto the coals. As it started to burn, he jabbed at it with the fire poker and stared intently at the flames as they licked and cracked at the dry wood. He wondered if, perhaps, a plan was beginning to manifest itself amidst the confusion clouding his mind. Slowly, but noticeably, as he gazed into the fire, he felt his anger begin to subside. It wouldn't disappear completely, nor did he want it to. He needed to be angry at these people. But, it was important he controlled the rage so he could remain focused and channel his anger in the right direction.

The fear he was feeling was in its right place now, too. Chap knew from his time in Vietnam that both anger and fear can make men react in different ways and often one of those ways was to panic. When faced with a life or death situation, he had learned that both these emotions, when controlled, could heighten one's senses and convey you to a place of disembodied but enhanced alertness and attentiveness and cause you to be more attuned to your surroundings. This was the place Chap wanted to be now.

Satisfied the fire was burning satisfactorily, he returned to his seat. As he sat there in the dim light, he thought about what Richardson said, about his telephone conversation with Tony Francis on the night he was killed, and about how the call was monitored. Did it mean that Richardson's people had managed to bug the phones at Police Headquarters? After some consideration, it was a scenario Chap gave little credence to. It seemed far too difficult, and risky, a task. But the alternative was frightening. Could one of his own people, someone from inside Major Crime, have heard the conversation and passed the details on to Richardson? This, too, was not a scenario he wanted to subscribe to but, at the moment, it seemed the most likely. The very thought of there being a crooked police officer inside Major Crime, or anywhere else within the force, did not bear thinking about.

To his surprise, but to his pleasure, he slept well. He was even more surprised when he realised, as he towelled himself dry following a shower, he was humming. Discordant strains of Neil Diamond's *Sweet Caroline.* His tuneless, hummed version was a long way from the melodic standard set by the great man himself, but it was at least recognisable. He looked at his image in the mirror as he ran a comb through his hair, and thought of Sally Prescott. Dear, sweet Sally. He recalled that she had commented once, early in their relationship, that he made a far better detective than he did a singer of songs. Chap smiled at the recollection.

His mood was light, and confident, perhaps even a little cocky. Although he knew he should be experiencing pangs of guilt because he felt so good, he wasn't. He was going to win, and it was this certain, unshakeable belief that lifted his spirits. He hummed some more as he made his way to the kitchen.

With his appetite soon appeased with his morning staple of toast and steaming coffee, Chap allowed his thoughts to drift to the business at hand.

First, there was Colonel Frederick W. Baxter. Somehow, he was involved in this mess. Eddie Dickson had said as much in his note. Now, Chap wanted to know just how he was involved. Given what Dickson had intimated, it would be a productive, not to mention enjoyable, experience if he could take the lying arsehole by the scruff of the neck and shake him until more than just his array of impressive medals rattled. But he could not travel to Canberra and be back in time for the twenty-four-hour deadline.

There had to be another way. As he poured himself a second cup of coffee, he decided he would ring Colonel Baxter.

It was not the same as being there, he conceded, but he could make it work. It was nothing more than a gut feeling, but Chap suspected Baxter would not be a hard nut to crack. He suspected that, behind the stiff, upright, military exterior, there lay a weakness he could exploit. If he could instil just the right amount of concern into the Colonel's mind, he might offer up some valuable information. It was an outside chance at best and, had he had the time to consider it more closely, he may well have discarded the idea, but outside chances sometimes paid off, and besides, it was the only one he had.

Things were not exactly as he would have preferred them to be but, given the limited information he had to work with, he was happy. He was feeling pretty good about himself. A plan of sorts had begun to materialise. It was not a clearly defined plan as yet, more a rough draft and he was bound to encounter obstacles during the execution phase, but nonetheless, the blueprint of a plan was there.

There was, of course, a distinct possibility that any plan

that manifested itself may never be crystal clear, and it was highly likely that, in coming days, he would find himself ad-libbing, sidestepping and detouring his way around, but he was glad he had at least some sense of direction, albeit obscure, to follow.

The first obstacle appeared sooner than he expected. It came when he placed a call to Central Army records in Canberra. Something was amiss. He sensed it as soon as he reached reception and asked to speak to Colonel Baxter. A prolonged pause followed, terminated a few minutes later by a request to hold. Military march music filled the earpiece while he waited, and he grimaced at the choice of 'hold' music. Finally, the same voice came back on the line, interrupting a brisk musical military march in mid-stride. The voice was soft, feminine and a little strained, Chap thought.

"Sorry to keep you waiting, Sergeant," the voice apologised. "I'm putting you through to the Colonel's secretary."

There was an audible *click* down the line, then a brief silence, followed by a voice he recognized.

"Hello, Sergeant Bouttell, this is Corporal Kelly."

Although Chap recognised her voice, it seemed different somehow, as if she had a cold, which was not surprising, he thought, given the weather in Canberra was worse than Adelaide. "Corporal Kelly," he said. "It's nice to talk to you again. It sounds like you have caught a cold."

"I'm sorry," she answered, a stammer evident in her voice.

An uncomfortable silence followed, punctuated by what sounded like gentle sobbing. Chap strained his ears to listen, remembering the bad line he had when he spoke to Tony Francis over the same distance. This was not a bad line. Corporal Kelly *was* crying. Or, she had been crying and was trying desperately to compose herself.

Chap found himself suddenly overcome by a strange, unwelcome, precognitive feeling. "Corporal Kelly," he asked, "are you alright? You sound upset."

"I'm sorry," she apologised again. "I'll be okay."

"I hope so," Chap said, with genuine concern. "I rang to speak to Colonel Baxter. I wonder if he would be available to talk to me?"

The corporal's response was a renewed bout of sobbing, and sniffing. The feeling of foreboding was stronger now and Chap's intuition kicked into overdrive. "Corporal Kelly, are you sure you're alright?"

Chap had never been adept at dealing with a crying woman. Back in his uniform patrol days, delivering news of the death of a loved one to a wife or parent was a task he always tried to avoid. Whenever he could, he would delegate the thankless task to his more junior partner and, on the few occasions he simply couldn't escape the duty, he found it to be perhaps the most difficult part of his job.

As he listened to Corporal Kelly on the other end of the line, he found himself becoming a little agitated, even frustrated, at her lack of honest response to his concern. Something was wrong, his intuition told him, and Corporal Kelly's sobs confirmed it. There was little he could do other than wait until she composed herself.

"I'm really sorry," she said finally, "it's just that… it's just that we received some more bad news this morning, about… about Colonel Baxter."

Chap knew what was coming next. How he knew, he couldn't explain if he tried. Intuitively, he knew the answer to his next question, but asked it anyway. "Colonel Baxter, what about Colonel Baxter?"

"He… he's… he's dead," Kelly announced, through a renewed burst of heavy sobbing.

Neither of them spoke for a few moments. Eventually, Chap could tell by the nose-blowing and sniffing on the other end of the line that Corporal Kelly was slowly regaining some degree of composure. He took advantage of the lapse in conversation to absorb the news and found it strange that he was not entirely surprised by it.

"What happened?" he asked finally.

There followed another momentary pause, this time without the accompanying crying. "The office security people found him this morning, in the building basement. He hanged himself," Kelly revealed.

"Suicide? Colonel Baxter committed suicide?" Chap was shocked. This was not what he expected. Somehow, he knew Corporal Kelly was going to tell him Baxter was dead, but he didn't expect his death to be suicide; he expected murder.

"The police said he probably did it last night, after everyone left the office," Kelly elaborated.

Chap's mind raced. "Are you sure? I mean, are the police sure it was suicide?" The instant the words were out, he regretted them.

"Wh… what do you mean?" Her tone was one of surprise. "Of course they're sure. What else would it be?"

Chap gathered himself quickly. "Nothing, nothing at all," he lied. "It's just that I never took the Colonel for the type to take his own life."

"Nobody did," Kelly agreed. "It was a shock to everyone."

"Yes, I'm sure it was. Do the police have any theories as to why he would do such a thing? Did he leave a note or anything that might explain his actions?"

"I don't know. They asked me to lock his office and allow no one in, and the basement has been put off limits to all staff until further notice. The police are still here. They said they want to talk to me later, to get a statement or something."

"You don't need to worry about that. You are the Colonel's secretary, it's natural they would want a statement from you, it's routine procedure."

When she didn't answer, Chap continued. "Listen, I've already taken up too much of your time. Please accept my sympathies. I know you admired and respected your boss."

The tremor returned to her voice. "Yes… I did. Thank you."

"You're welcome," Chap said. "You take care of yourself."

"I will. Thank you. Goodbye."

The line went dead as Corporal Kelly hung up. Chap held the handset to his ear for a few seconds, and then lowered it to its cradle. "Suicide, my arse!" he said aloud.

So now Baxter was dead. Chap did not know the man, and he had never been able to figure out why anyone could be driven to commit such a desperate act as suicide but, in this case, suicide did not wash with him. This was far too coincidental to be anything but murder.

"This is becoming a fucking pandemic!" he announced, to no one but himself.

These people were good; Chap had to concede that about them. They were bloody good. He could pre-empt the police findings with confidence. Baxter's death would be officially declared a suicide. That's how good these people were. They could easily make murder look like suicide, even under the closest investigative scrutiny.

There was some tiny part of his being, somewhere deep inside, that felt what could only be described as admiration for whoever they were. He was appalled that he should feel that way. However, whatever they did, including murder, they did with precision and efficiency. Their timing was perfect; impeccable, in fact. They were to be despised and reviled, he knew that, but somehow, strangely, they also had to be, on some level, admired. It was trite, of course, but he could only speculate at the good which might be derived if energies as efficient as these were to be channelled in a direction other than the path to evil.

Not for one moment did Baxter's death leave him disillusioned. In truth, if anything, it made him more determined. Until now, Chap had not given a lot of thought to the eventual outcome of his investigations and, as he did so now, he had to concede that it was highly unlikely anyone would ever be arrested and charged with the string of murders. It was a very real possibility that no one would be required to atone for their deeds. Not in this lifetime, anyway. That prospect made Chap angry, but it did not, and would not, dampen his determination.

He waited until mid-morning, filling the time with speculative scenario upon speculative scenario. His immediate plan was to pay another visit to the morgue, but he had to be sure that Dr. Lee Richardson would be there.

He checked his revolver. The Smith and Wesson Model 10 fitted snugly in his hand. Lately, it was becoming like an extension of his arm. He flicked open the revolving cylinder. It had the capacity for six rounds of .38 caliber ammunition but Chap only ever loaded it with five. He always left the chamber immediately to the left of the hammer empty. It was a safety precaution he had learned early in his career. Besides, he figured if he was ever faced with a situation where he was forced to use his weapon and five rounds wasn't enough to get the job done, it wouldn't matter, anyway. If a given situation reached that stage, a hundred more rounds would not save him. He clicked the cylinder shut and holstered the gun, then pushed the holster well back on his belt so it was out of sight when his jacket hung open. He breathed deeply, and felt the adrenaline rush through his veins. Now, he was ready, as ready as he was ever going to be, to take the fight to the enemy.

Chapter Twenty-Nine

The pathologist's car was parked in its usual place. As best as Chap could recall, the vehicle had been parked in the same place every day for as long as Richardson had worked at the morgue. Chap had seen the car almost every time he had reason to visit the city mortuary. However, when it had been following him, he had failed to recognise it as belonging to Richardson. Sometimes, the most difficult things to see were those under your very nose.

He found a vacant space next to the doctor's car and pulled into it. For a moment, he sat in the relative warmth of his rental car and looked at the other vehicle. Just before he got out, he removed his weapon from its holster and once again checked the ammunition. He was not planning on shooting anyone, and hoped he would not be placed in a position where he might have to, but, if the worst happened, it seemed appropriate to be adequately prepared.

As he had hoped, he found Richardson alone in the morgue. The pathologist was hunched over a long bench upon which sat a dozen or more large, sealed glass jars containing an assortment of human anatomy specimens. Livers, kidneys, lungs, and a variety of other grisly items Chap did not recognise, all preserved in a formaldehyde solution in the name of medical science.

One of the jars that always seemed to draw his eyes whenever he entered this place contained a human foetus in its early stages of development. To Chap, and he suspected, most people, it was a grotesque display. But this was pathology. It had to take a certain kind of character to do this kind of work every day. The gruesome display was the very thing that would raise the excitement levels of most people in the medical profession. It did very little for Chap's excitement levels, except perhaps to stimulate his morbid curiosity.

Dr. Lee Richardson did not hear Chap enter the dissection room, and he did not hear the *click* as the lock engaged on the doors behind him. He had his back to Chap as he leaned over a microscope, obviously engrossed in the study of some minute piece of cellular matter. As he worked, the findings of his examination were being recorded to tape to be transcribed in a later report. He did not hear Chap approach.

Silently, Chap removed the revolver from his hip and placed the muzzle against the nape of Richardson's neck, just below the hairline. Richardson stiffened, and tried to stand upright. The gun hurt as it ground hard into his neck, and he remained hunched over the stainless-steel workbench.

With his free hand, Chap reached around Richardson and pressed the off button on the suspended microphone. It would be best, he thought, if the ensuing proceedings remained strictly between the two of them.

A rush of panic surged through the pathologist. He tried to speak, but only managed to emit a stifled groan. His knuckles turned white where he gripped the edge of the bench.

Chap pressed the gun harder into the back of Richardson's neck, grabbed a fistful of his laboratory coat and yanked him roughly upright. "Good morning, Doc," he snarled. "The rain's gone, for the moment. The sun's out, and the birds are singing. It's a lovely morning for a nice, friendly chat, wouldn't you say?"

"Chapman!" Richardson croaked. "It's you. Shit, you scared me half to death!"

"That was the general idea," Chap confirmed. Holding the doctor tightly by the coat collar, he turned him around, hustled him across the room, and slammed him against the tiled wall. Now, they were positioned away from the bench where Richardson had been working, and out of view of the doors lest anyone should happen by and look through the window that filled their top half.

Richardson turned his head at the last second and avoided getting his face smashed against the wall. He could not, however, completely avoid the inevitable collision, and there was a loud crack as the side of his head smacked against the tiles.

Chap lifted the muzzle of the gun a couple of centimetres and saw that a dark, red circle, which would soon become a bruise, had formed on the back of Richardson's neck. Under his grip, he felt Richardson begin to tremble, and he had to tighten his hold to prevent the pathologist from collapsing to the floor.

He looked across to his right. Not two metres from where he stood, the naked body of a young woman lay lifeless on one of the cold, stainless-steel dissection tables. A crisp white sheet had been folded down and now covered only her feet and lower legs. Chap felt his eyes unavoidably drawn to her. She was pretty, even in death. Long, black hair flowed around her naked shoulders. Her pale, serene countenance reminded him of a sacrificial offering, lying in a potion-induced coma, awaiting the final act that would appease the gods. Chap estimated her age at twenty-two or three and, as he looked at the woman, he could see no signs of what had might have killed her. Death was not selective in who it chose, and that was a pity, he thought as he returned his attention to the pathologist.

In one sudden movement, he spun Richardson around so they faced each other. The hand that had gripped the collar of the lab coat now clutched the lapels, and Chap pulled Richardson a few centimetres away from the wall. Then, just as suddenly, he slammed him back against the tiles. Richardson's head hit the wall with a sickening thud, and the air rushed from his lungs. His breath in Chap's face smelled of coffee. The eyes staring back at Chap were filled with terror.

Chap squeezed tighter, twisting and bunching the material of the lab coat, giving it the ridiculous appearance of being several sizes too small for the doctor. He raised the revolver and placed the muzzle against Richardson's nose, at the corner of his left eye.

Richardson's eyes crossed and widened in fear as he tried to focus on the gun. Instinctively, he tried to pull away from the pressure of the gun against his face, an action which only served to throw his head backwards and it cracked again against the wall. He felt nauseated and wanted to faint, couldn't, and wished he would.

Chap moved his face closer to Richardson's, their foreheads almost touching. "You got Baxter, didn't you?" he hissed.

Shock registered on the doctor's face. "I… I don't understand. Wha… what do you mean?"

"Oh… that's right, I forgot. They only found him this morning, of course you don't understand. Never mind, perhaps your friends will send you a fax a bit later in the day and fill you in." The sarcasm in his voice was not lost on Richardson.

"What… what do you mean about Colonel Baxter?" Richardson stammered.

Chap pressed the gun harder into Richardson's face. "Oh please, don't insult my intelligence, Doc. No more lies. You know who Baxter is, or, should I say, *was.* You admitted as much when you were at my home. You know, just as you know of Dickson, Cobb and Elliott. You are not the small cog you claim to be. You are not the big boy, either, I admit, but you know far more than you have told me. It's time for the truth. It's confessional time. Time to wipe the slate clean."

Chap pressed his advantage. "The truth, Doc, or I'm going to kill you, and then I'll lay your pathetic corpse on a slab next to that pretty girl." He inclined his head towards the naked girl on the dissection table. "No one saw me come in here, and I guarantee you no one will see me leave. This gun"—he pressed a little harder into Richardson's face—"is a throw-down, and can never be traced to me," he lied. "Talk to me!"

"What about Baxter?" Richardson almost whispered.

"He's dead," Chap said. "Hanged himself, so I hear. Suicide is the official line. Suicide? Suicide, bullshit! Baxter was murdered, and you fuckin' well know it! You better start looking behind you, Doc. Your pals seem to be doing a bit of spring-cleaning. Perhaps they are a tad overstaffed and need to get rid of some of the dead wood."

"Baxter was not one of them," Richardson blurted.

It was the first positive response confirming what Chap already suspected; Richardson did know more than he had previously offered. However, this was a revelation Chap did not expect. He had assumed Baxter was one of them, and silently cursed himself for jumping to premature conclusions. This whole damn business had him imagining all sorts of bizarre scenarios. Was Richardson still lying? Was he really that stupid? Or that brave?

"Perhaps you didn't hear me, Doc. No more lies. You are in no position to bullshit to me anymore. I want the truth, and I want it now." With his thumb, he pulled the hammer of the revolver back, cocking the weapon. The audible *click* sent a new wave of terror through the pathologist. There was no fear of the gun discharging, as the act of cocking it rotated the cylinder clockwise one chamber, placing the empty chamber directly under the raised hammer. Even if the hammer were to fall accidentally, it would fall harmlessly on the empty chamber. Richardson, however, did not know that, and that was exactly how Chap preferred it.

"Jesus, Chapman, don't shoot me! Please!" Richardson was perspiring heavily. "It's the truth, I swear. He was not one of us. He was trying to blackmail us."

Blackmail! It was something Chap hadn't considered. It came as a complete and confusing surprise. Blackmail! He thought about it for a few moments. Slowly, ever so slowly, it began to make some sense.

Chap's oversight was the note from Eddie Dickson. He remembered the words at the end: *see Baxter, he's involved.* Chap wrongly assumed those words indicated Baxter was involved with the same people as Richardson. What it really meant was Dickson, and Baxter, were involved with each other, and with Cobb and Elliott, in blackmail. He didn't want to believe his former friends were involved in something as sinister as blackmail, but he hadn't seen any of them for forty years and people change. It was all starting to get too hard and it would be so easy if it would all just go away.

"Okay," Chap said finally. "Explain."

Richardson's legs were shaking. He knew that, if Chap let him go, he would crumple in a heap on the floor. "Please, Chapman," he pleaded. "Put the gun away."

"The gun stays," Chap said, emphasising his point by pushing the muzzle harder into the corner of Richardson's eye. "Now, explain."

"Dickson found the document by accident," the pathologist began. "He was doing some kind of research, and stumbled across it. It was supposed to have been destroyed immediately after the ambush, and both the CIA and ASIO thought it had been. Something went wrong. Somehow, it disappeared, and got buried in the system." He paused. His eyes crossed as he looked into the barrel of the revolver, and then he re-focused on Chap.

"Don't stop now," Chap prompted.

"At first, Dickson didn't know what to make of it. Of course, he realised its potential, but he didn't know what to do with it. He decided to show it to Cobb and Elliott. We believe that, after discussing it with them, a decision was made to take the document to Colonel Baxter. He was Dickson's commanding officer, and they needed to show the document to someone they could trust, so Dickson went to Baxter. Then, when Baxter realised the potential of the document, he decided to turn the information to his advantage."

"Blackmail," Chap offered.

"Yes. We think it was all Baxter's idea. He was a Colonel, and he was important. He also happened to be the National President of the Australian/American Armed Forces Association. Prior to his posting to Central Army Records, he served two years attached to the Australian Embassy in Washington." Richardson's voice was coming in short, laboured gasps. Chap hoped he was not about to have a heart attack. "He had access to the kinds of people he needed to approach in order to make blackmail demands."

"Go on," Chap ordered.

"Jesus, Chapman," Richardson pleaded. "I'm too old, and too weak, to overpower you. You can see I'm no threat to you. Please put the gun away."

"The gun stays. Get on with the story."

"Okay… okay." Richardson leaned back against the wall for support. "Baxter was well connected with politicians, embassy officials and other high-ranking military personnel, both in Australia and the US. He mixed in all the right circles."

"Come on, Doc, why blackmail? Baxter was a Colonel, for Christ's sake. A career soldier. He would have been making plenty of money. The army's a well-paid occupation these days. The only thing you've said that makes any sense so far is that it was all Baxter's idea. I find it hard to believe the other three would have gone along with it. I knew those blokes, and I would stake my life on all of them being honest and upright."

"We don't think any of them knew about Baxter's plans. He needed the money because he was touching the till," Richardson blurted.

"What?"

"Baxter was ripping off the government. His department received a large slice of the budget allocation each year to finance their continued research. He had control over the funds, and was siphoning off huge amounts to pay for a gambling addiction he developed in Washington, and continued when he came back to Australia. This was his chance to score big."

"What about the document?"

"Now, Baxter had a copy of it—Dickson kept the originals. Baxter rightly guessed there would be someone, somewhere, who would want the existence of the document to remain a secret. He told Dickson he would take care of everything, but we think that, somehow, Dickson found out what his boss was up to and called him on it. We also believe Baxter tried to buy his way out by offering Dickson and the others a cut of the proceeds in exchange for their silence."

"And Dickson refused and threatened to turn him in?" Chap speculated.

"Yes, we think that is what happened," Richardson confirmed.

"So, you think Baxter killed Eddie Dickson?"

"No. Dickson and the other two were doomed the minute they laid eyes on the document. Their deaths had nothing to do with Baxter's ambition to get rich."

Suddenly, it became still and quiet in the room. For a few moments, no words were exchanged between the two men.

No sound from outside the building filtered down this far into the heart of the Forensic Science Centre. In the distance, from another place deep within the basement, Chap could hear the soft hum of the electric motors keeping the body storage drawers at just the right temperature.

Richardson's breathing was more a laboured panting now, and perspiration flowed freely down his face. His pallor was ashen, not dissimilar to the colour on the face of the dead girl on the table nearby.

Chap's thoughts turned briefly to his friends and their betrayal by Colonel Baxter. He was certain none of them would have been involved in anything illegal. It had been a long time, and he knew that some people do change and, for reasons sometimes unfathomable, they do things which seem totally out of character. He conceded it was possible that one of his three old mates may possibly have fallen into such a category, but not all three. He dispelled the thought from his mind.

"What happened then?" he asked Richardson.

"Baxter went about asking discreet questions here and there," Richardson continued. "It was always only going to be just a matter of time before it got back to the right, or wrong, people. Eventually, someone made contact and apparently, Baxter produced his copy of the document to verify its existence."

"What was his price?"

"Two million dollars. In return, he would surrender the original as well as his copy of the document."

Two million dollars! It was a lot of money, even by today's standards. "But he didn't have the original," Chap reminded him. "Eddie Dickson did."

"They didn't know that." Richardson shrugged. "I suppose he believed he could convince Dickson to hand it over, for a price."

"Not bloody likely," Chap said. "Remember, I knew the guy."

It was not the amount that surprised Chap. Organisations like ASIO and the CIA had access to funds far greater than this amount, and he knew that much of it made up an unaccountable slush fund of sorts, used for all manner of nefarious schemes.

No, it was not *this* amount that surprised Chap; it was their paltry offer to him of one hundred thousand dollars that paled in comparison. He wondered if it was appropriate that he should feel slightly insulted. Given the lethal potential of the document, it was probably worth far in excess of the two million Baxter asked for. Perhaps he should have told Richardson to tell them to up their offer a few hundred thousand.

But Chap knew what Colonel Frederick W. Baxter obviously never considered; these people were never going to pay him one cent. Like Eddie Dickson, Charles Cobb and Brian Elliott, Baxter's life expectancy was severely abbreviated the minute they discovered he had the document. And, by extension, Chap also knew the likelihood of ever seeing the hundred thousand they offered him was similarly unlikely. He wondered, also by the same process of extension, if his own longevity might now be just as abridged.

Without realising it, Chap had lowered the gun slightly. It now pointed at Richardson's throat. The doctor's eyes followed the movement, but Chap left the weapon where it was now aimed. Richardson was right; he was no threat. He was a snivelling, cowardly excuse for a human being.

"Obviously," Chap concluded, "they were not prepared to deal."

"Of course not," Richardson confirmed. "Instead, they retaliated by eliminating Cobb and Elliott, both as a warning, and a demonstration, of just what lengths they were prepared to go to. They demanded the immediate, unconditional surrender of the document. There would be no deals, and no caving in to blackmail."

"If Dickson was aware of Baxter's plan," Chap posed, "why didn't he just turn him in to the authorities?"

"He wasn't aware, not at first. He thought Baxter was going to bring the document to the attention of the appropriate people, there would be an investigation and those responsible for the ambush would face justice. But then, Cobb and Elliott were killed and he began to suspect Baxter had betrayed him. Dickson confronted him and found out about the blackmail. Baxter was not expecting anyone to get hurt, but he had grossly underestimated who he was dealing with. He became consumed with greed and wanted to push on with the blackmail.

"He offered to cut Dickson in on the spoils but Dickson wanted nothing to do with it. The murder of his two friends was the end for him. If he wasn't aware of the volatility of the document before, he was when his friends were killed. He now knew the document's true worth, and it wasn't monetary. He knew what it meant for both Baxter and himself. He knew neither he nor Baxter were likely to survive, even if Baxter had a change of heart and abandoned his blackmail plan."

That would explain the argument between Dickson and Baxter that Corporal Kelly had overheard, Chap surmised. It was incredible. Like something out of an intricately plotted movie script. He believed Richardson now. The doctor was too afraid to tell him anything but the truth. Now, more than ever, Chap was convinced they would come after him, and soon.

"Baxter knew about you," Richardson was saying. "Dickson told him about you, and told him he planned to come here to see you and tell you everything."

Chap filled in the blanks. "Baxter acted as though I was just a cop investigating a murder. He was not about to tell me about any illegal activity he might have been involved in, like trying to blackmail the CIA, and ASIO. But, he let it slip that I was friends with Cobb and Elliott. Shit, where was his brain —on holiday?"

Richardson continued. "Greed possessed him. He foolishly believed, now that Dickson, Cobb and Elliott were dead, he could still carry off the blackmail."

"But," Chap interrupted, "he had nothing substantial to deal with. Dickson had the original document. How did he expect to…?"

The pathologist pre-empted the question. "We didn't know Baxter did not have the original document. He made the initial contact and the cash demand. It was assumed he had what he claimed he had. After all, he produced a copy. We had no way of knowing that Dickson had the original until it was too late. He had already mailed it to you. Baxter was sure we would assume *he* had the original, and would pay him the money on the strength of that assumption. Accordingly, he was convinced he could bluff his way through with a successful blackmail attempt."

Now, for Chap, it was all starting to make some sense. The terrible black secrets of the past, which had lain dormant and all but forgotten for the last forty years, had suddenly been unleashed, with a vengeance. It was starting to get out of hand, and those responsible for the atrocity against his unit were getting nervous. The body count was rising, and it was not over yet. How many more would die, Chap wondered, before it was over?

He relaxed his grip on Richardson, and was now more supporting him against the wall than holding him upright. However, Richardson, oblivious to Chap's slightly more casual stance, still exuded a countenance of fear.

"I assume," Chap said, "Dickson's trip here came as a surprise to your people?"

"It caught us off guard, yes. He had obviously decided it was time to get out of the mess that had been created, and that you were the one to help him. The fact that he made the trip in person led us to believe he had the original document on him. We never anticipated he might have mailed it to you."

"So, you intercepted him, and murdered him." Chap raised the gun and again placed the muzzle against Richardson's nose.

"Please, Chapman… it wasn't me," Richardson moaned. "I've never killed anyone. Please… you have to understand the extent these people will go to. They cannot afford to be exposed, and they cannot afford for the document to become public. They will prevent that at any cost."

"That's painfully obvious," Chap observed. The sight of the pathetic, pitiful, trembling figure in front of him disgusted him. Cowardice did not sit well with him.

"Stop snivelling, Doc. You made a conscious choice to do the things you have done. You must have known that one day, your deeds would come back and bite you on the arse. That day has arrived. The least you can do now is start behaving like a man. Grow some balls and accept the consequences of your actions."

"Are you going to kill me?" Richardson asked, his eyes pleading.

"I don't have to kill you, Doc. You're already dead. You died a long time ago. You died the day you said 'yes' to these people. Now, you are just a poor, pitiful excuse for a man. You make me sick, and while killing you would probably give me some measure of satisfaction, I can't bring myself down to the level to which you and your friends have sunk." Chap thought he saw a flicker of relief in Richardson's eyes. "I want you to take a message to your superiors…"

"They won't listen," Richardson wailed. "They have given you the deadline. You have no choice. You have to cooperate."

"Bullshit!" Chap spat, between clenched teeth. "You tell them this. Tell them to shove their deadline fucking sideways! I've got the document. You know it, they know it! Now, they play the game by my rules. You tell them there is a new deadline and I'm setting it."

"I… I don't understand," Richardson stammered.

"I want a meeting. Tell them I'm through with dealing with their spineless hired help. I want a meeting with the big boy, the boss cocky. Tell them they have until six p.m. tomorrow to contact me with the meet details."

"They'll never agree," Richardson insisted.

"They'd better," Chap countered. "Tell them if I haven't heard from them by six o'clock tomorrow night, they should tune into the late news on television. I'll be going public with everything I've got."

"Jesus, Chap, they'll kill you."

"Maybe, maybe not. At any rate, that is for me to worry about, not you. All you have to do is deliver the message."

Richardson moaned. "Jesus, Chapman, don't do this, you'll get us both killed. Jesus!"

"You may well call on Jesus, mate. Perhaps he will forgive you, because no one else will." Chap released his grip on Richardson's lab coat, and the doctor only just managed to regain his balance and support himself against the wall.

Chap lowered the hammer and re-holstered the revolver, leaving Richardson slumped uncomfortably against the wall. He turned away, crossed the room, and unlocked the doors. He could feel Richardson's eyes burning into his back. He turned to face the trembling medico.

"Oh, by the way," he said, casually, "the one hundred thousand dollars you offered me, tell your boss to bring it with him, and tell him to add another one hundred thousand to it." He paused. Something drew his attention to Richardson's feet. He glanced at the floor. A puddle slowly formed. The eminent, respected pathologist had pissed himself.

"Have a nice day." Chap smiled as he stepped from the morgue.

Chapter Thirty

The *Advertiser* lay on Chap's front lawn where it had been tossed in the cold, pre-dawn hours of the morning. Newspaper delivery, especially in the middle of winter, was a job he did not covet. He dashed across the wet grass, retrieved the paper, and hurried inside. With a steaming mug of hot coffee in front of him, he sat at his kitchen table, removed the plastic bag on the paper, and gasped at the headline blazoned across the front page.

GOVERNMENT PATHOLOGIST DEAD

Prominent Adelaide forensic pathologist, Doctor Lee Richardson was found dead late last night, slumped in the driver's seat of his car. While an official statement has not yet been released by investigating police, it is understood a firearm was recovered from the vehicle and…

The article continued for several paragraphs, and concluded with the suggestion that police were treating the death as a possible suicide.

"You have got to be kidding!" Chap exclaimed. Disgusted, he hurled the paper across the room. There was that word again. "Suicide."

For a long time, he sat at the table, sipping coffee and staring at the discarded newspaper on the floor. Eventually, he rose and recovered the paper. He discarded the bulk of the paper, and re-read the front-page article. Much of it was taken up with details of the pathologist's many achievements throughout his long and distinguished career. The sobering reality was, Chap thought, no one would know any different. There would be a lavish funeral, almost certainly funded by the taxpayers of the state and attended by politicians who would push each other aside for the opportunity to deliver a eulogy and thus show the voting public the soft and caring side of their character. Dr. Lee Richardson would be remembered as great and wonderful man whose contribution to medical science was second to none. What a crock, Chap thought.

It was a pathetic joke. Chap felt cheated. Not for himself, particularly, but for all the honest, hardworking people in the medical profession, not to mention Richardson's own family. It was plainly wrong that Richardson should be remembered with the glowing praises and tributes which would surely be bestowed upon his memory. Chap wanted to tell the world the truth about Dr. Lee Richardson. He knew he could not, and that angered him.

He had been a cop for a long time, and while he was prepared to admit there were examples from time to time of incompetence within the Police Department, it was not intrinsic. In any police force, anywhere in the world, where there were hundreds if not thousands of members, the sheer amount of numbers almost guaranteed there would be a degree of incompetence, even criminality, within the ranks. The South Australian Police Force could not expect to be excluded from this but, for the most part, Chap believed it to be second to none in the way it went about the job of policing. Still, he was finding it hard to believe Baxter's death, and then Richardson's, were both declared as suicides.

These conclusions were not arrived at as a result of incompetent investigations by police, by the ACT in Baxter's case, or by the South Australian police in Richardson's case. To Chap, this was another example of the effectiveness of the people who would stop at nothing to get their hands on the document of which he now had both knowledge and possession.

Had he died any other way than by gunshot, Chap might have entertained the suicide theory. Knowing the calibre of the people the pathologist worked for would be enough to drive anyone to the point of suicide. But, Chap knew how Richardson felt about guns. He was terrified of them. Chap doubted that the late doctor could even hold a gun, let alone put one to his head and blow his brains all over the interior of his car. As senseless as suicide was, it required a certain amount of courage and, in Chap's opinion, Richardson did not possess the intestinal fortitude required to shoot himself.

They had got to Richardson. He was weak. Chap had seen that in him; his killers would have seen it also. Richardson failed them. He failed to complete his assignment, and he knew too much. He was expendable and, once again, they fixed the problem swiftly and surely. It was simplistic, really; get rid of the problem and it is gone.

It did not escape Chap that Richardson had been his only link to these people. Perhaps his last link. Had Richardson delivered his ultimatum before they disposed of him? Chap could only hope so, but some small doubt niggled at him. Maybe this was their way of notifying him that they had received his message, as well as ridding themselves of a liability. The effect of killing Richardson was two-fold—it disposed of their problem, and sent a strong message to Chap.

All he could do was wait; he seemed to be doing a lot of that lately. He had to believe they would take his threat to go public seriously, but, with Richardson now out of the game, he was fast running out of options.

It was a long morning. He wanted to phone Sally. When he last saw her, she was afraid. He wanted to reassure her he was fine, but he dared not tie up the telephone. If a response to his ultimatum was to come, it would come here, to his home. They knew where he was. Lately, they seemed to always know where he was.

Their response could come in a number of ways. If they chose the telephone, he didn't want to miss it because he was tied up whispering sweet nothings down the line to Sally. He promised himself he would contact her as soon as he could.

When the phone finally rang, it startled him. It came exactly at noon. He stared at the phone, and listened to it ringing. When he finally picked up the receiver, he did not have to speak. The deep, monotone, robotic-sounding voice on the other end of the line ordered him not to. A deliberate and successful attempt had been made to disguise both the tone and the timbre of the caller's voice. Chap listened, and wondered if the person on the other end could hear the pounding of his heart against his chest.

The instructions would be given once, and once only, the voice insisted. Chap scrambled for a pen and paper, cursing himself for not being prepared. The instructions were delivered clearly and concisely. In less than thirty seconds, the line disconnected. The caller stayed on the line not nearly long enough to trace the call, even if he had been equipped to trace a call from his home. He held the handpiece to his ear for a moment. The voice was gone. Still, he waited. Finally, gently, he lowered the handpiece to its cradle.

Two p.m. was the time the anonymous voice had set down

for the meeting. Chap looked at his watch. He had two hours. He looked at the notepad on the table and noted the address. It was simple enough—a room in an office block, on the outer, eastern fringe of the city.

The possibility that he could be walking into a trap crossed his mind briefly, and he tried to discard the thought. If they wanted him dead, they had demonstrated they were more than capable of killing him at any time they chose; it was hardly necessary for them to lure him to some potentially fatal rendezvous. However, he knew his hasty and premature demise would be guaranteed if he was to take the document and all copies to the meeting as they demanded.

He gave little thought to what he was going to do or say when he got to the meeting. He only knew he was not going to give in to their demands. It was not rocket science. As long as he controlled the document, the odds were in his favour that he would maintain his continued good health.

He arrived at the designated office building early, thirty minutes before the appointed time. He wanted to get a look at the building before he went inside to face what was an uncertain reception.

Chap parked directly across the street and stared at the building opposite; an abandoned office complex, four floors of concrete, steel, and glass. He rummaged in his pocket and reviewed the directions. The address was correct.

The building was set to the rear of a large allotment, the front portion of the block being set aside as a car park. Adjacent to the entrance driveway, close to the footpath, there was a large real estate billboard advertising that the valuable investment property therein was for sale and would certainly appeal to the discerning property investor.

He looked beyond the sign, and ran his eyes slowly over

the facade of the building. It was familiar to him in that he had driven past it many times, although he had never afforded it anything greater than a passing interest. It had once been a government-owned building, leased to one of the large power supply companies. As best as he could recall, the building had been empty and the *For Sale* sign in place for a long time. Indeed, as he paid closer attention, he noticed small tufts of grass had pushed their way up through the asphalted surface of the car parking area.

From his vantage point across the street, Chap had a good view of the building. He deduced that anyone who might be inside the premises would also have an uninterrupted view of him. But that was fine. He wanted them to know he was there. He wanted them to know he was ready. Chap sat, watched and waited, occasionally glancing at his watch.

As the appointed hour approached, he felt himself becoming restless, his senses on high alert. He reached under his jacket, and touched the comforting shape of his revolver. Again, his eyes roved slowly over the facade of the deserted office complex. He could detect no movement in or around the building and the car park was empty. It appeared to be exactly what it was, a deserted office building.

Two p.m. exactly. He looked up at the entrance doorway. There, behind the glass, stood a figure. The doors seemed to be of heavily tinted glass, and it was difficult to see clearly, but there was someone in there, standing just inside the building, staring across the busy road at him, waiting for him.

For a few moments, they watched each other. Occasionally, a vehicle would pass along the road separating them, driving for a split second through their mutual line of vision. The stranger inside gave Chap no indication he was about to exit the building. It was obvious he was waiting for Chap to come inside.

Slowly, deliberately, Chap got out of the car. He stood alongside his vehicle for a few seconds, watching the building and the man inside. He allowed several cars to pass. The cold wind whipped a dirty spray from the passing cars, and he turned his face away. When he looked back, the stranger had not moved.

With a conscious effort not to appear anxious, Chap walked slowly across the street and into the car park. As he approached the entrance to the building, he saw the man had not moved and was still watching him as he crossed the car park. Chap glanced quickly around. Suddenly, he felt very alone, and very vulnerable.

He paused in front of the doors, only the thickness of the glass separating him from the man inside. If he entered the building, he was entering their territory. There would be no turning back. He recalled something one of his jungle training instructors said all those years ago: "The first step to winning a war is to know your enemy."

"Okay, let's get to know you," he murmured softly, as he reached out, grasped the heavy chrome door handle and pulled it toward him. The door swung open easily. He stepped inside.

The stranger took a pace to one side. "Please, step away from the door," he ordered.

Chap eyed the man for a moment, then turned his head and watched the door close behind him. He did not move. He looked back at the man. He was big, every bit of two metres tall and then some, he guessed. And he was not just tall. Underneath the dark suit jacket, he had muscles on his muscles. Shit, Chap thought, this bloke had muscles on his breath!

Chap looked at the man's eyes. The eyes were the mirror to the soul, or so they say. The man's eyes were cold and calculating. It took Chap just a few seconds of staring into those eyes to arrive at the conclusion that the man who loomed over him almost certainly had no soul. He was not your everyday, brain-dead, steroid-gulping, iron-pumping moron. He was,

Chap quickly deduced, fit, alert, and very dangerous. Mildly intimidated by the man's size, Chap refused to let him see it.

"Please, step away from the door," the man said again.

Chap stepped away from the door.

Silently, and with an agility at odds with his size, the man-mountain moved in front of Chap and slipped the bolts on the doors, locking them. Escape, should it become necessary, was not going to be made easy for Chap. And, should he have brought reinforcements with him, waiting discreetly somewhere nearby, they would be unable to gain easy access.

The stranger turned and faced Chap, his eyes expressionless. He held his hand out, palm upwards. "Your weapon, please," he demanded.

Chap stood his ground and returned the gaze. "Sorry, if it's all the same to you, I think I'll hang on to it."

This was not a man used to being disobeyed. He did not even blink. It was as if he hadn't even heard Chap. He remained standing with his hand out. "Your weapon, please," he insisted again.

Now was the time, Chap concluded, to exercise some authority. He took one step closer to the giant and looked him straight in the eye, although he had to crane his neck to do so. He was determined not to show any weakness. "Listen, Bozo," he said quietly but firmly. "This is my party. I sent the invitations. Now, we do this my way, or we don't do it at all. I'm a cop, but then you know that. I was taught a long time ago never to surrender my weapon. You, my newly acquired friend, and I use the term 'friend' very loosely, will have to kill me to get it, and I would suggest such drastic measures on your part would not exactly endear you to your boss."

He glared up at the hulk of a man, who was quite obviously not intimidated or moved in any way by Chap's oration. The man was a stone. It wasn't that Chap expected his display of machoism to turn Bozo's rock-solid resolve crumbling into a quivering jelly of fear, but he had hoped to make some small impression, at least. If there was any advantage to be had at all, Chap decided to press for it. “Now, shall we go?” He indicated to the empty foyer behind the man he had now christened Bozo.

Bozo looked at Chap, as though weighing up his options. Chap guessed this was probably the very first time he had ever met resistance from anyone. Finally, the big guy stepped to one side, allowing Chap to move ahead of him.

As Chap expected, Bozo fell in behind him. Not so close as to place himself in a position of danger, and not so far behind as to be unable to react quickly should it become necessary. Bozo was good, sharp, and every bit the professional, Chap thought. He decided then and there, he was not going to give this bloke any reason to tackle him; those arms could hold a bull out to piss!

This was Chap’s opportunity to take in his surroundings. They were in the entrance foyer of the complex. Being empty, it looked too large for its intended purpose. In front, and to his left, there was a lift. Assuming this was where it was intended he should go, he made his way across the tiled foyer to where the lift stood with its door open. As they moved across the foyer, he glanced quickly around the vast, empty space, looking for what, he did not know. He paused momentarily in front of the open lift door, and then stepped inside. Bozo followed.

The big man, whose bulk seemed to fill half the confined space, positioned himself behind Chap. “Remove the door jamb,” he ordered.

Chap looked down at the lift door track and saw a piece of strong timber dowelling had been placed there to hold the door open. He bent down and removed it. With a loud hiss, made louder by the cavernous emptiness of the foyer, the door slid closed. Suddenly, for the first time in his life, Chap felt claustrophobic. A small plate attached to the control panel indicated the lift was licensed to carry twelve people. It seemed overcrowded as he felt Bozo's breath on the back of his neck.

"Fourth floor," Bozo said.

Chap pressed the corresponding button on the control panel and, like the hiss of the closing lift door, the sound of the lift motor was amplified in the empty, hollow office complex. He felt the gentle, stomach-churning feeling as the lift ascended through the first three floors. Then it jolted to a halt. The lift door hissed open.

"Fourth floor!" Chap announced. "Ladies' lingerie, petticoats, bras and crotchless panties!" He turned his head and smiled up at Bozo.

If Bozo was amused, he did not show it. Was there no pleasing this guy? This was one mean, humourless prick who really needed to get out more. He must have the social life of a gnat, Chap thought.

Chap stepped from the lift and found himself facing a smaller version of the ground floor foyer area. Like its much larger counterpart four floors below, this area, too, was empty and unfurnished. To his left and right, a long corridor ran the length of the building and along this corridor there appeared to be a series of individual offices.

With a not too subtle shove in the back, Bozo steered him to the left corridor. "Second door on the right," he commanded.

"Jesus, steady on, big boy!" Chap complained as he stumbled forward. "These old bones are getting brittle."

The first door they passed was closed. Chap glanced at the number on a small plate attached to the door jamb. It was one less than the number he had received in his instructions over the phone. The next room would be the one. His pulse quickened with anticipation. He reached the door and stopped in front of it. There was, he figured, no point in delaying the inevitable. He grasped the doorknob, turned it, and pushed inwards.

He found himself in a small room; a secretary's domain, it seemed to Chap. The room was empty—no desk, no chair, no furnishings of any description. Chap stepped further into the room. Bozo followed close behind.

Directly in front of him, on the other side of the small room, was a second door. It, too, was closed. Behind this door, Chap reasoned, would lie the main office. He did not linger. He walked across the faded carpet and opened the door.

He stepped into a spacious office, made all the more spacious by the lack of furnishings. Directly opposite was a wall of windows which he guessed overlooked the street below. From these windows, he suspected his arrival at the rendezvous had been observed. To the left of the door, and almost behind him, sat a solitary office desk he hadn't noticed when he first opened the door. He turned and looked at it. It looked out of place. There was nothing on it. No papers, no pens, no desk lamp, nothing. A solitary chair stood, unoccupied, behind the desk. Chap slowly surveyed the room. His escort, Bozo, stood at the ready in the open doorway, barring his exit lest he decide to make a hasty retreat, which, as it happened, was right up there on his list of things to do, sooner rather than later.

Chap smiled sarcastically at the big man. "Is that chair for me?"

Bozo responded with a cold, blank stare. Chap shrugged, turned and walked across the room. For a moment, he stood in silence and gazed out of the window into the wintry day beyond. Rain, heavy and unrelenting, crashed silently against the double-glazed window pane. He did not hear the third man enter the room. When he turned away from the window, he was surprised to see the chair behind the desk was now occupied.

Chap took a few seconds to study the newcomer. He was possibly in his late fifties, distinguished-looking, and immaculately dressed. His hair was dark, with hints of grey at the temples. His face was clean-shaven, and the clear, steel-grey eyes, set wide apart and focused, gave nothing away. Chap recognised immediately that there was a definite aura of authority about the stranger.

Chap lowered his gaze to the man's hands, resting, fingers laced, on the desktop. Even from across the room, Chap could see the man's hands were clean and well-manicured. You could tell a lot about a man by his hands, and his shoes. He could not see the man's shoes under the desk, but he was willing to bet they would be fashionable and highly polished.

For a few moments, the two men eyed each other, neither blinking. Chap's attention turned to the man's posture and bearing. He might have been a lawyer, or a doctor, such was his professional, business executive-appearance.

When the stranger finally spoke, his voice reflected a man of excellent education and obvious fine breeding. His tone displayed a quiet but distinct, even mildly pleasant timbre. Chap baulked inwardly at the thought that, in another time, another place, perhaps another lifetime, he might have found something in this man to like.

"So, Sergeant Bouttell, finally we meet." The man smiled.

The office door was closed now, and Bozo had taken up a position of determined vigil in front of it; his arms, as big as tree trunks, were folded across his huge chest. "He still has his weapon," he said to the man behind the desk.

Chap crossed the room, positioned himself directly in front of the desk, and glared down at the man seated there. He heard Bozo step up behind him, but he did not flinch; he refused to flinch.

The newcomer looked beyond Chap and gestured to his hired help. "It's alright," he said calmly. "Sergeant Bouttell is not about to do anything foolish, are you, Sergeant?"

"That depends," Chap answered. "Would killing you be considered foolish?"

"Extremely." The man smiled again.

Chap ignored the response. "You have me at a disadvantage. You know who I am, but, who the fuck are you?"

"Names are not important here, Sergeant. However, if it makes you more comfortable, you can call me… ah… Jones. Yes, Jones. It has a nice ring to it, don't you think?"

"And I'm Brad Pitt," Chap scoffed.

"As you wish, Sergeant," the man said dismissively. "May I remind you, we are here at your request. I do not intend to stay long. So, please, state your business."

It was just the sort of condescending attitude that lifted Chap's anger level into the stratosphere. He leaned forward and glared down at the man behind the desk. "Don't give me that inconvenienced executive crap, you fucking low-life!" he said, between clenched teeth. "You are no more of a man than that testosterone-overdosed gorilla behind me." He jerked a thumb in the general direction of Bozo. "When it comes right down to it, you are nothing but murdering scum, and the expensive suit and polished shoes can't disguise that."

Jones did not appear overly moved by Chap's outburst. He did, however, absently and instinctively smooth the lapels of his suit jacket. "I did not come here to be insulted, or to listen to your character analysis," he said. "I assume you are anxious to come to some sort of arrangement with me. Why don't we dispense with the peripheral insults and name-calling, and get on with it?"

Chap was repulsed by the self-titled 'Mister Jones'. He wanted to reach across the desk, grab him by the scruff of the neck, physically drag him across the top of the desk, and crush the life out of him. It would mean no more to him than swatting a fly. "Oh, we are going to come to an arrangement alright," he hissed. "Effective from today."

Jones leaned back in his chair. A smug smile formed on his face. "Good. That's why I'm here. I'm interested to hear your proposal."

"It's simple," Chap shrugged. "I want you to back off."

"What precisely do you mean, 'back off'?"

"You know exactly what I mean. Too many people have been murdered by your lot. The killing stops and it stops now!"

With what seemed like genuine surprise, Jones responded, "Surely, Sergeant, you are not threatening me?"

"Jonesy," Chap answered, "I'm not threatening you, you miserable, worthless piece of shit, I'm promising you! You seem to have forgotten, I have the way, and the means, to put an end to you and your people, once and for all."

"You would, of course, be referring to the document now in your possession?"

"Go to the top of the class, Dipstick."

His words still seemed to be having little effect. Jones was cool, calm, even appearing to Chap to be mildly bored. He leaned back casually in his chair and folded his arms across his chest. The wry, smug smile was still there. It was a posture a body language expert might deem to be an expression of non-aggressive superiority. This was a man who could take all that Chap had to give, and still maintain his composure.

"Sergeant Bouttell, let me make something perfectly clear." He paused. "I would have thought that, by now, you would be fully aware of the consequences, should you make the decision to go to the media with what you have learned in the last few days. However, in the event you are not, please indulge me while I enlighten you." He paused again and cleared his throat, choosing his words carefully. "Naturally, I do not wish to elaborate on the composition of the establishment I represent. Suffice it to say, we have a power base which extends across international boundaries. The chain of command reaches deep into the corridors of political, commercial and military power. Believe me when I tell you, Sergeant, that if the information which has unfortunately come into your possession were to become a matter of public knowledge, the fallout could conceivably destroy the very fabric of the democratic process as we know it, both in this country, and the United States.

"You are an intelligent man, Sergeant Bouttell, I've learned that much about you. The wisest course of action for you at this time is to hand over the document, and any copies you might have made."

An uncomfortable silence filled the room. Finally, Jones reached down beside his chair and lifted a large, black sports bag onto the desk. Without taking his eyes off Chap, he unzipped the bag and pushed it forward to the front of the desk.

Chap leaned forward slightly and looked into the bag. It was full of money, lots of money; neat bundles of one hundred-dollar notes. It was all Chap could do to appear unimpressed. In truth, it was damn near impossible. He dragged his eyes away from the bag and looked at the stranger.

"There is two hundred and fifty thousand dollars in there," Jones indicated the bag, and pushed it a little closer to the front of the desk. "As a token of our good faith, we have decided to increase the amount you asked for by fifty thousand. And, I might add, in case you are wondering, they are all used, unmarked, untraceable notes. You can take it now, right now, and walk away from here unhindered. All that is required of you is that you leave the document here with me and, of course, forget you ever saw it."

Chap lowered his eyes and looked again at the money in the bag. He took a step closer to the desk, leaned forward and placed both hands, palms down, on either side of the bag. He heard a shuffling noise behind him and turned his head to see Bozo had moved a little closer to him in an instinctive, protective reaction towards his boss.

"Easy, Bozo," Chap said over his shoulder. "Don't snap your lead."

Jones gestured to his minder, and Bozo stepped back to his original position by the door.

"I assume you have the document with you?" Jones asked Chap.

"You give me credit for intelligence," Chap scoffed, "and you expect me to have it with me? That's not why I called for this little get-together." For the first time since he entered the room, Chap was sure he noticed a flicker of annoyance in Jones's eyes.

"In that case, Sergeant," Jones said, his voice betraying a degree of impatience, "perhaps you would care to enlighten me as to why you *did* ask for this meeting?"

Chap pushed back from the desk and stood erect. He was enjoying this. "What we have here, you prick, is a stalemate. Here's how I see it. If I give you what you want, it is reasonable, I think, for me to assume I could not expect to live another twenty-four hours, and any promises you might make to the contrary are worth jack shit to me. If I choose to spill the beans with what I have, the shit will really hit the fan, and we both know my life expectancy would be about the same. You see, I'm on a hiding to nothing. I'm a dead man either way. I'm smart enough to figure that much out. The truth is," he added, "I'm not ready to die, and I assume you and your friends are not ready to be exposed for the scum you are."

Chap paused, smiled lightly, and stared at Jones. "Am I going too fast for you? If you give me a pen and paper, I could write it down for you."

"Please continue," Jones invited.

"I am going to walk out of here unhindered. And, what's more, I am going to remain unhindered until I die of old age, peacefully in my sleep. I am not going to give you the document. And it might also interest you to know that I have added to my insurance with this..." He reached into his pocket and withdrew a miniature tape recorder. It was one he sometimes used for conducting records of interview with suspects. He held the recorder out in front of Jones. The tape was running, and the muscles in Jones's face tightened visibly. "Our entire conversation here today is on tape," Chap continued. "Along with two other conversations I had at my home, and at the morgue with the recently deceased Dr. Lee Richardson. You remember the good doctor, don't you?"

Had a crack finally appeared in the facade presented by the mysterious Mr. Jones? Was that a tiny hint of concern Chap saw reflected in his eyes?

"You will make no attempt to retrieve this tape, or the document," Chap advised. "Of course, the tape will be duplicated, and you will never how many copies I might choose to make."

"And, if I agree to your conditions, what's in it for us?"

"My silence." Chap smiled.

Jones shifted in his chair. "It would seem you now have *me* at a disadvantage, Sergeant Bouttell."

"I've got you by the short and curlies, mate!"

"Yes… quite. However, you must know we have conducted considerable research into your background over the years. Together with the records we already have in relation to your military service, we have compiled a rather substantial profile on you."

"If that is designed to impress me, it doesn't," Chap countered.

Jones dismissed the interruption. "Given all the information we have gathered, you come across as an honest police officer. You have a tendency to deviate from acceptable procedure from time to time, and we know that has brought you into conflict on more than one occasion with your superior. But by and large, you have never exhibited any blatant dishonesty. In recent times, you have attained knowledge of a conspiracy between the United States and Australia, to commit murder, if I may put it bluntly." He paused.

"Please," Chap invited with undisguised sarcasm, "put it

bluntly."

Jones ignored the remark. "Let's not be pedantic. After all, that's what it amounts to. Murder. I'm interested to know how you propose to live with that knowledge and do nothing about it."

It was a fair question, one Chap had been asking himself ever since he first read the document. He shifted his weight from one foot to the other, becoming ever so slightly restless. He wanted to be away from this room, and these people.

"Let me make myself perfectly clear, Mr. Jones," he began. "You and the people you work for disgust me! The citizens of this country, and those of the United States, deserve and are entitled to expect that the people they entrust with the job of making decisions for the benefit of their country are of the utmost integrity. You and your misguided band of thugs have betrayed that trust, not to mention making a mockery of the constitution under which we live. So, I agree, let's *not* be pedantic. You are gangsters! Common crooks! All of you! Fucking vermin! I will live with what I have learned. It will bring me no peace of mind—only anger, bitterness, and contempt. Contempt for you, and all you stand for, and contempt for myself for not acting on the information I have in my possession. But I *will* live with it!"

Chap's fists were clenched tightly at his sides, his knuckles white. How simple it would be to reach inside his coat, pull out his revolver, and place a .38 caliber bullet neatly between Jones's eyes, or perhaps not so neatly; he had little concern for the aesthetics of the man's death. The urge to put one in his forehead was, nonetheless, strong. Just as it had been with the late Dr. Lee Richardson. It had been a long time, forty years, but killing was akin to riding a bike, he figured. Once you learn how to do it, you never forget.

He unclenched his fists. Bozo had, once again, moved from the doorway, and was standing close behind him. He was sure to be fast on his feet, despite his huge bulk. That was not blubber under his clothing that was stretching his shirt tight across his chest. It was pure, unadulterated muscle, primed and ready to explode. Even if Chap were to succumb to temptation and dispatch Jones to the hereafter, where he surely belonged, Bozo would have him cold. He fought against the urge to act, and slowly regained his composure. Once more, Jones gestured to Bozo. This time, the big man promptly left the room and closed the door behind him.

Chap was left alone with Jones. Now, thoughts of killing him returned. He did not think Jones would be armed. People like him did not do their own dirty work. That's why they had buffoons like Bozo on the payroll. Chap wondered if Bozo knew what a knife-edge between life and death he actually walked. If it became necessary to protect themselves from exposure, men like Jones would terminate men like Bozo in a heartbeat, and not lose a minute's sleep over it. So much for job security!

Both men stared at each other. In the silence that followed, Chap wondered where Bozo had gone. Perhaps his little tête-a-tête with Jones was over and he was expected to leave, too. A minute or two passed without a word between himself and Jones. It bothered Chap a little that Bozo had not yet returned. He couldn't put his finger on it, but something pricked at the back of his mind, telling him to stick around a little longer. Finally, Jones spoke.

"You do realise, Sergeant Bouttell, that you will carry this knowledge around with you for the rest of your life, however long that may be." The bastard was smiling again; that smarmy smirk Chap would love to wipe off his face.

"Yes, I realise that," he responded.

"And, for the rest of your life, the rest of mine, and for many years thereafter, the people I represent will still be around. Their operations will continue and yes, it is possible that, from time to time, it may be deemed necessary that others may have to be silenced. You do realise that, don't you, Sergeant?"

"I realise that."

"There is one thing that concerns me, however," Jones admitted.

"I'm sorry to hear that," Chap said, with as much sarcasm as he could muster.

"Tell me, what assurance do I have that, at some time in the future, you won't have a change of heart?"

"No assurances." Chap shrugged dismissively. "If I decide my conscience weighs too heavy and it's time to unburden, so be it. You and your people will have to fend for yourselves."

"Of course, if it were to come to that, you would be signing your own death warrant."

"If it were to come to that, I would have already come to terms with the consequences."

Jones shifted in his chair. "It would appear, Sergeant, that our meeting is almost at an end. I deeply regret that we were unable to arrive at a compromise. However, there is one more thing before we part company."

"I can hardly wait."

"Your little display earlier, with the tape recorder. Extra insurance or something was the term you used."

"I like the term 'covering my arse' better." Chap shrugged.

Jones ignored the remark. "In some ways, we are very much alike, you and I."

"Only in respect of the fact we both have differing opinions as to how alike we are. Why don't you get to the point?"

"As you wish." There was that slimy, lizard-like smile again. "Insurance, my friend, insurance. You see, I anticipated you would have a trick or two up your sleeve. So, I had the foresight to take out some insurance of my own."

"Okay," Chap said, "I'll play the game. What insurance?"

"We know from our comprehensive research that you are a man more than capable of committing the supreme act."

"What the fuck is that supposed to mean?"

"Heroic martyrdom, Sergeant, heroic martyrdom."

"You're full of shit!"

"Obviously, we could hope you would keep what you now know to yourself, but that is a gamble we are not prepared to take. Not on nothing more than your word alone. Besides, even if you decided to risk your life and make public what you know and then go into hiding… you know, witness protection or whatever, it is conceivable that you might escape our retribution for some time. Such a situation would, of course, be unsatisfactory."

"Spare me the rhetoric, mate," Chap glared. "Get to the bloody point. You are really starting to piss me off."

"As you wish. Please turn around, Sergeant."

Chap turned to see the door swing open. He gasped audibly as Sally Prescott was pushed forcibly into the room. She had obviously been crying. Her cheeks were dark with smudged mascara. The big gorilla, Bozo, was right behind her, wearing a smug, self-satisfied smile. Chap wanted to pistol-whip the smile from his face.

"Jesus Christ," was all he could manage to say.

When Sally saw him, she almost collapsed. She stumbled forward and fell into his outstretched arms. Chap crushed her tightly to him, and she clung desperately. Her hair was untidy, and Chap found himself running his hand over it, straightening it.

Sally began to sob. "Oh, Chap… oh, Chap." Her voice was muffled as she buried her face into his jacket.

"It's okay," Chap whispered into her hair. "It's okay. Everything is going to be okay. Shh…. shh, I'm here." He took her face in his hands and gently lifted it so she was looking at him. Chap smiled reassuringly and kissed her lightly on the forehead. Sally placed her head against his chest again and clung even tighter.

Chap looked over the top of her head and glared at the

smiling, gloating Bozo. "I'm gonna wipe that smile off your face, you fucking retard." He turned back to face Sally. "Did he hurt you?"

"N... no," she sobbed, her chest heaving against his. "Who are these people, Chap?"

"They are scumbags," he heard himself say. "Lowlife scumbags."

"What do they want?"

"I'll explain it all to you later, I promise. Are you sure you're alright?"

"I'm scared, Chap."

"I know, I know, Sally."

Chap's anger was rising; fast. He raised his arm and pointed directly at Jones. "Why her?" he spat.

"It is as I explained," Jones shrugged. "Extra insurance. You have already demonstrated you are familiar with such precautions."

"But why her? Jesus Christ, she has nothing to do with any of this."

Jones shrugged. "I don't expect this to be of any consolation to you, but our involving Ms. Prescott is a regrettable course of action for us. After all, now there are two outsiders who are aware of our existence. However, given the need for the utmost security, and given your very obvious feelings for Ms. Prescott, it has been decided that her continued good health would be sufficient incentive for you to keep your end of the deal." He paused for effect. "The lovely lady has not been harmed, with the exception, perhaps, of her pride. Her presence here is a practical demonstration of our ability to reach you, and those close to you, at any time we choose. I trust my little demonstration will produce the desired results."

Jones stared at Chap, waiting for some response. None came.

Chap reached into his pocket and removed his car keys. He turned to face Sally, gently pushed her away from him and held her at arm's length. He looked into her eyes and saw her fear. His heart leapt out to her. He just wanted to hold her close and take away her pain and fear. He leaned forward, his face close to hers, and offered her the keys. "My car is parked across the street, in front of the building. It's a rental, a white Ford. The lift you came up in is just a few doors away, down the corridor. Take it to the ground floor. The main doors are probably locked from the inside. It's just a bolt. Unlock the doors and go to the car. Wait there for me."

Sally began shaking her head before he could finish his instructions. "No," she insisted. "No, Chap. You come with me, please."

"I'll be right behind you, Sally. Go. I'll be okay. I'll be right there, I promise." Chap escorted her slowly but deliberately to the door. Sally looked up at him, her eyes pleading.

"I'll be right behind you, I promise," Chap said again. He leaned forward and kissed her lightly on the mouth.

Only the big man stood between them and the door. He held his ground. Chap placed a hand in the middle of his broad chest and pushed. Bozo did not move, but he did glance across at Jones. His boss gave him a sign, and he stepped aside, exposing the open door.

As Chap gently ushered Sally through the door, he placed the car keys in her hand and closed her fingers over them. There was a pleading in her eyes that he found almost too painful to resist and he almost followed her from the room. He watched her as she backed slowly, hesitantly, towards the outer door and into the corridor beyond. Just before she turned and disappeared from his view, he saw her mouth the words, "I love you." His heart ached anew.

Chap stood in the open doorway and waited until he heard the lift door open and then close. Only when he heard the soft, distant whirring of the lift motor did he move. He turned, and looked across at Jones. Then he walked across the room, stood in front of the window and looked out into the street four storeys below.

It seemed like forever that he stood there watching his car across the road. Sally must be having trouble with the front doors, he thought. He was beginning to feel the first pangs of concern when, finally, he saw her. She stepped from the front of the building and began to walk across the car park, towards the street and his waiting car. Although it was raining now, she did not seem to hurry. Halfway across the car park, she turned and looked back at the building. She looked at the doors from which she had just come and then at the wall of windows above. She raised her hand to shield her eyes from the rain.

The window where Chap stood was tinted and he assumed all the others were the same. A person could see outside with ease but it would be difficult for anyone on the outside to see inside the building. He knew that as hard as Sally tried, she would not be able to see him watching her. He silently urged her on, willing her to get to the car. For a brief, frightening moment, he thought she was going to come back into the building. Suddenly, she turned away and hurried into the street. Chap breathed a sigh of relief. He watched as she waited for a pause in the traffic and then hurriedly crossed the street to the car. She fumbled with the keys momentarily, and then she was inside.

Satisfied Sally was safe for the moment, Chap turned his back to the window and walked slowly across the room to where Jones sat unmoved.

"If anything happens to her," Chap stated, "anything at all, I will kill you! I will find you and I will kill you. Do I make myself perfectly clear?"

"May I remind you, Sergeant," Jones answered, "that you, and only you, hold Ms. Prescott's safety in your hands. Provided you keep your part of our arrangement, no harm will come to her, or to you."

"Don't forget me, you arsehole," Chap cursed. "Take a

good, long look at this face and believe me when I tell you that if you, or anyone else," he paused and glared across at Bozo, "harms a hair on her head, I promise you, you will see me again, and I swear, you will regret the godforsaken day you were born!"

Both men stared at each other for a few seconds, each acutely aware of the power the other held.

Finally, Jones stood and held out his hand. "I wish I could say meeting you has been a pleasure, Sergeant Bouttell. Never mind." He shrugged. "Perhaps another time, and another place."

Chap looked at the outstretched hand with scorn. He slowly raised his own hand, reached out and picked up the sports bag containing the money.

"You're still going to take the money?" Jones asked.

Chap merely smiled, turned away, and crossed to the door. Bozo had resumed his position in front of the exit, and he stood firm as Chap stopped in front of him. "Move it or lose it, stupid," Chap ordered.

Bozo did not move. He glanced down at the sports bag in Chap's hand, and then at his boss. Again, he received a silent signal and he started to step aside.

Chap was anxious to get out of there, and Bozo's movements were just a fraction too slow for his liking. In one, lightning-fast movement, he launched from his left foot and thrust his right knee upwards, between Bozo's legs, with as much force as he could without throwing himself off balance. He felt the point of his knee sink deep into the big man's groin with a sickening thud.

Bozo gasped loudly. A rush of air escaped his throat with a loud whistle. He grabbed at his abdomen with both hands, and his legs began to buckle. His head lolled involuntarily forward, presenting Chap with target far too inviting to resist.

Chap hit him hard and fast in the face. He felt bone and cartilage crunch and tear as Bozo's broad nose collapsed into a mushy, bloody mess. It was two equal and opposite forces coming together. The knee in the groin caused Bozo's head to fall forward, and then the blow to the face caused his head to snap back with such force that he seemed to hang, suspended on wobbly legs, as though his body was wrestling with the decision of which way to fall. Then, as if in slow motion, his knees buckled under him, and he toppled, like a giant falling oak tree, to the floor. As he crashed headlong onto the carpet, Chap could have sworn he felt a mild tremor rumble through the office block

Chap waited for a moment, pain searing through his hand, and looked down at the crumpled heap on the floor. Blood from Bozo's smashed nose began to flow freely onto the carpet. Chap rubbed his sore hand and flexed the fingers. It felt broken, and hurt like hell. He bit down hard on his lip to prevent himself from crying out with the pain. Letting on that he, too, was hurting, was simply not an option.

He turned and looked back at Jones, who seemed unaffected by what he had just witnessed. "This prick's got a head as hard as a rock," Chap declared, flexing his fingers. "But his nuts are as soft as overripe kumquats."

Chap turned away, stepped over the prone form on the floor and, with a satisfied smirk on his face that no one could see, he walked quickly and confidently from the room.

Chapter Thirty-One

Sally was terrified. She did not deserve to be involved in all this, but she was, and Chap hated that. These people played by a set of rules of their own making, and their tactics were dirty.

He remembered the feelings that surged through him when he temporarily took Bozo, the mysterious Jones's hired help, out of the game. He hadn't wanted to stop until the bastard was dead. They were feelings not unlike those he remembered from the war, a lethal cocktail of fear, anger and hatred, fuelled by adrenalin. He had hoped such feelings were long gone, never realising until now just how close they had remained to the surface over the intervening years.

He explained everything to Sally. He felt he owed her at least that much after what she had been through at the hands of the testosterone-charged thug. Besides, it soon became apparent to Chap that she was not going to let him off the hook with little more than a brief synopsis of the facts. Nothing other than a full, detailed explanation would appease her.

Her insistence on knowing everything, however, was not the motivating factor behind his decision to be honest with her. He believed she deserved more than a précis of events. They were in this together now, and no matter how much he regretted it, he felt it was no less than her right to be fully informed.

There were other options available as to where they could go; his home, or hers, but his priority now was for complete privacy. No ringing telephones, no unexpected visitors, no interruptions. He took her back to the same motel where he had recently stayed.

He told her everything, right from the beginning, and he told her honestly. He told her about the training camp in the far north of Queensland where the nightmare had begun so long ago. He told her about the tattoo on his arm; the truth about the tattoo, not what he had led her to believe up until now.

Sally had seen the tattoo the night they made love for the first time. She had not given herself to another man since her husband's death, and Chap had been harbouring no small amount of bitterness and disillusionment as a result of his failed marriage. Baggage on both sides was carried into the relationship, but it seemed her abstinence and his resentment were, at this point in their lives, just the right ingredients.

Chap had made a habit of stopping at her restaurant for a drink to wind down at the end of an evening shift, and also for the company. She was pretty and interesting to talk to, as well as a much welcome relief from the inane ramblings on offer from rowdy, intoxicated, off-duty cops who frequented a pub nearby to Police Headquarters. And an empty house can be a desperately lonely place to go home to at times.

He couldn't recall exactly when his visits became more than just a social occasion. On reflection, he supposed it happened slowly, over a period of a few months. If either of them were to be asked exactly when they were first attracted to the other, there were certain to be two different answers. Only gentlemanly politeness would prevent Chap from confessing that for him, it was the first time he laid eyes on Sally Prescott, as inappropriate as that might seem given the trauma and grief she was experiencing. Then, one night, it happened, a late-night supper followed by a long walk on the beachfront near her restaurant, then coffee at his home. It was not a liaison either of them actively solicited; events just seemed to unfold that way and it seemed so right to both of them that neither resisted.

Sally asked him about the tattoo the next morning. Chap had stepped from the shower and was standing naked in the bathroom, towelling himself dry. Sally stood in the open doorway, watching him. Then she reached out and lightly, with her fingertips, touched the small diamond- shaped tattoo on his arm. A drunken, misguided antic with a couple of old army mates was how he explained it to her. She reacted as though it was believable enough; a couple of buddies, young, fit, and fun-loving soldiers, full of booze and bad decisions, having a great time together before shipping out to war. She accepted it with what seemed to Chap to be no more than passing interest, and she never mentioned it again.

Chap told her about Eddie Dickson, Charles Cobb, Brian Elliott and Colonel Baxter. How, and why, they all died. He told her how Baxter's foolhardy attempt at blackmail got them all killed. He told her about Dr. Lee Richardson and his involvement, and he told her how he suspected his death, and that of Colonel Baxter, were acts of murder as opposed to suicide. Sally listened in mesmerised silence, never interrupting, never asking for explanation.

Then, with a great deal of difficulty, he told her about the things he did in Vietnam. How he killed: shot men, cut the throats of men, and garrotted men with his bare hands. He told her about the ambush at the river and the escape through the tunnel. Then he told her about the Operations Order, how it had surfaced recently and how once again, after all these years, it was responsible for each of the most recent deaths, including the death of his partner, Tony Francis. He told her everything. He left nothing out. Occasionally during his narrative, she reached out and touched his cheek, or held his hand.

Not once in all the years since those days had he ever disclosed to anyone the things he disclosed to Sally. Not even to his ex-wife, in the days when he believed he loved her very much and theirs was a marriage which would last the distance. He opened up completely now, baring his very soul to her. When he was finished, he was left feeling exposed and vulnerable yet, at the same time, cleansed.

With the telling came the purging. It felt as though a great burden had been lifted from him. A crippling, suffocating weight of guilt and self-loathing slowly but surely eased itself from his life. A poisonous, weeping, ulcerated sore that was his conscience was at last treated. Now, the healing could begin. Chap needed no one's forgiveness but his own for the things he had done. Now, here, alone with Sally in his motel room, he gave himself that gift.

When it was over, he cried. He could not remember the last time he cried. The tears were long overdue. He cried great, heaving, gut-wrenching sobs. The tears flowed freely, occasionally stopped for a few seconds, and then returned, flooding again and again, with greater intensity each time, it seemed.

Sally held him, whispered to him, pledging her love and support. She held his head to her breast and caressed his face as he cried. The weeping, uncontrolled, and unabashed, continued for a long time.

He wept for his mates murdered in the jungle. He wept for Dickson, Cobb and Elliott. He wept for his partner, Tony Francis. He wept also for the enemy, soldiers just like himself, doing a job because their country asked them to. Finally, and perhaps most importantly, Chapman Bouttell wept for himself.

Sally insisted she loved him nonetheless for his unburdening. There were those, Chap believed, who would be seriously judgmental in regard to the acts to which he had openly admitted, but not Sally. She said she loved him even more, and told him as much many times that night. She watched him, listened to him and comforted him as he ran the gamut of emotions from anger, to fear, to relief, to forgiveness. Forgiveness mainly of himself, for making the decision not to expose the so-called Mr. Jones and his organisation for what they were.

He told Sally it was not the need for his own self-preservation that guaranteed his silence, but hers. He did love her, he admitted for the first time, and he did not want to lose her. These people would kill her if he went public. Nothing was surer in his mind, and he was not prepared to be the one responsible for precipitating the unthinkable. Too many good people had died already and, for some of them, like Dickson, Cobb, Elliott and Francis, as well as those who died that day in the ambush, he felt a degree of responsibility. He was not going to place Sally in a position of danger greater than she was already in. He had come to realise she was of far greater importance to him than the public exposure of a secret that had lain hidden for forty years.

With his mind now free of secrets, there came an exhaustion the likes of which he had never felt before. So, he slept. The tension and stress of the last few days finally caught up with him. Whether Sally slept also, he could not tell; he only knew she did not leave him. He fell asleep in the protective warmth of her arms and woke the same way two hours later. They made love then, furiously at first, with unchecked passion and, when it was over, they made love again, more slowly this time, lingering over every touch, every kiss. Those hours alone with her in the motel room were the most complete and fulfilling of his life. Until now, he had never really thought about what damage the past might have caused to his emotional wellbeing. The truth had brought with it a clarity and calmness greater than he could ever have imagined. Now he was whole again.

Chap wanted to believe his dealings with Jones and company were over. But in his heart, he knew they were not. For the rest of his life, however long fate might deem that to be, he would live with the feeling of eyes burning into the middle of his back. Could he live with that, constantly looking over his shoulder? As long as Sally was alive and by his side, he believed he could live with anything. They would live with it together. She knew it all now. She was aware of the dangers that might lie ahead—they both were. They would draw strength from each other if one felt themselves failing. She gave him a faith and a belief in himself that might easily have deserted him, if it were not for her encouragement and commitment.

They had dinner in a nearby restaurant rather than in the motel dining room, which lacked the comfortable intimacy they sought. There were many restaurants in the near vicinity and they narrowed their choice to either Chinese or Italian. On the toss of a coin, Italy won.

As they ate, they talked quietly and honestly. They drank a very nice Italian red wine, a touch too much perhaps, and it left them both giddy and light-headed. Whispering, laughing, holding hands across the table like young lovers—that was the way they felt, and that was the way they acted, oblivious to their fellow diners in the immediate vicinity and oblivious to the world outside and all its hidden fears.

For them, there were no others in the restaurant, just the two of them. For Chap, that was how it would always be from this point on, and Sally agreed. This night, despite the difficulties of the day, and those that may lie ahead of them, could not have been better if they had ordered it themselves.

Outside, the air was cold. The rain had eased to intermittent periods of drizzle and they walked briskly back to the motel, holding hands and huddled close together against the chill. Together, they looked up into the dark night sky and, as if on cue, a break in the clouds revealed an endless skyscape of flickering stars. They stopped and stood for a moment, staring in awe at the stunning display above. It was beautiful. As they watched in silence, Chap knew then that everything would be alright.

In contrast, the rain and freezing wind which accompanied Chap as he drove Sally to her house the next morning could not dampen their spirits. Their night together took them to a place neither of them had dared to venture to before. Now, as Mother Nature at her furious best hurled winter's worst against them, they were happy. Sally rested her hand on Chap's leg as he drove, and when he stopped at a set of traffic lights, he glanced across to see her looking at him. There was a look in her eyes as she watched him drive, a deep, thoughtful look he did not at first recognise, but interpreted as a look of peace and contentment. He had never seen her like this before. He sensed she wanted to say something but couldn't find the words.

He smiled across the gap separating them as he accelerated away from the intersection. "Everything okay?" he asked.

"Everything's fine." She smiled back at him.

After he left her, he continued on to his home and it was not until he pulled into his driveway that he remembered the money. He could not believe he had forgotten about it. He turned and looked into the back seat. It was still there, exactly where he put it when he left Jones. Two hundred and fifty thousand dollars! It had sat there, on the floor behind the driver's seat, all night. Only the locked car door between it and anyone who might be tempted to steal it. Chap shook his head and smiled. Thank God for winter, when those with a predisposition for breaking into motor cars, and Adelaide had its fair share of such characters, dared not venture out into the elements.

He reached behind his seat, lifted the bag into the front of the car, unzipped it, and looked at the bundles of cash. What was he to do with the money? It was on impulse that he instructed the pathologist Richardson to tell his people to bring it to the meeting, and it was impulse again when he picked it up from Jones's desk and walked out with it. Not for a moment had he ever considered what he might do with it.

It felt strange having that kind of money in his possession. Sort of wrong, somehow. Perhaps it was illegal. Did it really matter? Yesterday, it belonged to the bad guys, and they freely gave it to him, so what was the problem if it happened to be ill-gotten cash? He had the money, and Jones made no real protest when he took it from the room. Maybe there was no problem. As he sat in the car with the sports bag on the seat next to him, he came to the conclusion that there was no point in concerning himself with the legalities of taking the money. He should, however, give some thought as to what he was going to do with it now that he had it.

Chapter Thirty-Two

There was a note pinned to his front door. It was from Grahame Smith, one of the members of his detective team. The note was brief, and indicated it was urgent that he contact Superintendent George Baldwin.

"What does that dickhead want now?" Chap asked aloud.

As he reached to unlock the door, he heard the telephone inside his house ringing. He hurried inside, closed the door, and rushed to the phone. It was Smith. "Smithy," Chap greeted. "I just got home and found your note. What's up?"

"Shit, Chap, where have you been? We've been trying to find you since yesterday afternoon."

"I've been, shall we say, otherwise occupied," Chap answered. "I had my mobile phone turned off. I'm on leave, you know. What's so important that it can't wait until I get back to work in a couple of weeks?"

"I'm stuffed if I know," Smith said. "You know what this place is like. I'm just one of the mushrooms—kept in the dark and fed on bullshit. However, I suspect it has something to do with Tony's murder, and the Dickson case. What I can tell you is, Baldwin is having seizures. He's screaming at everyone, including the cleaning lady."

"I don't believe that!" Chap laughed. "George is never in the office early enough to abuse the cleaning lady."

"He's looking for you, Chap. You would think we were all hiding you from him as part of some bloody great conspiracy, for no other reason than we all hate the shithead."

"Well," Chap joked, "at least he's got that bit right. We *do* all hate him. The man's an idiot."

"We all know that, Sarge. But right now, he's an angry idiot. Can I tell him you are on your way? The lads and lasses here in the office could use a break from his ranting."

"Sure, go ahead," Chap said. "But don't tell him I have to shower and change first, or the bastard's likely to ring someone and get my water turned off."

"Okay, see you soon." Smith laughed, and hung up the phone.

Chap should have been angry at being summoned to the office. He was, after all, on leave; leave approved by George Baldwin himself. But he was not angry. Somehow, it did not matter anymore. At some point the night before, Chap's life had changed direction. Sally had done that to him, and he loved her for it.

He took a deliberately inordinate amount of time over showering, changing into fresh clothes, and making his way to Police Headquarters. He was anxious to find out what all the fuss was about, but he also wanted to piss Baldwin off. If there was money to be made by pissing George Baldwin off, Chap could have made a lucrative career from it. Sometimes it was the little things in life that brought the greatest satisfaction.

Chap delayed even longer when he stopped in the Major Crime squad room to exchange pleasantries with his colleagues. However, keen to have some respite from their boss, they quickly ushered him to Baldwin's office.

As usual, the door was closed. Chap went through the time-worn ritual of knocking once, waiting, and then knocking again, louder this time. He turned to the sea of faces in the squad room and gave them a collective, knowing wink.

As always, when he was finally invited to enter, George Baldwin was hunched over the same old file.

Chap left the door open and stood in front of Baldwin's desk. His superior looked up and peered over the top of his spectacles. "Shut the door," he ordered.

Chap turned and closed the door with his usual exaggerated enthusiasm.

"Where the fuck have you been?" Baldwin demanded.

"Careful, George, remember your blood pressure."

"It's Superintendent to you, Sergeant," Baldwin admonished.

Chap watched Baldwin's cheeks begin to glow softly to a pale pink shade. Soon, his whole face would glow like a stop-light. "Sorry, George… I mean Superintendent. For a brief moment, I forgot my lowly station in life. By the way, as I am officially on leave, I'm now on the clock. So, take your time, I could use the extra money."

"What the fuck have you been up to?" Baldwin demanded.

"You are going to have to be more specific. I've been up to lots of things. I'm on leave, remember? What I do on my own time is my business. Why don't you settle down, and tell me why you have dragged me into the office on this lovely Sunday morning."

"You have been snooping around in something, I know you have. I promised you I would get you and I am going to get you." He shook a fat, sausage-like finger at Chap.

There it was, Chap observed. The stop-light. George Baldwin's face was glowing. He wondered if it would be hot were he to reach out and touch it. Somehow, he managed to resist the urge to stretch his hand out and rest his palm against his superior's cheek. "I have no idea what you are talking about," he lied. "Why don't you enlighten me?"

"I've been trying to locate you since yesterday. You are wanted upstairs. I phoned them and told them I had found you."

"*You* found me? Don't be silly, George. How could *you* have found me? I doubt you've been out of this office since you came to work, except to take a piss, and then I expect you have to sit down to do that!"

If George Baldwin's face was glowing before, it was about to burst into flames now. "Get upstairs!" he ordered, then added, "They are expecting you. What do they want, Sergeant?"

"Who's 'they'?" was Chap's only response.

"The Commissioner, Assistant Commissioner Delaney, and some others. What is this all about?"

Chap was both surprised and confused at this latest turn of events but he was not about to let Baldwin see it. "The big brass, eh?" he said indifferently. He shrugged. "I don't know what they want. I'm surprised you can't tell me. I always thought you had your finger on the pulse around here. Won't the brass confide in you anymore?" He tapped lightly against the side of his nose. "Have we got our nose just a tiny bit out of joint?" he asked sarcastically.

"Just get up there!" Baldwin spluttered. "You're keeping the Commissioner waiting."

Chap turned, walked briskly out of the office and left the door open. As if on cue, he heard Baldwin curse loudly and then the door slammed shut. As he walked away from the office, he smiled at the curious faces in the squad room all turned his way.

As was his wont, he had been teasing Baldwin, baiting him. The truth was, he really did not know why he was being summoned upstairs to the Ivory Tower, as the administration floor of the headquarters building had become known. It had to be important, he knew that much.

In twenty-seven years on the job, Chap had never seen the

hallowed halls of power. It was only three floors above the Major Crime office, but he, like the vast majority of those who worked at the coal face of policing, had always thought he would almost certainly go through his entire career and never get the opportunity to see how the top brass lived. That was probably a good thing, he thought. He figured very little good could ever come from a summons to the Ivory Tower. This was a place generally accepted as being out of bounds to the rank and file members of the force. It was a place where those who worked there would tell you it all came together; the place where decisions were made and policy was formulated. It was a place of genuine power, or so they would have you believe.

That is what those who worked there might tell you, but, Chap didn't work there. He considered it a place where stale, aging, out-of-touch police officers went to polish the seats of their pants; a place that oozed syrupy, bureaucratic bullshit. But then, Chap had always been somewhat of a cynic. In truth, the administration floor was a place of structure and well-oiled efficiency. The police force could simply not operate without the ordered and structured participation of those who worked in the Ivory Tower.

There was no escaping the feeling he was experiencing. It was a gut feeling, gnawing at him, and he instinctively knew the summons upstairs had everything to do with the mysterious Jones and his network of miscreants. It was all too much of a coincidence to be mere coincidence, Chap thought. He headed for the lift that would take him to the corridors of power and those who awaited his presence.

Chapter Thirty-Three

Chap felt uncomfortably alien in the inner sanctum. This was not a place he had ever had any desire to work in. He found it an unimpressive, uninviting environment. The ranks of Commissioned Officers were for others to aspire to, he believed. The administration floor was nothing more than a series of offices, sized, it seemed to Chap, according to the rank and importance of those who inhabited them; namely, the Senior Police Executives, many of whom spent their working days composing meaningless memos, and drafting nonsense notifications on matters of procedure. He believed only a few of these men and women were still in touch with the real world of policing, the coal face, the front line. Most busied themselves with the task of trying to look busy while preoccupied with thoughts on how to keep their names prominent in the mind of the Commissioner. Cynical? Probably, but then, it could easily be said Chap was a cynical man.

He had never had much to do with any of those who worked here, most of whom he knew by name only. There were a few he had worked with in the past, back when they were on the streets, and before they moved onward and upward. There were a few he had never heard of. He had never been able to imagine himself as one of them, nor having anything in common with any of them apart from mutual membership of the police force.

He was greeted by a uniformed policewoman he had seen in the building many times but whose name he had never learned, or had forgotten. She was one of a handful of selected rank-and-file members, mostly attractive females— and what the fuck was that about, he wondered?— who worked on the administration floor.

She directed him to wait. Chap watched her disappear along a wide corridor. From somewhere in the distance, he heard her knocking on a door. Then he heard voices, too distant to distinguish. She would be announcing his arrival, he surmised. Almost immediately, she was back and, with a smile that looked a little contrived, she invited him to make his way to the Commissioner's office at the end of the corridor.

The door was open. Chap stood outside and knocked lightly on the jamb. He could see the commissioner seated behind a large desk, and several other people standing around the room. As he knocked, they all turned and looked in his direction.

The Commissioner spoke first. "Sergeant Bouttell, please come in and close the door."

Chap stepped into the room, and a quick glance around confirmed it was as he expected—a large office, comfortably furnished, and tastefully carpeted. The privilege of rank.

Police Commissioner Alan Bartholomew remained seated. Chap had known the Commissioner for a long time. They entered the South Australian Police Force at the same time, and came through the police academy together. Back in the early days, Bartholomew was one of those with whom he partnered on the streets.

Bartholomew earned the position he held today by hard work and diligence. He spent many years working in various roles, including a stint in a small country town in a remote part of the state, before slowly progressing through the ranks. He was well respected and admired as one of those who never forgot where he came from and as one who was never too proud to stop and offer words of encouragement to the most junior of police officers under his command.

While not incumbent on him to wear a uniform every day in his role as Commissioner, Bartholomew almost always did; it was his way of showing his respect for the job, and the position he held. It was a character trait Chap admired.

More slowly now, Chap cast his eyes around the room at the other occupants. Assistant Commissioner Geoffrey Delaney was also there. Delaney, together with Commissioner Bartholomew, was another of the very few senior officers Chap had any real time for. Both men enjoyed reputations of firmness but fairness, and for being strong campaigners for improved working conditions throughout all branches of the force. These were men who never, or at least very rarely, seemed to draw any negative criticism from the general membership. As Chap's eyes met Delaney's, the Assistant Commissioner nodded in recognition. There were two other men in the room, both strangers to Chap.

The Commissioner gestured to his second-in-charge. "Geoff, would you do the honours?"

"Of course, sir," Delaney responded, turning to face the two strangers. "Sergeant Bouttell, this is Mr. Richard Schaefer." Delaney indicated a man of around forty years of age, fit, tanned, and dressed in a suit that Chap estimated would have cost more than he himself would pay for three suits. Schaefer stepped forward and offered his hand.

"Mr. Schaefer is with the Australian Diplomatic Corps," Delaney added.

Chap tried to look suitably impressed. "Really, the Diplomatic Corps?"

"Yes, really," Schaefer said.

Chap took Schaefer's proffered hand. The Diplomatic

Corps. Surely that meant he was a spook. The diplomat's grip was firm and purposeful, and he wore an expression which said, "Don't fuck with me".

Chap turned to face the remaining man in the room.

"And this gentleman," Delaney said, "is from the United States Central Intelligence Agency. Agent… ah… I'm sorry," he apologised to the man.

"Rodrigues," the agent prompted.

Chap shifted his attention to the agent. His name, along with his olive complexion, suggested he was probably of Mexican/American extraction. Although never having met a real-life CIA agent, Rodrigues perfectly fitted the image Chap held of them. An image drawn from television and movie portrayals; that tough, no-nonsense, fit, good-looking, all-American, crew-cut look. Somewhere inside the neat, well-fitted suit jacket there would be the obligatory sunglasses, Chap figured. All the CIA agents he ever saw in movies carried sunglasses, regardless of the weather.

Rodrigues was younger than his counterpart, Schaefer, by at least ten years, Chap guessed. Either he was very, very good at what he did, or had influence in high places.

"Yes, Agent Rodrigues," Delaney completed the introductions, "Mr. Schaefer, Agent Rodrigues, this is Sergeant Chapman Bouttell."

Rodrigues stepped forward and shook hands with Chap.

Chap was confused and a little intimidated. There was some pretty heavy artillery in the room, so much so that he couldn't help but feel a touch insignificant. If there was ever any doubt in his mind that this little get-together was in connection with the Jones gang, the presence of the C.I.A agent in the room dispelled all of it. As to exactly why they were all there, he could only speculate. However, he knew it wasn't for the pleasure of his company. He stood in silence, mildly uncomfortable, and waited for someone to speak.

Finally, Assistant Commissioner Delaney spoke. "Sergeant,

I'm going to let Mr. Schaefer begin. He is more familiar with the details than I am, and I'm sure you are wondering why we asked you here. Richard…" He offered the floor to the diplomat.

Schaefer stepped confidently into the centre of the room and faced Chap.

Chap looked him up and down, feigning genuine interest. *Diplomat, my arse,* he thought.

Schaefer cleared his throat a little too noisily. "Thank you, Assistant Commissioner. Sergeant Bouttell, firstly, perhaps I should brief you on exactly why I am here today." He clasped his hands in front of him and looked intently at Chap. He looked, Chap thought, like an astronomy lecturer about to expound his theories on the vastness of the universe and the origins of the black holes therein.

"Basically," Schaefer continued, "my job, without getting too technical, is to act as a liaison officer between the Australian Security Intelligence Organisation and the Central Intelligence Agency, represented here today by Agent Rodrigues." He gestured towards the American and then paused, looking at Chap, his eyes inviting some response.

"I think I understand," Chap nodded. "You're not a politician, and you don't want to be seen as a cop." It was vintage Bouttell sarcasm at its best.

Schaefer looked slightly embarrassed. "Well… I… ah, let's talk about why we are all here."

"Let's do that," Chap said, with a condescending smile.

Schaefer continued. "It appears, Sergeant, you have unwittingly stumbled into a top level, top secret, joint investigation between ASIO and the CIA."

"Really. 'Unwittingly stumbled'—a nice turn of phrase. What investigation would that be?" Chap asked.

"Perhaps I should let Agent Rodrigues explain." Schaefer stepped from the centre of the room and his place was taken by the CIA agent. Chap watched Schaefer step back. "Nice buck-pass," he wanted to say; he chose instead to remain silent.

Rodrigues smiled at Chap. "Sergeant Bouttell," he began. "I will not, as you Australians would say, beat around the bush." *Well-schooled and well-spoken,* Chap thought. *Not a trace of a Hispanic accent.* He found that odd.

"As I understand it," Rodrigues continued, "you have recently become aware of a particular group of people we are investigating." He paused, as if waiting for a response from Chap. When none was forthcoming, he continued. "You have, no doubt, discovered that this particular group of people is vast in size, with tentacles reaching deep into the security organisations of both our countries. The membership of this group boasts personnel from all walks of life: politicians, solicitors, doctors, law-enforcement officers, businessmen, and many other high profile, professional people. Indeed, they have, over a period of forty or so years, managed to infiltrate and recruit members from the government, and private sectors, both here and in the United States. They are highly motivated, extremely efficient, and it seems they have access to unlimited funds. Their command structure has proven to be as capable as any military command we have knowledge of."

He paused and looked at Chap. There was no doubt in the agent's mind that Chap knew exactly what he was talking about. It remained only for Chap to confirm it. For the moment, Chap decided to continue with his 'admit to nothing' approach. "What has all this to do with me?" he asked.

"As explained previously," Rodrigues continued, "we have been conducting a joint operation with your security people—ASIO—investigating these people and their activities. We have known of their existence for many years and, for most of that time, we have employed a wait and watch approach in regard to their activities. But a more determined investigation began back home, in the States, about a year ago. A high-ranking member of the group was diagnosed with terminal cancer. He was given just a few weeks to live. Naturally, he took the news very badly. He suddenly found religion, thinking it would bring him some measure of comfort in the last weeks of his life. He decided he wanted to go to his grave with a clear conscience. He came to us."

"Why the CIA?" Chap asked.

"As opposed to his local police station, I assume you mean?"

"Something like that," Chap answered. "Or if, as you say, he found religion, why not just go to his priest and take confession?"

"He came to us because he was one of us," Rodrigues explained.

"You mean he was CIA?"

"For nearly thirty years," Rodrigues confirmed.

"And no one knew he was part of this band of evil misfits?" Chap asked, finding it hard to believe.

Chap knew very little of the CIA and its operations. In truth, he had heard more about them in the last few days than he had ever heard before. It was reasonable, however, for him to believe, or anyone to believe, they were, arguably, the best intelligence organisation in the world. It was incomprehensible to him that an active member of the CIA for thirty years could also be a member of such a lethal group of people and for his alliance to the group to remain undetected.

"Hardly 'misfits', Sergeant," Schaefer interjected rudely.

Agent Rodrigues turned and glowered at Schaefer, who immediately retreated a few steps and sat in an empty chair against the wall. ASIO and the CIA might well be working together, but it was obvious to Chap who was calling the shots.

Rodrigues turned back to face Chap. He could see the confusion in Chap's expression. "Perhaps," he said, "things may become a little clearer if I give you some background information."

"If you think it would help," Chap said, with mild

sarcasm. At this point, anything would help. He looked around the room. Everyone was now seated with the exception of himself and the young CIA agent. There was another empty chair in the room, a few paces from where he stood.

"Would you like to sit, Sergeant?" Commissioner Bartholomew asked.

"Thank you, sir. I would prefer to stand," Chap answered, looking across at the chair. It was a little too close to where Schaefer sat for his liking. He had only known the 'diplomat' a few minutes, but that was long enough for Chap to decide there was something about the man he didn't like.

"The group was born in the ranks of the Central Intelligence Agency about forty years ago, give or take." Rodrigues said. "A small, select band of operatives was hand-picked from within the Agency to form a special squad tasked with the duty of covertly investigating alleged corruption and other forms of illegal conduct amidst the ranks of government and law enforcement agencies throughout America. To do this effectively, it was often necessary to recruit civilians who were in a position to get the information we needed without raising suspicion. Being that these investigations were of a covert nature, the existence of this elite group was known only to a handful of trusted people within the CIA's Executive Office."

Chap remembered the Executive Office—it was from where the document, the Operations Order, originated.

"Initially," Rodrigues continued, "they were formed to investigate two specific instances of illegal activity deep within the White House administration. Their results were so impressive that the decision was made to keep the unit together and expand their role to include any alleged illegal activity, in any government organisation, anywhere in the country. Somehow, somewhere along the way, after some years had passed, and members of the special unit came and went as a result of natural attrition, something went wrong."

"In what way?" Chap asked.

"Very slowly, over a period of years, the lines became blurred and the rot began to set in. An example of the very corruption the group was established to expose would be identified and a blackmail approach would be made. A small number of members became extremely wealthy. It was all too easy, and their numbers slowly grew as they recruited from outside the Agency. Before anyone really knew what was happening, this group of people— they call themselves the Coterie—was born."

"The Coterie? What is that?" Chap asked.

"The dictionary interpretation is a small, exclusive group. Kind of like a subunit within the main unit. A small splinter group of the original squad at first, it became bigger and took on a life of its own. We believe there is a core group still active within the Agency, but the majority of the current members of the Coterie are from outside the CIA."

"And the Agency has never been able to stop them?" Chap asked incredulously.

"The initial squad, which comprised CIA personnel, was all very hush-hush and top secret. Oh, there were unsubstantiated rumours from time to time of a criminal element within the squad, but they were only rumours. No one knew for sure if this splinter group actually existed, let alone who might be part of it. Who was honest, and who was not. Eventually, when the rumours persisted, it became an embarrassment to the Agency, and the special squad was disbanded."

"What happened then?" Chap asked.

"Unfortunately, it was too late. Unbeknownst to everyone, the Coterie had become well and truly established. The very act of disbanding the special squad only served to remove suspicion and doubt from the minds of those who held such suspicion and doubt. In fact, it made the activities of the group less likely to be discovered."

"So," Chap concluded, "they have been allowed to proceed unchecked for all these years?"

"It is not that they were allowed to proceed unchecked," Rodrigues emphasised. "That suggests the Agency knew of their existence and did nothing to halt their activities. That could not be further from the truth. Again, when the special squad was disbanded, it was assumed that the Coterie, if in fact it still existed, would simply cease to operate. In reality, their activities were so secret that they had a chain of command and system of accountability, which guaranteed their own members did not know the identity of other members beyond those in their own cell. Each fewer than four members, and no more than six."

Chap allowed his eyes to wander over the faces in the room. There was silence. Everyone was poised, listening, hanging on the agent's every word. Chap was not the only person in the room hearing this account for the first time.

Commissioner Bartholomew finally broke the silence. "How did the activities of this so-called Coterie come to fruition here, in Australia?"

"It is important to understand," Rodrigues began again, "that it would be a mistake to think that the activities of these people were, or indeed are, confined to the United States. Unfortunately, it is like a disease, a cancer, and it is far more widespread than you might think. Australia, in fact any free world country, would be wrong to assume they are immune from the influence of the Coterie. We have learned that a massive, clandestine recruitment campaign was conducted as early as some twenty-five years ago, and it was, it would seem, very successful. We believe those enthusiastic young recruits, from countries around the globe, account for some of today's more senior members of the group.

"Australia did not escape the recruitment drive. We suspect there are some very prominent Australians, men and women, who were working for the CIA at the time, and who were recruited to the Coterie back then, or have been since. These are people from a wide range of backgrounds. Some are in powerful positions in both the government and the private sector, people of great influence and in some cases, great wealth. Others are your average, hard-working, next door neighbour types. They could be running your local service station or your corner store. The truth is, Australia provided more potential members than you could imagine. Now, today, the Coterie has an embarrassing number of members right here in Australia."

"Embarrassing to whom?" Chap asked.

Rodrigues shrugged. "Your government for one, and the general public—should the general public ever become aware of their existence." He paused momentarily, allowing his words to be absorbed, and then continued. "Do you know what a sleeper is, Sergeant?"

Chap nodded. "In the context of what you have been saying, yes, I think so."

"We believe many of the members of the Coterie are so-called sleepers, probably the majority, if truth be known, and it is highly likely that many have never been called on to perform any sort of duty, and it is also likely they may never be in the future. But the truth is, most sleepers never know when the Coterie might call in an old favour, so to speak."

Chap decided to try a bluff. He needed to know how much the people in this room knew about how much he actually knew. "I still don't know what all this has to do with me."

Everyone in the room turned their attention to Chap.

"You are here, Sergeant Bouttell," the diplomat, Schaefer, stated emphatically, "because you couldn't follow orders."

Chap turned and glared at Schaefer, who simply smirked. Chap looked away and glanced at the faces around the room. Commissioner Bartholomew was looking at him, Assistant Commissioner Delaney was looking at him, and Agent Rodrigues was looking at him. He wished he could learn to keep his big mouth shut. Four pairs of eyes burned into his face.

"Pardon?" Chap questioned, finally.

Schaefer turned to face Commissioner Bartholomew, and then back to Chap. When he continued, his tone was condescending. "I am led to believe," he began, "that you were specifically ordered to drop your investigation into the murder of Edward Dickson. You were advised, correct me if I'm wrong, that the investigation was to be handed over to, and completed by, the Federal Police. But you couldn't let it go. How am I doing, Sergeant?"

"Dickson was a friend of mine," Chap hissed at Schaefer. "Any investigating I did, I did in my own time, at my own expense. Besides, I learned the Feds knew sweet fuck-all about the murder, contrary to what I had been informed. Perhaps you might like to explain that."

Schaefer remained stoically silent.

"I thought that might be your response," Chap said, glowering at the diplomat.

Assistant Commissioner Geoffrey Delaney interrupted him. "Chap, this is not a witch hunt. This meeting is not designed to persecute you for any breach of discipline which may, or may not, have occurred." He scowled at Schaefer with an expression that said, "Ease up, mate", and then spoke to Rodrigues. "Perhaps, Agent Rodrigues, you might like to return to the issue at hand."

Rodrigues nodded to the Assistant Commissioner. "Of course." He turned, faced Chap, and continued. "Assistant Commissioner Delaney is quite correct, Sergeant. "I am not here, and neither is Mr. Schaefer, to question your involvement in the Dickson case, but merely to deal with it as best we can. Be it a blessing or a curse, you are in this thing now, and it stands to reason we should turn your involvement to our advantage."

"What do you want from me?" Chap asked.

"The high-level member of the Coterie I referred to earlier, who rolled over on the group, was, along with his immediate family, placed in a witness protection program where he remained until his death from cancer a few months ago. In the time we had him under protection, he gave us a good insight into the internal workings of the group."

"A risky thing to do," Chap suggested. "Given the lengths to which these people have demonstrated they are prepared to go."

"Absolutely," Rodrigues confirmed. "His motivation, however, was more for the safety of his family than for himself. Immunity from prosecution never entered the equation. He knew he would be dead long before any court proceedings could ever be instigated. The wheels of justice turn annoyingly slowly in my country, Sergeant."

"Tell me about it," Chap responded, with undisguised sarcasm.

"He was dying and he knew it. His own wellbeing was of no concern to him. It was not until he was satisfied we could guarantee the ongoing safety of his family, and the protection of his considerable financial worth, that he gave us all he knew."

A momentary pause gave Chap a fresh opportunity to study the other faces in the room. Everyone was transfixed with obvious interest, with the possible exception of Schaefer, who appeared to be more intent on studying his immaculately manicured nails while he waited for another opportunity to have a crack at Chap.

"Unfortunately," Rodrigues continued, "although he gave us a great deal of background information, our man's health deteriorated more quickly than expected. He died before we had the complete picture."

"So where do you stand now?" It was Assistant Commissioner Delaney who spoke.

Rodrigues turned to Delaney. "We stand, sir, enthusiastic, encouraged and determined, albeit frustrated. We believe we are tantalisingly close to shutting the Coterie down once and for all, but we are not quite there."

"How so?" Delaney asked with obvious interest.

"Naturally, we had hoped our man would live long enough to provide us with more detailed information, but that was not to be. However, he did give us enough to launch our own top-secret investigation into the activities of the Coterie."

"And?" Delaney prompted.

"With the information he gave us, combined with what we have been able to uncover ourselves, we think we have identified several currently active CIA and ASIO operatives who belong to the group. Unfortunately, if we move on them, we take the chance none of them will talk and we will really be no closer to shutting the Coterie down completely. However, we do have one thing in our favour."

"Which is?" Delaney asked.

"We have been able to infiltrate the Coterie."

"Infiltrate?" Chap heard himself say.

"Yes. Before our informant died, he told us the Coterie is still actively recruiting members, and how they go about seeking and indoctrinating new prospects. We subsequently placed a number of expert operatives in areas where we thought they would be noticed and, fortunately, a few were approached. It took a long time. The Coterie are naturally very cautious as to who they trust. Eventually, we had a small number of undercover agents embedded within the lower ranks of the group. However, it was not without its frustrations."

"I don't understand," Commissioner Bartholomew said. "I would have thought that successfully infiltrating the group would have been a major coup."

"Oh, it was, it was," Rodrigues said. "But it's important to understand that the very reason these people have existed so long, and so successfully, is due to their tight internal security. You see, we estimate their numbers worldwide to be in the hundreds, and yet each member of each internal cell knows only the other members in that cell. Their recruiting system works along similar lines to that used by some large commercial business enterprises, what we have come to know as multi-level marketing. It has taken several decades for them to become the established outfit they are today. Our people on the inside are new, and few, in their ranks. None of them are in positions of authority, and we have already lost two under suspicious circumstances, which indicates they are aware we have agents within their ranks; they just don't know how many, or where they are. Even if our people remain undetected, reaching a position of power and authority in the upper echelon takes years and, needless to say, our frustration is mounting."

"Not to mention the body count," Chap observed.

Rodrigues ignored the snipe. "We consider ourselves extremely fortunate to have infiltrated the group but, for the moment, and possibly for years to come, we have to tread very carefully. We do not want to lose any more agents."

"So, what exactly are you saying?" Chap asked. "It sounds very much to me like you are treading water here."

Schaefer, perhaps feeling he had remained silent for too long, cleared his throat. "All is not doom and gloom, Sergeant Bouttell. Pessimism is often interpreted as a weakness, you know. After a great deal of top level, ongoing discussion and consultation between the CIA and ASIO, we have been able to insert covert operatives of our own within the Australian arm of the Coterie. Not, I hasten to add, in the same numbers as our friends from the CIA, but with slightly more success in recent times, I am pleased to be able to announce."

Chap thought Schaefer made it sound like any success at all was due to his efforts alone. "What do you mean 'slightly more success'?" he asked.

"Schaefer smiled and deferred to the CIA agent. "Agent Rodrigues."

"We don't know," Rodrigues began. "But it seems we lucked out here in Australia. One of your ASIO operatives, recruited a long time ago, landed a position with one of the top people in the organisation here in Australia. I'm told he is one of the best undercover agents you have. It's a lucky break for us."

"And for Mr. Schaefer's career, no doubt," Chap offered sarcastically.

"Pardon me?" Schaefer said.

"Nothing." Chap smiled.

Rodrigues continued, ignoring the obvious tension between Chap and Schaefer. "Until recently, we have been concentrating our efforts on cracking the group at home in the United States. We never anticipated the breakthrough would come from the other side of the world."

Chap wondered if he should feel offended on behalf of the members of ASIO. Rodrigues made it sound surprising, even embarrassing, that ASIO got the jump on the CIA.

"What have you learned from the man on the inside?" Delaney queried.

"This is where Sergeant Bouttell comes in." Rodrigues smiled and nodded at Chap.

"Oh, really?" Chap asked, genuinely surprised. "How might that be?"

"We have been able to ascertain that you met with one, Douglas Wallechinski, just yesterday."

"Douglas Wallechinski? I've never heard of him." Chap shrugged.

"To give the gentleman his correct title," Schaefer interjected, "it is *Sir* Douglas Wallechinski. You might know him by another name. 'Jones,' I believe he called himself."

Of course. Chap always knew the man in the empty office complex was using an alias, and now, having heard his real name, the man himself became more real, more alive. He was someone; he had a name. In his mind's eye, Chap could see

Wallechinski, seated behind the desk in the abandoned office complex. He could see the smug expression on his face, the inconvenienced air about his attitude. Now Jones was real to him.

Chap was also surprised that Rodrigues, and now everyone else in the room, was aware of his meeting with Wallechinski, and he wondered just how much more they knew. "Who is this Wallechinski character, exactly?" he asked the agent.

Schaefer decided to answer the question and jumped in before Rodrigues had a chance to respond. "Sir Douglas Wallechinski is third generation Australian of Polish extraction. He is an extremely wealthy merchant banker. Before turning to banking, he owned a large share of several mining companies in Western Australia. He was as big in the mining industry as his late counterpart, Lang Hancock, but without the same high public profile. He preferred relative anonymity, and still does. His vast business investments are worldwide and he owns palatial mansions in several international locations. These days, he spends much of his time in Europe, where he has at least three homes that we know of. We are not sure of his exact wealth, but it is estimated to be in the billions."

"Lucky old Dougie," Chap observed.

"As it happens," Rodrigues interrupted, "we suspect him of being the money end of the Coterie, at least here in Australia."

Astounded, Chap asked, "Why haven't you picked this prick up and shaken the truth out of him?"

"We have no evidence of any illegal activity on his part. He is very, very good at what he does. We know he is an integral part of the Coterie, perhaps even the highest-ranking member here in Australia, but, until we get some hard evidence against him, evidence that will stand up, he will continue to do whatever it is he does. He has the fiscal resources and wherewithal to buy the very best legal team the world has to offer and we can't afford to mess it up by showing our hand too soon. All we can do for the moment is sit on him and hope he slips up somewhere."

"Good luck with that," Chap mocked.

"We are going to need a bit of that, too," Rodrigues said seriously.

"Tell me," Chap said, "how is it you know I met with this guy yesterday? Am I being followed?"

"No, that wasn't necessary," Rodrigues answered.

"Then how?"

"We found out from your man inside, the ASIO undercover operative."

Chap, confused, shook his head. "I'm sorry, you've lost me."

"You met him yesterday also." Rodrigues smiled again. "He didn't give you his name, but I understand you gave him a name of your own. 'Bozo', wasn't it?"

Chapter Thirty-Four

In the office of the South Australian Police Commissioner, listening to an agent from the American Central Intelligence Agency talking about matters of national security, sleepers from a rogue unit of the CIA, and undercover agents, seemed to Chap like an incredibly inopportune time to be reminded of incidences from his childhood, but sometimes, things like that happen.

Having spent his youth growing up in the orphanage in Adelaide, he recalled there were times during the years he spent in that place when life simply became too difficult for one of his tender years. Under the stern, watchful eye, and tutorage, of a bevy of extremely straight-laced and strict Catholic priests and nuns, there were times when he just wanted to be alone, with his own thoughts, and with his dreams of someday leaving that awful place.

Lying in his small, uncomfortable bunk at night did not, could not, offer the solitude he so often sought; solitude was conspicuously absent when you had to share your nights with fifteen other boys of various ages in dormitory-style accommodation. Some boys, mostly the very young, and sometimes a sensitive older boy, sobbed long into the lonely night, night after night. Chap, very early into his time at that place, knew he had to find a quiet place of his own.

The orphanage was a very large place and the imposing facade of the building was considered a wonderful example of nineteenth century architecture. It was, however, to many of the young inmates who had the misfortune to be housed and schooled there, a foreboding and imposing structure offering little more than a constant, nagging hunger, and a cold misery which shrouded them all the days they lived there. It was a place sadly devoid of the laughter that should, by rights, accompany the young as they gambolled and frolicked through the innocence of youth.

In the centre of the main entrance hall, there was a large, elaborate stairway ascending to the dormitory level above. Underneath the stairs, on the ground floor, there was an enclosed storage area. This cramped and stuffy space was a place where old chairs in varying states of disrepair, dusty cardboard boxes overflowing with long-ago-filled exercise books, journals, and old stationary items were stored. As he recalled, there was also the odd dilapidated desk or two, their tops scarred with deep scratches etched in the surface by bored, lonely, sad children who would surely have paid a harsh price for their reckless vandalism.

Empty, the space might have appeared large and spacious. Crammed full as it was with outcast bits and pieces, Chap remembered it as a small and mildly claustrophobic place; ideal as a temporary, secret refuge from the ever-present torments of his young life.

One day, for reasons no longer clear to him, young Chap was in this storage area and, while quietly exploring the contents for the umpteenth time, he came across a small niche tucked behind several boxes, not visible from the small doorway should anyone enter. This was not a place Chap entered with any trepidation; rather, it was a place of mystery and wonderment for him. It was a place where his imagination set him free from the harsh discipline and suffocating constraints of orphanage life. The tiny niche became his sanctuary, his stronghold—a safe hideaway from the world outside, and from the priests and nuns and their heavy-handed, often cruel administrations.

He told no one of his secret place. It was a special place. It felt like it was something of his very own that no one else had, or could take from him. Often, quietly and unnoticed, he would go there when he was depressed, or being sought by a member of the staff intent on administering punishment for an indiscretion Chap considered to be minor, but which the tough disciplinarians who ran the place would consider to be irrefutable evidence of Satan's influence on his naïve and impressionable young mind.

The young Chapman Bouttell would squeeze himself into the niche and sit on the floor, surrounded by boxes, listening to the sounds of the search outside. Sometimes, one of the staff would open the door to the storage area and peer into the gloom inside. Crouched silently in his sanctuary, Chap was never discovered. Later, when he was confident the coast was clear and he thought his tormentors had expended their energy searching for him, or when he got just plain hungry and he knew it was almost mealtime, he would slip unseen from his secret place. Strangely, he would always feel better than when he went in there. Perhaps it had to do with him successfully evading detection. It gave him a feeling of victory over the system. No one ever found his special place, and its existence remained his secret, right up until it was time for him to leave the wretched orphanage forever.

Now, as he stood in the Commissioner's office, Chap wished he was back in the orphanage. How he would love to get up and run from this room and secrete himself in his hideaway. He wanted to be anywhere but here in this room. Everything was beginning to close in on him, just like when he was a kid. He wanted to turn his back on it all and have it disappear, if only for a short while.

But Chap was not a child anymore, and this was no hidey-hole under the stairs. What was happening was real, and he knew there would be no running away from it. No hiding. No amount of daydreaming or fantasising about better, nicer things was ever going to change anything.

Chap stared at Agent Rodrigues. "Bozo is your man?"

"Ours, actually," Schaefer answered, from his seat across the room. "He's an ASIO operative, deep undercover, as I'm sure you can imagine."

Chap, totally ignoring Schaefer, was stunned. He must have looked it, with eyes wide, and focused on the CIA agent, Rodrigues. Suddenly, he thought of the last time he saw Bozo. "How is he?" was all he could think of to say.

Rodrigues frowned. "I understand you got a couple of good licks in. He has a badly broken nose, and is walking with considerable pain and discomfort."

Through his embarrassment, Chap could see a humorous side to all this. He wanted to laugh, but managed to contain the urge.

Rodrigues continued. "Bozo, and for the moment we will use your name for him, has been able to pass on some valuable information to us regarding where Wallechinski goes, who he meets, who he telephones, that sort of thing. He doesn't have unfettered twenty-four-seven access to Wallechinski, but we are getting some useful intelligence from him. It's a huge task, and a dangerous one. He has to separate Wallechinski's genuine business dealings from Coterie business, but, slowly, we are making progress. We are starting to compile a healthy dossier on Wallechinski and some of his colleagues, thanks to… ah… Bozo. We hope it won't be too long before we can start to move against some of these people."

"Why do I get the feeling that politics has a hand in all this?" Chap speculated.

Rodrigues shrugged. "It's sensitive. We have reason to believe there were, way back in the early days, high ranking politicians who owed their careers to the Coterie. We also believe there are a few around today, in various positions of power and influence. If we move too soon, our whole investigation could be shut down with the stroke of a pen, and these people would be allowed to continue their evil unmolested. We are very fortunate to have a handful of people, like Mr. Bozo, as you call him, in positions where they can report back to us on some of the activities of the people they are assigned to watch."

"I never called him 'Mr.' Bozo," Chap insisted. "But, if it's any consolation, he does his job very well. Perhaps you could pass on my compliments." As an afterthought, he added, "As well as my apologies." Then Chap thought about how Bozo had manhandled Sally. "On second thoughts, forget the apology."

Rodrigues seemed to ignore Chap's sentiments. "As I said earlier, he is one of your country's best field agents, extremely competent. Of course, while he is experiencing some discomfort at the moment, it has to be said that your altercation with him would only have strengthened his cover, rather than weakened it."

"I guess I did good, huh, Mr. Schaefer." Chap looked at the diplomat and smirked. It was a good point. In hindsight, belting Bozo was perhaps not such a bad thing. Somehow, though, it did not make him feel all that much better about decking an ASIO agent. On the one hand, he wasn't sure if he ever wanted to meet Bozo again. On the other hand, he remembered Bozo's size and bulk, and thought perhaps it would be more prudent, not to mention healthy, if he just put the whole Bozo incident behind him. Right now, that hidey-hole under the stairs was looking more and more inviting. He wondered if it was still there.

Rodrigues was still speaking, and Chap's mind raced to catch up. "We were alerted by ASIO to recent activity by the Coterie," he was saying. "A man by the name of Baxter, a colonel with the Australian Army, who we understand you also met recently, was reported to be asking discreet questions about the existence of the Coterie. Baxter was placed under immediate close surveillance. Ultimately, he led us to…" Rodrigues opened a file he held in his hands and briefly referred to it, "Edward Dickson, Charles Cobb and Brian Elliott." He closed the file and looked at Chap.

"And, I assume," Chap added, "Baxter's blackmail attempt."

"Yes," Rodrigues confirmed. "I flew out here from the U.S. immediately. A member of the Coterie eventually made contact with Baxter, who made certain demands."

"Like a big pile of cash," Chap offered.

"And now, Sergeant, this is where we need your help," Rodrigues said.

Chap looked across at Schaefer and winked. "I knew we were going to get to this at some point. My help—in what way?"

"Two million dollars is a lot of money. Baxter made a blatant, yet amateurish attempt at blackmail when he finally made contact with a representative from the Coterie—or, more accurately, when they made contact with him. But, until yesterday, we did not know the nature of the attempt, that is to say, the motivation behind it. We now know it involved what has been referred to as a document of some sort. We know nothing about this so-called document. I believe you can shed some light on that for us."

Chap glanced in the direction of Assistant Commissioner Delaney. He saw no hint of response. Chap was on his own. Swinging in the breeze.

It was Commissioner Bartholomew who finally spoke. "Chap… Sergeant, before you continue, I would like you to be aware of exactly where you stand, officially."

"Are you going to read me my rights? Do I need to have a lawyer present, or, at the very least, a Police Association representative?"

"If I tell you you don't need either, is that good enough for you?"

"Of course, as long as it's coming from you, and no one else in the room." Chap looked directly at Schaefer.

Commissioner Bartholomew continued. "We are aware that you have been conducting enquiries into this matter outside the sanction of the department. I would like to take this opportunity to reiterate what was mentioned earlier, and that is, I do not intend to make this a forum on the rights or wrongs of your actions. Suffice it to say, in recent days, there have been a lot of deaths which, it would seem, can be directly related to the activities of the so-called Coterie. Not the least of which was the murder of a very good police officer." He paused momentarily, as though carefully choosing his next words. "You should understand that it is not anticipated that you be the subject of any disciplinary action from within the department, in relation to any of these matters."

"Can you tell that to Superintendent Baldwin?" Chap interrupted.

"Forget about Superintendent Baldwin. He won't give you any trouble." It was a statement spoken with a conviction Chap trusted immediately.

The Commissioner continued. "All that is required of you at this time is your complete cooperation and your word that when you leave this room, you do not repeat, to anyone, anything you hear here today. I also require your word that you will discontinue, immediately, your private, individual investigations into the Coterie. I'm told these are matters of some delicacy and potential embarrassment to both our and the United States' government. They are to be dealt with by the joint investigation team that has been watching these people for a long time. Do you fully understand that?"

It was quite a speech. Impressive, even. Chap remained silent for a moment, allowing the commissioner's words and their significance to digest. Perhaps it was time to stand up and be counted. He had to trust someone. This whole business was far more intricate than he could ever have imagined. It had gone far beyond a routine murder investigation. He had to take a chance on someone—why not the people in this room? If he could not trust the two most senior police officers in the state, then he was fresh out of luck. He cleared his throat. "Yes, sir, I understand."

The commissioner smiled. "Good, thank you." He turned his attention to Rodrigues. "Please continue," he invited.

"Thank you, Commissioner," Rodrigues responded. He fixed his gaze on Chap. "Now, Sergeant Bouttell, what can you tell us about this document? We know that it exists, and we know, as the Commissioner has alluded, that it is sensitive and potentially damaging to both our governments, but that is about all we know about it."

Chap cast his eyes around the room and returned his attention to Rodrigues. *Well, here goes,* he thought, *straight in at the deep end.* "It dates back to the Vietnam war," he began cautiously. "It is an Operations Order. It originated from some clandestine branch within the Executive Office of the CIA, and was countersigned by some bloke from ASIO here in Australia."

"Like a joint operation between both security organisations?" Rodrigues suggested.

"That's how it would appear," Chap answered.

"Sergeant," Schaefer said, "I would suggest that security operations conducted jointly between ASIO and the CIA are not an uncommon event."

Chap shrugged. "I'm a police detective, Mr. Schaefer. I

know nothing about the activities of ASIO or the CIA, so I'll take your word for that. This, however, was different."

"In what way?" Schaefer probed.

"Well…" Chap looked slowly around the room. All eyes were directly on him. "I have seen the document, and the truth is, it is nothing less than a joint conspiracy between ASIO and the CIA to commit mass murder!"

A silence followed, which seemed to last longer than it actually did.

"That's outrageous!" Schaefer insisted; somewhat lamely, Chap thought.

"You got that right," Chap responded.

Commissioner Bartholomew leaned forward across his desk and spoke quietly but directly to Chap. "Sergeant, while the conversation in this room is confidential, I agree with Mr. Schaefer. That is a very serious allegation you are making, and I should caution you to be very careful where you tread."

Everyone was watching Chap, waiting for him to continue. He ignored the commissioner's warning. He was in too deep now, and there was no turning back. He paused, glanced around again at the intent, focused faces, and continued. "I was a member of a specialist covert unit during the Vietnam war. There were ten of us. Dickson, Cobb and Elliott were members of the same unit. Without going into graphic details, the tasks we were required to carry out were clandestine, extremely top secret, very dangerous, and very illegal. Illegal because we operated inside the borders of Cambodia, a neutral country in the conflict. Each member of the unit was required to sign a secrecy agreement before we left Australia. It was, in effect, an agreement never to discuss what our duties were. To do so would bring disgrace and embarrassment to both our governments. I have recently discovered it was intended from the very beginning that none of us were to survive the war."

"What the hell does that mean?" Schaefer asked incredulously.

"It means that a unit of US Special Forces led by CIA agents, code named T Force, and with the full knowledge and support of ASIO, was to lay an ambush and await my unit's return from its last mission. The instructions in the document are quite clear: none of us were to survive."

"Jesus Christ!" Assistant Commissioner Delaney murmured aloud.

"What happened?" Rodrigues probed.

"The ambush took place," Chap said, beginning to feel uncomfortable with the telling of it. "It was well planned and well executed. We walked right into it. We never stood a chance. Six of my unit's ten members were killed almost immediately, including our patrol leader."

"How did you manage to get out alive?" Delaney asked.

"Unbeknownst to the U.S. special force, the ambush was set up not far from a well concealed but disused North Vietnamese tunnel complex. We were familiar with it because it was shown to us some months earlier by the Montagnard tribe, with whom we were based while we were in Vietnam. We used it from time to time to store supplies and ammunition when we were on a prolonged operation. But it was close to a large river and it was often very damp and dangerous, so we stopped using it a few months before the ambush. We were heavily outnumbered, and the enemy was well concealed. We had no idea we were being fired upon by allied forces. We assumed we were under attack from a far superior enemy force." Chap paused, looked down at the floor and brushed at a bead of perspiration on his forehead.

"We didn't even have time to carry away our dead, or even call for air support," he continued reflectively. "We scrambled into the tunnel and escaped. There were only four of us left alive. Charlie Cobb was badly wounded, and we had to carry him. For a while, we thought he wasn't going to make it. By the time we were far enough away from the ambush site to safely leave the tunnel, he was close to death. We eventually made it back to the village where we were based and called for a medevac chopper. Everything happened pretty quickly after that. We were all at the end of our tour and within a few days, the four of us were sent home." Chap wiped at another trickle of perspiration.

Schaefer rose from his chair and stood facing Chap. "Top secret, specialist unit! United States Special Forces! CIA led ambush! T Force! A mysterious Operations Order! Mass murder! Do you have any idea how fanciful all that sounds?"

Chap glared at the diplomat. "You know, Mr. Schaefer, I don't give a rat's arse how it sounds, I'm just telling you how it was, and you can please yourself whether you believe it or not."

Suitably chastised, but hardly appeased, Schaefer returned to his chair and sat.

"And the document?" It was a question from Rodrigues.

"Dickson found it. Apparently, it was supposed to have been destroyed forty years ago, after the ambush, but somehow it wasn't. He found it by accident, buried in the archives at Central Army Records in Canberra."

"Some find," Commissioner Bartholomew commented.

"To anyone else," Chap continued, "it might have appeared insignificant and been ignored, but Dickson recognised it immediately because it referred to our old unit."

"How?" Schaefer asked.

Chap tugged at his sleeve, pushing it above his elbow. He turned his arm so the small, diamond-shaped tattoo was visible to everyone in the room.

"What is that?" Rodrigues asked.

"It's an identifying tattoo. We all had it put there before we left for Vietnam. Our job was such that we could not wear the conventional dog tags worn by other soldiers, nor could we wear a recognisable uniform. The tattoo was to identify us as the correct target and confirm the success of the ambush. Reference to the tattoo is made in the document and that was how it came to Dickson's attention." He adjusted his sleeve to cover the tattoo. "Realising what he had discovered, Dickson went to Cobb and Elliott, and eventually to Colonel Baxter."

"And Colonel Baxter's blackmail plan was hatched," Delaney concluded.

"How did you get involved?" Bartholomew queried.

"It started as a routine murder investigation," Chap said. "Then, on seeing the tattoo on his arm, I discovered the victim was Eddie Dickson, my old army mate. As I understand it, Baxter's plans began to fall apart when Dickson refused to go along with him and, when Cobb and Elliott, were murdered, Dickson decided it was all getting too hard. He mailed the document and flew here to ask for my help. Unfortunately, he was killed before he reached me. Then, when I was ordered to hand over the murder file and drop the investigation without any explanation, I had to find out why." He looked around at the faces watching him and he shrugged. "It just seemed like something I had to do. I felt I owed it to an old friend to find out who killed him, and the others."

"We have the file on Dickson," Rodrigues confirmed, "and on Cobb and Elliott, too."

"I know that now," Chap acknowledged.

As if by explanation, Rodrigues continued. "We could not afford for a cop somewhere, a cop like you, for instance, to dig too deep and discover the existence of the Coterie and then broadcast his newfound knowledge to all and sundry. We needed, and still need, to keep a tight lid on this thing."

Obviously affronted, Chap said, "I'm not in the habit of talking about cases to anyone other than those involved. What exactly are *you* doing about the murders?" He watched the CIA agent take a step backwards, place both hands in his pockets, and adopt an easy, relaxed stance.

"It's like I said, Sergeant, we have to keep a lid on… "

"You're not doing a fucking thing, are you?" Chap interrupted angrily.

"Now, Sergeant Bouttell, let's not get all fired up. There are a great number of things to be taken into consideration."

"Like what?" Chap demanded.

"Like internal security," Schaefer interjected. "Both within Australia and the United States."

Chap turned to face Schaefer. "Is that the 'diplomatic' answer?"

"Call it what you will," Schaefer said, "it just happens to be the truth."

"You know what I think, Mr. Schaefer? Fuck internal security! I think it's time you started telling the truth!"

"What do you mean?" Schaefer asked.

"Why don't you start by admitting that you are with ASIO, and not the Diplomatic Corps. Do you really expect us to believe that, as serious and potentially damaging as the document is to both the CIA and ASIO, ASIO is not represented in this room? Do you expect me to believe the CIA obviously considers this important enough to send Agent Rodrigues all the way over here from the U.S. and yet ASIO doesn't consider it worthy of sending their own representative? You are their man in this, and everyone in this room knows it, so why don't you cut the 'diplomat' crap and stop pretending to be something everyone in the room knows you're not!"

Schaefer shuffled his feet and remained silent.

"The files will remain with the joint investigation team," Rodrigues added hurriedly. "And they will remain open until we shut the Coterie down."

"In other words," Chap observed, "no one will ever be brought to justice for the murder of my friends."

"Sergeant," Rodrigues said sternly. "We don't like this goddamned situation any more than you do. The fact remains, however, that national security is at stake here, and this is the way it must be handled. The truth of the matter is, we don't know who in the Coterie is actually responsible for the murders."

Chap turned to face the Commissioner and his assistant. Immediately, he saw in their faces that, if there was to be any satisfaction forthcoming, it was not going to come from his superiors. "Sir," he addressed the Commissioner. "Are you aware that our forensic pathologist, Lee Richardson, was involved with the Coterie?"

"So I have been informed," Bartholomew acknowledged.

"I have reason to believe his reported suicide was in fact murder," Chap continued.

"Can you prove that, Chap?" Assistant Commissioner Delaney asked.

"He hated guns, for Christ's sake! He was terrified of them! He could no more have used one to shoot himself than fly to the moon on a broomstick! Jesus, I stuck a gun in his face and he pissed himself!"

"I'm going to pretend I didn't hear that," Bartholomew said. "And I'm not sure that proves he didn't kill himself," he added.

"Jesus Christ, this is crazy!" Chap said, with unbridled disgust.

"For what it's worth, Chap," Delaney said, "we agree with you. It *is* crazy. We are just as disappointed as you that the investigation has to take this tack. We lost a good police officer in Tony Francis, and you are right, someone should pay for that. However, our hands are tied, at least for the moment. Unfortunately, there is nothing we can do about it. Our instructions are quite clear on this."

"Instructions!" Chap said incredulously. "Instructions from who?" He glared at Delaney. "Well?" Chap spat at him. "Since when have we allowed politics to influence a police investigation?"

"Since right now," Schaefer interjected. "You don't seem

to understand, Sergeant Bouttell, that this is completely out of your hands. It's out of the hands of the South Australian Police. This is a joint investigation conducted by the CIA and ASIO. You really do not have any choice in the matter. You are to disassociate yourself from these matters and forget you ever heard of the Coterie."

"The only joint operation between the CIA and ASIO I am aware of is the one where they murdered Australian soldiers in Vietnam forty years ago, so forgive me if your current joint operation doesn't exactly fill me with confidence."

Agent Rodrigues spoke. "Sergeant, both our countries have undercover people deep within the Coterie, men who have placed themselves in extremely compromising positions. Their lives are at risk every day they stay undercover. Our investigations must be conducted with both delicacy and patience. It may very well take years. In any event, it has been decided that there must never be any risk of the Coterie and its dealings becoming public. The only reassurance I can offer you is that, in due course, the Coterie will be no more."

"So you keep telling me," Chap said. "But how exactly how do you propose to ensure that?"

"Okay, let me explain." Rodrigues sighed. "You are already familiar, in the examples of Colonel Baxter and Dr. Richardson, with the ability of these people to exact retribution on those who cross them."

"And make it look like suicide," Chap completed, for the benefit of everyone in the room.

Rodrigues continued. "It would be naïve of you to assume the CIA and ASIO, by their very nature as national security establishments, were unaware of the effectiveness of such methods."

That statement was, Chap knew, tantamount to an admission that both ASIO and the CIA employed similar tactics, when it was deemed necessary that a particular individual's silence was important to the continuance of national security. They 'neutralised' people who they considered a threat. They did it in the jungle that day forty years ago, and he suspected they still did it today. In his eyes, it made them no better than the people they claimed to be hunting. If there was a difference, it was that, in their case, they would have you believe it was legal and justified because it was carried out in the interests of national security.

It led him to wonder about all the accidental deaths, all the suicides, all the unsolved murders of prominent, and some not so prominent, citizens over the years. Not great numbers, but they happened occasionally. Was he drawing too long a bow? Perhaps, but he thought most likely not. How many of those deaths were genuine? How many of them were considered a threat to their country's security and had to be 'neutralised'? It was wrong that Mr. Average, Mr. Joe Citizen, went off to work each day and toiled to provide an honest and comfortable life for his family whilst remaining ignorant of the shit, the corruption, the lies and dirty tactics going on around him. It was just plain wrong.

"So, what now?" Chap posed the question to anyone in the room who cared to answer it.

The CIA agent took up the invitation. "We know it had to be something big to bring Wallechinski out into the open, and now, thanks to you, we know it was the document. I'm sure you can appreciate its value as evidence. As was stated earlier, it is important that you leave the investigation to those of us in the best position to handle it. You must treat everything said here today as strictly confidential. We believe that, in the fullness of time, the Coterie will implode. With the surfacing of the document, and the reaction it has caused, we are already seeing signs of weakness in their resolve. We are making positive ground, and it goes without saying that the document is a powerful weapon for us to have in our arsenal."

Chap turned his attention to the two senior police officers.

"With respect, sirs, I would like my next comments to go on the record." He waited until both men offered a nod of approval. Then he turned back to Rodrigues.

"I am a police officer," he began. "I took an oath to protect society, and to bring criminals to justice. In the last ten years in particular, that has meant murderers. Recently, I have come into possession of evidence indicating that six men were murdered on the same day forty years ago, in the jungles of Vietnam. And, lately, there has been a series of murders right here in this country directly related to those killings. Correct me if I'm wrong. You are asking me, with the full knowledge and approval of my superiors, to ignore that evidence and do nothing about what I have learned." He turned back to face Commissioner Bartholomew. "Sir, I want it known that I object in the strongest possible terms to what I am being asked to do. You and I both know there is no statute of limitations on murder, so you will have to order me to comply."

Commissioner Bartholomew sat stoically and matched Chap's gaze. "I understand your concern, Sergeant Bouttell. And, your objections are duly noted. However, prior to this meeting, I took the liberty of checking the bona fides of both these gentlemen and I am satisfied the matters discussed here are of national significance and should be handled by the appropriate authorities. You should therefore consider yourself ordered to comply with the request."

Chap stared at his commissioner, and slowly shook his head. "Since when have the police not been the appropriate authority to investigate murder?"

"Since these matters straddled international borders," Bartholomew responded, with a shrug of his shoulders.

Schaefer stood once again, and stepped closer to Chap. "We are all policemen here, Sergeant Bouttell, and we all follow orders from a higher command."

Rodrigues stepped between Schaefer and Chap. "It only remains, Sergeant, for you to give me the document."

Chap didn't know why he chose to lie. It was not a decision he had the luxury of time to think about; the lie just came out. Perhaps it was the natural survival instinct in him. He still felt that, as long as he had the original document, he was safe from harm. Or, maybe he was deluding himself once again. Nevertheless, he was loath to part with it and, in an instant, he decided not to.

"I only have copies." Chap patted his jacket pocket. "I have two here with me, one is lodged with my bank, and another with my solicitor. A copy of the original was all I received from Dickson. I can only assume he considered it too risky to send the original through the post, if in fact, there ever was an original. I have no way of knowing whether he ever discovered the original, or if what he found in the archives was a copy. Everyone who might have known is dead. Dickson himself, Cobb, Elliott, Baxter, Richardson… the list goes on, and seems to be getting longer."

A look of genuine surprise registered on the face of the agent, or was it disbelief?

Chap reached inside his jacket and removed the sealed envelope containing the two copies of the Operations Order. He offered it to Rodrigues.

Rodrigues paused, looked at the envelope, and then reached out and took it from Chap. He did not open it. He turned it over, looked at the back, then at the front again. Seemingly satisfied, he tucked the envelope away inside his jacket.

Strangely, Chap felt some mild relief. Now, someone else knew what he knew and he no longer had to live with the enormity of what he had learned. He was bitterly disappointed that he was excluded from ongoing investigations, and he was sceptical about how thorough the joint ASIO/CIA investigation would be. As had been pointed out to him a number of times, it was out of his hands and, despite his reservations, from somewhere he had to find some semblance of faith and trust in the system of justice. That would be the hard part.

"What about the money?" Schaefer said, from his position behind Agent Rodrigues.

"What money?" Chap asked.

"The two hundred and fifty thousand dollars Wallechinski gave you. Did you think we didn't know about that? The money is also evidence."

"Go fuck yourself!" Chap suggested.

Agent Rodrigues turned to Schaefer. "Forget about the money."

Schaefer was astounded. "What?"

"Forget about the money," Rodrigues repeated. "I'm sure Sergeant Bouttell will put it to very good use."

"But..." Schaefer protested.

"Forget it!" Rodrigues insisted.

Chapter Thirty-Five

The room was suddenly engulfed in uncomfortable silence. Chap was not about to blow his sudden good fortune by admitting he had the money, and he was certainly not prepared to surrender it. It had never been his intention to keep it for his own use, but he was not about to tell them that; certainly not Schaefer, the smarmy, so-called diplomat.

Also, he had no way of knowing who in the Commissioner's office actually believed him when he said he had never seen the original of the document. Their expressions gave nothing away. However, exactly who believed him and who didn't was a detail he was not going let concern him too greatly. He said he did not have the original, and now he had to maintain that position, or risk his credibility. It was too late to turn back. Rodrigues, he was sure, did not believe him. Like the others in the room, the agent's expression remained unrevealing, but there was something about the young CIA man that Chap found disconcerting, despite his generosity in allowing him to keep the money.

Chap decided to take the initiative and addressed Rodrigues. "How old are you?"

Rodrigues was plainly surprised. "Excuse me?"

"How old are you?"

"Sergeant, I don't see…"

Chap smiled. "Humour me. How old are you?"

Rodrigues glanced at the Police Commissioner, as if looking for support. He saw none forthcoming. Obviously, Commissioner Bartholomew was going to give his lead homicide detective some leeway, given the circumstances he found himself in.

Rodrigues looked back at Chap. "I'm thirty-one."

"Thirty-one." Chap nodded. "Thirty-one," he said again. "The Vietnam war was over before you were born."

Rodrigues shrugged. "I don't see the relevance."

"How long have you been with the CIA?"

"Ten years. I applied from college, and entered the training academy when I was twenty-one."

"Do you carry a firearm?"

"Not in your country."

"In yours?"

"Of course."

"Ever used it?"

"I don't understand where you are going with this line of questioning, Sergeant," Rodrigues said.

"Like I said," Chap answered. "Humour me, please."

"I've used my weapon in training, and I attend the range back home every few weeks."

Chap nodded in understanding. "I've been a cop for almost thirty years. I've only ever had to take my firearm out of its holster in the line of duty a couple of times."

"You've been very fortunate," Rodrigues observed.

"I take it, from what you have told me, you have never killed a man."

"I, too, have been fortunate, Sergeant."

Chap fixed the agent with a steely glare. "They flew us

home on a military transport plane a couple of days after the ambush. Charlie Cobb was still in a bad way, but he was stable and, thankfully, he was going to recover. He was on a stretcher, accompanied by a nurse and an army medic. It was a long flight, Agent Rodrigues. I remember none of us spoke much during the flight. I had plenty of time to think. I tried to count, in my head, how many men I had killed in the previous twelve months."

He paused, and looked away vacantly for a few seconds before continuing. "I got to nineteen, but I remember being sure I was missing a few. I remember thinking about the fragility of life, and the finality of death. Unless you've actually killed a man, you cannot imagine, not even in your wildest imagination, what it feels like. Do you know what I'm thinking about now, Agent Rodrigues?" He swung his eyes to Schaefer. "Mr. Schaefer?"

"No," both men said in unison.

Chap continued. "I'm thinking about the men who ambushed us, the men who were ordered to kill us and succeeded in killing six of us. I hope those of them who have since passed away, and after all this time I'm sure there will be a few of them, attained some degree of inner peace before they died. Those who are still alive have lived all these years with those murders on their conscience. They must have known they were not killing the enemy, but their allies. The men in my unit also committed murder—at least I think of it as murder. Even though the men we killed *were* the enemy, I find little justification in what we did. However, nothing justifies what the men who ambushed us were ordered to do. They have to live with their actions. I have struggled over the decades to imagine how they do that."

"Sergeant Bouttell..." Rodrigues began to speak.

Chap raised his hand and stopped the CIA agent. "When you two gentlemen leave here today, I want you to think of the men who died on that day in the jungle, and those who have died since. I want you to count the lives that have been wasted because some penis-obsessed bureaucrat made a decision forty years ago that, to this day, defies any logical explanation." Chap paused as if inviting a response.

Commissioner Bartholomew spoke this time to Schaefer. "Tell me, Mr. Schaefer, what would happen if the document ever became public? I mean, forty years is a long time. Chances are the original draftsman of the document is dead. Probably most of those involved in its planning and eventual implementation are dead, or at least very old. I can understand the CIA and ASIO being severely embarrassed if their involvement were exposed, not to mention both our governments. However, both the U.S. and Australian governments have changed many times in the last forty years, and both have suffered embarrassment to some degree over one scandal or another over that time, so what real damage would be done if the document were to find its way into the public domain?"

Schaefer cleared his throat and spoke in a soft, almost effeminate voice. "You're right, Commissioner, most of those originally involved would be either dead or old men by now. And you are also right when you say there would be some very red faces all around if this were to become public. But it is more than mere embarrassment that concerns the CIA, ASIO and both our governments. If this were to become a matter of public knowledge, I can almost guarantee there would be calls for a Royal Commission of Enquiry here in Australia, and I know Agent Rodrigues's superiors would demand a Congressional Enquiry in the United States would be a given.

"Not everyone involved would be dead, despite the passage of time. Many would be brought to task over this thing, many would go to prison, and more than likely die there. The political fallout for both our countries would be devastating. Particularly if any of those involved have since attained positions of power and influence or, heaven forbid, are currently sitting politicians. And let's not even think about the ammunition such knowledge would give to our enemies and detractors in other parts of the world. I'm sure we would all agree that there is no shortage of those who would love to see Australia and the U.S. as the subjects of international contempt and ridicule. No, Commissioner, we cannot afford to let this get out. We must shut this down as quickly and as quietly as we can, regardless of the cost."

"And regardless of how many more must die?" Chap added sarcastically.

"You know, Sergeant," Agent Rodrigues said, "this is not, and never was, about what you and your unit were sent to Vietnam to do. If what you did was to become public, it is conceivable, albeit unlikely, that it could be glossed over, trivialised, even glamorised with all the political spin and double talk you can imagine. After all, politics in your country is really no different from politics in mine; it's all smoke and mirrors. No, this is not about what your unit did. It's about what the CIA and ASIO did. This is about what *they* did. They were ordered to set up an ambush, kill every member of your unit and, apparently, a document exists out there somewhere, verifying just that. No amount of political spin or buck-passing will save your country or mine from the effects of the fallout."

"Let me see if I've got this right," Chap suggested. "All you guys *really* want is the document. And, when you have it, you want to put it through the shredder, or dispose of it in some way as to ensure it never sees the light of day, and all those penis-obsessed morons I was talking about a moment ago can sleep easy for what remains of their worthless, fucked-up lives. As for my friends who were murdered in Vietnam, well, that was a long time ago, wasn't it? Nobody cares what happened in a stinking jungle, in a war-torn land, in another part of the world, forty years ago, do they? And, if no one ever sees the inside of a courtroom over this recent spate of killings, that's okay, too, as long as you have the document.

How am I doing?" He looked at Rodrigues, and then at Schaefer. "I guess that's why you really don't care about the money. It would never be used in evidence, and would probably find its way into some crooked bureaucrat's pocket."

Schaefer struck a pose that suggested he was pissed off, even insulted. He was about to speak when Rodrigues beat him to the punch.

"Sergeant, we know the Coterie is responsible for all the deaths that have occurred recently; which particular member, or members, we may never know. And, now that we know what the document contains, we could, with a little old-fashioned digging, find out the names of all those who took part in the ambush and go after them, or those who are still alive. But that would tip the Coterie off, and we can't afford to jeopardise our investigation into their operations. We have been on their trail far too long. Although I hate to admit it, it's true that no one may ever face justice over any of these killings, but our priority is the total dismantling of the Coterie, and the ongoing security and reputations of our respective countries. We must focus our attention and efforts on achieving that end."

"I see you are pretty good at the political spin yourself," Chap noted.

Assistant Commissioner Delaney stepped forward. "This 'Coterie', as they call themselves, what do they want? What drives them? What do they care if the document were to become a matter of public knowledge? How would that hurt them?"

"All very good questions," Schaefer elected to answer. "The simple answer is it *wouldn't* hurt them. Given the document dates back forty years, and no one knew of its existence until Major Dickson found it recently, it is reasonable to assume there is no one involved with the Coterie today who was involved with the so-called T Force, back then; if in fact they ever *were* involved. Their motivation is misguided. The original Special Operations Group, from where T Force would have originated, was a legitimate section within the CIA's Special Activities Division. These were highly trained and multi-skilled people. They were dedicated to maintaining the security and integrity of their country. Obviously, this was a 'one-off', and a mistake in judgment, a bad one admittedly, but that doesn't alter the fact that they were all prepared to give their lives, if need be, to save their country from international ridicule."

Rodrigues took over the narrative. "To be honest, we don't really know what motivates them. We can only surmise that the original concept of saving their respective countries from disgrace and international ridicule still holds true for the handful of original members who date back to the days of the Coterie's inception. These elder statesmen in the group seem to be obsessively patriotic, and prepared to go to any lengths to maintain the equilibrium. Many of their members, like Wallechinski, for instance, are extremely wealthy, and they have the ear of politicians of all persuasions and levels of importance. Hell, it's conceivable that some of them may even *be* prominent political figures.

"Exposure would put the fortunes they have amassed, and the global business empires they have built, at risk. So, is it the risk of poverty and facing the rest of their lives in prison, or simply obsessive patriotism that drives them? We don't know for sure. We suspect, for those like Wallechinski, it is poverty and prison, because it has been a long time since the days of the T Force and other units like it. We believe that, for many of the people associated with the Coterie, the original connection to ASIO and the CIA has been clouded, even lost with the passing of time. What we do know is we have to keep working away at them until we can shut them down once and for all. At this time, that is our priority." He paused.

Chap addressed his next words to both Rodrigues and Schaefer. "You know, I have listened to everything you have said, and I can only draw one conclusion. You, and the Coterie, both want the original document, you for reasons of so-called 'national security' and the Coterie for saving their wealth and keeping their rich arses out of prison. I don't believe for one minute that your country, Agent Rodrigues, or ours, *Mr.* Schaefer, gives a flying fuck one way or the other about bringing killers to justice. It's all about the complicit atrocity that occurred in the jungle forty years ago and how you can keep that quiet so politicians in both our countries can sleep at night and can keep their snouts in the trough without having to constantly surface to look over their shoulder."

"Chap," Commissioner Bartholomew said, "let's try to keep this in perspective. Arguing the point, and criticising the methods and motivation of the joint investigation, is counter-productive." He turned to face Rodrigues. "What about the original of the document?"

"Unfortunately," the agent answered, "it seems the original is not to be had." He glanced knowingly at Chap, who looked questioningly back at the CIA man. "We can only speculate as to where it might be, or who might have it. Hopefully, it was destroyed when it was supposed to be."

"Obviously not before a copy, or copies were made," Chap observed.

Rodrigues agreed. "Obviously." He gave Chap that disbelieving look again. "Let's also hope the original has not been secreted away somewhere, by someone waiting for the right moment to produce it."

Chap remained expressionless. "Can you be certain that the copies I just gave you will remain safe from unwanted scrutiny?"

"I trust you are not casting aspersions on the internal security precautions of ASIO or the CIA?" Schaefer asked with disdain.

Chap was casting aspersions as big as boulders on the CIA

and ASIO; full stop. But, he chose not to dignify the question with a response. His main concern, for the moment at least, was for Sally, and himself. He knew he was in no position to demand the document copies remain a secret. A little of the security he felt earlier, when he was in charge of the copies, had been removed, but he could live with that. He didn't particularly like these two shifty-looking men in expensive suits, Schaefer even less than Rodrigues, but he had to trust them. Besides, he still had the original, and as long as they didn't know for certain that he had it, he felt like he still had the upper hand. "What about my partner?" he asked, changing tack.

Schaefer answered. "As far as anyone is concerned, the media, the public and, for that matter, the rest of the police department, your people are investigating his unfortunate death and the investigation is ongoing."

Chap turned to the commissioner for confirmation. "Sir?"

Bartholomew leaned forward and lightly touched a file that lay on the desk in front of him. "Following your meeting with Wallechinski," he began, "we know that Francis conveyed the document, or should I say a copy of the document, to you, and he was killed because of it. We also know he was not the intended victim, you were. We don't know who the killer is and, sadly, we may never know. This whole shitty business has been taken out of our control."

"Tell that to his family," Chap scoffed. "His father has an office here on this floor, just along the corridor, doesn't he? What are you going to tell him when he comes knocking and wants to know how the investigation into his only child's murder is progressing?"

"Sergeant," Bartholomew sighed, "I know how you feel. When a fellow police officer loses his life on the job, we are all angry and saddened. I will tell his father we are doing everything we can to find out who is responsible." He indicated his assistant. "I have appointed Assistant Commissioner Delaney as head of the investigation, and it will appear to be as thorough and detailed as any other investigation."

"*Appear*?" Chap asked.

"I'm afraid so, for the time being, anyway. But"— he looked at Rodrigues and Schaefer—"I trust we won't have to keep the charade up for long. Not being able to do what we are sworn to do because of political interference sickens me." He held the agents' eyes for a moment before continuing. "Gentlemen, while I accept this investigation is no longer a matter for the South Australian Police, I want it understood, by both of you, that I am not happy about murders being committed in my jurisdiction and not being able to do anything about it. I expect to be regularly updated on the progress of the investigation, even if only as a matter of courtesy."

He focused on Schaefer. "Mr. Schaefer, I am this close," he placed his thumb and forefinger a fraction apart, "from lodging an official complaint with your superiors in regard to your supposed identity. You come into my office and expect us to be honest and forthcoming with you, and you don't have the common decency to disclose your true calling. Like Sergeant Bouttell said, everyone in this room knows you are with ASIO. You may well use the Diplomatic Corps as a cover, but don't insult me, my Assistant Commissioner, and my most experienced homicide investigator, with any more of your bullshit. This is not a game of *'Spy versus Spy'*. That sort of shadowy, black-suit, white-shirt, black-tie, Oakley-shades shit does not work here. We are police officers and, among other things, we investigate murder. Those of us in this room who have dedicated our working lives to just that, are not happy at the prospect of murderers going unpunished just to save our country from some international embarrassment. So, if you ever find yourself in this office again, for whatever reason, please leave your cloak-and-dagger bullshit, and your ego, at the door."

Duly chastised, Schaefer dropped his eyes and focused on a spot somewhere on the carpet.

It seemed to Chap that this was the end of the meeting. One by one, he shifted his eyes to the faces of the men in the room. No one spoke. When his eyes met those of the Commissioner, Bartholomew nodded almost imperceptibly. Finally, Chap looked at the CIA agent. "Is there anything else?" he asked.

"The tape," Schaefer interjected bluntly.

Chap's eyes swung to face Schaefer. "The what?"

"The tape, Sergeant." He paused. "The tape of your conversations with Wallechinski and Dr. Richardson. We want it."

The miniature tape recorder was in Chap's pocket at that very moment. "I haven't got the tape. That is, I haven't got it here with me now," he lied.

Schaefer fixed him with the same disbelieving look that Rodrigues had given him a few minutes earlier. Chap was sure he heard him emit an almost inaudible huff of disdain.

Chap glared at Schaefer. "What?"

"Nothing," Schaefer shuffled.

Rodrigues said, "I have to fly out of Adelaide tomorrow afternoon. Do you think you can get the tape to me by then?"

"I'll see what I can do," Chap answered. "Where can I find you?"

"I'll find you. Perhaps I could stop by your house on my way to the airport."

Although he found it strange that Rodrigues would want to come to his home, Chap decided not to question the agent's motives.

"Suit yourself." Chap shrugged. He rose from his chair and turned to leave the room.

Rodrigues stepped in front of him and offered his hand. "Until tomorrow then."

Chap shook the agent's hand and turned to leave. His

departure was impeded by Schaefer, who also offered his hand. Chap smiled at the 'diplomat', stepped around him and left the office. Schaefer stared wide-eyed after him, eventually realised he was still standing there with his hand extended and, obviously embarrassed by the deliberate snub, quickly stuffed it into his trouser pocket.

Chapter Thirty-Six

Within walking distance from Police Headquarters there was a hotel Chap and many of his colleagues frequented from time to time; some more frequently than others. He was not a regular pubgoer but, when he did go, he never stayed long and, if he was going to have a drink, he preferred it to be with those with whom he worked, rather than drink alone—although, over the last few days, he had blotted his copybook in relation to drinking alone.

Today was different. Today, he wanted to be alone and he hoped he would not run into anyone he knew. He wanted the comfort of his own company and not to feel obliged to listen to some half-intoxicated colleague bitching about the stresses of the job, or crowing about how he had cracked a case all on his own.

The hotel dated back to the days of early settlement and had, over the long history of its existence, undergone many cosmetic changes. Recently, it had been extensively renovated by the present licensee to such a degree that it no longer bore any resemblance to the pub of old. Chap chose the relative solitude of the lounge bar, away from the front bar area which was the preferred haunt of off-duty cops. The proprietors had installed booths, tucked away against one wall in a dimly lit, secluded area of the room.

The lounge bar was accessible through its own entrance from outside, allowing Chap to avoid passing through the front bar and risk meeting any of his colleagues. He could lose himself here, engrossed in his own thoughts, and hopefully remain undisturbed. He purchased a whisky and slipped into a booth, accompanied only by his thoughts, and a glass of Johnny Walker.

His thoughts, and there were many of them, came in no particular order of importance. He thought about Eddie Dickson, Charles Cobb and Brian Elliott; about the pathologist Dr. Lee Richardson, and Sir Douglas Wallechinski.

How was it, he wondered, that someone like Wallechinski, with so much to lose both financially and personally, could get so deeply entrenched into such an evil organisation as the Coterie? Perhaps he got involved before he had a cent to his name. Perhaps they gave him his start in life, and now he felt obliged to repay that early leg-up.

His mind was also on the undercover ASIO man, 'Bozo'. His thoughts lingered on Bozo for a moment and strangely, he never felt any real regret for leaving him somewhat incapacitated. He wondered if his lack of remorse was something he should be concerned about, and quickly decided it wasn't. If Bozo was going to play rough with Sally, he deserved all he got.

He sipped his whisky and thought about Vietnam and his mates who died there, murdered by their own government. How could that have happened? Who instigated the plan? Were any of the culprits still alive? Would they ever be called to account for this horrendous obscenity of a crime? Chap thought not. He wanted to scream this atrocity from the highest mountain. He wanted every media outlet in the country to run with the story and then sit back and watch just who scurried down their rat holes. Then, he thought about the meeting he had just come from, and something deep inside him, some instinctive thing he couldn't explain, niggled at him. Something was wrong. This whole Coterie thing just didn't sound right. Something stank, and he just couldn't put his finger on it.

Without realising it, his glass was suddenly empty. He stared at the slowly melting ice cubes in the bottom of the glass as his thoughts turned to the CIA agent, Rodrigues, and the so-called 'diplomat', Schaefer. As he rose from the booth and crossed to the bar to get another drink, he thought of Colonel Frederick W. Baxter and the role he played in this ongoing saga.

When he was seated again, he thought about his late partner Tony Francis and found he was swamped by a foreboding feeling that confused him. For some inexplicable reason, and without success, he tried to direct his mind away from thoughts of his partner. Why should he not want to think about Francis? He was midway through his second whisky when it dawned on him—or perhaps crashed down upon him like a tree felled by a lightning bolt was a more apt analogy.

Chap gagged on a piece of ice, and almost choked as the possibility ran through his racing mind. It was impossible—or was it? Tony Francis part of the Coterie? No, it couldn't be, could it? Surely not? He cursed inwardly for allowing his thoughts to drift to such an outrageous scenario. But, as the possibility lingered in the front of his mind, he found himself analysing the facts as he knew them.

He looked at the time he and Francis had been partners. It seemed to correspond, albeit roughly, with the time Colonel Baxter was hatching his blackmail plan. There were other coincidences which came to his mind, and he hoped he was not creating them as a means of justifying the seriousness of the thoughts he was having.

He sipped at his whisky, and shook his head in an effort to clear it of negative thoughts in respect of Tony Francis. Francis could not have been involved with the Coterie. Despite not wanting to entertain the possibility, he could not drive it from his mind.

Was it possible that, after Chap phoned Francis from Canberra and learned the envelope had arrived, Francis then contacted the Coterie and told them the same thing? No— if that were the case, why not simply hand the envelope over to them? It was, after all, exactly what they wanted.

But, perhaps Francis couldn't hand it to the Coterie because he had already told Chap it had arrived at Headquarters, and he knew Chap would ask for it when he returned. Did Francis tell the Coterie about the envelope, only to be instructed to hold onto it and await further instructions? Was Francis set up? Was he always intended to die in the explosion that was also supposed to destroy the document? No, how could they have known he would be in Chap's car? Was Tony Francis a Coterie sleeper? Chap looked at it from every conceivable angle and, although hating himself for it, he still reached the same conclusion. Detective Senior Constable Tony Francis was dirty!

Oh, how he wanted to be wrong. He could forgive himself for the terrible thoughts he was having if only he could see some way he might be wrong. Disgusted with his doubts on the honesty of his former partner, Chap placed his glass on the table, and pushed it away.

Suddenly, he was overcome with a deep sadness. He felt depressed and alone. This thing called the Coterie was evil. It was a cancer which had spread throughout the ranks of ASIO, the CIA, through the private sector here and abroad, and almost certainly through both the Australian government, and the U.S. administration. There appeared to be no immediate solution. There would be, Chap knew, no quick fix, no miracle cures. Just as highly-skilled medical researchers spent years and uncountable dollars on efforts to find a cure for the human cancer strains, so would honest investigators toil to cure the cancer of lies, deceit, and death slowly eating away at the very fabric of society, perpetrated by the Coterie.

Chap guessed he would never know, not for sure, if he was wrong about Francis, and that saddened him. Francis's family, his friends and his colleagues, all believed him to be one of the finest police officers in the job. There were those, Chap knew, who even saw him as a future Commissioner. In the absence of any evidence suggesting he was anything other than an honest, dedicated, career cop, he deserved a funeral with full police honours, and perhaps it was best that those who knew him were left with only good memories.

Confused, Chap didn't know which way to lean. He was sitting on the fence and quite simply did not know what the truth was anymore. Perhaps Agent Rodrigues was a part of the Coterie. Or Schaefer. Or maybe both. Who would know with Schaefer? The man was a dipstick.

Who was telling the truth, and who was not? Right now, Chap trusted no one. Not the CIA agent, and certainly not the pseudo diplomat, Schaefer. He hated these feelings and wanted to believe he was doing Francis's memory a grave disservice, but he just didn't know.

He rose from the booth and left the hotel, feeling tired and despondent. Nothing seemed to matter anymore—not the document, not the Coterie, not even his job. For the first time he could recall, Chap Bouttell no longer wanted to be a cop.

After a sleepless night haunted by images of a long-ago war and wild, speculative thoughts of corrupt cops and politicians, Chap finally got up at four-thirty in the morning, dressed warmly, made coffee, and went to his computer. Now, several hours later, he sat in his lounge, complete with ripped cushions, and drank more coffee.

While dawn slowly surfaced outside, he stared absently into the crackling flames licking from the fireplace, creating dancing shadows springing from every corner of the still dark room. The effect was almost hypnotic, and he was able to drift to a place where nothing entered his mind to disturb the quiet, peaceful ambience. He even dozed occasionally throughout the morning, only getting up twice to refill his coffee cup.

Agent Rodrigues arrived in a taxi in the early afternoon. He alighted from the cab and looked up at Chap's house, confirming the address. He spoke briefly to the driver, perhaps asking him to wait, and then walked up the driveway towards Chap's front door.

Chap had not long stepped from a hot, reviving shower and was beginning to feel human again. He watched as Rodrigues approached, stepped onto the porch, and knocked lightly on the door.

"Come in," Chap called.

Rodrigues opened the door, and stepped into the house. He stopped just inside, closed the door behind him and glanced up the hallway towards the bedrooms, obviously looking for possible threats. He turned and saw Chap sitting in the lounge room. He moved into the room, noticed the fire, and crossed to the hearth where he turned his back to the flames and faced Chap. He smiled politely. "Good afternoon, Sergeant Bouttell." He placed his hands behind his back and rubbed them together, enjoying the welcoming warmth. "Cold outside," he said absently.

"It's winter." Chap shrugged, as if by explanation.

Agent Rodrigues looked around the room and eventually noticed the ripped, dishevelled cushions. He raised his eyebrows and nodded towards one of the lounge chairs. "Have an accident?" he asked.

Chap followed the agent's eyes. "No," Chap answered. "I suspect it's the work of your undercover man, or someone just like him."

"Really?"

"Yes, really."

"Well," Rodrigues said, as if offering justification, "he does have a cover to protect." His eyes were drawn to the coffee table in front of Chap. More particularly, to the small cassette tape which lay there. "Is that the tape?"

Chap leaned forward, picked up the tape, and tossed it casually to Rodrigues. "Think quick," he said.

The agent scrambled to catch the tape before it landed in the fire behind him. He clutched at it, gave it a perfunctory glance, and slipped it into his pocket. "Thank you."

Chap had copied the tape the previous night, and now his own copy lay nestled amongst his Neil Diamond music collection in the stereo cabinet across the room.

"Did you make a copy for yourself?" Rodrigues asked.

"No," Chap lied.

Rodrigues looked Chap in the eye. "You still have the original of the document, don't you?"

Chap returned the agent's stare, and lied straight to his face. "I told you yesterday, I have never seen the original."

Rodrigues did not believe him, and it was obvious. "You do still have copies though, right?"

"Of course," Chap answered.

"I wish you didn't," Rodrigues said.

Chap shrugged dismissively. "Just covering my arse."

Rodrigues stepped a pace away from the fireplace, towards where Chap sat. "You know, I didn't believe you yesterday when you said you didn't have the original, and I don't believe you today."

"That's your prerogative," Chap said. "Personally, I don't give a shit one way or the other."

"Do you have it?" Rodrigues asked bluntly.

Chap smiled. "For one so sure I *do* have it, you seem to be having some doubt."

"I guess maybe I was hoping I would hear you admit it," Rodrigues said.

"Sorry to disappoint you," Chap apologized, with little conviction. "The truth is, nothing has changed since yesterday. I told you then I had no idea where it might be, or what might have happened to it. Nothing has changed in the last twenty-four hours to make me change my position on that."

The CIA agent raised his hands in a gesture of surrender. "Okay, okay, Sergeant. I guess there is very little left for us to say to each other. I'll be on my way." He made to move towards the door, and stopped. "Oh, there is something that's been bothering me. I've been meaning to ask you…"

"What?" Chap interrupted.

"The blackmail attempt by Colonel Baxter. Were your army buddies part of that?"

"Come again?" Chap asked, shocked. The question came at him out of nowhere, taking him by surprise. But, he was determined not to make it easy for this guy.

"Well, you know, it had crossed my mind," Rodrigues said.

"What difference would it make if they were?" Chap posed. "They're all dead."

"We have no evidence to suggest they played a part in it, but then I guess we never will know, will we?"

"That's right," he agreed, "I guess you never will."

Rodrigues started again towards the door. When he reached the small entrance foyer, he turned back to face Chap, who had not moved from the chair. "One more thing," he said.

"I can hardly wait," Chap said sarcastically.

"There is still the small matter of the money."

"What about it?"

"Two hundred and fifty thousand dollars, I believe the amount was," Rodrigues said. "Where is it?"

"Safe." Chap smiled.

"You don't deny you have it then?"

"Given Bozo's allegiance to ASIO and the CIA, denying it would be pointless, don't you think?" Chap suggested. "Are you withdrawing your generous offer to let me keep it?"

Rodrigues laughed. "No, but Schaefer was right. You know, the money is technically evidence."

"Evidence of what? As I understand it, you and your joint investigation team are not going to do anything about the murder and mayhem the Coterie have caused, and are still causing. What would happen to the money if you had it? You say it is evidence, but we both know it would never be produced as such in any legal proceedings."

Chap focused intently on Rodrigues's face, lest his eyes be drawn automatically to the loft hatch cover in the ceiling above the agent's head. The money was stashed there, just a metre from where Rodrigues stood. "I spent some time, a few hours as it happens, sitting at my computer this morning," he said.

Rodrigues arched his eyebrows. "Oh?"

"I Googled everything I could on Sir Douglas Wallechinski."

"And…?"

Chap shrugged. "I found nothing. Not a single reference anywhere, not in merchant banking, not in mining, not even on Australia's 'Rich List', nothing. It's almost like he doesn't exist. Don't you find that strange?"

"He chooses a low-profile life," Rodrigues offered as explanation.

"And I think you are full of shit," Chap answered.

"Really?"

"Yes, really. Would you like to know what I believe to be the truth?"

"It's not important what you think, Sergeant, but I guess

you are determined to tell me anyway, so go ahead." Rodrigues made no move to step back into the room.

"I believe the Coterie exists, but I don't believe it has anything to do with any rouge group of ex CIA or ASIO members. I don't believe for one minute that Wallechinski, or whatever his name is, is a banker, or a miner. I expect the closest he's ever got to mining is to dig a hole in the garden for his wife's rose bush. I think he is one of your—or, more likely, one of our — operatives. The Coterie is an active, clandestine group of operatives from the CIA and ASIO. They are an assassination squad, a killing squad. Set up to do whatever is deemed necessary in the interests of national security, and their actions are never going to be exposed. In fact, their very existence will never be acknowledged, by your country or mine. How am I doing?"

"Do I detect some bitterness in your voice?" Rodrigues asked, choosing not to answer the question directly.

"Oh, I'm bitter all right." Chap scowled. "And fuckin' angry. When it comes right down to it, and you take away all the gloss and bullshit, you are police officers. A little more sophisticated, perhaps, and with a lot more resources at your disposal than us common state coppers, but police officers nonetheless. You are supposed to uphold the law, and devote your time and energy to exposing the existence of shit like the Coterie. Instead, you *are* the Coterie! How the fuck you sleep at night is beyond me!"

"Believe what you will, Sergeant Bouttell," Rodrigues countered. "We have some of the best law enforcement people you will find anywhere working their butts off on this thing. Some of them, as was explained to you yesterday, are in positions of great personal danger. Sometimes there are matters of such importance to national security that we must place that security before all else, and, no matter how much as law enforcement people we may dislike it, we are sometimes forced to look beyond obvious offences and see the big picture.

This is the way it has to be done, and I'm sorry you can't see that."

In his heart, Chap knew Rodrigues was lying. He had no proof, and knew he would never have any. This was what it was, and his suspicions alone, unsupported by any real evidence, were never going to change that.

"Look, Sergeant." The agent's tone softened a little. "I don't like this any more than you do. Really, I don't. I would like to see these assholes strapped to a gurney and I would like to press the plunger myself but, the truth is, there really *is* no other way. The consequences of this going public are far too frightening to think about. And, regardless of your, and my, involvement, the decision is not ours to make. You are a cop, you were a soldier, you know how these things work. Folks like you and me, we're just the foot soldiers for a much higher authority. We don't give orders, we follow them, despite how unfair or unjust they may seem to be. There are forces at play here bigger than both of us." He glanced at his watch. "I've got to go. I've got a flight to catch." He turned back towards the door.

"I think Tony Francis might have been dirty," Chap said to the agent's back.

Rodrigues stopped, and turned back to face Chap. "What?"

"Detective Francis, my partner. I think he was dirty."

"You're wrong," was all Rodrigues said.

"How the fuck do you know I'm wrong?" Chap pushed.

"Believe me, Sergeant, you don't want to know how I know. Francis was a good cop. Do yourself a favour and remember him that way. Don't get yourself all screwed up believing anything different. Francis was not dirty. He was just in the wrong place at the wrong time." He opened the door, paused, and pulled his collar high around his neck against the cold and rain waiting outside. "Don't waste your life letting all this crap get to you, it's not worth it. Be happy." He winked at Chap, and then stepped outside.

Just before he closed the door, he stuck his crew-cut head back into the foyer and said, "Spend the money wisely."

"Ah, shit!" Chap murmured to the door as it closed. "Don't go yet. You can't leave it like that. If Tony wasn't dirty, who the fuck is?"

Epilogue

With a military history dating back to the days of early colonisation, Torrens Parade Ground and its impressive old barracks building was located on the very edge of the Adelaide CBD, and within a short walking distance from the National War Memorial. With a large central drill hall bordered by offices, the barracks building was once used as a staging place for troops departing for war, and more recently as headquarters for the Citizens Military Force and Army Reserve. It also housed the South Australian branches of ex-service organisations such as the Returned and Services League, the Air Force Association, and the Vietnam Veterans' Association.

Before he left the city, and headed south, Chap took the bag of cash to the Torrens Parade Ground.

The Vietnam Veterans' Association occupied several rooms to the rear of the first floor, above the huge indoor drill hall of the beautiful old building. Casually carrying the sports bag with its cash contents, Chap made his way up the staircase to the second floor and followed a long, narrow corridor around to the rear.

Earlier, he had attached a note to the closed bag identifying it as an anonymous donation, with instructions that the money be used for the future health and wellbeing of Vietnam veterans in need. For the many Vietnam Veterans who had fallen on hard times, or who had never, after all these years, adjusted to a so-called normal life after the horrors they experienced, the money would be a godsend. There was no shortage of these desperate and, in many cases, physically and emotionally ill men, and Chap figured they needed the money more than he did.

He never saw anyone, and never spoke to anyone. When he reached the reception office, he stopped and listened for a moment to voices coming from inside the room. Not wanting to be discovered, he placed the bag on the floor where it would be seen by anyone who stepped from the office, and then turned and walked briskly away in the direction he had come.

As he walked quickly down the stairs and out of the building, he realised he was smiling. Most people who had just come into a quarter of a million dollars would not look upon the matter of giving it away as something to smile about, but Chap smiled widely.

He could have bought a new car, or a new lounge suite. Lord knows he needed both. He could have done many things to enhance his life with that amount of money but, somehow, his needs seemed individualistic and self-indulgent in comparison to the needs of those whose lives were forever changed for the worse as a result of the Vietnam War. What *he* wanted, or needed, was unimportant. No matter how he looked at it, for him, the bag contained blood money and he wanted no part of it for himself.

He could not explain why he felt good now, and he was not going to try. It had been a long time since he felt this way. He embraced the feeling as he climbed into his rental car and drove from the Parade Ground car park. When he exited, he turned south, drove through the city, and kept driving.

At Chapman Bouttell's home, the two intruders were thorough. They searched the house systematically, room by room, leaving no cupboard, drawer or crevice unexamined. They searched Chap's clothes hanging in the wardrobe, and those tossed aside in the laundry hamper. Nothing was overlooked, not the narrow space under the bed, not under the mattress, not inside the freezer, or inside the toilet cistern.

One of the men, the smaller of the two, removed the loft hatch cover, climbed into the dusty, claustrophobic roof-space and shone a torch into every possible hiding place. While he searched the cramped space, his partner disconnected the hard drive from Chap's computer and placed it at the front door, then waited for his partner to clamber down from the ceiling.

"Anything?"

"Nothing. If it was ever up there, it's not now. There is nothing up there except dust and spiders!"

Then they searched the house a second time, even more thoroughly than the first, with the same results. They searched the small shed in the backyard, and then the backyard itself, looking for any signs of fresh digging where someone might have recently buried something, like a bag full of cash, for instance. They found nothing.

Satisfied Bouttell had not stashed the money anywhere at his home, they left the house. Once settled inside a nondescript grey sedan parked on the street in front of the house, one of the intruders flicked open a cell phone, punched in some numbers and spoke almost immediately. "It's not at the house." He listened to the voice on the end of the line for a few moments and then disconnected the call.

"Well?" his partner queried.

"Another team has been following him. He took the money with him and dropped it off in the city. He gave it away! Can you believe that?"

"He gave it away? A quarter of a million bucks! Who's the lucky bastard?"

"Bastards, plural. He gave it to the Vietnam Veterans' Association. What do those broken-down old farts want with a quarter of a million dollars? Come on, let's get out of here, there's nothing more we can do here."

David Crofts was a respected and admired man, considered by those who knew him to be honest and above reproach. However, his honesty notwithstanding, every man has his price. Sadly, Crofts had his.

As a bank manager, he was paid well, but that hadn't always been the case. Before his current position, he spent many years working his way up the banking ladder, firstly as a Customer Service Officer, then a Senior Customer Service Officer, and then an Assistant Branch Manager, all somewhat more junior positions, and all somewhat less lucrative in regard to salary. They were also positions which required years of service at each level before one might be considered for advancement to the lofty heights of Branch Manager.

Crofts was nearing retirement age, and he knew he had nowhere near enough money in personal savings or in superannuation to see him into what he hoped would be a comfortable old age. Certainly not after that bitch he was married to declared, in an exceedingly unsavoury manner, that she was hell bent on cleaning him out financially. And, as if that wasn't enough, she was also shooting for half his superannuation entitlements!

Publicly, David Crofts was a personable enough character.

He did his job satisfactorily without setting the world on fire, he was reasonably popular with his staff and the bank's customers but, privately, he was an emotional wreck. Since his separation from his wife, he had become a bitter and resentful individual. Then, like manna from heaven, half a million dollars appeared in an offshore account he had recently opened. Earlier, he had checked and there it was, as promised. The money was in his nominated overseas account, and all he had to do was get rid of one envelope stored in a safety deposit box in his bank. It was just too easy.

Now, all his monetary problems were solved and, importantly, his greed-obsessed ex-wife and the team of vultures she called lawyers would never know. He smiled warmly at his sudden good fortune.

It was not unusual for Crofts to work late, particularly since he lived alone these days. His being alone in the bank long after it had closed for the day was not something that would draw undue attention. Besides, there was nothing, and no one, to rush home to these days. There was nothing worse than going home in the middle of winter to a cold and empty house; more accurately, it was a two-bedroom unit since his ex-wife was enjoying the luxury of the big house he still paid the mortgage on, as well as an exorbitant rent in his current, sparsely furnished abode.

Two hours after the last of his staff had left, he locked the doors and made his way to the vault containing the safety deposit boxes. He glanced at the number he had previously written on a scrap of paper and then, with a master key only he had control of, he scanned the hundreds of drawers. When he found the one he wanted, he gave a low grunt of satisfaction, inserted the key, and opened the box assigned to Chapman Bouttell.

There was just the one item in the box—a sealed envelope. He did not know what the envelope contained, and he did not want to know. He removed it, slid the drawer back, and locked it. If the safety deposit box records were ever audited, there would be no record of box number 386 ever having been assigned to anyone named Chapman Bouttell. Crofts had seen to that as well; he could do that, he *was* the bank manager after all. He whistled softly to himself as he walked casually back to his office where, without opening the envelope, he put it through his office shredder.

Satisfied he had covered his tracks as far as the bank was concerned, he turned off the office lights and left the bank through a back door which opened into a dimly lit rear access lane that ran behind the bank. As he strolled along the lane towards a small, non-public parking station where he and other city business operators parked their vehicles, he did not notice he was being followed. All Crofts was thinking about was half a million dollars, and how he would now be able to have the retirement he always dreamed of. He did not hear the footsteps gathering speed and falling lightly on the pavement behind him as a large, dark-clad figure emerged from the shadows.

The fire that raged through the city office complex destroyed the business premises of Brandt and Carter, Barristers and Solicitors. The fire was so intense, five fire units and their crews battled in vain for several hours trying to bring the inferno under control. It was not until the early hours of the morning, and after the building had been razed to the ground, that they were able to extinguish the last of the flames.

There was nothing left. Just a pile of sodden, smouldering debris. Everything contained in the building was irretrievably lost, including all the computers and all the hard copy files. One of the files lost forever, along with its contents, was a single, sealed envelope bearing the name *Chapman Bouttell.*

The subsequent Fire Investigation Report would reveal

that the fire was deliberately lit. It started in office filing room and, fuelled by an as yet unidentified accelerant, quickly spread to all parts of the building, destroying everything in its path. Ultimately, insurance would replace the building, but nothing would replace the hundreds of files and documents stored within.

A lone rower found the body. It was wedged in the undergrowth of the very old willows lining the banks of the River Torrens that wound its way lazily through the city.

At first, he thought it was a bag of refuse carelessly and wilfully discarded by an unthinking passer-by. When he rowed his single skiff over to the bank and nosed the prow into the reeds, he disturbed the bundle and it rolled in the water. He found himself staring, both mesmerised and horrified, into two wide open, lifeless eyes set in a pale, equally lifeless face. Blue, almost black swollen lips, exposing the teeth, smiled back at him in a grotesque grin of death.

When the police arrived, they used a boat hook to drag the heavy, sodden bulk unceremoniously from its prison of reeds and tree roots. Finally, they manhandled the body onto the bank and stood back to observe their find.

Bozo lay on his back on the river bank, with his death smile fixed, his lifeless eyes staring up at the drizzling rain, and a neat, round bullet hole in the centre of his forehead.

At Police headquarters, upstairs on the Administration floor, in an office next door to that of the South Australian Police Commissioner, Assistant Commissioner Geoffrey Delaney closed the door, walked casually to his desk and made himself comfortable. On his face, he carried a self-satisfied, smug half-smile.

It had been a long time since Chap had been to the Cape, and the journey was quicker than he remembered, due largely to the fact that the weather was so bad, it kept traffic to a minimum.

The wind howled and buffeted against the momentum of the car. The wipers battled to keep pace against the rain as it sprayed furiously against the windscreen. Despite some of the worst driving conditions he could recall, he made good time.

As he deftly manhandled the hire car over Main South Road, arguably one of South Australia's most dangerous roads, his thoughts were occupied once again with the faces of his dead mates. One by one, their faces appeared on the windscreen before him, their features distorted by the driving rain storming against the glass. It was his imagination, he knew, but he felt the men were really there, riding with him. He saw no sadness in their faces, not even in death. They all smiled, and he smiled back at each of them. Nine of them, all dead, all smiling at him through the windscreen.

As each face appeared, he softly called the soldier's name: Ryan 'Fergie' Ferguson, John 'Billy' Bunter, Ray 'Rayman' Porter, James 'Jock' McAndrew, David 'Girly' Galway, Colin 'Big Fella' Lewis, Charlie 'Cobby' Cobb, Brian 'The Brain' Elliott. The last face to morph in the glass was that of Eddie 'Dicko' Dickson. Eddie seemed to smile the widest of them all. Chap felt it was a welcoming smile, and it caused the hair at the nape of his neck to bristle eerily.

Near the small Fleurieu Peninsula community of Delamere, Chap slowed, and turned off the main road onto a well-maintained gravel by-road heading west, towards the sea.

In front of him was Starfish Hill where twenty-three huge, wind-powered turbines, part of the first wind farm established in South Australia, stood sentinel over the rolling hills and adjacent Gulf St. Vincent. Painted white, the sixty-eight metre towers stood stark and majestic against the contrasting green of the surrounding countryside. On top of each tower, and geared to turn at a constant speed in normal weather conditions, the great rotor blades powering one-point-five megawatt turbines were still; purposely shut down in the face of the howling wind.

As he drove, slower now over the narrow, winding access road, Chap focused on the ocean which lay to his front, just beyond the great turbines, and disappeared beyond the distant grey gloom of the horizon.

He stopped the car at a small parking area which doubled as a viewing site for those who came in much more favourable weather to observe the wind farm at close quarters. As he climbed out, an icy blast, with a wind chill factor that had to be near freezing, hit him front-on. He gasped at its power, pulled his collar high around his neck, and thrust his hands deep into his pockets.

Although it had been a long time, Chap had fond memories of this place. It was once a favourite spot to retreat to at times such as he was experiencing. Whenever he felt his life was in disarray—and over the years that had been more than once—he found a solitude bordering on loneliness here which, strangely, gave him comfort. This place had become his sanctuary under the stairs in his adulthood. He moved to the front of the car and leaned against the bonnet, feeling the warmth of the engine through his clothing.

He stood there for what seemed like a long time, staring out over the wild gulf waters which opened to the vast Southern Ocean away to his left. A short distance from where he stood, beyond the fence which defined the parking area, the land ended abruptly where steep cliffs dropped over a hundred metres to the sea below. Chap pushed himself away from the car, climbed over the low fence and, hunched over against the might of the wind in his face, walked unsteadily towards the cliff top.

When he reached the edge, he inched forward, leaned into the face of the tempest, and looked down at the raging, boiling sea below. The ocean here was engaged in all its winter fury. Huge waves, many metres high and whipped to a frenzy by a howling south-westerly wind, crashed against the rocky shoreline in a dense and deafening explosion of foam and spray which carried all the way to where he stood, a hundred metres above.

From his vantage point, Chap tasted the salt of the surf on his lips as the sea-spray, mingled with the icy needles of rain, rose to meet him, stinging his face. It was freezing cold, but at the same time oddly refreshing, cleansing.

He moved closer still to the edge and looked down again at the rocks so far below. For a brief moment, he realised how easy it would be to take just one more step out into the void, and end all the chaotic madness which now accompanied him daily. He shuddered, and stepped back, away from the precipice.

Many thoughts came to him as he stood there leaning into the wind and rain, not the least of which were the words the CIA agent, Rodrigues, had said as he left his home. Could it be he was wrong about Tony Francis? How could he possibly have thought his partner was dirty? Chap had always considered himself a fairly good judge of character, and he hated himself for having judged Francis that way. He silently cursed and damned the Coterie to hell for making him feel that way.

Chap had lost a lot of faith in the last few days; faith in the government, faith in the police force, faith in the free and democratic process, faith in the whole damn system. Now, more than ever before, it was clear to him that the taxpayers, the voters of the country, those who elected and paid the wages of the leaders of the country, knew jack shit about what went on behind their collective backs. How naïve the citizens of the country really were, he thought. While they worked, paid exorbitant, ever increasing taxes, ate, slept, made love, and took for granted that the people they elected to office would ensure their continued wellbeing, they were being duped. Blinded by their own innocent ignorance, they were being shafted.

"Why does it have to be so fucking hard?" Chap screamed into the driving windstorm.

Chap did not see, or hear, the vehicle approaching from behind. He did not see it stop and park some two hundred metres from where he stood, staring out over the raging sea. He did not see the driver reach across into the rear of his vehicle and move the long carry case into the front seat. He did not see the driver's side window slide silently down and the rifle barrel protrude out into the wind and rain. Nor did he see the driver brace himself against his seat and take careful aim.

From this distance, it would not normally be a difficult shot, not for this man—he was one of the Coterie's best. But the wind was strong, and the rain was in his face, so he took longer than normal to steady his aim. He did not want to mess this up. He pulled the butt of the rifle back hard into his shoulder, locked his elbow against the window jamb and turned his wrists slightly in opposite directions until the weapon was rigid and did not move in the wind. He deliberately slowed his breathing. As he inhaled, the barrel rose. As he exhaled, it fell. He inhaled again, and began to slowly exhale. The barrel began to fall. He took up the first pressure on the trigger. When the scope crosshairs were exactly where he wanted them, he held his breath. Satisfied, he began to take up the second and final pressure on the trigger.

Chap did not feel the cross hairs of the high-powered Remington .308 caliber hunting rifle as they focused on the back of his head. With the roar of the wind, and the pounding of the sea drumming in his ears, he did not hear the shot. He did not feel the bullet as it slammed into him and took off the top of his head.

Chapman Bouttell never did see the man who killed him.

Dear reader,

We hope you enjoyed reading *The Coterie*. Please take a moment to leave a review, even if it's a short one. Your opinion is important to us.

Discover more books by Gary Gregor at

https://www.nextchapter.pub/authors/gary-gregor

Want to know when one of our books is free or discounted? Join the newsletter at

http://eepurl.com/bqqB3H

Best regards,

Gary Gregor and the Next Chapter Team

You might also like:
A Game For Assassins by James Quinn

To read the first chapter for free, head to:
https://www.nextchapter.pub/books/game-for-assassins-cold-war-espionage-novel

The Coterie
ISBN: 978-4-86747-890-5

Published by
Next Chapter
1-60-20 Minami-Otsuka
170-0005 Toshima-Ku, Tokyo
+818035793528

28th May 2021

Ingram Content Group UK Ltd.
Milton Keynes UK
UKHW012007140323
418553UK00004B/385